Through Each Tomorrow

Books by Gabrielle Meyer

TIMELESS

When the Day Comes
In This Moment
For a Lifetime
Across the Ages
Every Hour until Then
Through Each Tomorrow

TIMELESS • 6

Through Each Tomorrow

GABRIELLE MEYER

BETHANYHOUSE
a division of Baker Publishing Group
Minneapolis, Minnesota

© 2025 by Gabrielle Meyer

Published by Bethany House Publishers
Minneapolis, Minnesota
BethanyHouse.com

Bethany House Publishers is a division of
Baker Publishing Group, Grand Rapids, Michigan

Printed in the United States of America

All rights reserved. No part of this publication may be reproduced, stored in a retrieval system, or transmitted in any form or by any means—for example, electronic, photocopy, recording—without the prior written permission of the publisher. The only exception is brief quotations in printed reviews.

Library of Congress Cataloging-in-Publication Data
Names: Meyer, Gabrielle, author
Title: Through each tomorrow / Gabrielle Meyer.
Description: Minneapolis, Minnesota : Bethany House, a division of Baker Publishing Group, [2025] | Series: Timeless ; 6
Identifiers: LCCN 2025006546 | ISBN 9780764243028 paperback | ISBN 9780764245688 casebound | ISBN 9781493451296 ebook
Subjects: LCGFT: Christian fiction | Time-travel fiction | Novels
Classification: LCC PS3613.E956 T47 2025 | DDC 813.6--dc23/eng/20250407
LC record available at https://lccn.loc.gov/2025006546

Scripture quotations are from the King James Version of the Bible.

This book is a work of fiction. Names, characters, places, and incidents are the product of the author's imagination or are used fictitiously. Any resemblance to actual events, locales, or persons, living or dead, is coincidental.

Cover design by Jennifer Parker

Published in association with Books & Such Literary Management, www.booksandsuch.com.

Baker Publishing Group publications use paper produced from sustainable forestry practices and postconsumer waste whenever possible.

25 26 27 28 29 30 31   7 6 5 4 3 2 1

To my first critique group and lifelong friends,
Lindsay Harrel, Alena Auguste, and Melissa Tagg.
Thank you for your unwavering support, your priceless wisdom,
and your loyal friendship. I'm so happy that God called us
on our writing journeys at the same time.

TIMELESS FAMILY TREE

Theodosia
B. 1733 & 1973

Libby
B. 1755 & 1895
(book 1)

Maggie
B. 1841, 1921, & 1981
(book 2)

Grace　　　**Hope**　　— *cousins* —　　**Rachel Howlett**
B. 1667 & 1887　　B. 1667 & 1887　　　　　　B. 1672 & 1862
(book 3)　　　　(book 3)

Kathryn　　　　　　　　　　　　　　　　**Anne Reed**
B. 1865 & 1915　　　　　　　　　　　　　　B. 1692 & 1892
(book 5)

Cecily　　— *step-* —　**Charles**　　　**Caroline**
B. 1542 & 1892　　*siblings*　B. 1539 & 1859　　B. 1706 & 1906
(book 6)　　　　　　　　　(book 6)　　　　(book 4)

1

CHARLES

JUNE 1, 1883
FREDERICKSBURG, VIRGINIA

Hardship seemed my constant companion. The only difference was that in 1563, I had money and a title to overcome the difficulties life threw at me. But here in 1883, nothing had been easy since the war. Something needed to change soon, because I was running out of time.

The last rays of sunshine spiked through the bank of low-lying clouds, painting the sky with vibrant colors. As I leaned against the open barn door, admiring God's creativity, I had to force myself to lower my gaze on the failing horse farm I'd inherited from my father.

"Don't let Mama see your glum face." My sister, Ada, stepped out of the gray weathered farmhouse and walked toward me, one hand on her low back, the other holding an envelope.

I smiled as I pushed away from the barn, not wanting to pile more worry onto her weary shoulders. Widowed less than six months after she married her childhood sweetheart, she'd come back to the farm pregnant and destitute. The baby wasn't due for another two months, but she was exhausted.

"I don't mean to look glum." I pressed a kiss to the side of her head. "Sometimes I get lost in my own thoughts." I studied her as she pulled back. "How is Mama today?"

Ada let out a sigh. "I had hoped the baby would give her something to look forward to." She put her hand on her rounded belly, sadness in her blue eyes. "She hasn't eaten in three days, Charles. I don't know what we're going to do."

This bout of melancholy was the deepest we had ever seen. Mama had suffered on and off since Papa's death, but it had never put her in bed before. The weight of her unhappiness had fallen on us ever since we were children, and though I tried to tell myself it wasn't my fault, I always wondered if things would have been different had I been able to make something of the farm.

I had one more long-shot idea, but it would be a miracle if it worked.

"I'll check in on her before supper and see if I can get her to join us," I promised.

There was curiosity in her face as she handed me the missive. "I almost forgot. This arrived for you when you were in the field. I wouldn't have bothered you about it since I know the mares are due back any minute, but it's from New York City." She frowned. "Why would someone from Whitney Shipping in New York City send you a letter? Is it another bill?"

My pulse pounded as I took the envelope, knowing exactly what it might contain.

The miracle.

I couldn't share it with Ada. Not yet. "I told you not to worry about the bills." I tried to chide her, distracting her from the letter. "We'll get by."

She put her hand on the back of my head where my time-crossing mark sat just above my hairline. Her face was serious. "You don't have much time left, and Cecily needs you more than we do."

"You both need me." I moved away from her touch, not wanting to worry about Cecily today. I had enough troubles to contend with. The letter in my hand could be the answer to the most pressing problem, but it would involve the most risk.

With another sigh, Ada glanced at the road, where a horse-drawn trailer was about to turn into our drive. "It looks like the girls are back."

My attention was torn from the important letter, though I wanted to read Drew's response immediately. I'd asked him for two favors, one that might have ramifications in 1563 and the other that could change the course of our lives in 1883. Yet, I'd been waiting for months for my two broodmares to return after using every bit of savings to send them to a stud farm. Stella and Faye were the only two thoroughbreds I had left from Father's prize-winning stock, and the fate of our farm rested on their ability to breed. It would be months before I knew if we had succeeded, and many more months until the foals were born and ready to sell. For now, we were living on the butter and egg money Ada earned and the goodwill of the bank.

I hesitated only a moment before handing the letter back to Ada. "Take it to my office. I'll see about it later."

Her pretty eyes had been full of life at one time, but now they were dull and disillusioned. She was only twenty-six, but she looked much older from her grief. "I'll keep supper warm for you."

"Thanks." I wanted to read Drew's letter more than anything, but the mares would need to be tended to, and there was no one else to do it.

I waited for the driver to pull up to the yard, trying not to feel embarrassed by the state of the farm. Vibrant before the War Between the States, our property was now a shadow of its former glory. Papa had been a prosperous horse breeder before the war broke out, but he'd died in the conflict, and then the farm had become a field hospital for Union soldiers during the last Battle of Fredericksburg. The only things that had survived were the house and barn. I'd been trying to rebuild the farm since I was

9

old enough to hold a hammer, but without money, I had worked in vain, eking out only enough to get by.

It took some time to unload the mares and get them into the barn. After the driver left, I set about grooming them, speaking in low tones, checking on their health.

As I lifted Stella's hind leg to pick her hoof, I immediately noticed a foul odor and discovered that her hoof was infected with thrush. After checking her other hooves and those of Faye, it was obvious they hadn't been cared for properly at the stud farm. Faye's hoof was so infected, she whinnied in pain when I tried to clean it.

I took several deep breaths, trying to calm my anger as I calculated how much it would cost to have the farrier visit the farm. It was an expense I hadn't anticipated, and with no ability to borrow more from the bank, I wasn't sure how we'd afford it.

Still, it wasn't the farrier bill or the other debt we owed that pressed against my thoughts.

An hour later, I left the barn and washed my hands at the pump before heading into the house. The letter from New York was all I could think about as I stepped into my office and found it sitting on top of my desk.

Without hesitating, I opened the seal and took it out of the envelope, dropping into the chair to read it.

Whitney Shipping
New York, New York

Charles,

I'm going to start my letter by saying that both of your requests would involve great risks, and I'm not sure I want to take them. Though I would be honored to serve our queen, if anyone discovered the truth, both of us would face the Tower—or worse. And what if I accidentally change history? I might forfeit my path in 1563 before I'm ready. I was prepared to say no. However, something came up, and I realized that perhaps we could help each other.

You need a physician that the queen can trust in 1563, and I am suddenly in need of an English aristocrat in 1883. I know that sounds strange. Let me explain. Mother has been in a terrible rivalry with my aunt for years, perhaps you've read about it in the papers. It's become a legendary fight, each one trying to prove that she is the Mrs. Whitney, the queen of the nouveau riche. They've both built enormous cottages in Newport and ridiculous mansions in New York City. They've thrown elaborate parties, costing hundreds of thousands of dollars, and purchased the most outlandish things to try to outdo one another. Their chief aim is to be included in Mrs. Astor's 400, a list of the most important people in American society— according to Mrs. Astor. Because the Whitney money is new, Mrs. Astor has snubbed them for years, but it hasn't deterred them. Whichever one gets the first invitation will be the winner, and my mother wants it more than anything.

The biggest issue, and the only one that really concerns me, is that both women draw from the same financial source: Whitney Shipping. Frankly, their lavish feud is starting to threaten our company's stability. One of them needs to win soon, or I fear they will do irreparable damage.

When my aunt informed the New York World that she was on her way back from Paris with Vicomte Deville, and that she would be entertaining him in Newport for the summer, my mother insisted that I find an aristocrat with higher standing so she could outdo my aunt. Mother believes that if she can bring an earl or a duke to Newport, Mrs. Astor won't be able to ignore her any longer.

It goes without saying that Whitney Shipping needs this rivalry to end.

I know you're not an earl in 1883, but you are one in 1563, and you have all the knowledge and mannerisms of an earl to pull it off for a few weeks. You can even tell Mother your real name from 1563, Charles Pembrooke, the Earl of Norfolk, so you won't mess anything up.

I just need you to show up at a few parties and impress a few of her friends, hoping to draw Mrs. Astor's attention.

Charles, if you are willing to come to Newport, I will agree to see the queen. And, regarding your other request, I will see what I can do. I think I can convince my father to invest in your horse farm, given the right angle. He's always been an avid horseman, but his shipping business has kept him too busy to pursue his passion. He's in Europe and won't return to New York until September. He has no plans to go to Newport, since he and Mother are not speaking.

I propose that you come to Newport for July and August as Lord Norfolk, and then we will go to New York when Father returns in September and you can meet him as Charles Hollingsworth, the owner of the Hollingsworth Horse Farm.

Mother and Father's social and business lives do not intersect, so neither one will be the wiser. If all goes as planned, your horse farm could be financially stable by the beginning of next year—before your twenty-fifth birthday when you need to make your final decision. If you choose to stay in 1563, you can have someone in place to keep up the farm so your mother and sister have an income. And, if you choose to stay in 1883, you'll have all the financial backing you'll need.

If you're willing to come, I will wire you enough money to get to New York, and enough to take care of your mother and sister until your return at the end of the summer. I will meet you in New York to outfit you as the Earl of Norfolk before we head to Newport.

I await your reply,

Drew

I folded the letter and ran my hand over the stubble of a beard I hadn't shaved that morning. In 1563, I was the Earl of Norfolk, an esteemed and respected member of Queen Elizabeth's privy council, and the heir of Arundel Castle. It was there that I met Andrew Bromley, the carpenter's son. I had recognized the time-crossing mark on the back of his head, and we'd learned that we occupied the same two paths—only, he was the son and heir of a massive shipping fortune in 1883, and I was the destitute son of a widowed mother. Our lives were complete opposites, but because of our time-crossing marks, we had been lifelong friends, though I'd never met him in person in 1883.

"You must eat, Mama." Ada's voice filtered into my office from our mother's bedroom across the hall. "You haven't touched anything in days."

I set the letter on the desk and left my office, Drew's request sitting heavy on my heart. Could I pretend to be the earl in this path? It would mean leaving my sister and mother for a few months, but with Drew's financial help, I could hire a farmhand while I was away.

"Mama," I said as I entered her room and found Ada sitting on the bed next to her, holding a bowl of steaming soup. "Ada is right. You must eat something."

Mama turned her gaunt face toward me, desperation in her eyes. "Charles. Did the horses come home? How are they?"

I sat on the other side of her bed and took her free hand in mine, trying to sound positive as I smiled at her. "They're back and looking fine."

A spark of hope warmed her blue eyes. "Do you think there will be foals? You know it was your father's greatest hope that this farm would succeed and prosper. If he knew—" She stopped, her lips trembling. "He'd be so disappointed in me for letting things get this bad. I never wanted to fail him or his memory."

"There will be foals, Mama." I tried to reassure her, knowing full well that the failure of the farm was my fault alone. One disaster after another had befallen us. As soon as we thought we were ahead, another calamity would strike. "The driver brought a letter from the studmaster, and he is confident that the mares

13

are in foal. Stella and Faye are young and healthy and should do just fine. Things will look up, Mama. God will provide for us as He always has." Though I wasn't sure I believed it, the promise seemed to strengthen Mama.

She studied me, the lines around her eyes deep and troubled. "Do you promise, Charles? Because things have looked up before."

Drew's request echoed in my mind as I thought about the ramifications. This wasn't the best time to leave the farm, but it couldn't be helped. And if it meant that I could meet his father and possibly get financial backing to expand our farm, it would be the best possible outcome. I could pretend to be an earl for a couple of months.

In turn, Drew would meet with the queen. If all went as planned, he could diagnose what was ailing her and help her recover. I could then give my attention to my younger stepsister in 1563, Cecily. Mama and Ada weren't my only responsibilities. Cecily was also on my mind. I needed to make sure she was taken care of if I left her.

As part of my time-crossing gift, I had to choose which life I wanted to keep on my twenty-fifth birthday next March and which one I would forfeit. If I could find a husband for Cecily before then, I would stay with Mama and Ada. If the farm was financially secure, I would stay with Cecily.

Either way, I had a lot of work ahead of me and not enough time.

With a smile, I squeezed Mama's hand. "I promise I will do everything I can to ensure that the farm succeeds. You have my word." Perhaps this was God's answer to my many prayers.

Hope sparked in her gaze as she squeezed my hand back and then took the bowl of soup from Ada.

I wasn't sure how I would keep my word, but I could not fail.

2

CHARLES

NEWPORT, RHODE ISLAND
JUNE 27, 1883

Midcliff was a Tudor-style mansion sitting proud on Ochre Point in the most fashionable neighborhood in Newport. A misting rain made it appear ethereal as it overlooked the white-capped waves of the Atlantic Ocean. A storm had followed us all the way from New York City and didn't appear to be clearing any time soon. Dark gray clouds hung low overhead, and a cool wind rocked the ornate carriage Mrs. Whitney had sent for our arrival.

I took a deep breath, hoping and praying I would not regret coming to Newport.

"What do you think, Charles?" Drew asked, sitting across from me in the carriage as it pulled into the circular drive. His arms were crossed as he leaned back in his seat. "It's not Arundel Castle, but it's a lot more comfortable than that drafty monstrosity."

I smiled at my friend's description of my ancestral home in 1563. As the 2nd Earl of Norfolk, I took great pride in Arundel Castle, even if it was drafty. "Midcliff will do," I said, affecting my cultured British accent for the role I was about to play. "For now."

Drew grinned at me.

Even though I sounded confident, I wasn't feeling it.

"I hope this works," I said to Drew as the carriage began to slow near the main entrance and our charade was about to begin.

"There is a lot riding on this," Drew agreed, his good humor disappearing as his face became serious. "It could either be a magnificent win for my mother's social status and finally end her expensive rivalry with my aunt, or it could be an abysmal failure, ruining her chances to ever show her face in polite society again. There isn't much room in between."

I scoffed. "Thanks for taking the edge off my nerves."

Drew's affable smile returned as he unfolded his arms. "It's going to be fine—better than fine. Just think of it as a summer holiday. As long as no one learns the truth about your identity, you won't need to worry about a thing. And when we're done here, we'll meet with Father in New York and see if we can convince him to back your farm."

"Don't forget your end of the bargain. The queen's health continues to decline. If something happens to her, another war could break out in England and thousands of people could die."

Drew's smile fell. "Thanks for taking the edge off *my* nerves."

As soon as the carriage came to a stop, a footman opened the door and a gust of wind sprayed us with rain.

I hoped I wouldn't regret my decision to come to Midcliff as the Earl of Norfolk—or my decision to ask Drew to serve Queen Elizabeth as a royal physician. While he wasn't a doctor in 1563, he was a medical student in 1883, and he knew more than any other physician or apothecary who had previously examined the queen.

But that was a problem for a different day.

As Drew and I exited the carriage, the front door of Midcliff opened and an elegant woman appeared. She was easily in her mid-forties, with her graying hair styled high on her head and wearing a light-colored dress. Large diamonds drooped from her earlobes.

"Drew!" She held out a hand to him, her eyes shining. "You're finally here."

"Mother." He went to the woman and embraced her. "It's good to see you again."

A butler stood at attention just inside the door, staring at the opposite wall. Waiting.

I followed Drew into the foyer, out of the rain.

Mrs. Whitney pulled back and smiled at her only son before she turned to me. "Lord Norfolk." She gave me a practiced curtsy. "It is an honor to welcome you to our humble cottage."

The mansion in question was not humble by any stretch of the imagination, but it was what high society called their summer cottages in Newport.

I did not have to pretend to know how to behave as I offered her a bow, taking her hand to kiss it. The courtly manners drilled into me as a child in the 1500s followed me to 1883. Whether I was greeting Queen Elizabeth or a leader of American High Society, I knew what to do. "It is an honor, Mrs. Whitney," I said, using my British accent. "Thank you for your invitation."

Her cheeks were pink with delight as she demurred. "The honor belongs to us, my lord. You have no idea how pleased I am to have an earl as our guest of honor this summer. My sister-in-law, the *other* Mrs. Whitney, has a lowly vicomte visiting from France." Her laughter tinkled perfectly, though I knew the rivalry was fierce.

"You must be tired and famished from your travels," she continued as the butler closed the door behind us. "I have arranged for refreshments on the veranda." She linked arms with Drew and motioned toward the back of the house. "Prescott," she said to the butler, "see that all their luggage is brought to their rooms."

Prescott nodded as we left the bright foyer and moved through a large parlor.

The house was decorated in various shades of white. The wallpaper was cream with white flowers, the trim was cream, the drapes were cream, and the furniture was covered in white brocade. Only the floors were natural wood. It was airy and bright—and made

17

me uncomfortable. Whitehall Palace, where we resided with Queen Elizabeth for most of the year, and Arundel Castle were grander in scale, but rough in comparison. The farmhouse in Virginia was small and sparsely furnished compared to this cottage, and almost always covered in a layer of dust.

The sound of laughter and conversation filtered into the parlor from a distant room.

Drew's steps faltered. "Are you hosting a party, Mother?"

"Just a few close friends," she said with a wave of her hand. "And Evelyn, of course."

My pulse picked up speed at a "few close friends" as I shared a look with Drew.

"Mother." Drew paused, his voice serious. "I told you that Charles didn't want a lot of fuss."

"It's not much fuss." She patted his arm. "Just a few neighbors, really. They're so eager to meet our guest."

I touched the cravat at my throat, trying not to feel like I was choking. Uncertainty was a new experience for me. I had no reason to feel apprehensive when I was the earl in 1563 or Charles Hollingsworth in 1883. But being the earl in 1883 was an entirely different matter.

Mrs. Whitney led the way onto the veranda. The archways facing the ocean had been battened down with green-striped canvas, but the room was still cool. It was a semicircle, wrapped around the curved parlor windows.

And it was full of wealthy women. At least two dozen. Young, old, and in between, covered with jewels and expensive clothing.

A hush fell over the group as they examined me like a fresh piece of prized horseflesh.

"Ladies." Mrs. Whitney clapped her hands, presumably to quiet them, though everyone had already stopped speaking. "It is my greatest honor to introduce you to Charles Pembrooke, the Earl of Norfolk!" Her voice had risen a notch with excitement, and she turned to me, her eyes sparkling. "My lord, these are my dearest and closest friends."

The ruse had begun.

I offered them a charming smile as I bowed deeply. "It is an honor to be in your presence."

They twittered and chirped as older women discreetly nudged their daughters with enthusiasm and determination.

"My lord," Mrs. Whitney said as she motioned toward a table at the front of the room and closest to the rounded parlor windows. "Won't you sit here?"

Three young women and two older women already sat at the table. One of the younger women had blond hair and wide blue eyes, and the other two had darker hair. All three sized me up. The one with light hair didn't look impressed, while the others offered warm smiles.

"Evelyn, dear." Mrs. Whitney motioned to the indifferent young woman. "Rise and greet our guest of honor."

Evelyn rose as her clear gaze held mine. It wasn't hostile, but neither was it welcoming. Her hair was swept up in a bun, and the tight bodice of her light-colored gown was stiff and ruffled. She was pretty, but not in a classical way. Her features were unique—distinguishable in a room of other pretty girls.

"Lord Norfolk," Mrs. Whitney said, more enthusiastic than before. "May I present my daughter, Drew's younger sister, *Miss Evelyn Whitney.*"

Evelyn gave me a small curtsy, and I bowed.

"It's a pleasure to meet you, Miss Whitney."

"The pleasure is mine, Lord Norfolk."

I glanced at Drew and lifted a brow. He hadn't told me he had a sister.

He just shrugged.

"And this is Mrs. Reinhold and Miss Isabel Reinhold," Mrs. Whitney said. "Congressman Reinhold's family."

Again, I bowed.

"How do you do, Lord Norfolk?" Isabel asked as she rose and curtsied.

I bowed, taken with her gentle voice and sweet demeanor.

"Next"—Mrs. Whitney lifted her chin, her voice cooling, though she seemed quite pleased with herself—"is Mrs. *Clarence* Whitney, my sister-in-law."

This was the woman who had tried to outdo Drew's mother whenever possible.

Mrs. Clarence Whitney pursed her lips as she extended a hand to me. "How fortuitous that Drew should have a noble friend, available at a moment's notice, to visit for the summer."

"I was fortunate to receive the invitation," I said as I bowed, harnessing all my aristocratic charm, ready with the story we had agreed upon. "Drew and I met in London when he was on his tour last summer, and he made me promise to drop in when I visited New York. When I did, he invited me to accompany him to Newport."

I hated to lie, but no one would believe the truth.

"May I introduce *my* daughter," Mrs. Clarence Whitney said as she motioned to the other young woman. "Miss Marianna Whitney."

She stood to curtsy, and I bowed.

A footman appeared and pulled out a chair for me between Evelyn and Isabel—which was not a coincidence, if Mrs. Whitney's private smile meant something.

The moment the conversation shifted toward Drew, Evelyn turned to me.

"If you think you've come to marry an heiress," she said in a quiet, even voice, "then I'm afraid you will be disappointed, Lord Norfolk. I am not for sale."

My eyebrows lifted at her boldness.

But I wasn't unnerved. I had no intention of wooing her or anyone else until I made my final decision next March when I turned twenty-five. Even if I was searching for a wife in this path, I wouldn't look for a wealthy heiress who couldn't survive on my Virginia farm.

"If you think you're going to buy a title," I said, just as frank as I lifted a glass of punch, "then *you* will be disappointed, Miss Whitney. My earldom is not for sale."

It was her turn to look surprised as I turned my attention to Miss Reinhold.

"How has your summer been thus far, Miss Reinhold?"

Her lips tilted into a charming smile as she glanced from Miss Whitney to me and said, "It has been lovely, my lord, but I believe it just got more interesting."

I couldn't agree more.

Three hours later, I stood near the windows in my large bedchamber, staring at the tumultuous Atlantic. My room was curved and sat right above the parlor with the veranda roof below. It was probably the nicest bedchamber in the cottage, with panoramic views of the ocean and the other mansions along the rocky shoreline.

I wished I could enjoy it, but knowing that Mama and Ada were alone at the farm, with just enough money to scrape by for the summer, haunted my thoughts. It seemed cruel that I was here enjoying the finest luxuries available while they worked so hard. They knew I had gone to New York to seek an investor—they just didn't know how I was going about getting one.

I hadn't stopped praying since I'd left the farm. This was my last hope.

A knock at my door pulled my attention away from the ocean. "Come in," I called.

Drew entered the large bedchamber and fell into one of the plush seats near the window. "Sorry about that, old chap. I didn't know Mother was planning a luncheon."

"You didn't tell me you had a sister." I crossed my arms and leaned against the window frame. "Does your mother think I'm here looking for a wealthy heiress?" The newspapers were always full of details of one American heiress or another marrying into the British aristocracy. Many wealthy families with new money, who weren't accepted into Mrs. Astor's circle, took their daughters to Europe to find titled gentlemen to marry them. In exchange, the destitute aristocrats were given large dowries to save their family estates.

"Even if she does—" Drew yawned—"you have nothing to worry about. Evelyn has no intention of nabbing an earl." He paused. "Honestly, I don't know what Evelyn wants. She's changed so much over the past year and a half, she probably doesn't, either." He grinned. "But Miss Reinhold was enjoyable. Mother would like me to escort her around this summer. Father would benefit having a congressman for an in-law."

"Speaking of your father, have you heard from him? Does he still plan to return in September?"

Drew dropped his feet on the floor. "I forgot to tell you that his plans changed. He wrote and said he's coming home early. I left him a message at his office, outlining the investment opportunity in your farm." He shook his head. "He'll probably be so surprised that I'm dipping my toes into the family business, he'll contact me the moment he gets back."

"I hope you're right. It would be nice to know if he's interested before September." And maybe I could quit this charade sooner. But it made me pause. "You're sure he won't come to Newport?"

"He detests this place. Nothing could persuade him to come."

"Good."

"For now," Drew continued, "just focus on what we're doing here. It wouldn't hurt you to flirt with Evelyn. Any rumor that my mother might have an earl for a son-in-law would escalate her rise up the social ladder, and perhaps she and my aunt would quit their feuding."

I turned from the window, thinking back to his earlier comment. "What do you mean your sister has changed?"

"She used to be more like Miss Reinhold. Teasing and laughing. Now she's reserved and serious, almost melancholy and prudish. Whatever happened, it took place while I was at Yale. I've asked Mother, but she doesn't know, either. It's a mystery to all of us."

"Have you asked Evelyn?"

"Of course I've asked her. But she says everything is fine." He clasped his hands and leaned forward, putting his elbows on his knees. "And speaking of sisters. Have you decided how we're going to convince Cecily that I'm a physician?"

I sighed and returned my attention to the ocean. Large waves rolled toward the cliff, breaking against the shore and spraying into the rain-drenched air. My stepsister, Cecily, was the only real obstacle I faced in bringing Drew into Windsor Castle, where the queen had moved the court earlier that month because of the plague sweeping across London. Cecily had known Drew since we were all children at Arundel Castle. She knew he was a carpenter.

"When was the last time you saw her?" I asked.

His brows came together as he looked at his clasped hands. "Five years ago." He spoke the words softly. "Before she moved to court."

"I think the best thing we can do is tell her the truth."

He looked up at me. "You think that's a good idea?"

"We're spinning a lot of webs. I think we should be honest when we can be. She knows you're a time-crosser, and when I explain that you're a medical student, hopefully she'll understand."

"Do you think it's wise? If the queen learns the truth, you and I could face severe punishment. I don't want Cecily to suffer with us."

"Cecily knows how to keep secrets. I won't tell her more than necessary."

"I hope you're right." He studied me for a moment. "How is Cecily?"

I pushed away from the window frame. "She wasn't doing well last time I saw her. It's been a few weeks since the court moved to Windsor."

"I wouldn't do well, either, if I lost one of my paths unexpectedly."

Cecily was grieving the loss of her second path in 1913, but she would come around. I would see to it. "Everything will work out for all of us," I tried to assure him, though the encouragement was more for my benefit. "Once you diagnose the queen, we'll establish her treatment, and then you can go back to Arundel. You'll be leaving 1563 in December, so even if you're caught—"

"I'll only spend six months in the Tower," he finished with a dry tone. "If you're caught pretending to be the Earl of Norfolk here, all you'll have to deal with is a scandal. I think you got the better end of this bargain."

"You forget, I could end up in the Tower with you. Besides, I have a lot to lose in 1883, as well."

A lot could happen between now and next March when I turned twenty-five. I'd known since I was small that I would have to decide if I wanted to stay in the 1500s or the 1800s. It was part of the time-crossing rules that governed my gift—if it could be called a gift. Ever since I was born, I had gone between my two lives. Tonight when I went to sleep in 1883, I would wake up in 1563. After I spent a day in 1563, I would go to sleep and then wake up again in 1883. Time stood still while I was away. I had two identical bodies and one conscious mind that moved between them. It was the same for Drew and had been the same for Cecily. I had inherited my time-crossing mark from Papa in 1883. It meant that on my twenty-fifth birthday, whichever path I wanted to keep forever was the one I would stay awake in past midnight. In the path I didn't choose, my body would die, and that would be the end of my life there.

Drew and I moved between the same two paths, but Cecily didn't. She had lived in the 1500s and the 1900s. She had always planned to choose her 1900s path when her birthday came—and I was going to choose my 1883 path to take care of Mama and Ada. But last January, everything changed. Cecily died of polio in her 1900s path, so her conscious mind had stayed in 1563, and she had no other choice.

Which meant my choices had changed.

"Let's just focus on what we're both planning to do," I said. "Tomorrow when we wake up in 1563, I will introduce you to the queen and you can examine her and find out what's wrong. If we're fortunate, it will be something simple."

Drew was still frowning. "What do her other physicians say?"

"She refuses to let them examine her."

He pulled back, his elbows coming off his knees. "What makes you think she'll let me?"

"She trusts me. And she'll like that you aren't part of the court. She doesn't trust the other physicians who are more interested in their own political gain than in serving her. If she likes you, she'll let you examine her."

"I'm only a student," he reminded me.

"But you're smart. I know you can help her."

He lifted his hands and leaned back in the chair. "I'll do my best."

"I'm not asking for anything else."

"And don't forget to flirt with Evelyn a little," Drew said as he stood. "My aunt would be livid if she thought Evelyn was going to become a countess."

"I don't want any complications this summer. And I don't want to break any hearts."

Drew grunted as he walked to the door. "I know that you're used to women falling at your feet, Lord Norfolk, but Evelyn isn't like the others. Mother has introduced her to dozens of European lords and princes and the wealthiest bachelors in America, and none of them have turned her head. I doubt you'll have to worry about breaking her heart."

"Maybe her heart has already been broken."

Drew paused, his hand on the doorknob. "Maybe it has, but I have no idea who would have done it. She wasn't serious with any of her beaus in her debutant year." He was about to leave the room when he said, "I hope you don't mind that Mother is making a fuss about you."

I lifted my shoulder. It helped keep my mind occupied, so I wouldn't worry about tomorrow. Because as confident as I tried to sound, I was nervous about Drew meeting the queen and Cecily learning about our plan. If the queen suspected that Drew wasn't a physician, or anyone thought I was trying to harm the queen, that could mean execution.

Drew had to be careful.

I had to be smart.

And Cecily would have to be quiet.

3

CECILY

JUNE 28, 1563
WINDSOR CASTLE

Sunshine warmed my shoulders as I stood just inside the main gate at Windsor Castle, watching carpenters construct the gallows Queen Elizabeth had ordered. They were a warning to anyone who tried to enter the castle without permission, or had followed the court from London, where the plague was ravaging the overcrowded city.

"They say a thousand people are dying a day in London," my cousin Aveline whispered, linking her arm through mine. "Do you feel guilty, running away to the safety of Windsor Castle when so many others are suffering?"

"Nay." I let out a sigh and turned her away from the gruesome reminder. I had no room for guilt. Grief had been my constant companion for six months and allowed few other emotions to rampage through my heart. But I squeezed her arm, knowing her anxious mind always needed reassurance. "We live to serve the queen, and 'tis our duty to ensure her safety. If coming to Windsor will keep her alive, then 'tis a necessary sacrifice."

Aveline nodded, though her face became more serious than before. "But she isn't well. What if she doesn't survive whatever ails her now?"

"The queen is strong and smart. Besides, we have other things to discuss." I steered Aveline toward the state apartments where we lived, needing her to remember why we had gone on this walk in the first place. We needed privacy. "We must find a way to secure your position as a maid of honour for Her Majesty. The competition will be fierce, and we need to show her that you are the most qualified lady of the court."

I had just learned that morning that one of the maids of honour was getting married later that summer, opening a coveted position within the queen's household, one I wanted for my cousin. Maids of honour were single women of noble families who lived at court to serve, entertain, and protect the queen. There were only six of us, and when this rare position opened, there would be at least twenty young noblewomen vying for the spot. Each of them would have a mother or grandmother or aunt to parade them in front of the queen. Aveline only had me, her twenty-one-year-old cousin, but I wouldn't let my age stop me. The queen liked me, and I would use that favor for Aveline's advantage. After being orphaned, Aveline had no dowry or inheritance to encourage a suitor. Becoming a maid of honour was her best hope.

Aveline let out a sigh. "I am not the most qualified. Lettice is far more beautiful, educated, and refined."

"That is precisely the talk I don't want to hear." I stepped closer to her. "If you do not believe you are the most qualified, the queen will not believe it, either."

"I hate competing," she lamented as her wide skirts brushed against mine. The stiff boning of our farthingale petticoats created the fashionable bell shape of our gowns but made it difficult to walk this close. "'Tis so demeaning and disheartening."

"Only if you lose." I smiled. "But you want the position, don't you?"

"Yes, of course. Who wouldn't? Everyone knows the queen's

maids of honour have the most advantageous marriages, and that is our highest aim, is it not?"

I would not respond to her question because I had no desire to marry. Until six months ago, I had not intended to stay in 1563, so a husband was inconsequential, and my heart was too battered and bruised to even consider such a thing now. "Let us go to the queen, and I will present you to her. We have a couple of months to convince her, but we must start now."

"Now?" Aveline's arm tightened around mine, and she pulled me to a stop. "She scares me, Cecily. I might faint away and embarrass myself in her presence, and then what would she think?"

"You would stand out to her, if that is any consolation."

Aveline's face was pale, and I knew she was in no mood to be teased.

"I will be there with you the whole time," I reassured her as sweat rolled down the center of my back from the heat of the sun and the pressure of the task ahead. I tugged her arm to continue. "Just be your sweet self, and she will love you. Later, you will perform, and I will show her samples of your embroidery and writing. The queen is intelligent and witty and loves people who can converse with her on multiple subjects. You are all the things she loves in a maid of honour. I promise."

Sighing, Aveline said, "I suppose we must get this over with if I want to find a decent husband."

I squeezed her arm and turned us into the quadrangle, a large green space made by the four sides of the Upper Ward of Windsor Castle. Ahead were the state apartments, and to the left was the Round Tower. We spent most of our time in this area of the castle since the Middle and Lower Wards were reserved for military and ceremonial buildings, including the beautiful St. George's Chapel.

Aveline's words troubled me because there were few options in 1563, especially as noblewomen. We could not seek higher education to become doctors or lawyers or professors, and we could not start businesses or offer services to be independently wealthy. Life was far too dangerous, and marrying a nobleman was the best course of action. It was the only option for Aveline, especially, because she had no father or brother to care for her. If she did not marry, and she found no position at court, she faced life in a convent. At least I had my stepbrother, Charles, and our home at Arundel, which was the only thing that brought me comfort.

As we followed a path through the quadrangle, we passed other courtiers of varying status and importance. Lords, ladies, gentlemen and gentlewomen, and servants all going about their business. There were usually over a thousand courtiers, but because of the plague in London, the inhabitants numbered less than three hundred at Windsor Castle. The queen had only kept her most important and trusted courtiers with her and sent everyone else back to their country estates to prevent the spread of the deadly disease. Aveline had nowhere to go and was only with us out of deference to her late father's position with the queen. Once the threat of plague passed, she would be sent away.

I could not let that happen to her.

After entering the state apartments, we made our way to the Queen's Ballroom, just outside the queen's Privy Chambers, and it was humming with activity. The stiff farthingale made it hard to maneuver, and the tight French hood with the sheer veil over my hair gave me a headache. I longed for something more comfortable to wear, but the queen's ladies were expected to exhibit the height of fashion.

There were more people in the ballroom than I anticipated. Now that we were settled into our quarters, our daily activities were starting to increase. Queen Elizabeth had called for amusement, so the maids of honour had practiced our dance earlier that morning in the sunny quadrangle and were ready to perform that evening. Others were preparing to read poetry, sing songs, and dance.

A familiar figure took shape at the end of the gallery, and my heart leapt with joy.

Charles.

With a grin, I broke free of Aveline's arm and hurried to my handsome stepbrother. He was dressed well in a doublet and jerkin, with trunk hose and a high collar. He wore a dark blue cape and a tall hat with a blue feather. He'd gone south to Arundel Castle to check on our servants and crops when the rest of court had come to Windsor.

But he was back, and I was so relieved.

The man speaking to Charles saw me first, looking past Charles's shoulder at my approach.

I slowed my steps, my smile faltering.

What was Andrew Bromley doing at court?

Charles must have seen Andrew watching me, because he turned, a question in his familiar blue eyes. When he realized it was me, he grinned and held out his arms. "Cecily."

Despite my uncertainty about Andrew, I went into my stepbrother's arms for a hug. Our stiff clothing made it a little awkward, but I didn't mind. Though Charles was my stepbrother, I had never known a time in my life without him. My mother had married his father when she was pregnant with me, and I'd been born with the Pembrooke family name.

He held me tight, banishing the melancholy I'd been feeling since he left us in London. It had been four weeks, and I'd missed him terribly.

"You've returned," I said as he let me go. "How is Arundel Castle?"

"'Tis doing well." He gently squeezed my hand. "And I've brought a surprise. You remember Andrew Bromley."

I faced the carpenter's son, looking up at the tall young man.

How could I have forgotten Andrew? He was the only man I'd ever loved—or at least believed I was in love with when I was a younger girl.

He had blond hair and brown eyes, the color of warm chocolate. His clothing was not as elaborate as my stepbrother's because he was not a nobleman, but it was well-made and looked new. It was brown with cream tones, accentuating his dark eyes and light hair.

Though Andrew's clothing wasn't as stunning as the rest, he wouldn't have trouble standing out. He was a fine-looking young man, with broad shoulders, long legs, a handsome face, and confidence that did not reflect his lowly status.

The queen was going to love him.

Andrew had grown and matured a great deal since I'd seen him last, and by the look in his eyes, he was thinking the same of me. My cheeks warmed at his perusal. In all the years I'd fancied myself in love with this young man, he'd never returned my affection.

"Lady Cecily," he said, bowing over my hand. "'Tis good to see you again."

My focus slipped to Charles, a question burning on my tongue. Why was our carpenter's son here? In the Queen's Ballroom? So far from Arundel?

The pair had been inseparable as children, so much so I'd often been jealous of their closeness. Charles and I had spent much of our childhood apart, learning different roles and expectations. He was only three years older than me but seemed to always be ten steps ahead in life.

"'Tis good to see you again," I said to Andrew.

"And you, my lady."

When he straightened and our gazes met, a wealth of memories flooded me. Did he remember the gifts he'd given to me, once upon a time? He'd been the first person who knew about my love for butterflies, and every time he found one, he would capture it and bring it to me in a glass jar to study. His simple gifts had propelled my passion to create a book dedicated to the life of butterflies in 1913—a book that had never been finished.

I pushed away the melancholy reminder of the life and dreams that had been stolen from me.

"What are you doing here?" I asked.

"The queen is in need of a new physician," Charles answered quickly. "I asked Andrew to accompany me to Windsor to see if he could be of service to Her Majesty."

"A physician?" I lifted an eyebrow at Andrew. "You?"

"Only just." Andrew readjusted his stance. "I've been studying for the past five years."

"Since I left Arundel?"

"Aye, my lady." He seemed uncomfortable, but was it from seeing me, from being in the Queen's Ballroom, or something else?

"Has Her Majesty agreed to see him?" I asked Charles, eager for someone to tell us what was wrong with our queen.

"I have not yet approached her," Charles confessed. "How does she fare today?"

Aveline finally arrived at our side, excited to greet Charles, who was her stepcousin, and pleased to meet Andrew.

After the introductions were made, I said to Charles, "The queen is in good spirits. Now would be the time to approach her."

"Will you see if she'll receive me?" he asked.

I glanced at Aveline. "I was planning to present our cousin to Her Majesty. There is an opening for a new maid of honour, and I intend to be Aveline's patroness."

"Her Majesty's health cannot wait," Charles said. "Mayhap you could present Aveline to the queen at a later time?"

I did not want to delay Aveline's pursuit, but the queen's health was more important. "Of course."

Aveline's relief was palpable.

I left the trio in the ballroom and entered the Presence Chamber, where ushers stood as guards on either side of the Privy Chamber doors. Andrew's sudden appearance still had me shaken. Andrew? A physician?

Since the ushers knew me, they didn't even acknowledge me as I knocked on the door to the Privy Chamber.

Kat Astley's voice called for me to enter.

The queen's Privy Chamber was dark, like most of Windsor Castle, with small windows. Dripping candles, set in wall sconces, did little to offer light. Tapestries hung on the walls to keep out the draft, but at the end of June, a draft was the least of our worries as the temperature continued to rise. Come winter, though, the castle would be freezing.

Queen Elizabeth sat at a table, looking over various pieces of parchment that were laid out before her, stacked up after days of being abed. This was the room where she spent the most time, working during the day and enjoying conversations, games, and meals with her intimate circle of courtiers by night. She was twenty-nine years old and dressed impeccably. Her famous red hair was curled in the front and then pinned up in a series of twists at the back. She wore a high collar, and her face was painted with Venetian ceruse, a thick white makeup made of lead and vinegar, which she had started to use the year before to hide the scars after her bout with smallpox. Some speculated that her current illness was simply from lingering symptoms of her earlier disease. Her hands and face were slightly swollen, making everyone fear the worst.

Her Chief Ladies of the Bedchamber, the two women who were closer to her than any others, sat on chairs nearby, embroidering. Kat Astley had been the queen's governess since she was three, and Lady Catherine Knollys was a cousin, though some rumored she was the queen's half sister, born to Anne Boleyn's sister, Mary, when she was having an affair with King Henry VIII.

Lady Catherine was also Lettice Knollys's mother, and Lettice was there with her, sitting decorously and embroidering silently.

It would be difficult to convince the queen that she needed Aveline as a maid of honour when Lettice was related by blood and always at her mother's side. But I would not give up the fight. Too much was at stake for Aveline.

When Queen Elizabeth glanced at me, I gave a low curtsy and dipped my gaze in deference. "Your Majesty."

"What is it, Lady Cecily?" she asked in a clipped tone. "Can you not see I'm busy?"

I had left her that morning in a good mood and feeling better physically, but her temperament had apparently shifted since then.

"My stepbrother has returned from Arundel Castle," I said as I straightened.

Her smile revealed yellowing teeth as she rose from the table.

"Lord Norfolk has been gone from us for too long. Send in my Eyes."

"Eyes" was the nickname the queen had given to Charles when he first joined her privy council. She was fond of nicknames for her favorites and had given Eyes to Charles because he was her eyes and ears at court, but more so because of the unique color of his irises. They were unlike any shade of blue I'd ever seen and were often commented on by enamored young ladies—the queen included.

I curtsied again. "Aye, Your Majesty."

Without hesitation, I returned to the Queen's Ballroom and motioned for Charles and Andrew to join me.

"Shall I come, too?" Aveline asked, looking terrified.

"Perhaps not now," I said. "But soon."

Charles, Andrew, and I passed through the Presence Chamber, and then I opened the door to the Privy Chamber.

Queen Elizabeth was waiting for Charles. She extended her bejeweled hand to him. "My Eyes have returned!"

He crossed the chamber quickly and bowed on one knee before her, kissing the emerald ring on her first finger. "Your Majesty," he said. "'Tis good to be with you again."

She motioned for him to rise as her attention turned to the stranger in the room.

Andrew's clothing would have immediately told her he was a commoner, but his height and breadth and good looks brought out a curious smile.

Andrew stood stiff beside me, his chest rising and falling on short breaths.

"Who is this?" the queen asked.

"Pardon me, Your Majesty," Charles said as he stepped aside so she could have a better look. "This is Doctor Andrew Bromley of Arundel Castle."

Andrew bowed low, staying close to my side, and did not approach the queen.

"Rise, Doctor Bromley," the queen said, "and come hither."

Andrew did as he was told.

She looked him over, walking around him with a keen eye. "Why have you come?"

"I've come to serve you, Your Majesty."

A slow smile lifted her painted cheeks as she looked at Charles. "Have you brought him to examine me, Lord Norfolk?"

"If it pleases Your Majesty. I know you haven't been feeling well, and Andrew is a kind, intelligent, and trustworthy gentleman. You have my word."

Something flickered in her dark brown eyes as she stopped in front of Andrew once again. He exhibited confidence, as well as humility. "It does please me," she said. "I trust my Eyes with my life." She motioned toward all of us. "Everyone but Kat and Doctor Bromley must leave our presence."

I curtsied as Charles bowed, and then we slipped out of the Privy Chamber, Lady Catherine Knollys not far behind.

When we were in the Queen's Ballroom once again, this time alone, I turned to my stepbrother. "Is he really a physician, Charles?"

He studied me for a heartbeat and then whispered, "No."

My eyes opened wide as dread befell me.

※

Evening had fallen on Windsor Castle as we dined in the Great Hall, also known as St. George's Hall. It was the first time the queen had joined us for a meal since leaving Whitehall Palace in London.

She sat at the head of the table, eating her sweets, as a court jester juggled before her. Though she smiled and seemed to enjoy herself, I knew her well enough to see that she still wasn't feeling well. Was she putting on an act to convince everyone she was healthy?

I sat across from Charles and Andrew at the large, U-shaped table with the other five maids of honour. Even though Charles was young, he was popular at court both with the smitten young women and the respected noblemen. He was wise in political matters, level-headed in the face of foreign troubles, and shrewd in his dealings with court intrigue. Not only did he advise the queen in those areas, but he was one of her most trusted correspondents, writing and receiving almost all her important letters. He was a good diplomat, and the queen placed her undivided faith in him. But he was also personable and charming, and the lord of a castle in the south of England. Many had sought his company since he'd entered the hall, and they had been curious to meet Andrew.

Charles's words to me, moments after we'd left Andrew with the queen, still rang in my mind. If anyone discovered that Andrew was not a physician, both he and Charles could hang. And if they learned that I knew the truth, I would hang with them. People would assume that there was a conspiracy afoot and we meant harm to Her Majesty. Others had died for lesser crimes, no matter how much the monarch had previously trusted them.

The jester continued his antics as I watched Charles and Andrew speak to each other. Since Andrew had come out of the queen's Privy Chamber, he had been quiet and reserved—though that wasn't unusual for him. It was one of the things I'd enjoyed most about him as a child. He hadn't been loud or obnoxious trying to prove himself, like so many other boys.

Andrew's gaze slipped to mine across the room, but it wasn't a passing glance. He intentionally looked at me.

"Come, Cecily," Henrietta Throckmorton, one of the maids, said as she appeared at my elbow. "Our dance is next."

I rose, mindful of my white gown, and followed her and the other four maids of honour. The queen loved it when we dressed in white, and because she purchased our clothing, we wore what she desired. I had other colored gowns, but when we appeared as a group, we always wore white. Queen Elizabeth wanted her court to portray purity.

The jester finished with a flourish and received applause from his audience, while the musicians began to play the recorder and the tambor. Queen Elizabeth clapped to the sound of the tune as the maids of honour stepped into the space the jester had just filled.

Aveline was in the audience at a long table in the back of the room. Before the night was over, I planned to present her to the queen.

I was on the side closest to Charles and Andrew as we began to dance. My stepbrother smiled at me as he took a sip of his ale, but Andrew did not smile. He watched the dancers, his gaze landing on me occasionally, though he spent more time watching Henrietta Throckmorton. Hen, as she was known, was often called upon to greet dignitaries who visited, paraded about as the standard for courtly beauty with her blue eyes and red hair. She was lovely and drew the most attention when we performed.

I always felt awkward and inelegant next to her.

But even as Andrew watched her, I could see something was wrong in the depths of his eyes. He was worried. Was it the queen? Or was he nervous because he shouldn't be here?

"Don't forget to smile," Henrietta said beside me through her teeth as she grinned. "The queen is watching you."

She was right. The queen was watching, and she didn't look pleased. She'd often said that the prettiest thing a woman could wear was her smile, and since she prized beauty, I must always remember to smile.

I complied, getting lost in the dance and the music, thankful for a distraction from my melancholy thoughts.

It had been six months since I'd died in 1913, and I was still reeling from that shock. Before contracting polio at Christmas in 1912, I had known exactly what I wanted to do with my life. I had been attending Girton College—a women's college in Cambridge—studying biology, hoping to become a teacher or professor, and I was creating a book of paintings about the life stages of butterflies. My parents, Kathryn and Austen Baird, were my rock. Mama was a time-crosser and had guided me, and Papa had taught me to paint. My older brother and sister were both married and starting families, and I'd loved being a new aunt. I was confident that

I would choose that path, though I would have missed Charles with all my heart. But I had everyone and everything else to look forward to.

Now, I was stuck in 1563, with no chance to study biology, no opportunity to teach, and no reason to create a book of paintings. In 1563, most people still believed that insects came from spontaneous generation, appearing out of nonliving matter, such as mice from grain and maggots from meat. They didn't understand the life cycle because few people had studied it.

Worse, Queen Elizabeth dictated and commanded every aspect of our lives, determining when and if we could travel home, who we could spend time with, what we could discuss, what we could wear, and whom we could marry. It was no life, at least not for someone who had more freedom in 1913. Though, I couldn't complain. Being a noblewoman at court offered more opportunities than if I was a commoner.

I kept the smile on my face, pretending to be happy, and the queen finally pulled her gaze away from me. The only benefit to smiling, besides pleasing the queen, was it reminded me of Mama. I had inherited her dimples and brown eyes, though my hair was as black as a raven's wings from my mother in this path.

When our dance ended, I found Aveline, who had worn her best dress for this very moment.

"Are you ready?" I asked.

"I believe so."

She had been presented to the queen before, but not as a potential member of her ladies in waiting.

Arm in arm, we approached the queen as she watched another group of dancers perform for her. These were young women, including Lettice, who were trying to impress the queen.

"Your Majesty?" I asked as Aveline and I curtsied. "Do you remember my cousin, Lady Aveline Spencer?"

Queen Elizabeth remained seated as she studied Aveline, her keen brown eyes taking in Aveline's appearance from head to toe. "I do, indeed. Her mother was Lady Temperance, your mother's sister, and her father was Bernard Spencer, the Marquess of Buckingham and a trusted servant of the Crown."

"You are correct, Your Majesty," Aveline said as she rose.

"Your father and mother passed away just last year," the queen added.

"Correct again." Aveline's voice shook slightly. "An illness took both of them."

"But you requested to stay at court," the queen said as more of a question than a comment.

"To be near Lady Cecily," Aveline replied. "She and I are as close as sisters, Your Majesty, and she has been a constant source of comfort since losing my mother." She paused and then said quickly, "And to avoid the convent."

The queen smiled at me. "Lady Cecily brings comfort to us all. I do not know what I would do without her and my Eyes at court."

"'Tis my pleasure to serve you, my queen," I said.

She looked back at Aveline. "A convent isn't the worst thing that could happen to you."

Aveline dipped her chin but did not respond.

"Marrying a man who mistreats you would be far worse."

"Yes, Your Majesty," Aveline said on a whisper.

"I suppose you are hoping to present Lady Aveline as a potential maid of honour." This was a statement directed at me from the queen—not a question.

"Aye, Your Majesty," I said. "I believe Aveline would serve you very well. She is quite accomplished—"

"We shall see." The queen sighed and returned her focus to the dancers. "The competition is fierce, but I will not make my decision until later this summer. I do hope Lady Aveline will make a good effort to convince me."

"I will, Your Majesty." Aveline curtsied again.

The queen dismissed us, and we walked away, our heads held high until we slipped out of St. George's Hall, and then we began to speak in excited tones.

"We must work diligently," I said. "We have much to do."

Aveline nodded—but then her gaze slipped over my shoulder, and she stood straight. "Doctor Bromley approaches, Cecily."

I turned, my heart beating wildly.

"I hope I am not interrupting," he said.

"No." Aveline curtsied. "I am just leaving."

Before I could stop her, she maneuvered around us and returned to the Great Hall.

"Your dancing has improved," Andrew said with a smile.

I wasn't sure if he had followed me on purpose, or if he had stumbled upon me. Either way, I was pleased to see him again. He was tall, but he felt taller as we stood alone in the corridor. "Thank you."

"I remember when you danced for your parents at Arundel," he continued. "I always thought you danced better than anyone else."

I smiled, thankful for good memories with my mother and stepfather at Arundel before tragedy had struck our family. "You were a child," I said, trying to deflect his compliment with laughter. "You didn't know better."

"Mayhap I didn't know better then, but I do now. You're still more accomplished than the others."

My cheeks warmed, especially since I'd been dancing next to Henrietta, who was a far better dancer. "You're even more charming than the last time I saw you, Andrew."

"I've been practicing at Newport."

"Ah." I nodded. "I'd almost forgotten your other path. You are quite important there."

It was his turn to laugh and deflect. "My father is important, and my mother is trying to be. I am a nobody."

"Perhaps not yet, but one day you will inherit your family's fortune and begin your own legacy."

He smiled, but the gesture didn't quite reach his eyes.

I'd loved hearing about Andrew's path in the 1870s and 1880s when we were children. I was familiar with the wealthy Americans who had infiltrated English Society during the Gilded Age, and how they had tried to purchase aristocratic titles for their daughters. I knew all about the splendor of Newport and the opulence of families like the Vanderbilts, the Astors, the Rockefellers, and the Whitneys.

He motioned toward a door that led onto the North Terrace, where the gardens were in full bloom. It was dark, but there were torches lining the pathways for moments like this. "Would you care to take a stroll?"

I had not walked alone on the terrace with a man, though many of the other maidens did. I had found no purpose in pursuing a romance when I'd planned to stay in 1913.

Things were different now.

But this wasn't a budding romance. This was an old friend.

Besides, I wanted to talk to him about the reason he'd come to Windsor Castle and warn him to keep his real identity a secret.

I took his arm as we stepped through a doorway and into the cool evening air.

The Thames River was less than half a mile away, and from the elevation of the terrace, we had views of the water under the light of the moon. Fragrant blossoms filled my nose as the torches flickered in the wind.

There were two other couples walking through the gardens on the terrace. They were both so far away, I couldn't even make out their identities. This was a quiet moment as Andrew and I meandered along the paths.

"I asked you out here to talk about something," he finally said.

I waited, unsure what he planned to say.

"Charles told you the truth?" he asked.

"Aye—and I wanted to talk to you about it, as well." I glanced around the terrace before saying, "No one must know who you really are."

Andrew nodded and then started to walk again. "'Tis true that I'm not an apprenticed doctor here, but I am a Yale medical student in 1883."

"That will not matter to the queen, or anyone else."

"I will keep the information close," he said in a low voice. "Only you and Charles know the truth, and there will be no one from Arundel Castle visiting here any time soon." His face was very serious. "I have no desire to lose my head, Lady Cecily."

We walked for a few paces, and I asked, "Do you not want to be a physician here?"

"My birthday is in December, and I do not plan to stay here." His words felt like a splash of water over a kindling fire, though I'd always suspected he'd leave. Why would anyone give up a wealthy family in Newport to live as a commoner in the sixteenth century?

"Do you plan to be a doctor in 1883?"

He was quiet for a moment before he replied. "My parents do not approve. They've agreed to let me go to medical school until I'm twenty-five, and then I am expected to start working with my father in January."

I paused and looked up at him.

The firelight from a nearby torch danced in his eyes.

"Why would you work so hard to attend medical school and then not be a doctor? It seems like a lot of hard work for no reward."

"Because I love it." He let out a sigh. "And I keep hoping my father will have a change of heart, though I doubt it. I am his only son, and the only Whitney male heir. My grandfather built the Whitney family fortune from nothing. He operated a ferry over the Hudson River, then purchased more boats until he had a small fleet and began a shipping empire. He eventually invested in railroads and then real estate. I have no choice but to continue in his and my father's footsteps. The Whitneys have no use for a doctor."

"I'm sorry to hear that, Andrew." I realized I was still holding his arm as we stood there, and he was cradling it close, but I didn't pull away. "I wanted to be a biology teacher in 1913 and to create a book of paintings about the life stages of a butterfly before I died there. And even though I cannot be a teacher here, or create a book, I still value the education I received."

"Your education is not a waste." He continued to walk along

the torch-lit garden path. "You can still study biology. Just think of all the things yet to be discovered."

"You and I both know I cannot knowingly change history." It was one of the rules that governed time-crossers. If we knowingly changed history, we forfeited the path we tried to change.

"How would that change history?"

"Because someone else was meant to discover those things."

"Who said it wasn't supposed to be you?" His voice was filled with certainty. "God knows the end from the beginning. When you died in 1913, that didn't surprise Him. He knew you were going to stay in 1563, and He gave you a desire to study biology and create a book of paintings. That hasn't changed." He stopped near a hibiscus and let me go so he could examine it under the light of a nearby torch.

I frowned as I watched him, wondering what he was doing.

After a moment, he smiled and reached under a leaf. When he pulled away, he held a Painted Lady caterpillar. It was spiny, with brown spots and fuzzy antennae.

He took my hand and gently transferred the caterpillar to my fingertips. It latched on and climbed over my skin, tickling me and making me smile.

"Paint caterpillars and butterflies and any other insect that catches your fancy," he said. "Watch them, document them, pursue what you love. You won't knowingly change history, Cecily, and you'll help others understand this amazing world that God has gifted to us."

Warmth filled my chest as I looked up at him. For the first time since January, a flood of excitement washed over me as I thought about his suggestion. I didn't have to give up my love of biology in 1563, or my desire to create a book. I'd been so lost in my grief, I hadn't contemplated such a thing. "Thank you."

He smiled and then motioned toward the castle as he offered his arm again. "I should return you to the queen before she thinks I've abducted you."

I put my hand on his arm to still him, my thoughts returning to my earlier fears. "Be careful, Andrew. You're smart and educated, but any misstep could get you and Charles in a lot of trouble. I can't risk losing him. He's all I have left."

He put his hand over mine. "I promise to be careful, Lady Cecily."

His hand was warm and strong, and I had to swallow the nerves that bubbled up my throat at his touch. We began to walk toward the castle as I held the Painted Lady caterpillar in one hand and grasped Andrew's arm with my other. "Will the queen die?" I whispered, dread in my voice.

The queen had not yet established her heir, nor had she found a husband. If she died, a war could ravage England for the throne, and as noblemen and women, we would be caught in the middle of it. That was how my stepfather lost his life and, ultimately, how my mother had lost her life when the queen's sister, Mary, had taken the throne. Mother had been pregnant with her second child, and she gave birth right after my stepfather was hanged for treason. She had been heartbroken and so weak that she died in childbirth and the baby died with her.

It was one of the reasons Queen Elizabeth placed Charles on her privy council at such a young age and asked me to be a maid of honour. It was a gift to our family for our parents' ultimate sacrifice.

I was quiet as I waited for him to answer my question. I needed to know if the queen would survive.

"There is a possibility she could die," he finally said, "but I will do everything in my power to ensure that she lives. I promise."

As Andrew returned me to the castle, I knew I could trust him.

But I also knew that God had plans that were out of our control.

4

CHARLES

JUNE 28, 1883
NEWPORT, RHODE ISLAND

The sun shone bright on my second morning in Newport. It felt good to be back in 1883, away from the problems at court. I loved seeing Cecily again, to know she was well, but I had already faced dozens of issues that the privy council needed to address. As the queen's councilors, we created and implemented policies, kept an eye on the spy network throughout Europe and abroad, advised her on matters that were both private and public, and oversaw the management of the kingdom. The most pressing issue was the plague, which was wreaking havoc on London and spreading like wildfire. We had to do something to stop its progress, or we might face unprecedented loss of life. The nineteen members of the council had already ordered the citizens to burn bonfires each evening to clear the air of miasmas that might be spreading the illness. Even though germ theory was in its infancy in 1883, I had enough knowledge to know that burning bonfires would not solve the problem. Instead, I lobbied for better sanitation and to quarantine the sick.

As I entered the breakfast room, I wanted to put thoughts of England aside for the day, though I still needed to speak to Drew about my concerns for the queen. I hadn't had a chance to talk to him privately at Windsor Castle because my duties had kept me too busy. Without an heir apparent, things could get dire if the queen died.

I paused in the breakfast room doorway, surprised to find Evelyn sitting alone.

She glanced up from the book she was reading as she dipped her spoon into a boiled egg.

I wasn't sure why her presence took me by surprise. I should have expected to see her there. I just hadn't anticipated that she would be alone.

"Good morning, Miss Whitney." I went to the sideboard where the breakfast dishes had been set out. There were boiled eggs, toast, fresh fruit, sausage links, oatmeal, and more.

"Good morning, my lord."

"Please, call me Charles," I said as I filled my plate with food.

She didn't respond as Prescott entered the breakfast room to hold out a chair for me to take a seat. Then he poured a cup of coffee and a glass of orange juice for me before slipping back into the butler's pantry, leaving us alone.

Evelyn continued to read as I began my breakfast.

Most young women, especially those who had been taught proper etiquette, would have set aside the book to converse with me.

Apparently, Evelyn wasn't like most women.

"Why don't you like me, Miss Whitney?" I finally asked, deciding to address the issue head on. The three times I'd been in her presence, she had treated me with cool indifference.

"I don't know you, Lord Norfolk," she said without lifting her gaze from the story.

"But you clearly have an opinion of me."

47

"I have an opinion of your kind." She finally looked at me, and I was struck again by her unique features. They were delicate, yet bold. Rare, yet classic.

"Ah," I said. "There is the truth. You decided not to like me because you think I'm after your inheritance."

"Isn't that why you've come?" Her eyebrows lifted. "Why I've met countless aristocrats like you in the past two years? My mother wants me to marry one of you so she can parade me in front of my aunt and her friends as a duchess or a countess."

"Perhaps those are your mother's plans, but they're not mine."

"You all say the same thing." She closed the book and put her napkin on her plate. "Every one of you. You pretend that you've fallen madly in love with me and that my money means nothing. You want to convince me that I'm the most intriguing woman in the world and that you cannot possibly live without me." There was pain behind her words, though she tried to hide it. "But your true colors will eventually shine, Lord Norfolk. And you'll break my heart, too, if I'm not careful." She rose—and I rose, as well, my manners ingrained in me. "I'm not as innocent and naïve as I once was," she said. "And, for your sake, I'm sorry. I'm sure you've spent a great deal of money you do not have to come here. But you're wasting your time. I will not marry you, or anyone else. Though there are other young ladies in Newport who will jump at the chance. I suggest you start with Miss Reinhold or, if she doesn't have enough money, my cousin, Marianna. They are sweet and eager for your attention."

My mouth opened to respond, but she didn't give me time.

"Please excuse me, my lord." She gave a curt nod and then walked toward the door.

Drew entered the breakfast room as Evelyn left, not even acknowledging her brother's presence as they passed each other.

"What did you do to her?" he asked.

"Nothing. Absolutely nothing."

He chuckled. "She doesn't like you, does she?"

I took my seat, trying not to let Evelyn Whitney get to me. "I'm not worried."

"When was the last time you met a young woman who didn't fall over herself to be noticed by you?" He grinned as he went to the sideboard. "She's going to drive you mad. Mark my words."

I took a bite of my toast and frowned. "She doesn't bother me."

"Maybe not yet, but when you realize you can't charm her, she will."

I ignored his comments and returned to my breakfast.

Prescott entered to clear Evelyn's plate and pour coffee and juice for Drew. When he left us alone again, I had a chance to ask Drew my pressing question.

"What is your diagnosis?"

He looked up at me, his fork half raised to his mouth. "What do you mean?"

"The queen," I said quietly as I glanced toward the door to make sure Prescott wasn't entering again. "What is wrong with her?"

Drew slowly lowered his fork. "I'm sorry, mate. I'm not at liberty to say."

I frowned. "What do you mean? I was the one who asked you to examine her, and I'm risking my neck to have you at Windsor Castle. I brought you there so I could find out what ails her."

"If the queen wants to share her diagnosis, then she will. I swore an oath to her that I wouldn't tell anyone. Not even you."

I stared at him, too bewildered to be angry. "I need to know how to best prepare the privy council."

"If she wants the privy council to be concerned, she'll tell you." He put his forearms on the table. "I will not betray her confidence, Charles. And if that's why you brought me to Windsor, then you will be disappointed."

My temper started to rise, though I tried not to let it show. "I have a country to protect, and if the monarchy is in danger, then I need to ensure it goes to the right person."

"The monarchy is always in danger."

"Is she very ill? Will she die?"

His face was serious. "There is a possibility she will not survive, but there is also a possibility that she will. I promise to do all in my power to ensure she lives." He paused. "But it won't hurt to proactively settle the inheritance issue."

My pulse escalated as I studied him. "Is it that serious?"

"Everything is serious when it concerns the queen."

"We've tried to get her to agree to a match for years. It's probably too late now."

"Why does she hesitate?"

"If she had a son, there are many who would try to destroy her life because they believe a man should be on the throne. She is safer if she has no heir. But that will not solve any problems, either. She needs a child to ensure the monarchy is passed down to a Tudor." My voice was serious as I asked, "Is she dying, Drew?"

"Her health is in jeopardy, as you know, but that is all I will say."

She'd joined us for supper the night before. How sick could she be? Or was she just putting on a show for the council so we wouldn't panic? Queen Elizabeth was a savvy politician, and though she considered our advice, she was steadfast in her own decisions.

Drew motioned to my plate. "Finish your food so we can leave. It does not pay to ruin today's enjoyment with problems that we face in another path." He smiled. "And I plan to challenge you to a tennis match this morning, so you'll need all your strength."

I did finish my breakfast, but it wasn't food or tennis on my mind.

For five years, the privy council had been encouraging the queen to marry and produce an heir. At least six of her closest relatives, including her cousin, Mary, Queen of Scots, kept a watchful eye on the queen's every move, knowing that the throne would be up for grabs if she died.

I couldn't let that happen. I would learn the truth about the queen's condition from Drew, no matter what it would take. And pray that we would be spared a war.

Drew called for a carriage to take us to the Newport Casino on Bellevue Avenue later that morning. He had told me it was a popular social club that housed a tennis court, reading rooms, a dance floor, theater, and more.

I was still thinking about our conversation at breakfast as we stepped outside Midcliff and found Evelyn getting into a separate carriage.

"Are you heading to the casino?" Drew asked, stopping her from entering the carriage. "You could come with us."

She paused, her skirt lifted in her hand. She had changed from her light-colored morning gown into a darker, more serviceable skirt and jacket. I didn't know a lot about women's fashion, but she didn't look like she was going on a social outing.

"I'm not going to the casino." She glanced toward the road, clearly anxious to be away. "But I hope you have a nice afternoon." She started to step into the carriage, but Drew called out again.

"Where are you going?"

She hesitated. "I'm doing charity work."

"Does Mother know?"

"Of course."

Drew frowned. "And she's allowing it?"

Annoyance creased her forehead. "Of course she's allowing it. Don't worry about me, Drew. I volunteer all the time."

"You do?" He pulled back. "Since when?"

"Since—since " She shook her head in exasperation. "It doesn't really matter. Go have fun at the casino." She glanced at me but didn't address me. "I'll be late if I don't leave soon."

I stepped forward to offer her a hand into the carriage. She paused, surprised, but accepted my assistance.

"Thank you," she said and then disappeared inside the conveyance.

The coachman pulled away from Midcliff as Drew and I watched Evelyn leave.

"I don't understand what happened to her," Drew said as he

stepped into the second carriage. "Or why Mother would let her spend her morning doing charity work when everyone in Newport will be at the casino, or swimming, or paying calls. Mother's sole purpose is to climb the social ladder, and her children are the rungs she uses to get higher."

I didn't offer an explanation, because I had none. And I wasn't about to start worrying over Evelyn Whitney. She had no interest in me, and I had none in her.

The storm clouds from the day before were gone, and the sky was a pristine blue. Heat warmed the carriage as we drove down Bellevue Avenue past dozens of mansions, ornate carriages, and pedestrians. Those who strolled on foot were well-dressed men and women, or governesses in black gowns with white aprons and mobcaps pushing prams and wrangling children.

Storefronts lined Bellevue the closer we came to downtown.

The casino was teeming with activity as the carriage pulled up to the main doors. The large building was made of red brick, brown shingle siding, and green trim with striped awnings over the windows.

I followed Drew out of the warm carriage and into the cool casino as people stopped to stare. There were whispered conversations as we passed, and more than once I heard my name. Mothers and daughters eyed me with curiosity and excitement—and intent.

"My mother told me this morning that she has already received five invitations from prominent families in Newport since your arrival," Drew said with a smile. "It seems our plans are working."

"No invitation from Mrs. Astor yet?"

"Not yet, though there is a rumor she is planning a large ball for later in the summer. Invitations have not yet been issued. We still have time to impress her."

I smiled, though the increased attention gave me more anxiety. I should have known I couldn't stay inconspicuous as the Earl of Norfolk.

"Mr. Whitney," an older gentleman with a southern drawl said to Drew as we waited at the counter to secure a time slot for the tennis court. "It's good to see you again."

"Congressman Reinhold." Drew shook the older man's hand. "It's good to see you. This is my friend and guest Charles Pembrooke, the Earl of Norfolk."

Congressman Reinhold offered his hand, which I shook with pleasure. He was a distinguished-looking man with a wide middle and graying hair. The laugh lines outside his brown eyes made me like him instantly.

"It's an honor to meet you, Lord Norfolk," the congressman said. "I believe you met my daughter at luncheon yesterday, Miss Isabel Reinhold?"

He motioned to Isabel, standing beside him. Her smile was just as warm as his.

"Yes, of course." I nodded at her. "It's a pleasure to see you again, Miss Reinhold."

She curtsied. "The pleasure is all mine, my lord."

"We were about to play lawn bowling," the congressman said. "Would you like to join us?"

Drew glanced at me, and I nodded. The tennis court wouldn't be available for several hours, so we had plenty of time.

As the congressman and Drew led the way, Isabel held back to walk with me.

"It is good to see you again, Lord Norfolk."

"Please, call me Charles."

"Then you must call me Isabel."

Her congenial personality was a stark contrast to Evelyn Whitney.

"I detect a southern accent," I said. "Where do you and your family live?"

"Virginia." She smiled, her love for her home state evident in the way she said the simple word.

I couldn't help but smile, as well, and almost told her I was from Virginia—but I stopped in time.

"And you?" she asked. "I know you're from England, but what part?"

I had to shift my thoughts from this path to my other one and remember who I was pretending to be. "Arundel, in West Essex, south of London."

"Arundel Castle?" She stopped and put her hand on my arm, though I wasn't sure if she realized it. "We visited there last year when we toured Europe. You must be so pleased with the changes being made. Are the carpenters finished?"

My pulse picked up a notch at the press of her hand and at Drew's cautious gaze. He didn't need to warn me to be careful. I had no idea who currently lived at Arundel, and the thought of someone else owning my family seat was a bit unsettling.

But then another thought came to me. Was the current owner a descendant of mine from my 1563 path? Perhaps the 12th or 13th Earl of Norfolk? Or would I leave there to stay in 1883 and surrender my family title to the relative next in line?

"Castles are a hindrance on the pocketbook," I said with a practiced laugh. "Always needing repairs and renovations."

"We were disappointed that your family was away when we visited," Isabel said as she removed her hand, and we began to walk again. "Who would have known that we needed to come to Newport to meet you?"

"You're from Virginia?" I asked, trying to steer the conversation away from Arundel Castle. "Where?"

"I was born and raised in Fredericksburg," she said, "but we live in Washington, DC, during the congressional season."

"When we're not in Newport," Congressman Reinhold added with a chuckle.

"Papa has promised me that we'll return to Newport next summer." Isabel smiled at her father. "This has become my new favorite place to visit."

"I knew it would happen." The congressman laughed, regarding his daughter affectionately. "If we came, she'd get a hankering to come back."

I was still reeling from her comment. Our horse farm was just outside of Fredericksburg, and we did business in that city all the time. No wonder the congressman's name sounded familiar. I hadn't even thought to put it together when I'd met Mrs. Reinhold and Isabel the day before.

We stepped outside onto the large back lawn of the Newport Casino. The two-story building enclosed three sides of the lawn, with galleries on the upper floor. People lounged in the galleries, sipping drinks and visiting. Women wore white gowns with large hats, while men were in light-colored linen suits and jackets with wide-brimmed straw boaters to shade their eyes. I was wearing one of the new linen suits we'd purchased in New York before we'd come.

The congressman led us to the lawn bowling rink, which was a level green space.

"Mr. Whitney, how about you and I play against Isabel and Lord Norfolk?" the congressman asked Drew.

"All right." Drew lifted his bowls, which were elliptical-shaped balls. We each had two and would roll them toward a smaller ball called the jack. Whichever team rolled their bowls closer to the jack would receive more points.

We began the game, and Isabel proved to be a competent partner. She was competitive and skilled but laughed when she made a mistake. When we lost, she put her hand on her father's arm with pride. "Papa has been playing since the war, so he has decades more experience than the rest of us. But some day I will beat him."

"You don't let your daughter win?" I teased with a smile.

"Never," the congressman said. "You don't learn anything if you're coddled. One must face their own battles to find the courage and confidence to fight."

"You fought in the Civil War?" Drew asked as we left the bowling rink and stepped onto the veranda for something to drink.

"I served with the Fortieth Virginia Infantry Regiment," the congressman said with pride, though he was standing on Yankee ground. The country was still healing from the war that had ended only eighteen years before, but most people had tried to move on. "We assembled in Fredericksburg in May of 1861 and fought valiantly until our surrender at Appomattox Court House in 1865."

His words caught me off guard for the second time that day, and I spoke before I had a chance to think. "Did you know Lieutenant Nathanial Hollingsworth?"

"Did I know him! Nate and I were tentmates. How did you know him?"

I paused, unsure how to respond. Nathanial Hollingsworth was my father from this path, the man I had inherited my time-crossing mark from. He'd died at the Battle of Sailor's Creek, just three days before the Civil War had ended. But how would the current Earl of Norfolk know a horse farmer from Virginia?

Drew watched me closely, and I knew I had to come up with a logical answer.

"My father, the last Earl of Norfolk, purchased horses from Nathanial Hollingsworth when I was a small lad," I said, trying to make the story as believable as possible. "I recall him speaking of Mr. Hollingsworth's passing in the war, and it captured my imagination as a child. He was the only soldier I had a personal, if somewhat distant, connection to."

"How very odd," Congressman Reinhold said. "This really is a small world."

He continued to talk about the war as I breathed a sigh of relief that he didn't ask any other questions. Though I was torn because I would have loved to learn more about my father in this path, I didn't ask him. Papa died when I was six but had left the farm to fight when I was only two. I had very few memories of him. It was his father, my grandfather, who had taught me about my time-crossing gift and told me about the other time-crossers before us.

It wouldn't be hard to believe that an earl had purchased horses from Nathanial Hollingsworth. Before the war, our horse farm was one of the most successful and prosperous in Virginia, and Papa's horses had been shipped to England, France, and Spain. It was during the war that we lost everything. Things had begun to fall apart as soon as Papa had gone to fight, and then they became dire during the First Battle of Fredericksburg in December 1862, when most of our farm was destroyed. The final blow came in May 1863, during the Second Battle of Fredericksburg, when everything we had left, which wasn't much, went to the Union Army. By the time Papa died, we were destitute.

"Do you plan to stay all summer in Newport?" Isabel asked me as Congressman Reinhold and Drew began a side conversation about New York City.

A waiter brought cold lemonade as we lounged at a table, watching another team start a game of bowls.

"I only plan to stay until the end of August," I said.

Her smile dimmed at the news, but she rallied and asked, "And will you return to Arundel right away or see more of America?"

The truth was, I would return to Virginia, but I couldn't say that to Isabel.

"I haven't decided."

Her brown eyes were gentle yet flirtatious as she said, "If you'd ever like to see Virginia, I'd love to show you around."

The congressman glanced at us for a moment before returning his attention to Drew, but I knew he was keeping one ear on our conversation.

"If I ever get to Virginia, I would like that," I said, and I meant it.

5

CECILY

JULY 4, 1563
WINDSOR CASTLE

I had tried to get into the garden all morning to look for caterpillars, but my duties had prevented me from slipping away. I also wanted to meet with Aveline to work on the skills she would demonstrate for the queen, but there hadn't been time. The ladies of the Privy Chamber, including the maids of honour, were the only women who were allowed access to the queen. That meant that we served as her household staff, cleaning her chamber pot, overseeing her baths, washing her clothing, preparing her meals, and tidying up her rooms. One of the Ladies of the Bedchamber, the most trusted position of all, was even tasked with tasting all the queen's food in case someone tried to poison her.

It wasn't until afternoon when I finally had a chance to step onto the North Terrace with Aveline. The gardens were in full bloom as I sat on the grass near one of the flowerbeds, inspecting it for caterpillars while keeping one eye on my cousin. It had been a week since Andrew had presented me with the Painted Lady caterpillar, and I had placed it in a jar and given it leaves to eat, waiting for it to spin a cocoon. In 1913, I'd made dozens and dozens of paintings for my book, but here, I would need to start over. Thankfully, I retained all the knowledge I had from 1913, and I wasn't starting from scratch.

"Does the queen prefer poetry or literature?" Aveline asked as she sat with a piece of parchment and a quill. "I could write a poem and recite it for her, or I could give a dramatic reading of a piece of literature. Which do you think?"

"She prefers to hear poetry." I turned over a leaf, disappointed that it didn't contain a caterpillar. "But she likes to discuss literature. If you are planning to recite something as part of your masque, it should be a poem, I think."

Masques were a form of entertainment popular at court. It involved music, dancing, singing, acting, and dramatic readings. I'd heard that Lettice Knollys and her mother were planning an elaborate masque for the queen, even hiring professional actors to coach Lettice and perform along with her. I didn't think it was necessary. The simpler, the better.

Aveline nodded enthusiastically. "I have an idea for a poem about the seasons. Shall I work on it?"

"I think it would be a good idea."

She began to write, dipping her quill into an inkpot, her tongue pinched between her teeth.

"There you are," Charles said as he approached me. "I've been looking for you for almost an hour." He held a letter in his hand as he frowned at us. "What are you two doing?"

"I am collecting caterpillars." I held up the jar where I had put the two I'd already found, grinning like a fool who had just been given a priceless gift. It felt good to smile again. "And our dear cousin is working on a poem."

A group of three noblewomen passed, whispering to each other as they sent suggestive looks in Charles's direction. He was handsome, strong, and courageous—a perfect combination for a nobleman and a trusted member of the queen's highest council. But he didn't seem to notice the women as he squatted next to me, looking at my caterpillars.

He, like me, had not planned to stay in 1563 and had never taken the time to find a wife.

Would that change now? Right after I'd died in 1913, Charles had promised to take care of me, but did that mean he would stay? I had thought so at the time, but as the months passed and he didn't mention it again, I had started to wonder.

I wanted to ask him, but I was too afraid of his answer.

"I have an urgent matter I need to bring to the queen," Charles said as he held up the letter. "It's a message from the archduke of Austria."

"Why don't you take it to her yourself?" I continued to look under the leaves of the hibiscus, hoping to find another Painted Lady. As soon as I had several samples, I planned to begin painting.

"This is a delicate matter." He spoke softly as he glanced at Aveline and then back at me. "I cannot take the chance that the queen is in a foul mood when I approach her."

"She was in good spirits when I left her."

"That's because she likes you."

I smiled. "She likes you even better, *Eyes*." Everyone knew the queen liked healthy, strong men who were confident, bold, and daring. She appreciated a good dancer and someone who could keep up a lively conversation. Charles fit all those descriptions.

"Please, Cec," he said. "You have a calming effect on her, and she might need that after she learns about the letter."

I sighed. "Aveline, will you be upset if I leave you?"

"No." She smiled, her hazel eyes filled with contentment. "I will spend my afternoon penning this poem. I'll see you at supper."

I nodded and lifted my hand so Charles could help me off the ground. "I will take you," I said, "but you must carry my caterpillars."

He gave me a look, reminding me of our childhood when I would ask for his help doing something trivial. It wasn't that I couldn't carry them myself, but I liked having my big brother care about the things that were important to me.

He shook his head with a smile as he picked up the jar, inspecting the little creatures.

As we walked into the castle, I couldn't help but marvel that God had brought Charles and me together. Neither his parents nor mine in this path had been time-crossers. Our marks came from our parents in our other paths. Yet, God had still put us in the same family. The fact that Charles's father had married my mother was remarkable.

And then we met Andrew, another time-crosser, which was even more amazing.

Over the last week, I had seen Andrew from time to time around the castle, mostly at meals or in passing as he came and went from the Privy Chamber. We hadn't spoken since our conversation in the garden, but that didn't mean I hadn't thought about him. On some days, he was all I could think about.

"I've decided it's time to find you a husband," Charles said.

My footsteps faltered as we walked down a long gallery with high windows to the right.

"Pardon me?"

He stopped and turned to me, and I could see by the deep creases around his eyes that the subject had been weighing on his mind. "I've waited as long as I dare, offering you time to mourn. But you're twenty-one. 'Tis time we secure an advantageous match for you. I might not always be here, and I want to know that—"

"Where are you going?" My heart hammered as I studied his face, looking for signs that he might leave me.

"Cecily, you know I have a mother and a sister in 1883."

"You're not leaving me here, are you?"

"The truth is, I don't know what I'm going to do." He ran his hand over the back of his neck. "If I can find you a husband, I will stay in 1883 to care for Mama and Ada. But if I secure financial investment in our farm, I will feel better leaving them to stay with you. I feel obligated to both families."

He carried a great weight on his shoulders, and I didn't want to be a burden—yet the thought of him leaving me here alone was terrifying.

"And what if you can't find me a husband, and you can't get financial backing for the Virginia farm? What will you do then?"

"I don't even want to think about that, Cec. If I had a choice, I would find a husband for you *and* secure investments. I cannot fail at either. But God has not yet answered my prayers, so I must do all I can to ensure you're all taken care of."

"What if I don't want to get married?" I asked quietly.

He lowered his hand, compassion in his gaze, knowing how I felt about the subject. "Even if I stayed here, you would still need to marry."

"I don't need a husband to be happy."

"'Tis not about your happiness. If something should happen to me. Or if the queen—" He took a deep breath as he glanced up and down the gallery to make sure he would not be heard. "Our positions in court are never secure. If the queen should die and there is no heir apparent, we might face a civil war." He studied me. "You need a husband, Cecily. I know it wasn't that way in 1913, but things are different here. Survival, especially for a woman, is found in her connections and alliances."

He put his arm around my shoulder as I took a deep breath, and we continued to walk down the gallery. The reality of my situation was out of my control. I wanted more time. I was still mourning my losses from 1913—and I hadn't met a single man at court who had appealed to me.

Except for one. But it would be out of the question, even if he did care for me.

Charles pulled away and said, "The Duke of Albany has expressed an interest in marrying you."

"No." I shook my head adamantly as I slipped my hand around his elbow. "He's old, Charles. And—and *old*."

"But you would be a duchess."

"It wouldn't be worth it."

We paused our conversation as a group of servants passed, their eyes lowered in deference.

I was about to reiterate my dislike of the Duke of Albany when Andrew stepped into the gallery from a door up ahead.

My heart did a little flutter in my chest, and I must have tightened my hold on Charles's arm because he turned his troubled face to me.

"It would never work, Cecily." His voice was low. "The queen has never given permission for one of her maids to marry a man beneath her."

My cheeks warmed. "I know not what you speak of."

"And even if the queen said yes," Charles continued, his voice quiet, though Andrew was still far enough away that he couldn't hear, "and Drew felt the same way about you, I know he is staying in 1883. He's the only male heir to the Whitney fortune."

"I didn't say anything," I protested, my irritation rising as Charles's rational comments made too much sense.

"And, more importantly," he said, "*I* would never approve."

I turned to him, surprised. "You love Andrew like a brother."

"As a man, there would be no one better for you. But he's a carpenter here, Cec. A servant at Arundel Castle. He doesn't have a farthing to his name. I want stability and safety for you."

"Please stop talking about this," I said through gritted teeth as Andrew came closer. "I have no intention of marrying Andrew Bromley—and he has no intention of marrying me."

"Good." Charles let out his breath. "You need to start thinking of your best options, and the Duke of Albany is at the top of the list."

I wrinkled my nose. I couldn't help it—but I met Andrew's gaze at that moment and heat filled my cheeks.

If he knew what we were discussing, I would be mortified.

※

Andrew joined us as we walked to the Queen's Ballroom on the main level of Windsor Castle. He was quieter than usual, but that didn't stop Charles from asking, "How is the queen feeling today?"

"She is much the same," Andrew said. He'd treated her every day since arriving at the castle, but he had not shared his diagnosis.

"Neither improving nor getting worse?" Charles asked.

"That would mean 'much the same,' Charles," I said with a cheeky grin.

He gave me a side-eye as Andrew smiled quietly beside Charles. I liked to make Andrew smile.

But Charles's earlier comments about Andrew made me sad, because all of them were true, and I was a fool to pretend otherwise. It didn't matter, though, since Andrew had given me no indication that he had romantic interest in me. I'd always suspected that he thought I was pretty, but beyond that, he treated me like all the other young women at court.

"I'll wait here for you," Andrew said as he stopped in the Queen's Ballroom.

"You should come with us," Charles insisted. "What I have to say to the queen will be strengthened with the presence of her physician."

Andrew pressed his lips together as if he wasn't sure but nodded his agreement.

We entered the Presence Chamber and passed the ushers guarding the door to the Privy Chamber. I knocked and was told to enter.

The queen reclined on a sofa with a plate of sweets. Her love for sugar was a luxury that few people could afford, but it had caused trouble for her with teeth problems and weight gain.

Kat Astley, Lady Catherine Knollys, and several other ladies in waiting were seated around the queen with their embroidery in hand, while Lettice entertained with a story.

My pulse increased knowing that Lettice was making headway with the queen while Aveline and I were in the gardens. I should have known they would gather here this afternoon. How was I going to get Aveline a position as a maid of honour if I didn't strategize better?

There was another person in the room who did not surprise me. Lord Robert Dudley, one of the queen's friends from childhood and her favorite courtier. He was master of the horses, an honorable position in the queen's household, which kept him close to her side. His apartments were connected to hers, and it was widely known that he had proposed marriage to her many times, though she would neither say yes nor no. He was also a member of the privy council, along with Charles.

"Lady Cecily," the queen said as she set her sweet down on the plate. "You've brought your brother and Doctor Bromley with you again. But where is your cousin?"

I curtsied as Charles and Andrew bowed.

"She is penning a poem for you, Your Majesty," I said. "She looks forward to entertaining you soon."

"I am anxious to hear her."

It was clear the queen was in a good mood, which boded well for whatever Charles had to say.

"If it pleases Your Majesty," I said, "my stepbrother would like to speak to you."

"Is this about the matter we discussed earlier?" Lord Robert asked Charles. "I thought I had made it clear where I stood on this issue."

Charles's face was hard as he addressed Lord Robert. They rarely saw eye to eye and did not hide their dislike of one another. It was something the queen encouraged. She didn't want her privy council to agree on everything and kept people with differing opinions close to her. "I wanted the queen to decide."

Queen Elizabeth looked between both men, her sharp gaze filled with suspicion. "Have you tried to keep something from me, Robert?"

"You will not be pleased, Your Majesty," Lord Robert said. "That is why I told Lord Norfolk to respond to the letter on your behalf."

"Is this what you are discussing?" the queen asked as she motioned to the letter in Charles's hand.

Her ladies watched with avid curiosity. Queen Elizabeth had forbidden each of us to get involved in court politics. She'd even kept Kat Astley, her most trusted friend, under house arrest for a month when she learned that Kat had secretly worked with Prince Erik of Sweden on courtship negotiations on the queen's behalf.

Even though she did not allow us to be involved in politics, she did allow us to gossip about them and even depended on us to carry important information to her and for her. But that was all we could do. Tell her what was being done—not try to do it ourselves.

Charles stepped forward and presented the letter to the queen. She handed her plate of sweets to Kat and accepted the paper.

Lord Robert stared at Charles as the queen opened it and began to read.

"The Archduke of Austria has asked permission to call on Your Majesty," Charles said. "And it is our belief that he intends to offer you a marriage proposal."

She continued to read the letter, her painted face giving nothing away.

"The archduke is Catholic," Lord Robert said, as if that was all she needed to know.

Queen Elizabeth's father, Henry VIII, had left Catholicism when the pope refused to give him a marriage annulment with his first wife. Instead, King Henry had become a Protestant and divorced Katherine of Aragon, declaring that their daughter, Mary, was illegitimate and couldn't inherit the throne. He'd married Elizabeth's mother, Anne Boleyn, next. What ensued was a religious battle that had raged for years, with Mary killing hundreds of Protestants after she took control of the throne. Upon her death, Elizabeth had inherited the throne and returned the realm to Protestantism. There were many who would not sanction a Catholic marriage.

Queen Elizabeth finally lowered the letter and addressed Charles. "It says he would like to come yet this fall."

Lord Robert stiffened.

"I do not think it prudent with the plague raging," she said. "Perhaps we should invite him to visit in the spring."

"You would encourage his pursuit?" Lord Robert asked.

"We are not in a place to discourage anyone." She handed the letter back to Charles. "Nor are we able to accept a marriage proposal. As soon as I have an heir, my life will be in constant danger. Even more than it is now."

"But, Your Majesty," Charles protested. "The privy council agrees that it is imperative that you marry and produce an heir immediately. There is too much at stake if you do not."

"Why have you not offered a proposal yourself, my Eyes?" the queen asked with a teasing smile, though her voice was serious. "Would you not make a good consort to the queen and father to an heir?"

Charles's lips parted in surprise as Lord Robert glared at him. Lord Robert wanted to marry her, and everyone knew it. Perhaps he would have, had he not been married to someone else when the queen ascended to the throne. But his wife's untimely and suspicious death, falling down a flight of stairs, had made it impossible for them to wed. Everyone already suspected that she and Robert had killed his wife. If the queen married him, it would only fuel the fires. And Queen Elizabeth needed to remain popular so her kingdom would defend her if her enemies attacked.

"Your Majesty," Charles said as he lowered his gaze, clearly uncomfortable. "It would be an honor to marry you—"

"I am only jesting, Lord Norfolk," the queen said with a sigh. "I am well aware of what's at stake." She leaned back on her cushions, sweat beading on her brow. Her mood changed abruptly, and she looked like she might become ill. "I want everyone but Kat and Doctor Bromley to leave."

The ladies looked surprised as they stared at one another.

"Now!" the queen thundered.

Everyone gathered their embroidery quickly and fled the queen's Privy Chamber.

I glanced at Andrew as Charles and I walked past him, but his concern was focused on the queen.

As we stepped into the Presence Chamber, Lord Robert stopped Charles.

"I knew it would make her upset," Lord Robert said. "She doesn't need the added stress of finding a husband at this point."

"Do you know what ails her?" Charles asked.

"She refuses to tell me." He took a step closer to Charles. "Do not bother her with marriage prospects, do you hear me? And do not get it into your head that she was serious about you."

"Why? So you can continue to woo her yourself?"

There were many, Charles included, who did not want the queen to marry Lord Robert. They believed a foreign alliance was a better idea, to strengthen ties between two European powers.

"Leave her be," Lord Robert said with clenched teeth. "Or you will have me to deal with."

He strode away as Charles's chest lifted with heavy breaths.

When he turned to me, he said, "I want you to speak to Kat. See if you can get the truth from her. Drew refuses to tell me what is wrong, but mayhap Kat will share with you."

"I doubt it. Kat is the queen's most trusted friend."

"Kat has gone behind the queen's back when she thought it was best for her."

"And was arrested."

Charles dipped his chin as he looked at me. "This *is* best for the queen—for all of us. I want to know what ails her."

I sighed and nodded my acquiescence.

"Good." Charles straightened. "In the meantime, consider what I've said. By the end of the summer, I would like you to secure a marriage proposal of your own. I know you want to marry for love, but love isn't necessary."

"And what if I do secure a proposal?" I asked. "Will you leave me here?"

"If I still need to get financing for the farm."

"Which path would you choose if you do?"

He was quiet for a moment and then said, "I know not. My

life has always been determined for me. If I had to choose, I'm not sure what I want."

"I know what I want." I put my hand on his arm. "I want you to be happy, Charles."

He touched my chin. "Worry not, Cec. When the time comes, I'll know what to do."

"I hope so."

He smiled. "I must be off to pen a letter to the Archduke of Austria."

After he left, I remembered the jar of caterpillars Charles had carried for me. They were sitting on a table nearby, almost forgotten, and reminded me of what I wanted to show Andrew.

I waited in the Presence Chamber for over an hour before Andrew stepped out of the Privy Chamber.

"Do not even ask what ails her," he said when he saw me.

"I wasn't going to."

"Then why have you waited for me?"

I suddenly felt nervous and uncertain. "May I show you something?"

"Of course."

Lifting the jar of caterpillars, I motioned for him to follow me.

"I see you've been collecting." He nodded at the jar.

I only smiled.

We walked through a maze of rooms and up several flights of stairs into one of the towers facing the North Terrace and the Thames River. I had asked the queen for its use earlier that week, and she had granted it.

Andrew did not ask me where I was taking him. When I glanced back, he lifted his warm brown eyes and my heart raced violently. I had not expected Andrew Bromley to reenter my life. I'd spent the past five years trying to forget my feelings for him, feelings I had never really entertained because of his lowly status and my desire to leave 1563.

But he was here now. And my feelings had returned like a raging storm.

I swallowed my nerves and took several deep breaths as we continued to climb. When we entered the highest room in the tower, light poured in from the large windows and the painting I'd created was on full display, right where I'd left it on the easel.

When I moved to the side, Andrew paused on the top step, his attention on my painting as wonder filled his eyes.

He looked at me, his lips parted. "You painted this?"

With an awkward nod, I tried to smile. I was so nervous, I suddenly couldn't remember why I had thought this was a good idea. I felt bare and exposed before him, my heart on the canvas I had painted. I hoped he liked it, but if he did not, it would crush me.

I didn't like feeling so vulnerable with anyone, least of all Andrew.

He walked to the easel to study it closer. "Lady Cec—"

"Please, just call me Cecily," I said as I stayed near the wall.

"Cecily," he said, his voice lower, his eyes on me again. "This painting is magnificent. It looks exactly like the caterpillar we found in the garden last week. Your talent astounds me. It reminds me of John James Audubon, have you heard of him? He's famous for painting—"

"Birds." I nodded. "I studied his work in my other path." I took a deep breath. "This is the first time I've painted since . . ." I couldn't bear to say it.

"Since you died in 1913?"

"Yes." I needed him to understand what he had done when he handed me that caterpillar. "The Painted Lady you found for me was a gift," I said, blinking away the tears that suddenly stung the backs of my eyes as I swallowed the last bit of nerves. "You gave me back my dream so I can look to the future, instead of the past. Will you accept this painting as a gift in return?"

He studied me, and I felt his gaze almost as if it was a physical touch.

"Do you not need it for your book?" he asked.

"There will be many others—a dozen or more of this species, perhaps. I will choose the best of my paintings for the book."

"Then I would be honored to accept it, Cecily."

I let out a little breath and smiled brightly, the tears banished. I removed the dried canvas from the frame and slowly rolled the painting.

He watched me silently, and when I handed it to him, our fingers brushed.

Fire raced up my arm, and I let the canvas go, hoping that I wasn't wearing my feelings on my face.

Perhaps I could not marry him, but I could become his friend. And that would have to be enough.

6

CHARLES

JULY 4, 1883
NEWPORT, RHODE ISLAND

"'We hold these truths to be self-evident, that all men are created equal, that they are endowed by their Creator with certain unalienable Rights, that among these are Life, Liberty, and the pursuit of Happiness . . .'"

The sun beat down on the citizens and visitors of Newport as we stood in Touro Park, listening to the reading of the Declaration of Independence from the town mayor. The sound of firecrackers could be heard in the distance, as children had been lighting them up and down the city streets since early that morning. Popcorn scented the humid air as people drank lemonade and children licked their dripping ice cream cones. Hundreds of people, young and old, poor and wealthy, had come together to celebrate Independence Day.

Congressman Reinhold sat on the stage, waiting to give the Gettysburg Address as his wife and daughter sat near the front. Isabel took that moment to glance in my direction. Her pink cheeks made her brown eyes sparkle as she smiled at me.

"Don't look now, my lord," Mrs. Whitney said from beside me, "but someone is watching you."

I glanced at my hostess, who was wearing a large white hat with white silk roses around the crown. She held her head high, receiving attention wherever we went in Newport as many people wanted to meet me.

It was strange how much these Americans revered British aristocrats when a hundred years before, they were fighting to have independence from them.

"The *other* Mrs. Whitney can't keep her eyes off you," Drew's mother said as she continued to look at the stage but spoke to me.

Helen watched me closely. I tapped the brim of my fedora when I met her gaze, and she nodded, but she didn't smile or look away. Her lips were pursed, and her eyes were calculating. Whenever possible, I avoided her company, not wanting to give her any reason to dig into my past. I wasn't worried that she might discover that my real name was Charles Hollingsworth—but if she inquired at Arundel Castle about the current Lord Norfolk, she would quickly discover that I was not him.

I didn't want to be scrutinized by her, so I stepped back, allowing Mrs. Whitney's large hat to cover me from her line of sight.

The portly vicomte Helen had invited as her guest was near the ice cream stand for the third time since the speeches had started. He seemed more enamored with American food than with the people. I'd met him and he was a good chap, but he wasn't there to play Helen's games, as far as I could tell.

As I watched him order another ice cream cone, a movement in the crowd caught my eye. Evelyn had been standing near our group just moments ago but was now walking toward the edge of the park, away from the stage. She glanced behind her for a moment and then continued toward Bellevue Avenue.

Neither Drew nor his mother seemed to notice her absence, but curiosity got the better of me. Where was she going?

I couldn't help but follow.

By the time I reached Bellevue, Evelyn was turning left onto Church Street, away from the celebrations.

The street was thick with people as I continued to follow her, more curious than before.

As I turned onto Church Street, I discovered that she had stopped at a stand selling firecrackers.

With a frown, I stayed back and watched. Carriages passed, and vendors tried to sell their wares to me, but I put up my hand and shook my head.

As soon as Evelyn finished paying for the bag of firecrackers, she continued down Church Street and turned onto School Street. I picked up my pace, not wanting to lose her.

School Street was much quieter as Evelyn entered the yard of a large brown building. It stood three stories tall with dormer windows on the top floor. At one time, it might have been a grand house, but now it looked more like a school. Children ran toward Evelyn from every direction. They were all wearing matching gray uniforms that were clean but worn. Excited chatter filled the air as she grinned at them and set down her paper bag before holding out her arms to accept their hugs.

My eyes caught on a sign above the front door.

The Newport Home for Friendless Children, established in 1866.

It wasn't a school, but an orphanage.

I stayed back so Evelyn wouldn't see me, though I had a good view of her.

"Children, children," said a matronly woman wearing a dress made of the same gray cloth who stepped out of the building. She carried a child on her hip, a baby of perhaps ten or eleven months old, though I could never guess those things properly. "Give Miss Whitney some space. It isn't as if you haven't seen her."

"I don't mind," Evelyn said in a gentle voice that did not resemble the one she used with me. "I miss them as much as they miss me." She smiled at the baby and held out her hands. "There you are, my darling."

The baby clearly knew Evelyn and bounced in the matron's arms as she was passed from one woman to the next.

"I have brought treats to help you celebrate the Fourth of July," Evelyn said as she indicated the bag. "But you mustn't light these unless you have Mr. Flanders's help."

"Are they firecrackers, Miss Whitney?" a little boy with missing front teeth asked, his eyes growing large.

"Take a look, Eddie." She hugged the baby and nodded at the bag.

"*Gee willikers!*" the boy said.

"Now, Eddie," the matron warned. "You know I don't like slang."

"I know, I know." He showed the contents of the bag to the other children who crowded around them.

Evelyn smiled at the children, but then turned her full attention to the baby in her arms. Her eyes shined as she looked the child over. "She's growing so fast," she said to the matron. "She'll need another dress soon. I'll bring one the next time I come."

"I don't know what we'd do without your generosity, Miss Whitney."

"I wish I could do more to pay you back for all you've done for me." Evelyn squatted with the child and put the baby on her wobbly legs, slowly letting go until the child was balancing on her own. She grinned at Evelyn, squinting into the sunshine. "Has she taken her first steps yet?" Evelyn asked.

"Not yet." The matron crossed her forearms over her waist and looked fondly at Evelyn and the child. "I keep hoping you're here when she does."

"So do I." Evelyn took a half step back, close enough to catch the little girl if she fell, but far enough away to entice her to take a step.

"Come here, darling," Evelyn said as she held her hands out to the baby.

The little girl teetered and almost fell, grinning the whole time, but she didn't take a step.

Evelyn laughed and then scooped the baby into her arms. "Perhaps tomorrow." Her face became pensive as she said, "I mustn't stay long, or I will be missed. Mother has agreed to let me come and visit only if I attend all the social events on her calendar. Today is full of them, I'm afraid." She sighed and kissed the baby's cheek. "I must go. But I'll be back."

Evelyn handed the baby to the matron and gently ran her hand over the child's wispy blond hair before saying good-bye to the others.

She would be walking right past me in a moment, so I turned and started down School Street toward Touro Park, hoping I would blend in with the crowd. My mind was spinning with everything I'd just witnessed and everything I'd already learned about Drew's sister.

In the past year and a half, she'd had a sudden shift in her personality, from fun-loving and carefree to sullen and melancholy. She had formed an opinion about me before I arrived and told me at breakfast that I was just like all the others, and if she wasn't careful, I could break her heart, too. She also volunteered at an orphanage every day, one that her mother allowed her to visit.

The most telling evidence of all was how close she was to a child who was not quite walking but was probably about ten or eleven months old. A child with fair hair and blue eyes—like Evelyn's.

As I approached Touro Park again, my pulse thumped with the revelation of Evelyn's secret. Did Drew have any idea what had happened to his sister?

My steps slowed as I entered the park and returned to Drew's side, hoping Evelyn hadn't seen me. Drew glanced in my direction but didn't seem concerned that I had left—or that his sister was gone. Had he even noticed?

As Evelyn made her way back through the crowd several minutes later, she didn't look at me or give any indication that she knew I had followed her. The smile she'd had for the children was gone, but the deep sadness behind her pretty eyes made more sense now.

She must have felt me watching her, because she lifted her gaze to look at me.

I hoped she didn't see pity on my face, because I didn't feel sorry for her.

I was sad.

Evelyn studied me for a moment, and for the first time since I'd met her, it felt as if she was looking deeper than surface level. She was mining for something—but what it was, I couldn't be certain.

All I knew was that Evelyn was not an easy person to read or understand, but now that I knew her secret, I had a better appreciation for her melancholy countenance.

Her heart had been broken. I just wasn't sure who had done it. Though I suddenly wanted to know, if for no other reason than to make him accountable and restore the light in her eyes that I saw when she held that baby.

The ball that evening would be held at the *other* Mrs. Whitney's home on Bellevue Avenue. Drew's mother had been fussing all day that she wished she had a husband who cared about her. Clarence Whitney would be at the ball—but his brother, Drew's father, William, was still in Europe.

I'd discovered that most of the men were either in Europe or stayed in the city while their wives and children frolicked in Newport. Some of them traveled to the resort town for the weekends, but very few stayed for long periods of time. Clarence Whitney was different. He spent all his time in Newport or Europe, and Drew had told me that he was rarely at the office in New York. He'd stopped working years before and let his brother manage the family business.

Not only were the two Mrs. Whitneys drawing financial support from the same business, but William was the only family member working for the company.

"Do you think your father will let you know when he returns to New York?" I asked Drew as we descended the grand staircase in Midcliff to wait in the parlor until the ladies were ready to leave for the ball. I pulled on the cuffs of my black evening coat, marveling at the fit. I much preferred the fashions in 1883 over the elaborate costumes in 1563. Not only were they more appealing to look at, but they were more comfortable and functional.

"I am not sure." Drew opened the door into the parlor, and we entered the bright room facing the veranda. All the shades were open today, allowing the last vestiges of sunshine to find their way into the room. The Atlantic rolled beyond the property, but it was serene compared to the day I had arrived. "I hope he's intrigued by my message about a possible investment."

I took a seat on one of the cream-colored sofas to wait for Evelyn and Mrs. Whitney. "And you're certain he won't come to Newport?"

"Quite. I fear he may have—" He paused, clearly disturbed. "I think he might have a mistress. The way Mother talks, I'm certain their marriage is over."

"I'm sorry, Drew." Even in 1563, affairs were a commonplace problem, especially at court, where people lived closely with one another. The queen frowned upon them and punished those who were caught, but it didn't stop them.

"It shouldn't come as a surprise." Drew crossed his arms and leaned against the fireplace mantel. "Mother is obsessed with her social status, and Father is consumed with his work. When they are together, they do nothing but fight about money. Neither seems satisfied, and both are seeking happiness in the wrong places." He stared at the cold fireplace, his thoughts far off. "In 1563, I might have nothing, but at least my parents love one another deeply. Their love is sacrificial and sincere. Instead of seeking what they can get from one another, they look for ways to serve one another." He finally looked at me. "I would rather be poor and loved unconditionally than be wealthy and have a shallow marriage to a woman who only wants me for my money."

"Perhaps you can have both love and money."

Drew scoffed. "That would be a miracle." After a moment, he uncrossed his arms and pushed away from the mantel. "Charles, I've been meaning to ask you something."

A noise in the foyer caught my attention, and I looked toward the open door. I hadn't stopped thinking about Evelyn or her visit to the Newport Home for Friendless Children earlier that day. It wasn't my place to tell Drew what I had discovered, though it would be hard to keep it hidden from him. He and I saw each other every day in both paths now. I trusted him implicitly, and I knew he would handle the information tactfully—but it still wasn't my place.

The butler, Prescott, walked past the door, and I felt strangely disappointed that it wasn't Evelyn.

"It's about Cecily," Drew said.

My attention focused on my friend. "What about Cecily?"

He started to speak and then paused, as if he didn't know how to address his concern. Finally, he said, "I know you've been speaking to the Duke of Albany about a possible marriage."

"It would be a good match."

"For who?" Drew asked, his reticence gone. "He is not only old, but he is a curmudgeon. You can't be serious. He would suck the life out of your sister."

"Cecily needs someone to protect her and provide for her. The Duke of Albany is wealthier even than the queen. She would be set for life."

"And so would you."

Drew's words felt like a punch to my gut. I stiffened. "You forget yourself, Drew."

"There are other men to consider." He didn't back down. "Men who could provide for Cecily and not only offer her protection, but a life. She's already lost so much."

"I know what she's lost." My anger increased. "Her loss has affected both of us."

"Don't force her to give up what little she has left." His voice was calm, almost pleading, and I suddenly realized how much he cared about her.

Cecily's response at seeing Drew in the gallery at Windsor returned to me. My stepsister also cared for Drew.

I recalled memories of Cecily and Drew from our childhoods, of the gifts he used to bring her and the way she always wanted to tag along when I was in his company. Was their relationship deeper than I realized?

"Don't get in my way, Drew." The words came out more forcefully than I intended, but I needed him to know I was serious. "Cecily is a lady from the House of Arundel, the stepdaughter of an earl, and a maid of honour in Her Majesty's service. You know as well as I do that she has a responsibility to marry well."

He stared at me, his voice cool. "I understand completely. You have nothing to worry about where I'm concerned, Charles, but I cannot stay silent watching you snuff the life out of her. That, I cannot abide."

"I have no intention of snuffing the life out of her." My anger increased at such a suggestion. Every decision I'd ever made for Cecily was for her well-being and happiness. "But you have no say in who she marries."

There was another sound in the foyer.

Drew straightened. "That might be Mother. She'll want to leave as soon as possible."

He walked to the door and left the parlor without looking back at me.

It took me a moment to even out my breathing. Why was I so threatened by Drew's words? Cecily was smart enough not to fall in love with him, even if she did have a fondness for him. And Drew would never overstep his boundaries. So then why was I upset?

As I moved toward the door, I knew that Drew was right. Forcing Cecily to marry the Duke of Albany would crush her spirits. Perhaps the duke wasn't the right person, but there had to be someone tolerable who could provide and care for her. I just had to look harder.

I stepped out of the parlor and found Drew talking with his mother in low tones. When she saw me, her face brightened. "Lord Norfolk! How splendid you look tonight. You'll be the talk of the ball. You will surely outshine the Vicomte Deville."

The reminder of the vicomte, and of Helen Whitney's ball, stiffened my shoulders. I would need to avoid the woman at all costs tonight. I didn't want her to ask too many questions.

A movement on the stairs drew my attention as Evelyn appeared.

She wore a stunning blue silk gown, which matched the color of her eyes to perfection. It was drawn up to a bustle in the back with ribbons dangling behind her. The straps on her shoulders and the décolletage accentuated her thin arms and slender neck. Her blond hair was styled high, and she wore a blue jeweled comb that matched the fabric. Everything about her shimmered and danced.

Everything but her eyes.

Her sad gaze fell on me but quickly moved to her mother as she descended the stairs, her gloved hand skimming the banister.

"You're breathtaking, Evelyn," Mrs. Whitney said as she turned to me. "Isn't she beautiful, my lord?"

"Very." I finally discovered my voice as Drew stepped forward to offer her his arm.

I couldn't find the right words to describe how beautiful Evelyn looked tonight. Seeing her with the children earlier had opened my eyes to so much and helped me to see her in a different light. She was no longer angry and bitter in my mind, but heartbroken and sad, and that changed everything. Somewhere in the world was a man who had misused her and was not shouldering her pain. And there was a little girl she was forced to abandon because of her position in society.

"You're staring, my lord," Mrs. Whitney said with a chuckle next to me.

Warmth climbed my neck. I couldn't remember the last time

81

I had been embarrassed. "Pardon me." I cleared my throat and looked away from her daughter.

"I don't blame you," she said. "You won't be the only man who notices her tonight. You'll want to secure your name on her dance card right away."

Prescott opened the front door for us to exit Midcliff.

Evelyn was not paying attention to me as Drew brought her a wrap and placed it over her shoulders.

Mrs. Whitney exited the house first as I stood by the door and waited.

As Evelyn finished with her wrap, the gentle fragrance of her perfume enveloped me. "You look lovely tonight, Miss Whitney," I said, though my words were stilted and awkward—and nothing at all like the polished comments I made daily to the courtiers at Windsor Castle. I felt like an inexperienced boy, all arms and legs and no charm.

"Thank you," she said as she walked past me.

I almost groaned, but Drew was standing nearby, a frown on his face.

The women entered the carriage, and then I stepped up with Drew behind me. We sat across from Mrs. Whitney and Evelyn.

Mrs. Whitney carried the conversation as we made our way to the other Whitney family cottage on Bellevue Avenue. Evelyn only added to the conversation when she was addressed. Her thoughts seemed a million miles away.

Or perhaps they were closer than that, as close as a Home for Friendless Children on School Street.

7

CECILY

JULY 5, 1563
WINDSOR CASTLE

White cumulus clouds filled the massive blue sky over the tennis court at Windsor Castle, though I only had a small view of it. The court was enclosed with tall stone walls on all four sides and sloping roofs over the spectator galleries on two of them. I sat next to the queen on the raised dedans, a platform behind the service end of the court, which had the best view. King Henry VIII had loved tennis and had the court built in the Lower Ward during his reign, not far from St. George's Chapel.

The queen was having a good day and had ordered a tennis tournament for the afternoon. Most of her ladies in waiting had been called to attend, and several noblemen had been asked to participate. I had brought Aveline with me and presented her to the queen, who had invited her to sit with our group. Lettice was also present, as were about a dozen other young ladies vying for the maid of honour position.

On days like today, it was hard to imagine that thousands were suffering from the plague in London.

As we watched one game after the other and listened to the echoing sound of the ball hitting the hard surfaces of the court, my mind was not on the matches but on helping Aveline present her best attributes to the queen.

"Aveline plays, Your Majesty," I said to the queen as one match finished and we waited for another to start.

"You play tennis?" the queen asked Aveline. "Are you any good?"

"I like to think so," Aveline said, lifting her chin. I had told her the queen didn't like simpering women, but prized confidence at all times. "My father was an avid player, and he built a court at our castle in Wales."

"Did you ever beat him?" she asked.

Aveline grinned. "I did, Your Majesty. Many times."

The queen clapped, and those around her joined in the applause.

Aveline's cheeks turned pink, and she smiled at me.

I returned her smile, considering this moment a victory, though we had a long way to go.

"My Eyes," the queen said when Charles appeared on the court, holding a tennis racket. He was wearing a pair of tighter hose, ballooned to the knee, with stockings. He also wore a white linen shirt and leather jerkin but had discarded the long-sleeved doublet for ease of movement.

Charles jogged across the court and bowed over the queen's hand, his face more sullen than usual.

There had been something different about him all day, but I hadn't had a chance to talk to him. He seemed pensive, almost distracted.

"Will you win today, Lord Norfolk?" the queen asked.

"I will try, Your Majesty," he said with a gallant smile.

"And who is your competitor?"

A second man stepped onto the court, and I sat up straighter, my heart skipping a beat.

"Ah, Doctor Bromley," Queen Elizabeth said with a wide smile. Her face and hands appeared to be more swollen today than usual, but she hadn't complained of a headache, which seemed to be her constant ailment of late. "I did not know you played tennis."

"I try, Your Majesty." He was also wearing hose, stockings, and a linen shirt, though he wasn't wearing a jerkin. Without his doublet, I had a better grasp of the breadth of his chest and his muscular arms. Not only was he tall, but he was built beautifully—and I wasn't the only woman to notice as others began to whisper his name.

It appeared that Charles had competition, not only on the tennis court, but in the eyes of the ladies in waiting.

"May the best man win," Queen Elizabeth said—and then added, "and the victor will get a reward of my choosing." She surveyed the ladies in waiting who were sitting near her, and a sly smile appeared on her face. "A kiss from one of my maidens—a maiden of the winner's choosing."

Heat warmed my face as I looked in Andrew's direction. He offered me a smile, and it went straight to my heart.

"Let the game begin." The queen motioned to Andrew and Charles to start.

They left the dedans and took their places on either side of the net. Charles was on the service end, so he served the ball, sending it along one of the slanted roofs over the spectator's gallery. Andrew hit it back, and the game commenced. Whenever one of them gained a point, the crowd of men and women cheered.

Half of the maids cheered for Charles and the other half for Andrew, including Lettice, who sat near the front of the gallery, her eyes shining as she watched the match.

I found myself hoping that Charles would win so I wouldn't have to watch Andrew kiss another maiden. And whoever was selected among the women would get special attention from the queen. If it was Lettice, it would only help her cause.

"Move to the front," I whispered to Aveline.

"What?" My cousin turned to me, her hazel eyes still bright from interacting with the queen.

85

"Slowly make your way toward the front of the group and take a seat next to Lettice," I whispered. "It will give you a better chance to receive a kiss, and whoever gets the kiss will be rewarded with the queen's attention."

"Do you think it will really matter in the long run?" she asked.

"Everything matters, Aveline. We must look for ways each day to gain approval, and if one of the queen's favorites chooses you for a kiss, it will show the queen you are desirable and valuable to her retinue."

"But one of the competitors is my cousin," she protested.

"Your stepcousin," I reminded her. "But it's even better. If Charles wins, I will catch his eye and motion for him to choose you. He will simply kiss your hand, but it will remind the queen that you are his cousin. Family ties are very important to her. They strengthen alliances and ensure loyalty."

Aveline took a deep breath and lowered her chin, as if she was preparing to go into battle. "I will do it."

"Good."

The match was warming up, and several spectators had risen to their feet. Aveline was able to move through the crowd to get to the front without much trouble.

Andrew and Charles were well matched as they battled for the win. Sweat beaded on their brows, and their focus was sharp and pointed on their opponent. Back and forth they went, making it impossible to know who might win.

"Lady Cecily," the queen said, tearing my attention away from the game.

"Yes, Your Majesty."

"Fetch my page," she said. "I would like some sweets from the kitchens."

I hesitated for a heartbeat, not wanting to miss a moment of the game, but I could not deny her request. It was my job to serve her without question.

"Yes, Your Majesty," I said with a quick curtsy.

Without wasting another moment, I left the dedans in search

of the page who had come with us to the tennis court. He was not in the spectator boxes, nor was he in the corridor behind them.

The crowd cheered, but I could not see the court. Who was winning?

Finally, out of breath and frustrated, I located the page just outside.

"The queen would like to speak to you," I told him. "Make haste."

He jumped at the sound of my voice and ran into the building.

The cheering grew louder as I reentered the tennis court.

"We have a winner!" the queen declared, her voice carrying over the others. "Doctor Bromley of Arundel Castle."

My heart picked up speed as I tried to get to the dedans.

"Take your pick, Muscles." The queen's laughter filled the echoing tennis court as her newest favorite received a nickname.

I stepped onto the dedans at the back, behind the queen. All the maidens smiled and tilted their heads in expectation. Lettice and Aveline were at the front, closest to Andrew. He glanced at all of them, the color high in his cheeks from his victory, though visibly uncomfortable picking a maiden to kiss in front of everyone.

I didn't move—couldn't breathe. I wanted to be in front with Lettice and Aveline, but I couldn't make a scene to join them.

"Go on and choose," the queen said, leaving no room for arguments.

Andrew approached the maidens and gallantly bowed before Lettice.

My heart fell as disappointment filled my chest.

Not only had he chosen Aveline's rival—but he hadn't chosen me.

I turned away as a cheer arose from the crowd. I didn't want to see Andrew or Lettice or watch as the queen beamed with pleasure. She would never approve of a match between a lowly doctor and her cousin's daughter, but she would encourage flirtation, especially with the handsome young doctor who now had a pet name.

I didn't know where I was going, but my feet seemed to have a mind of their own as I left the tennis court in the Lower Ward.

It was hard to be alone at the castle, but with everyone watching the tournament, there was no one in the Queen's Garden just outside of St. George's Chapel, offering me a rare moment of privacy. I went there, trying to staunch the flow of emotions warring within me.

The roses were in bloom, and I ran my finger over the soft petals, trying to understand the feelings wreaking havoc on my heart. It was ridiculous to be upset.

If I had been at the front, he might have chosen me. But he hadn't even looked for me, and he knew I had been there. Instead, he'd chosen Lettice.

The ache inside my chest was unreasonably deep and made me more frustrated.

Of course he'd choose Lettice. Who wouldn't? She was beautiful, graceful, accomplished, confident, and intelligent.

I tried to tell myself I was upset because it had been a win for Lettice's pursuit of the maid of honour position, but I knew better.

I sank to the grass near a lavender plant, the fragrant aroma wrapping me in an embrace. I plucked a stem and ran the small purple flower under my nose, trying to stimulate my senses so my feelings would not be so powerful.

"I was wondering where you went." Andrew's voice was gentle as he approached, his long legs bringing him to my side. He had his doublet slung over his shoulder as sweat still glistened on his brow.

My heart thumped wildly. Why had he come?

"May I join you?" he asked.

It would be so much easier if I didn't have to see him day and night. I wanted him to leave, to let me sulk over my silly childhood crush.

I began to stand, though it wasn't easy in my cumbersome dress. "I was just about to return to the queen."

He dropped his doublet and reached for my elbow to assist me. The pressure of his hand on my arm was too much. I pulled away the moment I was on my feet. My cheeks were on fire.

Instead of letting me go, he put his hands on my upper arms to still me. "Are you mad at me?"

"Of course not," I said, unable to meet his gaze, afraid he would realize it wasn't anger but jealousy that plagued me.

The word tasted bitter, and I detested it. I'd always struggled with Lettice, but I'd never been jealous of her before now.

"Then what ails you?"

He was still holding me, and I tugged against him, but only halfheartedly. "Nothing."

"You *are* mad," he said, a little surprised.

"No." I swallowed and finally found the courage to look at him, hating myself for the words that were about to slip out of my mouth. "I'm jealous."

His lips softened, and he slowly lowered his arms, searching my face for the truth. "Jealous?"

Anger finally appeared—but not at him. At myself. I turned away from him and touched the lavender, wishing he hadn't followed me and that I wasn't so honest. "Please leave, Andrew."

"Cecily." He said my name as if it was a question and put his hand on my arm again, gently turning me to look at him. His brown eyes were so tender, so dear. "Why would you be jealous?"

I couldn't tell him the truth. I would be mortified if he laughed or took pity on me. I could survive anything but his pity.

"Please forgive me." I knew I had to make an excuse. "'Tis nothing. Just a rivalry that I need to let go." I mustered a smile, though it was weak. "I'm embarrassed admitting the truth. It seems so immature and juvenile when I say it out loud." I lifted my chin. "Congratulations on besting my stepbrother." I was rambling but not sure how to stop. "He will demand a rematch soon, I'm sure." I pulled away from his touch again, and this time, he let me go.

If I ran away, he would suspect the real reason I was jealous, so I had to stay and pretend all was well. "Do you play tennis in 1883?"

He was still studying me, but he said, "Occasionally. Charles just beat me at the Newport Casino yesterday, though the game has evolved quite a bit. We do not play in a walled court, but on a lawn with larger rackets, lighter balls, and different scoring methods."

I smiled. "Yes, I know. We had lawn tennis in 1913."

He returned my smile. "I always forget that you lived thirty years later than me in your other path."

My smile fell as I ran my hand over the lavender again, not looking at him. "I'm envious that you still time-cross and spend a day away from here. I miss 1913 with every breath I take." It was true. But, more importantly, it was a safer topic than my jealousy of Lettice. "I miss swimming. Do you swim? I imagine you do in Newport. I also miss telephones and electricity and automobiles. Though, I suppose you don't have automobiles in 1883 yet, do you? And the telephone is quite new."

"Cecily."

"I miss my family most of all," I continued, not responding to my name, afraid of what he might say if I gave him the opportunity. "I miss speaking freely to my mama about time-crossing. Charles cares, but he isn't someone I usually confide in, especially about my grief. Mayhap he'd listen and offer advice, but I feel guilty knowing he has so many other things to worry about." I paused, not realizing until now that I had stopped confiding in Charles because I didn't want to be a burden to him.

"I'm here," Andrew said.

I turned, realizing I had put a great deal of space between us. "What?"

"I'm here. To listen. To offer advice, if you'd like. Talk about time-crossing."

My mouth suddenly felt dry. "You would listen to me ramble?"

He slowly walked toward me. When he stopped, he took the lavender out of my hand and slipped it above my ear. "You only ramble when you're nervous."

His finger brushed my ear and sent a tingle down my back.

"When you speak from your heart," he continued, "you are eloquent and thoughtful. But whether you ramble or opine or vent, I am here to listen."

My hands were trembling as I looked into his brown eyes.

His attention dropped to the locket I wore around my neck.

I slowly lifted it and unlatched the clasp to reveal the miniature photos within. "'Tis my mama and papa from 1913," I whispered. "I painted them right after I finished the caterpillar. I never want to forget what they looked like."

He slipped his gentle fingers behind mine, and I pulled my hand away so he was holding the locket. It was still on the chain around my neck, and he had to bend close to look at them.

"Their names were Austen and Kathryn Baird," I said quietly.

"You look like your mama." His gaze lifted to mine. "She was very beautiful."

My chest rose and fell as his breath tickled my lips.

Someone cleared their throat, interrupting the moment.

Andrew dropped the locket and took a step away, as if he'd been caught doing something improper.

I found my stepbrother watching us, his arms crossed.

"Charles," I said, discovering that my voice was trembling. I closed the locket and faced him. "Have you come to demand a rematch so soon?"

He looked between me and Andrew, his expression imperceptible. "The queen took ill," he said to Andrew. "I came to retrieve you."

Without another word, Andrew grabbed his doublet and left the garden, glancing back once as he walked toward the tennis court.

When he was gone, Charles turned to me. "What was that?"

"Nothing."

"It didn't look like nothing, Cecily. I thought you understood that this isn't a good idea."

I groaned as I started to walk away. "It was nothing. I assure you."

"No good will come of your infatuation with Drew."

"Infatuation?" The word seemed foul as I faced him. It was not at all how I felt about Andrew.

"I've sent word to Lord Wolverton to visit us here at Windsor," Charles continued. "He's been at his castle in northern England for the past three months and should not bring the threat of the plague with him."

"Lord Wolverton?" I frowned. "As a possible suitor? Are you that desperate to be rid of me?"

Charles's shoulders fell, and he walked toward me. "I am not desperate to be rid of you, Cec. I love you." He put his hands on my upper arms so I would look at him. "Lord Wolverton is only thirty-five, but he is wealthy, well-respected, and his home is far removed from London. More importantly, he is an earl and a distant relative of the queen. She would approve the match."

"I've never met him."

"That's why I've summoned him to court. I want you to keep an open mind."

I lifted my locket into my hand, holding it close, feeling the warmth of Andrew's touch still present as it mingled with the memories of my parents.

"The best way to forget is to move on," Charles said as he let go of my arms, his voice kind and understanding. "It's time, Cec."

My heart fell as I realized he was right. I let go of the locket, unable to hold on to the things that were no longer mine.

8

CHARLES

JULY 5, 1883
NEWPORT, RHODE ISLAND

The sky was partly cloudy as I left my room the next morning at Midcliff. I hadn't spoken to Drew since coming upon him and Cecily the day before in the garden because the queen's sudden turn for the worse had the entire castle in upheaval. She'd been rushed to her bedchamber with Drew at her side, and neither of them had been seen the rest of the day. Even Cecily had no word as to the queen's status.

An emergency meeting of the privy council had been called, and we had discussed what would happen should the queen die. Mary, Queen of Scots, was the most likely heir and the one the queen seemed to prefer, but she was Catholic, and the Protestant nobility of England would fight to keep her from the throne.

I needed to speak to Drew. To learn the queen's prognosis—and to discover what had happened between him and Cecily in the garden.

"You mustn't fight with me, Evelyn." Mrs. Whitney's voice carried into the hall as I passed her bedchamber. I didn't mean to overhear, but the door was cracked open, and Mrs. Whitney's voice held an edge I'd never heard before. "This was part of our agreement. I would let you volunteer at that—that *home*, and you would maintain my social calendar. The excursion to Fort Adams today has been on my calendar for weeks."

"I promised Mrs. Flanders I would be there today," Evelyn protested. "If I go on the excursion, I will not have the opportunity to see the children. And Laura is about to take her first step. I don't want to miss—"

"You vex me, Evelyn," Mrs. Whitney said in a tired voice. "I will remove my permission if you do not attend the excursion."

"Please don't," Evelyn begged, her voice filled with desperation. "I must see—"

"Then I suggest you forgo one day at the home and put a smile on your face. All the most important young people in Newport will be on the excursion today." Mrs. Whitney sighed. "At least try to have fun. And pay a little more attention to Lord Norfolk. He won't be here forever, you know."

I stood straighter at hearing my name.

"How much longer until he leaves?" Evelyn asked in an annoyed voice.

"Evelyn," she scolded.

"He's only here to use me, Mother."

"Nonsense. He is Andrew's guest. He didn't even know you existed until he arrived."

There was a pause. "Who told you that?"

"Andrew." There was a creak in the floorboard, and I imagined Mrs. Whitney had moved closer to her daughter. "Not everyone is out to hurt you, Evelyn. Lord Norfolk is a good Christian man."

I moved past Mrs. Whitney's door, not wanting to be caught, and walked down the stairs toward the breakfast room, feeling chastised by her words.

I wasn't a "good" Christian man. I went to church in both

paths, to satisfy my mama in 1883 and the queen in 1563, but it was out of obligation and duty, not always faith. Losing both of my fathers at the ages of six and fifteen had caused me to carry the weight of my family's responsibilities on my shoulders. And it had hardened my heart toward God. I prayed, but it often felt like my supplications were falling on deaf ears.

It wasn't a good excuse to be angry at God. I had many blessings in my life, but I still tried to control everything because I didn't trust Him to intervene.

I stopped in front of a mirror in the hall and faced myself for the first time in a long time, thinking about how Cecily must have felt yesterday. Did she really think I was trying to marry her off so I could get rid of her? Did Drew think I was selling her to the highest bidder to better myself? Their comments made me take a long, hard look at myself. Life had become too hard. Too serious. And God had become too untrustworthy. It was easier to rely on myself.

The revelation took me by surprise.

Drew appeared at the top of the stairs and paused when he saw me. He slowly descended, his jaw tight.

"You don't need to say it," he said as he walked down the last few steps. "We can't speak inside." He kept walking, past the breakfast room, through the parlor, and onto the veranda.

I followed him to the veranda, where we would have more privacy.

As soon as he closed the door, he said, "Nothing happened between me and Cecily."

"But would it have happened had I not come upon you?"

Drew ran his hands through his hair, something I'd never seen him do before. "I don't know."

I hadn't expected this—at least, not from Drew. I thought he knew better. "When did this start?"

He leaned against the veranda's stone railing and crossed his arms. "I honestly couldn't tell you. Maybe when I first got to Windsor Castle, maybe when we were children. I've always been fond of Cecily, but seeing her at Windsor—"

"It can't continue."

"I know." He pushed away from the railing and motioned to Midcliff. "I know that better than anyone. I'm a Whitney. I have an obligation to this family."

His words echoed my own thoughts. I was obligated to my family, as well.

"And what if you weren't a Whitney?" I asked, knowing his answer but needing him to accept the truth and say it out loud. "What if you only had 1563?"

He gave me a look. "Charles, you know as well as I do that it would be impossible. The only reason I've had confidence to speak to her is because I'm a Whitney in this path. I can't separate myself. If I only lived in 1563 and knew no other life, I wouldn't even lift my eyes to meet hers when I was in her presence." He paced away from the railing. "You don't have anything to worry about. I'll keep my distance."

"Do you love her?"

He took a deep breath as he looked out at the ocean. "I haven't even allowed myself to contemplate such a thing."

I wouldn't tell him that Cecily was struggling with her own feelings. He'd have to be a fool not to notice the way she'd been gazing at him in the garden.

"I summoned Lord Wolverton to Windsor Castle," I said. "If all goes as planned, he should be there in a fortnight. He is an honorable man and would make a good husband for her."

The muscles in Drew's jaw flexed as he looked at the coastline. "I will not stand in his way." He turned to me, and there was fire in his eyes. "But if he is not an honorable man, as you claim, I will do everything in my power to protect her."

I tried not to get upset at his passionate response, knowing that Drew was a healer. A fixer. It was part of the reason he'd gone to medical school, and why I had called upon him to serve the queen. He wanted to protect Cecily as much as I did, but we had different perspectives.

Instead of responding to his warning, I crossed my arms, needing to change the subject and address the other pressing matter. "How long do we have until the queen succumbs to her illness?"

He shook his head. "I don't know. She will be bedridden for some time, but she can still turn a corner. I am doing everything in my power to help her, but I can't change history, Charles. If I treat her with a procedure not yet known in 1563, I will forfeit my path there."

I stood straighter. "You will forfeit it on your birthday anyway—why not treat the queen and save her life now?"

"It's not that easy. And I don't want to forfeit my life this soon. I still have parents at Arundel that I am trying to care for. Everything I earn I send to them."

"I should just look in the history books and see if she survives this."

"You haven't already checked?"

"No. My grandfather warned me to never look for answers about my other path, and I heeded his words. He said there could be dire repercussions." I was reminding myself as I said, "History is supposed to play out as God wills."

"Then we need to let this play out. I am doing my best to care for her. That is all we *can* do."

He was right, but it wasn't easy to accept. If she died, war was inevitable. Mary, Queen of Scots, would fight for the throne and the Protestant nobility would probably try to give it to Lady Katherine Grey, Queen Elizabeth's cousin. My father had died because of the last succession controversy, and I hated to think of what might happen to myself, or worse, Cecily, should it become an issue again.

"We will be late if we don't eat breakfast soon," Drew said as he moved toward the parlor door. "The excursion party is leaving my aunt's house at ten."

I wasn't eager to spend the day at Fort Adams, but Drew's mother had asked us to attend, and as her guest, I had little choice.

"Carrie Astor has been invited," Drew added. "We will need to find a way to get an introduction made between you and her.

If she likes you, perhaps her mother will invite you to the ball—and, if you're invited, it would be rude not to invite your hostess."

"I will do my best."

When we entered the breakfast room, Evelyn was near the sideboard, filling a plate with food.

"Good morning," Drew said to his sister.

She looked up at our arrival, and her gaze caught on mine. It was no longer hostile, but more curious than before. Had she believed her mother's word that I wasn't here in pursuit of her fortune?

"Good morning," I said to her.

She nodded a greeting and then went back to selecting her breakfast.

"Will you be joining us today?" Drew asked as he picked up a plate and perused the offerings. "Or are you running off to do your charity work again?"

Her shoulders stiffened. "It seems I have no choice. Mother insists I join the excursion."

My pulse ticked up a notch as I realized I would get to spend the day with her. Until now, we had only crossed paths occasionally.

Could I get her to talk about the orphanage and open up with me?

I wasn't sure if she would, or why I cared so much—but something compelled me to try.

Over thirty people assembled on the lawn of Helen Whitney's chateau-inspired cottage that morning to visit Fort Adams, west of Newport. The Vicomte Deville was included, but he seemed more interested in eating than visiting with the others. As we had gathered, he'd spoken to a wide-eyed maid in broken English, making sure the lunch baskets were packed in the extra carriages that would follow the excursion party. Helen had saved the maid, steering the vicomte toward her daughter, Marianna.

When Carrie Astor arrived with a group of other young ladies, both Mrs. Clarence Whitney and Mrs. William Whitney descended on her like vultures.

"You won't be spared, I'm afraid," Drew said to me as he nodded in Carrie's direction. "Mother is beckoning us."

Drew and I crossed the lawn to join Mrs. Whitney.

"There you are," she said as she reached toward me, her eyes bright with excitement. "Miss Astor, have you met our very dear Earl of Norfolk?"

Carrie turned her pale blue eyes to me and shook her head. She was probably in her early twenties and was an attractive young woman, but her clothing hung on her thin frame, and she looked pale and sickly, with dark circles under her eyes. Drew had told me that Carrie was in love with a young man from a family her mother didn't approve. They were "new" money and from the South. People had been whispering all summer that she was so miserable without the man that she was starving herself to death.

"Lord Norfolk," Mrs. Whitney said, "may I present Miss Carrie Astor?"

I bowed over Carrie's hand. "It's a pleasure to meet you, Miss Astor."

"The pleasure is mine, Lord Norfolk."

"Oh—Vicomte! Vicomte Deville!" Helen said in a frantic voice, drawing our attention. She waved toward the vicomte, who was speaking to a group of people nearby. "You must come. There is someone you must meet."

Drew's mother lifted her chin with triumph as she turned her back to Helen. "Miss Astor, how lovely you look. Doesn't she look lovely, Lord Norfolk?"

I smiled at Carrie. "You look lovely, Miss Astor."

"Thank you, my lord."

Helen looked anxiously at our little gathering as the vicomte took his time to join us.

"And, Miss Astor, this is my son, Mr. Andrew Whitney," Mrs. Whitney added.

Carrie nodded at Drew. "Yes, we met at the casino last summer."

"Miss Astor and her partner bested me and Evelyn at a game of tennis," Drew said with a smile. "But we will get a rematch soon."

"I would like that." Carrie glanced over Drew's shoulder and said, "Oh, please forgive me. A friend has just arrived. I look forward to talking more later."

"Of course," Mrs. Whitney said as Helen approached with the vicomte. "You go ahead." She put her hand on Carrie's arm and turned her away from Helen and practically pushed her toward her friend.

As Carrie walked away, Helen arrived, her mouth parted. "Why, Minnie Whitney, you did that on purpose."

"What?" Mrs. Whitney asked, wide-eyed.

Helen narrowed her gaze on Mrs. Whitney and then took Vicomte Deville by the arm and called out, "Miss Astor! A moment of your time, please."

As they scurried off to approach Carrie, Mrs. Whitney smiled in triumph. "I love seeing Helen squirm."

"Mother," Drew cautioned, "it isn't becoming of you."

Mrs. Whitney seemed to remember where she was and who she was standing with. She smiled at me, embarrassment tinting her cheeks. "Pardon me, Lord Norfolk. My rivalry with my sister-in-law is a decade old, and I sometimes forget myself."

When it was time to assemble into the open carriages, Isabel Reinhold was seated next to me with Evelyn and Drew across. Mrs. Reinhold and Drew's mother were in another carriage with the older adults, but they kept a keen eye on all of us.

Several carriages with servants, blankets, chairs, umbrellas, and picnic baskets followed, creating a parade as we passed stately homes and curious pedestrians.

I studied Evelyn as we paraded through the tree-lined streets of Newport, wondering what kind of conversation might engage her interest. She held a cream-colored parasol that matched her gown. The dress hugged her small waist and accentuated her curves, and somehow made her large blue eyes seem bluer today than usual. She wasn't like the other women. If my suspicions were correct about Baby Laura, she had far weightier things on her mind than the average girl in our group.

Which meant she wasn't looking for frivolous or shallow conversation. She probably longed for deep and meaningful connections, and discussions about topics that truly mattered.

I spent most of my days thinking about weighty subjects in Queen Elizabeth's court and taking care of the Virginia farm. Here in Newport, with luxury and opulence all around, it had been easy to forget that there was real pain and suffering and injustice in the world.

But I suspected Evelyn rarely forgot.

When we finally arrived at Fort Adams, I took in the vista with appreciation. The fort was made of irregular-sized blocks, several stories tall, and took up the entire end of the peninsula. According to Drew, it was the third largest fort in America. To the right was Newport Harbor, and to the left was the passage out to the Atlantic. The grounds around the fort were pristine with low-cut green grass, which would make a perfect place to picnic.

Drew and I exited the carriage and then helped the ladies to alight as the servants began to set up the picnic area, with Helen overseeing their efforts and Vicomte Deville standing next to her, eagerly anticipating his next meal.

The older ladies stayed near the picnic area as Drew's cousin, Marianna, spoke to the young people. "Shall we take a walk around the fort while lunch is being prepared?"

The large group followed her and began to break off into smaller clusters as we progressed. Several of the young people, including Carrie Astor, cried out in excitement when they discovered two sailboats racing in the harbor. Drew offered Isabel his arm to walk her to the water's edge, but Evelyn continued to follow the path around the fort, her parasol partially covering her pensive face. She was looking up at the fort, so lost in her own thoughts she could have been there alone.

I vacillated between joining the others to get to know Carrie better—and following Evelyn, who was much more intriguing.

The decision wasn't difficult.

"The fort is quite impressive," I said as I approached Evelyn, my hands in my pockets. "I'm sorry you had to miss your charity work to come. It must be very important to you."

She turned her surprised face toward me, as if she'd thought she was alone. "It is important."

"May I ask what you do?"

Apprehension filled her countenance. Did she think I would suspect the truth if she told me where she volunteered?

"I—I volunteer at the Newport Home for Friendless Children."

Something warmed inside me as she chose to trust me with this small part of her life.

"That must be very rewarding work."

She nodded, still a little hesitant. "There are twenty-three children who live there. Mr. and Mrs. Flanders oversee all those children and only have the assistance of two servants, one inside and one outside. They need so much more help, but they can barely keep up with their current expenses. When I learned of their plight, I knew I must help. I can't do much, but I offer what I have."

"I'm sure they appreciate what you can give."

"I wish I could do more."

We continued to walk farther away from the crowd that had gathered to watch the sailboats in the harbor.

"Have you been volunteering there for long?" I asked.

She paused as if trying to decide whether she wanted to take the conversation deeper, but I could see that she was starved to discuss something that mattered to her. It was clearly near and dear to her heart. "I started working there shortly after we arrived in Newport earlier this summer. To be honest, I've been coming here for years and didn't even know there was an orphanage here before now."

This was the most she had spoken to me since my arrival, and I didn't want her to stop.

"How did you find out about it?" I asked, though I suspected that I knew. If Laura was her child, no doubt that was how she discovered the orphanage.

Again, she hesitated and studied me for a moment before she said, "Last fall while I was in New York, there was an accident on 5th Avenue and our driver had to divert our carriage to another street to get around it." Her focus shifted to the water, and I wondered if she was imagining that day. "It was not our usual way home, and suddenly we were in an area of the city I'd never seen before. I noticed a run-down orphanage with dirty children playing in the muddy yard. It was so cold and rainy that I knew they must be miserable, while I was sitting in a plush carriage. All night long and into the next day, I could think of nothing else." She brought her gaze back to my face, and I could see a myriad of emotions there.

"My entire world shifted in those twenty-four hours," she continued. "Why had God chosen for me to have this life and for those children to suffer through theirs? I'd been so blind to the needs of people around me, especially children, but suddenly that's all I could see, and I became so overwhelmed that I could no longer enjoy the life I was living. I've spent every day since then trying to do what I can, but my life isn't mine. It's dictated by the expectations and duties of my family."

I studied her, amazed at the depth of her conviction—and realizing how much we had in common. Expectations. Duty. Family.

She pulled back, just slightly. "I suppose you think I'm odd."

"No," I said quickly.

She motioned toward the servants setting up the food on blankets near the water's edge. "I am thankful for my life, but I feel ashamed that I have an excess of everything while most people don't have enough of anything."

"I don't think you're odd, Miss Whitney. And there is no reason to be ashamed of the life God has given you. You didn't choose to be born here. We don't know why God chooses to place some people in poverty and some in palaces, but He has an important purpose for each of us." Even if I wasn't sure that God heard me or would answer my prayers, I couldn't deny He was sovereign. I thought of my life serving the queen in 1563 and Drew's life as a carpenter. God had chosen where we would live and how we would serve. Neither life was more important than the other. "Instead of feeling shame, you should be thankful that He opened your eyes to see how you can use your blessings to serve others. It's a privilege to partner with Him, no matter what He has created us to do. And just think of how much more you *can* do in your position."

"How is this serving Him?" She motioned to the elaborate picnic again. "We eat expensive food and waste our days trying to fill them with parties and games and entertainments, while others are fighting to survive."

"These people are just as deserving of your time and talents as the friendless children at the orphanage. We don't know what they might be facing, or what trials they are under. Perhaps God placed you here not only to help those in need of food and clothing and housing, but also to open the eyes of those who might feel their lives are pointless and help them find meaning."

Evelyn's brow softened, and her eyes filled with tears.

My heart started to hammer. "I didn't mean to upset you."

She looked away as her tears fell against her cheeks and she wiped them with her gloved hand. "You haven't upset me, Lord Norfolk." She returned her tear-rimmed eyes to me. "For the first time in almost a year, you've offered me hope."

Relief caused my pulse to slow. "Please, call me Charles," I said in a gentle voice. "It's what my friends call me." I paused for just a moment. "I hope we can be friends."

She nodded, her tears subsiding. "I hope you'll call me Evelyn."

"I would like that." I took a clean handkerchief from my pocket and handed it to her, feeling compelled to tell her what I was thinking. Perhaps she hadn't heard it enough. "You have a beautiful heart, Evelyn Whitney. I'm not surprised God has called you to minister to the orphans, or to bring awareness to your peers."

She accepted the handkerchief and dabbed at her cheeks. "I

haven't done a good job bringing awareness to my friends. Mother doesn't want me to talk about my charity." She let out a breath. "It took a lot of work for me to convince her to let me volunteer at the orphanage. When I asked her for money to help them hire another staff member, she refused. I don't have the means to pay for one on my own."

"What about a fundraiser?" The suggestion slipped out before I had time to think it through. "The Reinholds invited me to attend a luncheon fundraiser for the widows' relief organization next week. Why couldn't we host a fundraiser for the Newport orphanage?"

"We?" she asked, her eyebrows lifting.

I paused. "I don't mean to be presumptuous."

A smile warmed Evelyn's beautiful blue eyes as warmth radiated through my chest. I suddenly wanted to make Evelyn happy, no matter what it took.

"I would like that, Charles," she said, her smile widening.

My pulse started to thrum at the sound of my name on her lips, and I knew I was in trouble.

What was I doing? It wasn't a good idea to offer to help her because it would mean spending more time in her company. And while it was exactly what I wanted, it wasn't a smart move. I couldn't let my heart get tangled up in 1883—and least of all with Drew's sister.

The irony of it was not lost on me.

Yet, I'd already offered to help, and I couldn't back out now without looking like a cad.

We continued to walk farther away from the group as we followed a path along the fort walls. The sounds of water lapping against the shoreline and people chatting with excitement as the sailboats continued to race floated on the gentle breeze. I should have turned back to join the others, but I couldn't tear myself away from her side.

"What kind of fundraiser do you suggest?" she asked me.

"Everyone does luncheons and dinners and balls. I'd like something unique—exciting."

I smiled because up until this conversation, *exciting* wasn't a word I would have associated with Evelyn Whitney.

"How about a tournament?" I asked, deciding that if I was going to do this, I was going to do it well. "A tennis tournament, at the Newport Casino."

"That's a wonderful idea. I love tennis and used to play all the time."

"Perhaps we should compete against each other sometime."

She turned to me, her parasol as a backdrop, and the corner of her mouth tilted up in a challenge. "Tomorrow? I can use the opportunity to speak to the owner to see if he has a date available for the fundraiser."

Seeing her enthusiasm was all it took to convince me that I needed to go through with this. That, and the fact that I was certain I could not say no to any request she made.

"Tomorrow sounds perfect."

Drew called to us, and though I wasn't ready for the interruption, it was best. I offered Evelyn my arm, and she hesitated for a moment but then slipped her hand through the crook of my elbow and allowed me to escort her back to the picnic.

The scent of her delicate perfume enveloped me, and all rational thought started to fade. I was surrounded by dozens of ladies at court and dozens more in Newport, but none had this effect on me, and it made no sense.

Evelyn was just another woman. Drew's sister.

So why did she feel different?

When we returned to the group, the older women were watching us. Evelyn's mother had a pleased smile on her face, but Helen's look was calculated, unconvinced.

As Evelyn let go of my arm to find a spot to sit, a new thought occurred to me. She had never told me how she came to volunteer at the Newport Home for Friendless Children. Had she intentionally ignored my question, or had she thought she explained because she'd discovered the orphans' plight in New York? Was that the only reason she volunteered there? Or did it have something to do with Baby Laura?

It didn't really matter. In a couple of months, I would leave Newport, and I would never see Evelyn again.

The sooner Mrs. Astor invited Mrs. Whitney to her ball and Evelyn's father returned from Europe, the sooner I could escape this charade.

9

CECILY

JULY 6, 1563
WINDSOR CASTLE

I paced inside the Privy Chamber as several of the queen's ladies sat quietly, whispering their worries over needlework. It had been twenty-four hours since the queen had been brought to her bedchamber from the tennis court, and none of us, except Kat, had seen her. Not even Lady Catherine Knollys had been allowed to visit the queen.

The door to the bedchamber opened, and I stopped pacing to look inside. The queen's bed was positioned against the far wall, and the drapery was pulled over her small windows, enshrining the room in darkness. It had been raining all day, making it drearier still.

Kat stepped out quietly with the chamber pot and then closed the door behind her.

"Is there any improvement?" I asked.

"She is resting quietly for now," Kat said as she repositioned the cloth over the chamber pot.

I had not been in the Privy Chamber all morning, knowing that there was little I could do to help the queen when none of us were allowed inside her bedchamber. Instead, I had spent the first part of the morning with Aveline, working on the masque she planned to give for the queen, and the second in the tower with my paints. I needed to focus on something other than the queen or Andrew or the impending arrival of Lord Wolverton.

But nothing helped. I was anxious and restless, and my paintings had suffered.

"Is Doctor Bromley with her now?" I asked.

"No. Lady Agatha has taken a turn for the worse, and the queen requested that he see to her."

Lady Agatha Throckmorton was an elderly noblewoman who had served the queen faithfully for years. She had been kind to me when I first came to court, and it broke my heart that she wasn't doing well.

Kat called one of the younger maids over and asked her to dispose of the chamber pot and then returned to the bedchamber.

I felt torn. I wanted to make progress with the queen on behalf of Aveline, but there was no telling when, or if, I would get the chance. I also wanted to go to Lady Agatha and show my support to her and her loved ones.

And I wanted to see Andrew again.

Without giving it much thought, I left the Privy Chamber, walked through the Presence Room, and then into the Queen's Ballroom. My dress felt especially cumbersome and heavy today, and my French hood was too tight. I longed for the cooler, lighter clothing I wore in 1913.

As my feet took me to the east wing, I continued to debate myself. Going to Lady Agatha wasn't wise or sensible, especially because she wasn't the only reason I was going.

The corridors were quiet as I walked the length of the east wing to Lady Agatha's apartment. Everyone was worried about the queen, and most courtiers had stayed in their rooms, praying, speculating, and planning should the worst happen. I'd been told

Through Each Tomorrow

Lady Katherine Grey was ensconced in her rooms in the castle with Charles and other Protestant privy councilors, discussing the possibilities of her becoming the next queen. I couldn't imagine what she was thinking, knowing her older sister, Lady Jane Grey, had been beheaded when she tried to take the throne after Edward VI had died. Lady Jane had been declared queen for nine days before Mary deposed her and later had her executed.

I shivered just thinking about it. Did Lady Katherine even want to be queen? Would she have a choice? And what if Mary, Queen of Scots, decided to make war against Lady Katherine to claim the title for herself? Charles would be in the middle of the battle.

At each window, I had a view of the dismal weather. Low, gray clouds hung above the castle, weeping onto the land. Did the weather know something we did not?

Two young servants stood outside Lady Agatha's chamber as I approached, whispering and giggling like schoolgirls. I heard one say Andrew's name. When they saw me, they quickly curtsied and then walked away from the door.

Doctor Bromley had quickly become a favorite not only of the queen, but also of all the fair maidens of Windsor Castle.

Was he as popular in Newport?

Jealousy wrapped its ugly grip around my heart as I contemplated such a thing for the first time. I'd never wondered if Andrew had a sweetheart in 1883 until now. Was his family arranging a marriage? Was he engaged? Surely Charles would have told me.

Then again, Charles had always kept his other path private. I knew very little about his life there. He was a farmer in Virginia, and he had an older sister named Ada. His father had died in the American Civil War when he was six, and his mother had remained unmarried. That was almost all I knew.

Were Charles and Andrew friends in 1883?

Not for the first time, I wished Charles confided in me more. He was so busy with the council, and both his work for the queen and his other life were things he didn't share with me. It made me feel like I was one more responsibility he was forced to shoulder.

I knocked on Lady Agatha's door, and it was opened by Henrietta, her great-granddaughter.

"How does Lady Agatha fare?" I asked as I stepped into her outer chamber.

"She will not be with us much longer, I fear," Hen said. "The doctor is with her now."

"I'm sorry." There were several family members and close friends in the outer chamber. Some were weeping, and others were sitting quietly in prayer.

"Lady Agatha enjoys visitors." Hen motioned to the door. "You may step in, if you'd like."

Smiling, I went to the door, which I opened slowly.

Lady Agatha's bed was on the far wall, and Andrew was sitting on the side, holding the elderly lady's hand—or perhaps he was taking her pulse. His back was toward me, and he didn't seem to know I had entered. Two of Lady Agatha's daughters were in the room, standing together on the other side of the bed. One of them glanced at me when I opened the door and motioned for me to come forward.

I stepped into the room a little farther but paused, not wanting to interrupt Andrew if he was examining the elderly woman.

As I watched, Andrew gently put his hand on Lady Agatha's forehead to brush aside a lock of her silver hair. Her eyes were closed, and her breathing was shallow, but she looked serene.

"Go in peace, Lady Agatha," Andrew said just above a whisper as he put his hand on her shoulder. "God is waiting for you, His good and faithful servant."

Lady Agatha took a final, shuddering breath, and then she was gone.

Her daughters began to weep as Andrew folded her hands over her chest.

Tears filled my eyes as I watched the scene. I'd never witnessed someone die. And even though Lady Agatha was old and she had lived a long, happy life, it was still heart-wrenching.

Had my parents watched me die in 1913? I'd only ever thought about my pain and what I had lost—but how had they survived my death?

The weight of their sorrow suddenly took hold of me, and I struggled to catch a breath.

Unable to stay in a room with death so close, I fumbled for the door latch as Andrew turned from the bed. Our gazes met a moment before I fled the bedchamber. It had been a mistake to come. The shadow of death still had a grip on my heart.

I attempted a poor excuse for my behavior as I passed Hen on the way out of Agatha's outer chamber.

The corridor was empty as I walked back toward the state apartments in the north wing, trying to catch my breath.

"Cecily." Andrew's voice drifted toward me.

I paused, my heart pounding.

It was the second time he'd come after me in two days. I wanted to believe it meant something, but I knew better. I had been a fool to come, and he was a fool to chase me.

Slowly, I turned and found him striding toward me, his face serious.

"I shouldn't have come," I said, voicing the truth that he already knew.

Andrew didn't stop, didn't hesitate, didn't speak, but drew me into his arms.

My mouth parted in surprise, and then my heart broke into a hundred little pieces as he enfolded me in his strong embrace.

"I'm sorry, Cecily." He spoke quietly near my ear. "I'm sorry you lost so much. And I'm sorry you had to witness death again today."

Tears fell down my cheeks as I realized he knew exactly what I was feeling. Somehow, he'd understood why the moment in Lady Agatha's bedchamber had affected me so deeply.

"How did you know?" I whispered.

"It was written all over your face. I can't imagine what it's been like for you to mourn without being able to share your grief with anyone. To tell them why your heart is so heavy. Charles would shoulder it with you if he didn't have the weight of the realm on his mind."

I could feel Andrew's heart beating under my ear as the heat of his arms warmed me. I recalled his tenderness with Lady Agatha as she passed from life unto death and how blessed she was to have Andrew's compassionate hands there to soothe her brow. He was a healer and was starting to heal my heart, whether he realized it or not.

"I have something for you," he said as he pulled back. "Lady Agatha's family needs time to mourn in peace, and I will not be missed. Will you come with me?"

I nodded, wiping the tears off my cheeks.

I would go anywhere with him.

Andrew led me away from Lady Agatha's chambers and back toward the state apartments. The corridors were still quiet as we walked side by side. My hand brushed his, and he glanced at me, his thoughts hard to read.

Neither of us spoke as we passed from one hall into another.

We walked up two sets of spiraling stairwells and then down another long corridor.

"Where are we going?" I asked, though it didn't matter to me.

"My apartment."

Heat filled my cheeks at his simple answer. Though Andrew was honorable and trustworthy, I had never been in a man's apartment except Charles's.

We finally stopped at a door, and he studied me for a moment. "Mayhap you should wait out here, in case someone should come by and see you enter my rooms."

"I care not what they think," I said, feeling a little reckless. I wanted privacy with Andrew to talk about what had happened in the garden. There was nothing I could do about my feelings for him, but I yearned to know if he returned them. It would be little comfort, but comfort nonetheless.

A gentle smile lifted his lips, and then he opened his door and allowed me to enter ahead of him.

His outer chamber was much like all the others, with a couch and other chairs to recline upon. There was a table strewn with books and papers, and tapestries hung on the stone walls.

As he closed the door, I noticed a framed painting perched on a table near the couch, with a stack of books holding it upright.

It was the Painted Lady caterpillar.

Andrew stood for a moment, leaning against the door as I studied the painting.

"I wasn't sure if it would be rolled up in a corner of your room, forgotten," I said as I turned to him.

"I would never do such a thing to one of my prized possessions."

My painting was one of his prized possessions?

The room was intimate, and we were completely alone. I wanted to return to his arms, but his embrace had not been romantic. It had been comforting and nothing more.

"What did you want to give me?" I asked, realizing I sounded breathless.

He moved away from the door and went to the table, where he picked up a book. When he returned, he held it out for me to take.

"It's Aristotle's *Historia Animalium*," he said. "He wrote it in the fourth century BC, and it is both an exploration of the animal world and the philosophy behind their existence. It's translated from Greek."

I looked from the book to Andrew, at a loss for words.

"Have you heard of his work?" he asked.

"Yes," I finally said, able to nod.

"Have you read it?"

"No."

He smiled, gently probing. "Do you want to read it?"

"Yes." I began to laugh. "Where did you find it?"

"In the castle library." He motioned to the table. "There are dozens of books that I thought you might enjoy reading. The knowledge they contain is limited, but they are still groundbreaking studies of the natural world and are foundational books for the works of scientists who will come after them. Scientists like you."

"I am not a scientist."

"You have a scientific mind, Cecily, and a desire to learn about the world around you. You are a scientist, an artist, a historian—whatever you wish to be."

I wanted to believe him, but I also knew that there were limitations placed on my life by the queen, by society—even by Charles. And, if my stepbrother succeeded, there would be limitations set by my husband.

But that didn't mean I couldn't learn and read and explore. Or paint pictures for my book.

I hugged *Historia Animalium* to my chest. "Thank you, Andrew. You've offered me another priceless gift."

He smiled. "Will I get another painting for my efforts?"

I grinned. "Do you want another painting?"

His face grew serious. "I would take every painting you created, if I could. But what would be left for your book?"

Without thought, I approached Andrew, and this time, I embraced him.

He hesitated and then put his arms around me and held me close.

It was dangerous to be in his arms, to allow my heart to fall in love with him again, but I couldn't help myself. Andrew was not only handsome and strong, he was also good and kind and intelligent. He was everything I had ever wanted in a man, and I was certain no one would ever compare to him.

I slowly looked up, craving more.

His gaze slipped to my lips and sent a river of desire flowing through my limbs. My breathing became shallow as time stood still.

His chest rose and fell on deep breaths, and he slowly lowered his head—but at the last second, he paused. Uncertainty returned to his eyes, and this time he didn't look directly at me as he pulled away. "I'm sorry."

Swift disappointment coursed through me, and embarrassment warmed my cheeks.

He took a step back and ran his hand through his hair. "I made a promise to Charles."

The book was heavy in my hands as I brought it back to my chest, not wanting to face the reality of what he was going to say.

"I will not stand in the way of his plans for you."

I swallowed and nodded. "Of course you won't."

"I—I care for you, perhaps more than I should, but you deserve better than me."

"Andrew, there is no one better than you."

"Please do not say such things." He put his hand on the back of his neck and walked away from me. "I have nothing to offer you."

I hugged the book close, knowing that he had offered me more than anyone else.

"I have no title or property, and I have an obligation to stay in 1883. If God had intended for us—" He paused and took a deep breath. "But He did not ordain such a thing, and it would be best if I kept my distance from you."

Tears burned the backs of my eyes as I nodded, though I did not agree with what he was proposing. It would be too hard to know he was so close yet out of my reach. It had taken me years to forget my feelings for him. How long would it take this time? Especially if he was nearby.

"I'm sorry," he said as he finally looked at me, anguish in his eyes.

I swallowed the emotions clogging my throat and nodded again, wanting him to know that I was not angry, and I did not blame him for his decision.

"Thank you." I walked to the door, clutching my book. "And I'm sorry, too."

With that, I slipped out of his room and leaned against the

closed door for a moment before walking away from Andrew's apartment.

My heart cried out in anger and confusion as I lifted my face to the ceiling. "Why?" I whispered to God. "Why do you continue to take everything away from me? Where is the joy and peace and love that you promised?"

God was silent as my heart broke yet again.

10

CHARLES

JULY 6, 1883
NEWPORT, RHODE ISLAND

I stood in the foyer at Midcliff, torn between my worries about Queen Elizabeth and my unreasonable nerves about spending the afternoon with Evelyn. I'd spent the day before in 1563, counseling Lady Katherine Grey and making plans for her accession should the queen not live. There were a few others on the privy council who believed Mary, Queen of Scots, was the rightful heir, and they were secretly meeting. If the Protestant advisors could get enough support for Lady Katherine, we would move in that direction. But if the Catholic advisors could convince the council that Mary should be the next Queen of England, we would be forced to put her on the throne instead.

It was a grim task, but without knowing what ailed the queen, we were forced to discuss the unthinkable. Lord Robert did not believe either side should be discussing the issue, and he threatened to tell the queen we were planning to overthrow her. Thankfully Lord Burghley, the Lord High Treasurer, had convinced him otherwise. For now.

There was little I could do about the inheritance question while I was in Newport, so I turned my thoughts to Evelyn, wanting to give her my full attention. I had enjoyed her company at the picnic, but we hadn't had any time alone to talk about the fundraiser. That morning at breakfast, she'd asked if I was still interested in playing a game of tennis at the Newport Casino.

She appeared at the top of the steps, wearing a blue-and-white-striped day dress with a bustle at the back and blue pearl buttons down the bodice. It was a little shorter than her other gowns, allowing her leather shoes to peek out from beneath her hem. She wore a straw boater with a blue band around the crown, and her blond hair was pinned up in a low bun at the nape of her slender neck.

But it was her smile that made her ensemble so stunning. It had been missing for the first part of my visit. Now I couldn't get enough of it. Her cheeks were pink as she met my gaze, and I was certain I was doing a poor job of hiding my reaction to her.

"Are you ready, my lord?" she asked.

I smiled and offered her my arm. "I thought I asked you to call me Charles."

As she slipped her delicate hand around my elbow, her smile fell. "I call you 'my lord' to remind myself that, despite your reassurance, you are still an aristocrat, and I promised myself never to be deceived again."

Her words were sobering and reminded me that this wasn't a simple summer flirtation, and I *was* deceiving her, though perhaps not how she assumed.

I opened the door, and we stepped into the sunshine. Without another word, I assisted Evelyn into the waiting carriage, and we sat across from one another as it pulled out of the drive.

"May I ask what happened?" I asked cautiously, wanting to address her earlier comment.

She clasped her hands and took so long to answer, I was afraid she wouldn't trust me with the truth. Finally, she said, "Someone I cared very deeply about deceived me. Sometimes I fear the damage to my heart is irreparable."

Through Each Tomorrow

"I'm sorry." The memory of seeing her with Baby Laura had replayed in my mind several times over the past couple of days.

"You did nothing wrong, though I confess I am struggling to believe that you are helping me with the fundraiser with no ulterior motives."

I wasn't sure how to respond, so I remained silent as I looked out the window.

"You are nothing like him," she said after a moment.

I returned my gaze to her and found her studying me.

"You took the time to ask what mattered to me. He never did. All he was interested in was himself, and in the end, his actions spoke louder than his words. It took the greatest sadness of my life to finally understand that my heart is mine alone to guard, and I realized I needed to do a much better job."

Anger for a man I'd never met continued to increase. "A real man guards the heart of the woman he loves," I said, unable to hide my feelings. "I don't know who he was, but not all men are as heartless and cruel."

She slowly nodded. "I know."

We were soon at the Newport Casino, and I helped Evelyn step out of the carriage. It was Friday, so the casino was busier than usual. We entered the paneled foyer and placed our names on the waitlist for a tennis court, then asked to speak to the proprietor, Mr. Bennett, who also owned the *New York Herald*. He was a prominent figure in Newport society and spent his summers operating the casino.

Evelyn and I waited outside his office for several minutes before he could be located, and when he finally arrived, he was gregarious and hospitable.

"Welcome to the Newport Casino," he said as he shook my hand and slapped my back. He had a thick mustache that curled on the ends and blue eyes that were almost translucent. "I'm James Gordon Bennett, Jr. It's a pleasure to have you with us, Lord Norfolk."

"The pleasure is mine."

After I introduced him to Evelyn, we went into his office.

"What can I do for you?" Mr. Bennett asked as we took the seats across from his large desk.

"Miss Whitney and I are eager to help the local orphanage on School Street," I said. "Currently, there is not enough staff or money to maintain it properly."

"I wasn't aware that there was an orphanage in Newport," Mr. Bennett said as he nodded and then waited for me to continue.

"We thought it would be helpful to host a fundraiser for them, not only to earn money but to bring more awareness to their plight."

"That sounds like a good idea," Mr. Bennett said. "But I've already given my quota to charity this year."

"We are not looking for your money," Evelyn explained. "We are hoping to host a lawn tennis tournament here in August and allow the proceeds to benefit the Newport Home for Friendless Children."

Realization dawned on Mr. Bennett's face. "Ah, I see now. But I'm afraid August would be a difficult month. We're hosting the third annual US Lawn Tennis Championship August 4 through 8. I do not believe we could successfully host two large tournaments back-to-back. I'm sorry. Perhaps next year, we could plan for June or July." He began to rise as if the conversation was over.

But I wasn't ready to concede. The orphanage needed money before next summer.

More importantly, I didn't want to disappoint Evelyn.

"Perhaps we don't host a tournament," I suggested, "but a charity event before the championship begins. A game with a local citizen playing against the reigning champion from last year's tournament, all in good fun and sportsmanship. We could host a dinner and dance afterward, right here at the casino."

"And we would not ask you to do a thing," Evelyn added quickly, "just provide the space."

Mr. Bennett squinted and ran his hand over his mustache, clearly taking our proposition into consideration.

Evelyn was on the edge of her seat as she waited, and I hoped and prayed Mr. Bennett would agree—not only for the orphanage's sake, but for her sake. I couldn't imagine how helpless it would feel to have a baby at an orphanage.

"I think it's a splendid plan," Mr. Bennett finally said. "I will speak to Mr. Sears, the champion from last year, and see if he would agree. If not, I'm sure we can get another player from this year's roster to compete against a local citizen."

"Could I propose the local citizen?" Evelyn asked. "Or, at least a visitor to Newport?"

Mr. Bennett smiled at Evelyn. "Lord Norfolk?"

"Yes." She beamed at me. "I've heard he's quite talented."

"Why not?" Mr. Bennett said. "I think we'll draw a bigger crowd to the charity event if we have an earl playing our national champion."

"I'm not sure that's a good idea." I didn't want to draw that much attention.

"Please," Evelyn said as she put her hand on my arm.

I was afraid I would be unable to say no to her again, so I quickly gave her an alternative idea. "Perhaps we host a small tournament among the local men to see who plays Mr. Sears? A week or so before the national championship."

"Only if you promise me that you'll compete in the smaller tournament." Her smile was so brilliant and hopeful, I found myself agreeing to her request.

When we left the meeting, we walked out of the building and onto the back lawn. There were several courts, side by side, and we had one at the end. Evelyn was beaming, and I couldn't hide my pleasure at her happiness. I'd never felt anything so satisfying.

"Lord Norfolk!" Isabel called to us, waving her tennis racket from the court where she and a young man played together. Mr. and Mrs. Reinhold sat nearby under an umbrella with another older couple.

I didn't want to share the moment with anyone else, but it

would be rude to ignore Isabel, so I smiled and veered off-course to greet her.

Evelyn followed.

"How wonderful to see you again," Isabel said as we joined her and the man playing tennis with her. "Lord Norfolk, this is Mr. Morgan Brent, an old family friend from Virginia." Her accent had deepened. "Morgan, this is Lord Charles Pembrooke, the Earl of Norfolk, and Miss Evelyn Whitney."

"Ah," Mr. Brent said with the ease of an aristocrat as he shook my hand, "so this is my competition."

Isabel's cheeks filled with color as she lowered her eyes.

His competition? Did she think I was competing for her affection?

"It's a pleasure to meet you, Mr. Brent." I accepted his handshake, trying to lessen the awkward moment.

He squeezed my hand harder than necessary, so I returned the gesture in kind.

Evelyn's gaze slid between me and Isabel, uncertainty drawing her inward again.

She and I had made so much progress, I didn't want to lose ground.

"It was nice to see you," I said to Isabel as I put my hand on Evelyn's lower back, "but Evelyn and I should start our game."

"How about a doubles match?" Mr. Brent suggested, swinging his racket as if he was serving a ball. "Isabel and me against you and Miss Whitney."

I started to decline, but Evelyn said, "I think that's a splendid idea."

"You've never seen me play," I teased her.

"*You've* never seen *me* play," she countered with a waggish smile.

I was starting to see some of the old spark in Evelyn that Drew had mentioned—and I liked it.

"We accept," I said with a grin.

After finding our rackets and tennis balls, Evelyn and I took our positions on one side of the net. Lawn tennis was like the game of real tennis in 1563, but I was more skilled at this version than the other. The rackets were bigger, the balls bounced higher, and the court was smaller. It was also played on grass as opposed to stone.

Mr. Brent served, and Evelyn easily hit the ball back into their half of the court. It was a marvel to watch both her and Isabel play in their full dresses, not only because it was hot, but because it couldn't be easy for them to maneuver. It was much the same for women at Windsor Castle.

As we played, I couldn't help but admire Evelyn's form and her effortless handling of the racket. She had a beautiful backswing, and she was naturally athletic.

Isabel was no match for Evelyn, and that soon became evident as Mr. Brent hit most of their shots.

Evelyn and I played well together, anticipating the ball, moving aside for one or the other with little communication. When we scored, she offered me the most brilliant smile, and when we lost a point, she squared her shoulders and returned her focus to the game.

In the end, we easily beat our opponents.

I shook Mr. Brent's hand.

"We'll need a rematch, of course," he said.

"Of course." I smiled congenially.

"I'll be in town for the next couple of weeks," he added, his chin lifted. "My parents have taken the rooms adjoining the Reinholds' at the Ocean House."

"It was such a surprise," Isabel said. "I had no idea the Brents were coming to Newport."

"I'm sure we'll be seeing a lot of you." I toweled off my face and neck, guessing that Mr. Brent had come to woo Isabel.

"We run into Lord Norfolk all the time," Isabel told Mr. Brent. "He's been a delightful companion."

"I'm sure he has," Mr. Brent said.

I ran the towel over the back of my head as Evelyn came up beside me. I glanced at her to smile, but her face had turned pale.

Instead of returning my smile, her eyes swam with dozens of questions, and I somehow felt guilty.

Frowning, I scanned the casino lawn, but nothing seemed unusual or out of place. "Is everything all right?"

She swallowed and said, "Excuse me," then left the court without looking back.

"I'm sorry." I laid my towel on a nearby chair as I left Isabel and Mr. Brent to follow Evelyn.

I jogged off the court, nodding at the Reinholds and their guests as they sat in the gallery, and entered the cool interior of the Newport Casino.

Evelyn sat on a sofa in one of the corners, a large fern almost blocking her from view.

When I approached, she stood, her hand on her forehead.

"What's wrong?"

She lowered her hand and shook her head. "Everything is fine."

"No." I led her to the couch. "Tell me what happened."

Her hands trembled as she tried to clutch them on her lap. "It's—" She swallowed and took a breath. "Your mark—on the back of your head."

My hand went to my time-crossing birthmark. It was usually hidden under my hair. Had she seen it while I was toweling off the sweat? Was she familiar with Drew's? Did she know what it meant?

I slowly lowered my hand. "Perhaps we should take a walk for a bit of privacy."

We left the casino's front door and stepped onto Bellevue Avenue. Without thinking, I led her to the north toward Touro Park.

"Do you know what the mark means?" I asked her.

Evelyn bit her bottom lip for a moment before asking, "What other time do you occupy?"

"1563."

"And how much time do you have left to choose?"

"My twenty-fifth birthday is next March."

We walked side by side down Bellevue. I wanted to offer her

my arm, but I kept my distance, suspecting that she needed space to process the information.

"Which path will you choose?" she asked quietly.

I let out a long breath and watched the carriages as they passed. "I was going to choose this path—but my stepsister, Cecily, is in 1563 and she needs me. She is also a time-crosser, but she unexpectedly lost her other path and is stuck there. I need to find her a husband before March, or I must stay to take care of her."

She nodded slowly, as if she was trying to take it all in.

"Drew never told you that I'm a time-crosser?" I asked.

Evelyn's head came up quickly as she came to a stop, a frown etched deep into her forehead. "Drew is a time-crosser?"

I stared at her, confused. "You didn't know?"

We had just arrived at Touro Park, and there was a bench nearby. Evelyn went to it and took a seat, staring straight ahead. "Drew is a time-crosser?" she asked again, almost to herself.

I joined her on the bench. "He never told you?"

"No." She finally looked at me, so much confusion in her eyes. "Drew spent much of his childhood at boarding schools, and when we were together, it was all very formal."

"You've never noticed his mark?"

"No." Evelyn shook her head. "I can't believe my brother is a time-crosser and I didn't know it."

Realization suddenly came over me. "Then how do you know what the mark on the back of my head means?"

Evelyn slowly lifted her gaze, and I could see the truth written all over her face.

"Are you a time-crosser, Evelyn?"

Her hand came up and rested over her chest. "My mark is here."

I wasn't sure what she meant. I'd only ever known time-crossers with a mark on the back of their heads. Me, my father, Cecily, and Drew all had marks just above our hairline.

She slowly lowered her hand. "Time-crossers with the mark on their chests only get twenty-one years to decide."

"And when is your twenty-first birthday?"

"August 31."

I blinked a few times, unsure how to process what she was saying. "You will need to make your final decision next month. Are you leaving here?"

Evelyn shook her head as she looked at her hands, grief and heartbreak sloping her shoulders. "Just like your sister, Cecily, I lost my other path without warning. I will remain in this path for the rest of my life."

I suddenly understood the depth of her sadness—at least part of it. "When was your other path?"

Tears gathered in Evelyn's eyes, and she stood. "I don't want to talk about it, Charles, and please don't ask again."

"Evelyn." I reached for her, but she pulled away.

"Perhaps we should go tell the Flanderses about the fundraiser." She wiped her tears. "I don't want to think about my other path. Not now—and not ever again." She continued to walk toward the north, but stopped when she realized I wasn't following.

"Evelyn—"

"Please don't ask." She pressed her lips together. "I died in my other path, and it no longer matters who I was there."

"How long ago?" I asked. "Will you tell me that much?"

She let out a heavy breath. "Last October."

I thought about what she'd told me about last October. "Around the time that you saw the children in the orphanage? In New York City?"

She looked away from me. "I couldn't tell you the whole story before. Yes, I saw the children, and it had a profound effect on me. But it wasn't the only thing that had broken my heart. That was the same day I realized I had died in my other path. All of it came crashing down at the same time, and the only thing that has brought me joy since then is helping at the orphanage."

"I'm sorry." I wished I could offer more. "I can't imagine the pain you've endured."

She bit her bottom lip and nodded, but then she said, "Until now, I didn't think there were any other time-crossers in this path with me. Now I find out that both you and Drew are time-crossers." She let out a breath. "You would think it would bring me comfort—but I know how difficult it is to live two lives, and it only makes me sad."

"Please don't worry about me," I said, feeling an inexplicable bond with Evelyn—and a desire to ease her pain.

She nodded and slipped her hand around my elbow. "Will you come with me to the orphanage? I don't want to think about our other lives anymore. I want to focus on this one."

"Of course."

When we arrived at the orphanage, several of the children were playing outside, and they greeted her like they had before. She smiled for them, though it didn't quite reach her eyes today.

But when Mrs. Flanders came out with Baby Laura on her hip, Evelyn's entire countenance lifted. She took the baby in her arms and nuzzled her affectionately as she introduced me to Mrs. Flanders.

"And this," Evelyn said with pride as she held the baby close, "is Laura."

I reached out and touched the baby's hand, thankful that despite all of Evelyn's heartache, this child brought her happiness. I disliked thinking of her with another man, but I hated even more knowing he'd hurt her. At least she had Laura. God worked in mysterious ways, bringing joy from the pain. "It's a pleasure to meet you, Miss Laura."

The baby grinned, her blue eyes shining.

"Come inside," Mrs. Flanders said as she watched me with curiosity. "It looks like we have a lot to talk about."

Evelyn followed her inside as Laura looked at me over her shoulder.

We did have a lot to talk about. I just wasn't sure if Evelyn would tell me what I wanted to know.

11

CECILY

JULY 20, 1563
WINDSOR CASTLE

A pall had fallen over the castle as we waited daily for the queen to recover. We had done our best to keep our spirits up, but without the presence of the queen, it was hard to enjoy the activities that made court life pleasant. In the evening, we still danced and participated in entertainment, but it wasn't the same.

Andrew and Kat kept most people out of the queen's bedchamber, though a few women entered to clean and take her food. It was Kat who saw to almost all her needs. I tried to get Kat to tell me what was ailing the queen, for Charles's sake, but she refused.

Finally, the privy council demanded answers, and the queen allowed Andrew to share his diagnosis. His best guess was that it was a complication from the smallpox that she had suffered the previous October. It was causing headaches, abdominal pain, and swelling throughout her body. Andrew had performed bloodletting, a practice still in use in the 1880s, and was giving her herbal diuretics while recommending complete bedrest and as little strain as possible so she could rest.

As I sat in my tower room, looking out at the North Terrace, my mind slipped to Andrew, as it so often did. I had done my best to avoid him for the past two weeks, spending most of my time painting. Two of my caterpillars had cocooned, and I was expecting them to emerge any day. There were now dozens of paintings, mostly of caterpillars, but also of the castle and grounds, scattered around my room.

"Cecily?" Charles paused at the top of the stairs.

I turned, surprised to find him there. He'd never come to the tower before.

"So this is where you hide away," he said with a smile. "May I come in?"

"Of course." I stood, wishing I had done a better job of keeping the place tidy.

He slowly walked around the room, admiring my work. "I didn't know you still painted."

"I just started again." I began to pick up my brushes and organize the table. "I am hoping to compile all of them into a book one day."

Charles stopped at the window, where I had several jars with caterpillars lined up on the sill. He lifted one that held a cocoon dangling from the wooden lid.

"Please be careful." I set down my brushes and gently removed the jar from his hand. "They're very delicate."

He released the jar into my care, and I put it next to the others.

"Why are you here, Charles?"

"Lord Wolverton arrived this morning."

A heaviness weighed upon my chest as I stared at my collection. I had known he would arrive any day, but I'd tried not to think about it.

"He is hoping to meet you before supper."

I slowly turned from the window, my arms crossed. "Has he come all this way expecting to marry me?"

"He came expressly at my invitation."

"To possibly marry me."

"Yes."

"And if I do not like Lord Wolverton and choose not to marry him, will he be angry that he came?"

Charles sighed. "I hope you'll keep your mind and heart open to him."

"I suppose I don't have much choice."

"You always have a choice, Cec, but I want this to be settled. I think you will be pleased with him."

I didn't think anyone would please me besides Andrew. But if I was married, Charles would have one less thing to worry about, so I would do as he asked and keep my mind and heart open.

"Meet me in my apartment in an hour," Charles instructed. "Lord Wolverton will be there." He stepped forward and placed a kiss on my forehead before saying, "I know this is not how you wanted things to play out, but life isn't always about what happens to us. It's about how we respond to what happens that makes all the difference."

"That's easy for you to say." The bitter words slipped out before I could stop them.

He was quiet for a moment, then he said, "My life is not turning out how I imagined, either. But I'm trying to do my best, for you, for the queen, for Evelyn—" He paused.

"Who is Evelyn?"

"It doesn't matter."

I put my hand on his arm. "Who is Evelyn?"

Sunshine poured through the window and bathed his face, causing his blue eyes to sparkle. At the moment, though, they were filled with uncertainty. As if he'd misspoken.

"Evelyn is Drew's sister in 1883."

My eyebrows came up. "Andrew has a sister?"

"I didn't know about her until I got to his house."

"You're at Andrew's house?" I squeezed his arm. "Charles."

He frowned. "Have I not told you?"

"You tell me as little as possible about your other path. I learned long ago not to even ask." But now that I knew, I needed all the details. "I was aware that you and Andrew lived during the same time, but I didn't know you were friends there."

He walked to my table, absently playing with the brushes, and I wondered if he'd finally tell me about his other path. "We didn't meet there until a couple weeks ago. He asked me to go to his summer cottage in Newport."

I followed him and stood on the other side of the table. "Does he live there alone?"

"His mother and sister are there."

"Aren't you a farmer in 1883? I wouldn't think it was socially acceptable to host you."

"'Tis not acceptable." He lifted his gaze to mine. "He told his mother, and everyone else, that I'm the Earl of Norfolk."

"Charles."

"It's a harmless fabrication. I *am* the Earl of Norfolk."

"*Charles*," I said again, disappointed in him.

He explained why he had done it and what he hoped Andrew's father could do for him in return.

It was all starting to make sense. "You went to Newport to pose as the Earl of Norfolk, and Andrew agreed to take care of the queen and petition his father to invest in your family's horse farm."

"Yes."

I studied him. "And what are you trying to do for Evelyn?"

He left the table and went to my paintings. Some were framed and leaning against the wall, others were drying on a rope I'd strung across the room, and some were stacked in a pile.

"It matters not," he finally said.

I put my hands on my hips. "Why have you always been hesitant to tell me about your other path? Are you hiding something from me?"

"Of course not." He lifted his shoulders. "My grandfather always told me to be careful about sharing too much information with other time-crossers, especially if it isn't necessary for them to know. It can mess up history in ways we might not understand."

"If we *knowingly* change history—but what could I change if I knew about your other path?"

"I don't know, but I don't want to take any chances. What if I told you about a person I knew, or an event, and you had foreknowledge from your 1913 path? If you gave me information I shouldn't know, it might affect me or my choices."

"You're overthinking." I crossed the room and put my hand on his arm so he'd turn and face me. "I have a feeling that you don't *want* me to know about Evelyn—or whatever else you've kept from me—because you don't want me to scold you."

"That's not it at all."

"Then tell me about Evelyn." A new realization made my heart skip a beat. "Are you in love with her?"

"No." He shook his head adamantly—too adamantly. "I've only known her for a month."

"Is she in love with you?"

"No."

"Do you want her to be in love with—?"

"Cecily." His voice held a warning. "The only reason I came up here was to tell you Lord Wolverton has arrived, and I want you to join us in an hour."

He walked toward the stairs.

"You're all I have left, Charles." I bit the inside of my mouth to control my emotions. "Please don't keep me shut out of your life."

Compassion filled his face, and he returned to me, drawing me into his arms, hugging me tight. "I'm sorry, Cec. I only want what's best for you. Please trust me."

"I do."

"Good. I'll see you in my apartment."

As I watched him leave, I took a deep breath.

I would keep an open mind about Lord Wolverton.

But it wouldn't be easy.

Charles's apartment was part of the state apartments, one floor up from my dormitory, where I slept with the five other maids of honour and our chaperone. All the chambers in this part of the castle looked out to the North Terrace and the Thames River.

I had quickly washed the paint off my hands and changed into a more suitable gown to meet the Earl of Wolverton.

The corridors were silent, as they had been for weeks. I passed a few servants, but no one else was out and about. Part of me hoped to see Andrew, since his apartments were close to Charles's, but he was probably with the queen on the main floor.

Surprisingly, my pulse wasn't thrumming and there were no butterflies as I stopped outside Charles's door. I was not nervous about meeting Lord Wolverton. On the contrary, I felt numb, unenthusiastic and almost detached. This man could very well become my husband, but I had no romantic or unrealistic expectations about our relationship. It was simply a business deal, meant to protect me and provide an heir for him. Nothing more. Nothing less.

I knocked on Charles's door and waited for a moment before it opened.

Charles stood on the other side, wearing a dark blue coat and matching blue hose. He assessed me with one quick glance and nodded his approval.

I might not be keen to meet Lord Wolverton, but I would put my best foot forward. I was Lady Cecily Pembrooke, after all.

Just inside Charles's apartment, a man stood from where he had been sitting on the couch. I wasn't sure what I had expected from a man named Lord Wolverton, but it wasn't the person standing before me. He was older than me, perhaps in his mid-thirties, and though he wasn't classically handsome, he had a very pleasant face with kind brown eyes.

"Lord Wolverton," Charles said, "may I present my stepsister, Lady Cecily Pembrooke?"

Lord Wolverton bowed over my hand. "'Tis a pleasure to finally meet you, my lady. I have only heard good things about you since my arrival at Windsor Castle."

I curtsied. "I'm pleased to meet you, as well, Lord Wolverton, though I fear I have heard very little about you."

"I thought," Charles said quickly, "that you might take a stroll along the North Terrace. Lord Wolverton has never been to Windsor, and who better to show him around? I will chaperone, of course."

"Would that please you, Lady Cecily?" Lord Wolverton asked, his expression eager.

"Of course."

"Wonderful." Charles went to the door and held it open for us.

I stepped out first, and then Lord Wolverton followed, with Charles at a distance behind us.

As we walked along the corridor, my mind went blank, and I wasn't sure what I should ask Lord Wolverton. But then I realized that I wasn't the one who had initiated this meeting, so I remained silent and waited for him to speak.

"I was under the impression that you and Lord Norfolk were blood related," he said after a while. "But he called you his stepsister."

Charles was far enough behind that he couldn't hear our conversation, but he could keep an eye on us.

"My mother was expecting me when my father was killed in a hunting accident," I explained. "Charles's father had been a widower for a couple of years, but he had known my mother when they were younger. When he proposed marriage, she was eager to accept. I was born a month later."

"And who was your father?"

Was he wondering if I had noble blood?

"The Marquess of Sterling, my lord."

"I'm very sorry for your loss."

"I have no memory of him. The 1st Earl of Norfolk was the only father I knew, and he was a good man. Charles is much like him."

We walked down a flight of winding stairs, and I led him through another corridor to reach the North Terrace. He wasn't much taller than me, but he appeared strong and his face was tanned, which told me he spent time out of doors.

"And where is your home?" I asked him.

"Alnwick Castle in Northumberland."

Northumberland was one of the northernmost counties in England, on the Scottish border, whereas my home, Arundel Castle, was on the southern border in West Essex County. They could not be farther apart.

"Do you go to London often?" I asked.

"Rarely, if I can help it. I prefer to stay at Alnwick as much as possible. Court life does not suit me."

We stepped into the sunshine on the North Terrace, and my first inclination was to go to the flowers and start to look for caterpillars, but that would have to wait. I had promised Charles I would keep my heart and mind open to Lord Wolverton. Still, it wasn't easy to imagine living on the northern border, so far from all the things I loved.

Charles stopped at a stone bench as we continued to walk. It was expected that we would stay within eyesight of him, but I had no desire to be alone with Wolverton, so he had nothing to fear.

"I believe you know why I've come," Lord Wolverton said, "so I won't pretend otherwise."

I admired his frankness.

"I am not keen on being at court, as I've just said," he continued. "I am not fond of flirtations and games and manipulations. I am straightforward in all my dealings, and I like it when people are straightforward with me. I need a wife. My first two wives succumbed to death in childbirth, taking my children with them to the grave. I long for a male heir to continue my family legacy, and I want to be young enough to teach him properly. I am now thirty-five, and I want my inheritance issues secured by the time I am forty, if possible."

I paused near one of the rose beds, my eyebrows raised high.

He regarded me. "You are prettier than I would prefer. I have no need for a pretty wife. All I require is that she be healthy and capable." He looked me over. "Though you do seem strong and competent enough. I don't want a wife who whines or complains or finds life in Northumberland to be tedious and boring. I do not want one who longs for a courtly life. Is that you, Lady Cecily?"

I blinked several times. "Which part, my lord?"

"Do you long for a courtly life?"

"I do not prefer it," I said honestly. "I am happiest at Arundel Castle."

"That is good to hear." He continued to walk, and I followed him.

Two people stood in a shadowed alcove near an entrance into the castle, out of sight of Charles. It was a man and a woman, but they were speaking so close to one another, I wasn't sure who it was at first.

As we continued walking, I realized it was Andrew and Kat. Neither of them noticed me at first, and by the looks on their serious faces, something was not right.

"I do not want to stay in Windsor longer than necessary," Lord Wolverton said. "I would prefer to leave within the month. Would that be acceptable to you?"

Frowning, I paused. "What do you mean?"

"I would like the wedding to be held as soon as the banns are read."

The Church required that a couple who wished to marry should let their intentions be known on three consecutive Sundays. If there were any reasons they should not be bound in holy and legal matrimony, people had time to make their claim.

"I do not want to be here when winter sets in," he continued, "or we might be required to stay."

"But I have not agreed to a marriage," I said, all but forgetting about Andrew and Kat. "I need time to get to know you and to make up my mind."

"I've already told you all you need to know." He frowned. "I do not want a wife who does not know her own mind."

"I know my mind," I assured him, "but I do not know yours. We are discussing a life-altering choice, one I will not enter without proper consideration and prayer."

He sighed. "I do not wish this to take longer than necessary. I've already been gone from Alnwick for a fortnight. You must understand my position."

"Aye. But you must understand mine. And there is the matter of the queen's permission. Right now, she is bedridden and is not to be disturbed. We cannot marry without her consent, and because none of us know you that well, I'm uncertain if she will grant permission."

Lord Wolverton pursed his lips. He seemed affable enough, though he also appeared to be headstrong. "I suppose you're right, but if I wait for you to decide, how can I be certain I am not wasting my time?"

"I'm afraid you cannot."

"What will it take to convince you?"

"Time."

"Which I do not have."

"I am sorry, but I will need time to decide."

"Will I need to woo you? I told you I do not care for flirtations and games and manipulation. But, if I must, I will put my best efforts forward."

"You do not need to woo me," I said, "but you do need to convince me."

He set his mouth in a line, though I could not tell if it was disapproval or determination.

Andrew looked up, and my gaze caught his.

Kat turned to see what he was looking at, and she nodded at me, then slipped into the castle.

"Excuse me, my lord," I said to Lord Wolverton. "I must find out if my queen is doing better, and I see her doctor." I also wanted to know more about Andrew's sister, Evelyn.

"Will you sit with me at supper?" he asked.

"I must sit with the other maids."

"When will I speak to you again?"

"After supper, if you'd like."

He let out a sigh and then bowed. "Very well. Until we meet again, Lady Cecily."

I curtsied and then lifted the hem of my gown and strode to Andrew, who was still standing in the alcove, watching Lord Wolverton.

"Is that him?" he asked as soon as I arrived at his side.

"Aye. Lord Wolverton."

"Was he kind to you?"

"Of course." But I didn't want to talk about Lord Wolverton. "How is the queen?"

"There has been little change."

"Are you doing everything—?"

"More than perhaps I should."

I frowned as I studied him. "What does that mean?"

"I've been researching her condition in 1883, and I am treating her with advanced medical knowledge."

My breath caught, and I put my hand on his arm. "Do not risk it, Andrew. Does Kat or anyone else suspect that you're not a physician here?" The threat of him getting thrown in the Tower was ever-present in my mind.

"I know not." His emotions were hard to read as he looked past me. "Lord Wolverton is watching us."

"I am not concerned about him."

"If he becomes your betrothed, you will need to take him into consideration."

"I'm not betrothed now."

His stormy brown-eyed gaze returned to me.

Warmth filled my chest, but I didn't want to continue with a conversation that would break my heart, so I said, "Were you and Kat discussing the queen? You looked very troubled."

"I wish I could tell you, but—"

"I know." I sighed, hating that he couldn't be open with me about the queen's health. There were so many secrets at court. It was one of the things I detested the most.

Which reminded me of my stepbrother's secrets. A quick glance over my shoulder told me that Charles had joined Lord Wolverton.

"You've never told me about Evelyn."

Andrew frowned in surprise. "How do you know about her?"

"Charles told me. He also said he's in Newport with you."

"Did he tell you why?"

"Aye."

"And do you think it unwise?"

"Aye."

He smiled. "I appreciate your honesty."

"I cannot abide lies or secrets."

"It seems my life is full of them."

"Does Evelyn love Charles?"

Andrew's lips parted. "What? Why would you ask that? She doesn't seem to like him at all."

"Oh." I frowned. "I just assumed, by the way he spoke about her—I thought that he loved her, but he claims he doesn't."

"He had better not." Andrew's body tensed. "There is no hope for a future between them."

Just as there was none for Andrew and me.

"I should depart." I did not want to continue our conversation, afraid I might say something I'd regret. "Good day, Doctor Bromley. Please remember to be careful."

I was about to turn away when he took hold of my hand to stop me.

My fingers curled around his as warmth raced up my arm.

"Will you marry him?" he asked, his voice low.

My heart wanted to say no, but my mind was more rational. "I know not."

He slowly let me go, but his eyes held mine. "I will pray that you know which path to take."

Lord Wolverton and Charles approached, so I went into the castle, not wishing to speak to them again so soon and needing to get away from the feelings Andrew elicited within me.

12

CHARLES

JULY 20, 1883
NEWPORT, RHODE ISLAND

I stood in front of the mirror in my room as I adjusted the cuffs of my suit. My valet had just left after helping me prepare for the evening activities.

Life in Newport had been one endless round of luncheons, afternoon socials, dinner parties, and balls. Thankfully, I was spared from making calls with Mrs. Whitney and Evelyn and had enjoyed spending many of my mornings at the casino with Andrew.

No matter how hard I worked at distracting myself, I could not stop thinking about the queen and her illness. Lady Katherine Grey was ready and willing to take the throne, but she was terrified. Not only because her sister had been beheaded fighting for the crown, but because I suspected she was in love with a nobleman out of her reach. Just like Queen Elizabeth, if Lady Katherine became the next queen, she would be pressured to marry and produce an heir as soon as possible, and she would have little choice in the husband she took. The sweet and docile Lady Katherine was nothing compared to the headstrong, stubborn Queen Elizabeth.

Yet, the privy council had been discussing Mary, Queen of Scots, with more fervor in the past week. They had asked me to pen a letter as the queen's correspondent and tell Mary to prepare to come to Windsor. I did not want Mary anywhere near Queen Elizabeth, or to even know she was this ill. It made the throne vulnerable in many ways, because unlike Lady Katherine, Mary was already a ruler and used to getting her own way. She would not be so easily influenced. She was only twenty years old, but she was already widowed. It was widely known that Queen Elizabeth favored Mary for her replacement, yet it didn't sit well with me or several others. Kat included.

Either way, with the queen's life at stake, we had sent out private missives to our armies throughout England, instructing them to prepare for war if need be, though I prayed it did not come to that.

A knock sounded at the door a moment before Drew stepped in. He was wearing his evening suit and carried an envelope in his hand. "This just arrived."

"What is it?"

"A letter from my father." He handed it to me.

I quickly took the letter, unsure how to read Drew's mood. He'd been distracted for the past two weeks and irritable all day. His tennis game had suffered, and I'd beaten him handedly that morning. I hadn't seen him in Cecily's company at Windsor, though I had seen him watching her in the Great Hall while we dined, and I worried that his morose mood was because of Lord Wolverton's presence at court. Yet, I admired them for setting their feelings aside to do the right thing.

I was starting to understand how hard it was after Cecily asked me if I was in love with Evelyn. I had told her the truth, but I couldn't deny that there was something about Evelyn—about her untold story—that had captured my attention. It wasn't just her time-crossing that had bonded us faster than I anticipated. I found myself looking for ways to see her and spend time in her company. It wasn't love, but I liked her, perhaps more than I should.

Without another word, I unfolded the letter and began to read.

Andrew,

It is good to hear from you, as I know your mother keeps you busy in Newport. I am counting down the months until you join me at Whitney Shipping in January. There is so much to teach you, and your involvement could not come at a better time. Your uncle Clarence is a disappointment to our family, and he, his wife, and your mother spend their time frittering away our money. Clarence has been in Newport all summer, entertaining on his yacht, and the stories I hear are difficult to stomach. I won't bore you with the details.

Suffice it to say, I need a good, solid partner I can rely on, and you are that man. Our family business will rest on your shoulders for future success, but I am confident those shoulders are broad enough to handle the weight of that responsibility.

I must confess, I am excited that you have an investment proposition for me. It tells me that you are ready to step into your role at our company. I am eager to hear more about your ideas, but, as you can understand, I cannot go to Newport to see you. Will you take the train into the city and meet with me next week? I will be in Philadelphia until Wednesday morning but plan to be in New York by midafternoon. Come then, and, if you are able, have the owner of the business meet with us at the office, as well.

I look forward to seeing you on Wednesday. Come prepared to impress me and convince me that your investment is sound.

Father

I lowered the letter and found Drew pacing to the window, his hands in his pockets.

"This is good news, isn't it?" I asked.

"For you, yes. For me, it's just another reminder of my responsibilities to my family." He turned to face me. "I like practicing medicine, Charles. And I'm good at it. I was with Lady Agatha when she died just a couple of weeks ago, and though I wasn't there to heal her, I was able to make her more comfortable and to walk her home to heaven. It gave me a sense of purpose I've never felt before. I don't want to sit behind a desk for the rest of my life. I don't want the weight of the Whitney legacy to rest on my shoulders."

"I don't know what to tell you, other than I understand. The Pembrooke legacy rests on my shoulders in 1563. It isn't what I wanted, either." I handed him back the letter. "Do you plan to go to the city?"

"Of course. Will you come with me?"

"As the Earl of Norfolk or as Charles Hollingsworth?"

"Charles Hollingsworth. It's your family farm that I'm asking him to invest in. You're the most qualified person to tell him about it."

"And what if he finds out I'm posing as the earl in his home?"

"Father will not come to Newport this summer. I've spoken to Mother, and they both agreed it would be best to spend this time apart."

I nodded, knowing we'd have our best chance if I went with him to see his father. But I hesitated.

"The local tennis tournament is next Thursday afternoon. Will we be back in time? I promised Evelyn that I would participate." We'd agreed that the winner of the local tournament would play last year's national champion. I had no intention of winning, but I would happily play for her sake.

"If we leave straightaway on Thursday morning, we should be here by afternoon." He folded the letter and slipped it back into the envelope, hesitating as if he wasn't sure how to proceed. "Cecily said something to me that I haven't stopped thinking about."

My shoulders stiffened. "Are you still meeting with her?"

He lifted his chin. "You saw us together after she spoke to Lord Wolverton on the North Terrace. I did not seek her company, if that's what you mean."

"I do not want you interfering." I couldn't help sounding irritated. I'd worked hard to get Lord Wolverton to the castle, and Cecily had hardly spoken to him since his arrival.

"He isn't good enough for her."

I frowned and walked to the window where he stood. "He's an earl with a castle and thriving farmland. He's also decent and respectable from all accounts."

"I sat with him at supper last night." Drew crossed his arms. "He's boring."

I rolled my eyes. I couldn't help it. "*That* is your only argument against him? He's boring?"

"He's far too pragmatic and predictable. There isn't a creative or clever bone in the man."

"Don't mess this up for Cecily."

"I don't plan to. I think the earl will mess it up for himself."

I sighed. "What did Cecily say that you can't stop thinking about—or do I want to know?"

"She asked me if you're in love with Evelyn."

An awkward silence filled the space between us before I asked, "What did you tell her?"

"I told her no. It was preposterous."

"Why is it preposterous?"

He narrowed his eyes. "What do you mean, why? She believes you are the Earl of Norfolk. When she finds out you're just a farmer from Virginia, she'll be angry and hurt."

"Just a farmer from Virginia?" I asked, my temperature rising.

Drew shrugged. "It is what it is, Charles. And I'm just a commoner at Arundel Castle in 1563. We both know what we are and what we aren't."

"Evelyn knows I'm a time-crosser."

"What?" He leaned forward. "How?"

"She saw my mark and knew what it was."

"How would she?"

"Because she's a time-crosser, too, Drew."

"Evelyn is a time-crosser?" He straightened as the information took him by surprise. "How is that possible?"

"I don't know. She won't tell me about her other path. Just like Cecily, she lost hers and she's stuck here."

Drew put his hands behind his neck and paced away from me. "How could I not know? All this time. I can't ever remember seeing a mark on the back of her head."

"That's because she told me hers is on her chest. I think that's why her personality shifted so drastically. Something happened in her other path that devastated her." Though I was still convinced that something must have happened in this path, as well. It was the only way to explain Baby Laura.

"That makes a lot more sense than what I was imagining." He lowered his hands. "There's something I've never told you about Evelyn."

I frowned, not sure I could handle more surprises.

"She was adopted by my parents when she was a baby. My parents had struggled to have more children after I was born, and my mother was seeing a doctor in New York. After another loss, the doctor wanted to ease my mother's melancholy and told her that his sister had given birth to a baby out of wedlock. Instead of sending her to an orphanage, the doctor wanted to find a good family for her. My parents decided to adopt her."

"Does she know?"

"Yes. But it baffles my mind that my parents adopted a time-crosser—and that I never knew."

"I'm still amazed that God chose for Cecily to be my stepsister."

Drew paused for a second and then said, "You haven't answered Cecily's question. You've spent a lot of time with Evelyn the past two weeks planning the fundraiser. Is something happening between you?"

"No." It wasn't completely true, because I was feeling something for her, but she'd given me no indication that she returned the feelings.

"I will warn you like you warned me, Charles. Evelyn is off limits."

His words rankled, but what right did I have to become angry? He was right. In this path, even though I was pretending to be the Earl of Norfolk, I was a nobody. I wasn't good enough for a wealthy heiress like Evelyn Whitney. And besides that, I had too much to worry about with Cecily in 1563 and Mama and Ada at the farm in Virginia. I couldn't complicate matters by falling in love with Evelyn.

Drew was about to leave my room when he turned and said, "I think that as soon as the tennis fundraiser is done, Lord Norfolk should plan on leaving Newport. And he should start to prepare my mother and sister for his departure."

I didn't respond as Drew left my room.

There was nothing left to say.

Chateau-sur-Mer sat proud on Bellevue Avenue, one of the most stunning cottages in Newport. The owner, George Wetmore, was a wealthy philanthropist and politician who had inherited his vast wealth and home from his father.

"This is the first time we've been invited to one of the Wetmores' parties," Mrs. Whitney said as she touched her hair and the carriage turned into the Chateau-sur-Mer drive. "We owe it all to you, Lord Norfolk. I'm sure the *other* Mrs. Whitney will be jealous when she hears of it!"

"Don't you think Aunt Helen will be invited since she has the Vicomte Deville as her summer guest?" Drew asked as he sat next to me on the forward-facing bench.

Evelyn was seated beside her mother, wearing a stunning purple gown that made her blue eyes seem almost violet tonight. Her hair was styled high, and her slender neck kept drawing my attention. It looked silky smooth and inviting.

I had to work hard to concentrate on something other than Evelyn, but it wasn't as difficult with Drew's warning still fresh in my mind.

If Evelyn discovered I wasn't the Earl of Norfolk, she might never speak to me again.

She glanced at me, her expression tender in the darkening shadows inside the carriage. Awareness was building between us, and every time we were together it only became stronger. Was she feeling the same attraction I felt? My pulse thrummed at the thought.

Mrs. Whitney sighed. "Perhaps you're right," she said. "Helen might be there tonight—but I still have an earl, and she only has a lowly vicomte. And a fat one, at that."

"Mother," Evelyn said with a frown.

"What? The man has done nothing but eat since he arrived in Newport. I wonder how Clarence and Helen can afford such a guest."

"I wonder how Whitney Shipping can afford it," Drew said under his breath.

Evelyn shook her head as she met my gaze again.

I could only smile.

"Regardless," Mrs. Whitney said, not keeping her rivalry with Helen a secret, "the Wetmores are part of Mrs. Astor's social set, and she will probably be there tonight. We are one step closer to social acceptance, and that's all that matters. I do hope you'll get a chance to dance with Carrie Astor tonight, Lord Norfolk."

"I will do my best, Mrs. Whitney."

Evelyn's chin came up a notch—hardly noticeable if I hadn't been watching.

Did she not like the idea of me dancing with Carrie?

When we finally arrived at Chateau-sur-Mer, every window in the three-story Victorian mansion was filled with lights and dozens of carriages were waiting in line to drop off their occupants.

A four-story tower and a prominent porte cochere gave the home an imposing feel.

As Drew and his mother continued to talk about the vicomte and Helen Whitney, I was doing a terrible job ignoring Evelyn and she was doing a terrible job pretending I wasn't watching her.

I couldn't help it. She was stunning.

Drew elbowed me in the side, and I turned to him. "What?"

"Get out of the carriage."

"Andrew," Mrs. Whitney scolded him. "That's no way to talk to our guest."

There was a warning in Drew's eyes, and I knew he'd caught me staring at his sister.

I didn't like how this felt, and I suddenly had a greater appreciation for how he reacted when I warned him off Cecily.

I exited the carriage and helped Mrs. Whitney and then Evelyn.

As she stepped down next to me, I inhaled a breath of her perfume and every one of my senses ignited.

We entered Chateau-sur-Mer and were presented to Mr. and Mrs. Wetmore. They lived full-time in Newport and were anchors in local society. Though they seemed impressed with my noble title, they did not fawn over me.

The house was full of people I'd met throughout the summer, though most of them were part of the older money crowd. Mrs. Astor stood in the Wetmores' massive entrance hall next to Mr. Ward McAllister, one of the self-appointed arbiters of society. He had made Newport a famous summer destination for the wealthiest Americans and was rumored to control the list that Mrs. Astor used to determine her party guests. I'd seen them at the casino and the Fourth of July celebrations, but we'd not been introduced.

"Have you met Mrs. Astor yet?" Mrs. Wetmore asked Mrs. Whitney.

"Not formally, no." Mrs. Whitney looked unaffected by the question, though I knew it was all that she thought about.

"Let's change that, shall we?" Mrs. Wetmore smiled as she motioned for Mrs. Whitney and me to follow her.

The Wetmores' entrance hall was filled with people, and it was hard to maneuver toward Mrs. Astor. We were almost to them when I noticed Helen Whitney speaking to them with Vicomte Deville at her side.

"We will have to arrange a gathering," Mr. McAllister said to Helen in a southern accent. "I would love to have you and the vicomte to tea one day soon."

Mrs. Whitney's body grew tense as Helen glanced at her with triumph. She'd gotten to them before we could.

"Mrs. Astor and Mr. McAllister," Mrs. Wetmore said, seemingly unaffected by Helen's presence, "I'd like to introduce you to two more guests."

The pair turned to us, and Mrs. Astor raised her eyebrow.

"Lord Norfolk," Mrs. Wetmore said, "may I present Mr. Ward McAllister and Mrs. Caroline Astor?"

I harnessed all the charm I could muster, realizing that I had lost sight of Evelyn before I could put my name on her dance card. It took all my self-control not to scan the room. Instead, I gave my undivided attention to Mr. McAllister and Mrs. Astor. They were, after all, the reason I had come to Newport.

"I am pleased to meet you," I said as I bowed over Mrs. Astor's hand and then bowed to Mr. McAllister.

"And this is Mrs. William Whitney," Mrs. Wetmore continued, "Lord Norfolk's hostess for the summer."

"How do you do?" Mrs. Whitney asked, giving a curtsy.

"The pleasure is ours," Mr. McAllister said as he bowed over her hand. He then turned to me. "I do hope you're enjoying our Newport summer, Lord Norfolk. I had hoped we could meet, sooner rather than later."

"It's been a lovely time," I assured him.

"Carrie told me she met you at the outing to the fort," Mrs. Astor said. "I do hope you have a chance to dance with her tonight"—she motioned to Vicomte Deville—"both of you, of course."

"I will find her immediately and ask for a dance." I bowed again, wanting to find Evelyn even more. "I hope you'll excuse me."

Freshly cut flowers perfumed the air as a five-piece orchestra played soft music in the ornate, three-story ballroom. The sound lifted toward the stained-glass windows high above the room.

Within moments, I was surrounded by young women and their doting mothers, all of them making introductions and asking me to fill their dance cards. I was forced to oblige, trying to keep at least one dance open for Evelyn.

As I took a card to fill in my name, I got a peek at Evelyn through the crowd. I hurriedly wrote my name and then said, "If you'll excuse me."

There were disappointed murmurs as I pushed my way through the crowd, ignoring the greetings of others, and approached Evelyn.

She was surrounded by a handful of men. Her cheeks were bright pink as she smiled at one man after the other.

Jealousy wound its way around my heart and choked any goodwill I felt for these gentlemen. If they had taken all her dances, I would not be pleased.

As she turned from one man to the next, her blue eyes caught on me and lit up with pleasure. "Charles."

My heart pounded hard at that look. I tried to see her between the shoulders of the men in front of me. "May I have a dance, Evelyn?"

She looked at her card and frowned.

"Two would be preferred," I said to a round of disapproval from the other men.

"I only have one to give," she said. "The waltz right before supper."

"I'll take it."

Time crawled along as I waited for the waltz. I danced first with Carrie Astor and then several others, but it was hard to focus on my partners when I couldn't keep my eyes off Evelyn.

Every time we passed one another, our gazes collided, and the tension in my stomach tightened. When it was finally time for our waltz, I approached her on the dance floor, every nerve in my body alive with awareness, and without a word, I took her hand and drew her into my arms.

Her breath caught as she looked up at me, but she came willingly and, I hoped, with as much anticipation.

"The music hasn't started, my lord," she whispered as we stood face-to-face, her hand in mine and my other hand around her waist.

"I didn't want to miss a moment with you."

The first strains of the waltz began as others found their partners, and we started to dance.

"My mother will be so pleased that we waltzed together," she said.

"Are you pleased, Evelyn?"

Her body was closer than necessary as we moved across the floor, but she didn't pull back or put space between us.

"Very," she breathed.

I inhaled the soft scent of her perfume, wishing this moment would never end, longing to be the Earl of Norfolk in this path. What would she think when she learned the truth? Would she understand because she was a time-crosser? Or would she never speak to me again, knowing that I had tried to deceive her and her mother, not to mention all the other people in Newport?

"Will you sit with me at supper?" I asked her.

"Are you not tired of me?" she teased. "We see each other all the time. Perhaps you want to sit with Isabel Reinhold or Carrie Astor."

There was a slight edge to her voice, and I wondered, again, if she was jealous.

I tried to tell myself it didn't matter. Because I wasn't who I said I was, and even if I were, I might not stay in 1883.

Suddenly, I wanted her to know me—the real me, just as I wanted to know her. But it meant I would need to risk everything.

Moments before the song ended, I asked, "May I take you outside? I have something I want to tell you."

"Of course."

We stopped dancing, and I led her toward one of the tall sets of French doors. There were so many people that no one paid attention when we slipped outside.

The air was much cooler as we stepped onto the manicured yard. The moon was full and bright, creating moon shadows on the lawn.

We walked to a stone railing and leaned against it.

My pulse was erratic as I thought about what I was going to tell Evelyn. The only way she might trust me with her past was if I told her about mine. And, to do that, I would need to be honest about this one, too.

Behind us, the music from the orchestra drifted out to the lawn, creating a cocoon of gilded warmth. Thankfully, there was no one else outside. What I had to say needed to be kept private.

"What did you want to tell me?" she asked.

I took a deep breath, knowing there was no going back now. "It's about my other path."

She turned to me. "You don't need to, Charles. I, more than anyone, understand how difficult it is to live two lives. You don't owe me an explanation."

"My other path is 1563," I said, not allowing myself to back down. "And it's there that I'm Charles Pembrooke, the 2nd Earl of Norfolk."

Evelyn didn't speak as she studied me, though her expression was wary. "And who are you here?"

"I'm Charles Hollingsworth." I allowed my accent to slip into the Virginia cadence I'd adopted in this path. "My father, Nathanial, was a time-crosser. He was a Confederate soldier in the American Civil War and died when I was only six, but his father taught me about my time-crossing gift. I grew up on a farm where my father was a successful horse breeder until we lost everything in the war, and I now live there with my widowed sister, Ada, and our mama, Meredith."

There. I'd said it.

Her expression didn't change. "You're not an earl here?"

"No. But in 1563 I am, and I'm also a member of the privy

council for Queen Elizabeth. I'm currently at Windsor Castle because there is a plague outbreak in London. Andrew and I grew up together at my castle in Arundel, and that's how we met. I asked him to go to Windsor to care for the queen, who is ill. In exchange, he asked me to come here and pose as the Earl of Norfolk for your mother's benefit. He is also trying to get your father to invest in my family's horse farm."

Evelyn wrapped her arms around herself and paced to the end of the railing.

My throat tightened with uncertainty. But I couldn't live with myself if I continued to deceive her. She deserved so much better.

"You lied to me," she said just above a whisper without turning back.

Letting out a breath, I took a step toward her. "I'm sorry, Evelyn."

"I can't abide lies or deceit, Charles." She hugged her waist, the weight of her pain rounding her shoulders. "I told you I was hurt by someone I trusted."

"I never meant to hurt you—truly." I took another step, afraid she would slip away from me, desperate to convince her. "That's why I'm telling you now. I didn't want the lies to continue."

"You're not the only one to blame. I'm just as disappointed in Drew."

There was nothing I could say to defend myself or Drew. Evelyn had every right to be angry and disappointed.

"I'll understand if you—"

"I know how difficult it is to be a time-crosser, Charles." She finally turned to face me, pain and anger still fresh in her eyes. "And I understand why you've done what you've done. But you still tried to deceive me."

"Please forgive me." It was all I could ask.

"If anyone else learns the truth, it would ruin our family." She walked back to me. "Mother must never know."

"I won't tell her." It took all my willpower not to reach out to her while she was standing this close. "Can you forgive me, Evelyn? I care too much for you to hate me."

She studied me in the moonlight, and I could see the war waging in her mind and heart. Finally, she said, "I could never hate you, Charles."

"It breaks my heart what happened to you," I told her as I put my hand on her cheek. It was as soft as I imagined. "And the last thing I want to do is add to your pain."

"Are you staying in 1563?"

"I'm not sure what I'm doing yet."

Evelyn took a step back, leaning against the railing as she faced the ballroom. "Someone I once loved told me whatever I wanted to hear to get what he wanted. He made me believe that I was in love with him, and I did unspeakable things because of it." She turned her head to look at me. "I like you, Charles, but I've already tried to manipulate God's plan for my life, and I won't do it again. If you are called to 1563, then you must do everything in your power to ensure that you end up there without harming anyone in your path."

"Drew believes I should leave Newport after the tennis fundraiser, and I think he's right."

She looked back at the ballroom, and I could see a dozen emotions passing over her beautiful face. "It's probably for the best."

I took a step closer to her, knowing that we didn't have much time left. "I really do hope you can forgive me. The last thing I wanted to do was hurt you. It's why I told you now, so you wouldn't find out another way."

She pressed her lips together for a moment and then let out a breath. "I won't pretend that I'm not upset. But if anyone knows how complex and difficult it is to be a time-crosser, it's me."

And with that, she slipped her hand around my elbow and led me back to the ballroom.

13

CECILY

JULY 25, 1563
WINDSOR CASTLE

The jousting tournament had been planned for weeks, but with the queen's ongoing illness, many had suggested canceling it. When the queen heard the rumors, she ordered Kat to tell the castle to continue with the plans. Even if she couldn't attend, she wanted others to enjoy the entertainment and communicate to the world that there was nothing wrong. She had commanded Lord Burghley, her Lord High Treasurer, to be the presiding noble. He sat on a raised dais and reigned over the tournament.

Hundreds of courtiers, servants, and guards stood or sat in the Lower Ward near the tiltyards, where the jousting took place. Events such as this one were usually held during wedding feasts or when dignitaries visited, but with the ongoing plague still ravaging London, we were cloistered in the castle with little to break up the monotony of the days. A jousting tournament was exactly what everyone needed.

The day was overcast, but the rain had held off as we watched various noblemen compete for favors from the queen's ladies in waiting. Throughout the day, the winners had been given scarves, ribbons, and veils, and the queen had ordered that the best jouster be given a gold ring from her collection. That evening, we would have a feast in the Great Hall.

"Do you joust, my lord?" I asked Lord Wolverton, who sat next to me in the stands.

Aveline sat on my other side. Because the queen was bedridden, our efforts to convince her that my cousin would be a good maid of honour had stalled. So Aveline, like everyone else, was looking for ways to pass the time.

My only consolation was that there were no other maidens gaining the queen's favor. It gave us more time to prepare Aveline.

"No." Lord Wolverton shook his head. "I do not joust. There is enough danger living along the Scottish border. Why increase the odds of injury or death to try to prove my strength or courage?"

"Is there any entertainment to be had at Alnwick Castle?" I asked, trying not to sound gloomy.

"Do you require entertainment, Lady Cecily?"

I had to think about that for a moment. I'd had it all my life. I couldn't imagine not enjoying a bit of entertainment from time to time. "I do not require it," I said, "but I enjoy it when it's available."

He pursed his lips in disapproval.

"There is no entertainment at your home, my lord?" Aveline asked.

"When others insist upon it," he told her, "but if I had my way, we would not waste time, money, or energy on anything that did not serve a purpose."

"Entertainment serves a great purpose," I countered. "Life is full of difficulties and hardships. Entertainment exists to ease those challenges, if just for a moment. To help us forget about the ongoing troubles that surround us, and to make us laugh and smile and cheer. I propose that it is an essential part of life."

"Then we have differing opinions." He crossed his arms. "It will be something you'll need to work on."

"If you are trying to convince me to marry you and travel to the ends of nowhere," I said, my voice a bit dry, "perhaps you should make that life sound more pleasing."

"I do not wish to make it sound unappealing." He uncrossed his arms. "But I want to be realistic, so you know what to expect."

"Is there no ability to change how things are done at Alnwick Castle?" Aveline interrupted, no doubt trying to ease the tension between me and Lord Wolverton as two jousters entered the lists, the field in which they would compete. One of them was Charles. His match was the last of the day and highly anticipated by all the spectators.

Lord Wolverton squinted as he watched the jousters mount their horses. "I suppose I could be persuaded, if Lady Cecily had enough evidence to support her case. I am nothing if not reasonable."

Aveline smiled and nodded encouragement at me, but I had to press my lips together to keep from responding. Though Lord Wolverton was kind, he was also very opinionated and hardheaded. Reasonable was not a trait I would have assigned to him.

Charles was in his full armor with the Norfolk Crest on his shield. He was a crowd favorite, and many of the ladies fluttered their scarves at him to gain his attention as he paraded in front of the stands. He waved at the noblewomen, creating a round of enthusiastic chatter.

And though I enjoyed entertainment, jousting was not my favorite. I had watched Charles joust most of my life and hated it every time. The idea of two men galloping toward each other with ten-foot wooden lances pointed at their opponent was ridiculous. It was designed to show strength, bravery, and fighting skills, but in my mind, it was only for pride.

Charles did look handsome and strong on his horse, wielding the family crest. I could only shake my head and hope and pray that God would keep him safe. What would his Evelyn think if she saw him now? Would she be like the simpering noblewomen, trying to gain his attention? Or was she serious and withdrawn? It was the first time I'd wondered about the kind of woman who could capture his attention.

Andrew stood on the side of the tiltyards, ready to assist should the worst happen. I'd seen many men injured over the years, some dying from their wounds. Even King Henry VIII had been seriously injured during a jousting match, creating problems for years to come.

The heralds called out the names of the competitors, issuing the challenges to fight. When Charles's name was proclaimed, a raucous cheer arose from the crowd.

He saluted his opponent by lifting his lance high in the air as the spectators cheered again. My heart fell with a new thought. What if Charles was killed and I was left in 1563 alone? He would still have his path in 1883, but I would never see him again. It was a prospect I did not want to consider, not only because I would miss him dearly, but also because I would be left with few options. I would not have the liberty of taking my time to marry Lord Wolverton if that happened.

Out of the corner of my eye, I saw a woman join Drew on the sideline. It was Lettice.

She was wearing a colorful gown made of rich burgundy satin, with an impressive matching headpiece. Drew turned to her and offered a brilliant smile as she put her hand on his arm.

Whatever she said made Drew laugh as his attention was torn from the jousting match. He nodded and did not pull away from her touch.

Had they been getting closer while I kept my distance?

The trumpet fanfare blew, and then Charles and his opponent lowered their lances. Both competitors spurred their horses into a gallop, and I held my breath. The lances were designed to break easily in noncombative jousting, and the blunted ends eased the impact, but it didn't mean there wasn't risk.

The horses galloped at a deadly pace, their hooves beating the earth, on either side of the tilt. I closed my eyes and turned to Aveline, not wanting to watch as the sound of splintering wood pierced the air.

A gasp arose from the crowd, and I opened my eyes in time to see Charles fall to the ground. His opponent's lance hadn't shattered as his had done.

Charles was motionless as part of the crowd cheered for his opponent, still seated upon his horse.

I stood, my heart pounding hard, and pushed my way through the ladies in waiting who were now standing to get a better look.

Andrew was already on his way across the tiltyards as I stepped onto the grass and lifted my skirts to run to Charles's side.

He had not moved or attempted to rise, making me fear the worst.

Several squires ran up to clear the horse as the opponent took his victory lap.

"Charles," I said as I fell to the ground on my knees beside him.

Andrew was still running toward us. "Remove his helmet!" he yelled.

One of the squires helped as we took off his metal helmet.

Charles was unconscious.

"Charles," I said again, putting my hand on his cheek. "Wake up."

Andrew finally arrived and knelt beside my stepbrother. He lifted Charles's eyelids and felt the pulse at his neck. "He lives," he said. "We must get him into the castle, where I can better examine him." He motioned to the squires standing around us. "I need all the help I can get."

"I'll go ahead and prepare his room." I rose, breathless. The Lower Ward and Upper Ward were at a great distance.

"I don't want to take that much time." Andrew motioned to the nearby building. "Let's move him into the knights' lodging."

"He can use my bedchamber," one of the knights said. The military knights were retired soldiers who lived at Windsor and performed ceremonial duties in exchange for room and board.

They were housed in the Lower Ward with the active soldiers who protected the castle and the queen.

"This way," the knight said as the squires lifted Charles, his armor rattling. He was like a ragdoll in their hands, his head lolling back and his body limp.

I wanted to cry out, but I would not embarrass myself or Charles in such a way.

I followed them to a room within the Lower Ward, not far from St. George's Chapel. It wasn't very large, but it had a bed and would serve the purpose Andrew sought.

"We must get him out of the armor," Andrew instructed.

Several of the squires, more familiar with armor, stepped forward to assist Andrew as I stood back and watched. Under the metal armor, Charles had on a coif to protect his head and neck, a gambeson, which was a padded jacket, as well as other material and clothing to protect all areas of his body from bruises and wounding. After they had removed everything but his gambeson and hose, Andrew began to assess his body to check for broken bones or other wounds.

"Why is he unconscious?" I asked Andrew. "I do not see any blood."

"He was probably rendered unconscious from the blow or from falling and hitting his head." Andrew called for a candle and then lifted Charles's eyelids again, running the flame of the candle in front of his eyes to watch his pupils. He glanced at me, and I could see he was concerned.

The squires left the room while Andrew continued to examine Charles. As I waited, I paced and prayed. I didn't want God to take one more person from me. Charles was all I had left in this path. I could not bear to lose him.

Finally, Andrew stood.

"What?" I asked. "Why hasn't he woken up?"

"I'm not sure, Cecily. I know a little about head injuries, but not enough to offer a prognosis."

"What will we do?"

"I think he's stable enough to move to his apartment. From there, we'll monitor him and hope he wakes up soon."

Charles groaned and began to move his body.

"Charles!" I fell to the side of the bed and took his hand. "Please wake up."

Slowly, he opened his eyes, blinking several times as confusion and pain played across his face.

"Do you hear me, Charles?" Andrew asked as he stood beside me.

Charles continued to blink as his gaze focused on Andrew and then on me. A frown deepened his brow.

"My head is pounding," he said.

"You were knocked off your horse in the jousting tournament." I squeezed his hand tight. "We think you hit your head when you fell."

"Jousting tournament?" His hand was limp in mine as he looked at Andrew. "Where am I?"

Andrew leaned forward, resting his hand on Charles's shoulder. "You're at Windsor Castle, in one of the knight's chambers."

"Knight's chambers?" Charles looked at the room, confusion in his face. He slowly brought his attention back to me and pulled his hand out of mine. "Who are you?"

My breath caught. "It's me, your stepsister, Cecily."

"My sister's name is Ada." He started to sit up, but Andrew put pressure on his shoulder.

"Lie still," Andrew said. "You've had a brain injury, and I don't want to make it worse."

Thankfully, Charles did not fight him.

"What are we doing here, Drew?" He no longer spoke in his British accent. I'd only ever heard an American southern drawl in a play on the West End in my other path. He used the same diction and cadence. "Where is Evelyn?"

"Evelyn is in 1883." Andrew straightened, concern tightening his voice. "We're currently in 1563, in our other paths, Charles. Don't you remember?"

Charles frowned and studied Andrew as if he was telling him a lie.

"Don't you remember me?" I tried not to cry, but panic made my voice shake. "I'm Cecily, your sister here. You're a time-crosser, Charles, all three of us are. You are currently living in 1563 and 1883. Both you and Andrew."

Charles squinted his eyes in disbelief. "You're not making any sense." He looked around the room again. It was sparse and small. "Is this a prison cell? Am I being held against my will?"

Tears burned my eyes as I shook my head. "This is a room at Windsor Castle. A knight's bedchamber. Your apartment is in the Upper Ward, near the queen's apartment. You are Lord Norfolk, one of the queen's privy councilors."

He put his hand over his closed eyes. "In 1883, I am *pretending* to be the Earl of Norfolk to help Drew's mother. Is this a bad dream? Am I now dreaming I'm the earl in a bygone era?"

I could no longer contain my tears as I looked up at Andrew. They fell down my cheeks, and I had to brush them away, not wanting to worry Charles. I pleaded with my eyes for Andrew to do something, but he lifted his hands and shook his head.

"Drew." Charles opened his eyes. "Please tell me this is a joke. That you moved me to this—" he motioned to the room—"this prison cell at Fort Adams and put on these silly costumes, and that when I woke up, you and this woman"—he motioned to me this time—"would try to convince me that I have a second life."

"This is not a joke, Charles," Andrew said. "Tomorrow, when you wake up, you will be in 1883 again. But here your brain must be swollen from your concussion, and your memories of this place are being impacted. Hopefully after some rest, the swelling will go down and your memories will be restored."

Charles listened intently, but he still didn't look convinced.

"And what if they are not?" I asked Andrew. "What if he can never remember this path?"

"We will deal with that if and when the time comes," Andrew assured me. "But I pray it does not come to that."

"How would we deal with it?" Panic was building as it coursed through my limbs, making me shake. "If he cannot remember me, why would he choose to stay here with me?"

"Stay here?" Charles asked, frowning. "I don't want to stay here."

"Please do not say such things, Charles," I begged. "You are my only family. I do not want to stay in 1563 by myself."

My words appeared to distress him, so Andrew stepped forward. "We will have Charles moved to his apartment, and I will keep an eye on him. If all goes well, he will be restored soon."

"How long might it take?" I asked.

"It could be a few hours or a few weeks. There is no way of knowing. I will do more research in 1883 and see if I can find answers."

Charles had closed his eyes, but I wasn't sure if he was unconscious again or simply trying to cope with what was happening to him.

Andrew put his hand on the small of my back and led me out of the room. The squires and knight were waiting in the hall.

"Please prepare to move Lord Norfolk to his apartment," Andrew told them. "I must speak to Lady Cecily in private."

The men walked toward the room, but Andrew stopped them. "He is speaking very strangely, but do not be alarmed with anything he tells you. He is not in his right mind at present."

They nodded and left us in the corridor alone.

"I only know a little about brain injuries." He spoke quietly to me. "But I don't know why he can remember 1883 and not recall his life here. I promise I will do everything I can to return his memory, but it might take some time."

I realized my hand was on his arm, holding him as if he was an anchor in an uncertain storm. I started to pull it away, but he captured my hand in his.

"You are not alone here, Cecily." He put his other hand on my upper arm. His touch was gentle and calming. "I will not leave your side through this trial. I promise."

"Thank you," I whispered, trying to hold back the tears again.

But despite his reassurance, when he left me to move Charles, I felt utterly alone.

Darkness had fallen on Windsor Castle as I stood in my tower room, watching the stars from the high window. I had wanted to stay with Charles, but my presence agitated him. Andrew was the only person he recognized and wanted by his side.

Hours had passed since his accident, and still he did not remember his life in 1563. Andrew only allowed one or two male servants to enter Charles's apartment to care for him and warned them that Charles might say strange and unusual things.

I had paced in the tower all evening, alternately praying and crying, as a headache wrapped around my skull. The feast was held as scheduled, but I did not want to dance and make merry when my stepbrother's life was in peril and I was in so much pain. Lord Burghley excused me from the evening's festivities, and I had fled to the tower.

Before long, it would be time for bed, and the others would be worried if I didn't show up in my dormitory.

With a sigh, I left the tower and decided to check on Charles one more time before I went to bed. Perhaps something had changed.

As I exited the stairs and entered the corridor, Kat Astley passed by.

"I was just coming to find you." She took my hand and pulled me back into the stairwell and closed the door. We were standing in utter darkness. "I heard Lord Norfolk has sustained serious injuries." She spoke in low tones. "Are the rumors true? Lord Robert has been drinking and crowing about Lord Norfolk's demise all evening."

My raw emotions felt close to breaking. "Has he no shame?"

Kat sighed but didn't address my question. "I've also heard that Lord Norfolk isn't in his right mind. Is that true? I could not be seen going to his apartments to inquire. No one must know I've spoken to you, either."

Concern folded my brow as my eyes adjusted and I had a better view of her. "When he awoke, he could not remember me or anything else. I am going to check on him now to see if he has improved."

"I trust you, Lady Cecily." Her voice was serious. "You are the only person I can ask this favor, but you must swear to keep it a secret."

I pulled back as far as the stairwell would allow, uncertain I wanted to be privy to Kat's secrets. She knew more than anyone—and probably more than even the queen. But if it had something to do with Charles, I would do whatever was necessary.

"You have my word."

Kat took a deep breath. "No one must know Lord Norfolk is suffering. No one. I will tell everyone that he has sustained injuries, but he is recuperating and will continue to work from his apartments." She moved a little closer to me. "Lord Norfolk is working on a very important letter for the privy council." She paused, as if weighing the wisdom in telling me more. "Several council members were able to convince the majority that the throne should pass to Mary, Queen of Scots, and they ordered Lord Norfolk to write her a letter, apprising her of the situation and telling her to prepare to come to Windsor Castle."

"I thought the privy council was positioning Lady Katherine Grey to take the throne."

"The council is split, but a majority believe Mary, Queen of Scots, is the rightful heir."

"And you do not?"

"Nay. Lord Norfolk and I agree that Mary should not be allowed anywhere close to this castle. Even if the queen should survive, I do not trust Mary. She would have the queen killed, if it were up to her. And I don't think 'tis wise to tell Mary how dire the situation is. She is liable to raise an army to attack." Kat studied me closely. "The council expects a letter to be sent to Mary, but Lord Norfolk is drafting a different one. If he is not in his right mind, you must find the letter and keep it safe. We must stall the privy council as long as possible, until he is well again. We cannot let anyone see that letter, and we cannot let the privy council have someone else write the letter they want. Do you understand?"

"Aye. But how long can we stall before the privy council demands the letter or for Charles to show himself?"

"I know not—but we must try to keep them at bay for as long as it takes." She put her hands on my arms. "I need you to stand in his place. We will have his work sent to his apartments, and you must oversee it. You will be the go-between with him and his secretary. Do you understand?"

I wasn't sure what I was agreeing to, but I trusted Kat and Charles, so I nodded. "I will do whatever it takes."

"Thank you. And no one must know you're doing this or that I spoke to you."

"What about Doctor Bromley? I cannot hide it from him."

"He already knows too much, but it cannot be helped. He's proven trustworthy, so you may tell him. But he must understand that absolute secrecy is demanded of him."

I nodded again.

Without another word, Kat left me.

There was nothing left to do but go to Charles's apartments. I prayed he had returned to his senses, and I wouldn't need to worry about the letter or carrying out his work for the foreseeable future. Though I had a vague idea about what he did, I couldn't be responsible to maintain the charade for long.

As I moved through the darkened hall, another person appeared up ahead.

Lord Wolverton.

I paused, prepared to turn the other way, hoping he hadn't seen me when I heard, "There you are, Lady Cecily."

With a groan, I continued.

"Do you have word of your brother's condition?" he asked.

"I am going there now." My stomach felt queasy from the pain in my head. I'd suffered from migraines before, but it had been months since the last one. "Doctor Bromley thought it best that I leave Charles in peace as much as possible. I want to check on his progress before I retire for the evening."

"Doctor Bromley is the man you spoke to the day that I arrived? The one in the alcove on the North Terrace?"

"Aye." I continued to walk toward Charles's apartment.

"I've heard he comes from Arundel Castle." Lord Wolverton followed me. "That you have known him since you were young."

"Aye," I said again, trying not to appear concerned. Would Lord Wolverton inquire after Andrew's experience as a physician?

"Are you in love with this Bromley?"

I finally turned to look at him and saw that there was no anger or animosity in his gaze, just simple curiosity. I didn't know what to say, because I couldn't lie.

"I only ask because I need to know what I am up against," he said. "I cannot control who you love or who you might have loved before we met. I also know the queen would never approve of a marriage between the two of you, but one's heart cares little for such things. If you love him, I do not want you pining after him while trying to build a life with me."

"If I did love him, would you drop your pursuit for my hand?"

He was quiet for a moment, but then he shook his head. "No."

"And if I said I might spend the rest of my life mourning the loss of his love. Would that deter you, my lord?"

"If you can promise me that you will not let it interfere with your duties as the mistress of Alnwick Castle, or your ability to produce a child, then no."

I let out a breath, reminding myself that marriage in 1563 was rarely about love and almost always about political and social status. At least for nobility.

To find true love was a rare gift.

"I must check on my stepbrother and then return to my dormitory." I curtsied. "Fare thee well, Lord Wolverton."

Without another word, I strode down the corridor, wanting to be rid of the man who would have me become his wife.

When I finally arrived at Charles's door, I knocked lightly and then stepped inside, not knowing what I would find.

Andrew sat at the table in the outer chamber with a single candle offering light as he read a book. He was alone, since Charles's bed was in the next room.

He looked up at my arrival, and I could see the tension and worry in the lines of his face.

"Is there no change?"

"None." He sighed and pushed the book away. It was entitled *Hippocrates Corpus*. "I am trying to learn all I can about brain injuries, but the knowledge here is so limited."

"You'll have access to more in 1883?"

He ran his hands through his hair and stood. "Aye. But I don't know how much I can do without changing history. I've bled him twice already, hoping to take down the swelling in his brain. But it has done no good."

The candlelight flickered, casting shadows on one side of his face while leaving the other side in darkness. He was an attractive man, in both body and soul.

"What will happen when he wakes up in 1883?" I asked, my headache so intense I could hardly think straight.

"I know not, but I'm eager to find out. We are currently staying in my family's townhouse in New York City and are supposed to meet with my father tomorrow to discuss Charles's family horse farm. If he cannot remember anything there, it could threaten those prospects."

"Do you think he'll not remember 1883 when he has such a clear memory of it here?"

Andrew shrugged. "I really couldn't say. I don't know what will happen. I have never spoken to a time-crosser who has dealt with amnesia before. This is uncharted territory." He paused and studied my face. "Do you not feel well, Cecily?"

"'Tis just a headache," I said, dreading that I would have to tell him what Kat had asked of me.

"Do you get them often?"

"Only in times of great duress."

"Where does it hurt?"

"All over, but mostly around the back of my head and into my neck."

"How long has it persisted?"

I tried to smile, but it didn't form. "'Tis nothing to worry about, Andrew. I need to speak to you about something else."

He took a step closer, resting his hand on the side of my face, concern in his eyes. "How long has it persisted, Cecily?"

His touch was so soft, so tender, I forgot all about Kat. "It came on shortly after Charles's accident."

"Will you allow me to ease the pain for you?"

My voice caught in my throat, and all I could manage was a slight nod.

He took the candle off the table in one hand and put the other on the small of my back, leading me to the other side of the room. "Have a seat while I get my things." He left my side and retrieved his medical chest from Charles's bedchamber. When he came back and set the chest on the table next to the candle, he said, "Charles sleeps peacefully."

"I need to speak to you about Kat—"

"Let us take care of your headache first, and then we will speak. I'm certain it can wait."

I liked the idea of forgetting about my troubles for a moment. Andrew was right. It could wait.

"What will you do for my headache?" I asked instead, already feeling a little better knowing I was in his care.

"Bloodletting with the use of cups." As he spoke, he removed a lancet from the case.

I cringed. "I hate bloodletting. 'Tis going out of use in 1913."

"'Tis an ancient practice," he told me. "Dating back thousands of years. It balances the humors and restores order in your system. I learned how to do it at Yale."

"'Tis also painful and slightly disturbing."

He smiled.

It was fascinating to watch him work as he removed several clear glass cups from his case and then some rags and ointment. His face was so serious, so intent, that he seemed to be in another world.

Without looking at me, he smiled again.

"Do you mind if I watch you?" I asked, my voice low. "'Tis a rare privilege."

"Nay. I do not mind." He continued to gather his things as he said, "I enjoy watching you, as well, Lady Cecily."

My heart beat hard, which made my head hurt even more.

When he was ready, he faced me. "Have you ever had cupping done?"

"Nay. Though I've seen it."

"I will explain everything in detail so you are not concerned." He lifted the lancet and showed me the small blade. "First, I will make very small incisions in the skin of your upper shoulders with this, and then I will warm the cups over the flame of the candle. Next, I will place them over the small incisions, and as the cups cool, they will create a suction, which will draw out the blood and ease the tension in your neck and shoulders. Hopefully, this will alleviate your headache."

"My shoulders?" I asked, suddenly aware that I would need to remove my upper garments for him to proceed. I had worn bathing suits in 1913 that were beginning to show more skin, but in 1563, I was usually ensconced in layers of fabric. If Andrew had been any other doctor, I would not have thought twice about it. But he wasn't any other doctor.

He was Andrew.

"'Tis just your upper shoulders." He studied me. "Would you like me to proceed?"

My head had never hurt as much as it did now, and if he thought he could lessen the pain, it would be worth it.

"Aye."

"You'll need to remove your outer gown and kirtle and farthingale," he said without any awkwardness or discomfort. "But you can leave on your smock and petticoats. I'll step into the bedchamber and wait."

My smock was a linen garment worn under all my other clothes, like a chemise. The farthingale, a stiff cone-shaped hoopskirt, was worn on top of it, and over that went the kirtle. The kirtle was the main part of the gown, including the stiff bodice and skirt. And over all of that went the decorative gown, which was more like a robe, open in front to reveal the skirt of the kirtle.

"I will need help with the back laces on my kirtle," I told him in a quiet voice as he began to rise.

Without a word, he offered me his hand and helped me to stand, then he turned me around as I untied the front of the gown and let it slip off before setting it aside.

His hands were gentle as they untied the kirtle. I held my breath, never feeling more vulnerable, or safer, at the same time.

"I'll let you do the rest from here." He left the outer chamber to step into Charles's bedchamber.

I removed the kirtle and then the farthingale and set all the clothing on a chair nearby with my French hood. I had on my smock and my thick petticoats, and I was fully covered and modest, but it still felt strange.

After I was done, I sat on the couch and waited.

The door slowly opened. "Are you ready?" Andrew asked.

"Aye."

He stepped out and paused for a moment at seeing me sitting there, but then he closed the bedchamber door and approached.

"You'll need to lie on your front," he said, his voice a little lower than before.

I did as he instructed, yearning for my headache to subside.

"I will pull the smock down just enough to expose the skin of your shoulders and upper back," he explained.

There was little for me to say or do, so I simply remained silent.

He knelt beside me, then his hands touched my neck, just above the top of my smock, and moved the material down until my shoulders were exposed.

I closed my eyes as gooseflesh rose at the feel of his skin against mine, trying desperately not to shiver under his touch.

Andrew ran his left hand over my skin, and I held my breath again. His hand was warm and slightly rough, but also achingly tender and gentle.

I wanted to know how this was affecting him, but I kept my eyes closed, trying to focus on *why* he was touching me.

"I will now make the first incisions," he said. "This shouldn't hurt too much."

He kept one hand on my upper back as he reached for the lancet, and then a moment later, I felt the pressure of the blade making small incisions. It hurt a little but was nothing compared to the headache.

"Now I'm warming the first cup," he said as he removed his hands.

I finally opened my eyes and watched as he ran the cup over the heat of the candle, dimming the room even more.

When he turned back to me, our gazes collided, and I saw everything I needed to see.

This was affecting him as much as it was affecting me.

"This will be warm," he warned as he returned to my side, "but it will not hurt."

With one hand on my upper back again, he placed the warm cup over the incisions, and as it cooled, it began to suction my skin. I could feel the blood rising from the incisions and pooling in the rim of the overturned cup.

He repeated the process three more times, placing the cups on various parts of my upper back and shoulders.

When he was done, he cleaned the lancet and set it back in his box.

"How long will the cups stay on?" I asked.

"About fifteen minutes, unless they begin to hurt." He returned to my side and knelt by me again. "Close your eyes, Cecily. And try to relax."

He began to massage my temple with the pad of his thumb,

slowly drawing it down my jaw and then under my ear, before wrapping his hand around the base of my skull to massage the area that hurt the most.

I sighed as my entire body began to relax, and all my cares and tension slipped away, if only for a moment.

"You're beautiful, Cecily."

I slowly opened my eyes again and found him watching me.

"But 'tis not just your outward beauty that I admire," he continued. "Your inner strength and kindness are just as lovely."

"Thank you," I whispered.

He continued to massage my head as we waited, and when it was time to remove the cups, he did so with just as much tenderness as before. When that was done, he applied an ointment over the incisions.

"How do you feel?" he asked when he was done.

My headache was almost completely gone, but whether it was from the cupping, the massage, or Andrew's gentle care, I couldn't be certain.

He left the room again, and I put on the kirtle, then he came back and laced it up for me. I put on the gown next, and then my French hood. When I was done, I turned to face him.

"Did you want to tell me about Kat?"

I sighed, not wanting to bring up the subject, but there was little choice. "She swore me to secrecy and demanded that you agree to the same. It is a dire situation Charles is in, for more than one reason, and Kat is calling upon me to help."

He studied me closely. "You have my word, Cecily. I will not let you bear this burden alone."

I smiled despite the uncertainty and repeated what Kat had said to me.

"I will come back in the morning and look for the letter," I told him. "And then spend my days here, intercepting any messages that come for Charles. We must not let anyone know he is unwell. This needs to stay between you, me, and Kat."

His face was grave. "I understand."

"Thank you." I placed my hand on his forearm. "I am in your debt, Andrew. For keeping this a secret and for easing my pain."

"I am only doing my job."

I stood on tiptoe to kiss his cheek. When I pulled back, I said, "That does not mean you don't deserve compensation."

He smiled at me. "If that's the compensation I get, I might have to administer daily treatments."

I returned his smile. "May your soul be in God's keeping as you rest tonight, Andrew."

And with that, I left Charles's apartment, my head and heart feeling the healing touch of Andrew Bromley. Even if my mind was overburdened by Kat's request and Charles's injury.

14

CHARLES

JULY 25, 1883
NEW YORK CITY

Sunshine streamed through the window, making me blink my eyes open. Drew and I had arrived at the Whitneys' brownstone mansion the day before in preparation for our meeting with Mr. Whitney. We were expected at his office later that morning.

I rolled over, trying not to be uneasy about our meeting, though the future of the Hollingsworth horse farm rode on the back of what was said and done today. I wanted to make my father's memory proud and care for my mother and sister. But more than anything, I wanted to accomplish something worthwhile if I was forced to leave this path.

"Charles?" Drew knocked on my bedroom door. "Are you awake?"

"Yes." I sat up, stretching my hands over my head. "Give me a minute."

I stepped out of the bed, grabbed a dressing robe, and then opened the door. "How much time do we have before we need to leave?"

Drew studied me as if he was searching for an answer to a puzzling question. "How do you feel?"

I frowned. "Fine. How do you feel?"

"Do you remember what happened at Windsor Castle yesterday?"

"Of course. Why do you want to know?"

"Tell me what you remember."

Moving away from the door, I tied the belt to my dressing robe tighter, trying to think back. "There was a jousting tournament." I paused, realizing that my memories of the day before were a little hazy. "I was supposed to joust last. I remember waiting for my turn and putting on my armor." I frowned, unable to remember anything past that. "Did I joust?"

"You don't remember jousting?"

"I don't recall anything after I put on my armor." That was strange. Why couldn't I remember anything beyond that? "Did something happen?"

"You did joust and were hit off your horse. You sustained a serious concussion, and when you woke up, you had amnesia."

"Amnesia?" I pulled my head back. "What do you mean?"

"You didn't remember anything about your life in 1563. You didn't know Cecily, and you didn't recollect any of your memories there. But you did remember me and your life here. And you asked me where Evelyn was."

All I could do was stare at Andrew as I tried to put all the pieces together. "You said I woke up there—correct?"

"About twenty minutes after you fell off your horse."

"If I woke up there, why can't I remember what happened after that? Why can't I remember the conversations we had?"

"I don't know." Drew continued to study me. "I believe your brain is swollen in 1563, and it's causing memory loss of that time and place. But, for some reason, your conscious mind still recalls this life, and your brain here is unaffected."

"That's so . . . odd." I paced away from him. "Cecily must be distraught."

He was quiet, and when he didn't respond, I turned back to him. "What?"

Drew took a seat and placed his elbows on his knees, not looking at me. "She is extremely upset," he finally said. "You were so anxious when she was around that she couldn't stay by your side. She spent hours alone in the tower. But she came to check on you last night."

I crossed my arms, sensing that his story wasn't finished. "What happened after that?"

"Nothing—I mean, she had a headache, and I bled her with cups." He still wasn't looking at me as he swallowed. "And massaged her neck."

"You were alone with her?"

"Of course I was alone." Drew rose to his feet, defensive. "I was doctoring her, nothing more. She was in distress—"

"And you took advantage?"

Drew clenched his fists. "Never. And I will not allow you to say something so foolish again."

"You could have had a servant there to chaperone. Her reputation could be ruined, and then what? Who would marry her? The queen would throw you both in prison. You need to be more responsible."

"She was in pain. I knew how to alleviate the tension. I am a doctor—at least, that's what they believe. No one would find fault." He shoved his hands into his pockets and walked to the window. "Her headache came on because she's distressed."

"That's ridiculous. I remember everything just fine here. I'm sure I'll have my memory restored when I return there tomorrow."

"I hope so—for your sake, as well as hers."

"I won't worry about it. We have far greater things to concern ourselves with today."

He turned and hesitated.

"What?" I asked.

"Cecily said that Kat visited her and told her she must stay in your apartment and intercept anyone who comes to see you. Kat said that you are working on an important letter—"

I groaned as I ran my hand over the stubble on my cheek. "The letter to Mary, Queen of Scots."

"Kat doesn't want anyone to see your real letter—and she doesn't want anyone else to take it upon themselves to write to the Scottish queen on behalf of the privy council, for fear Mary will attack Queen Elizabeth while she is incapacitated."

"We both fear Mary's response," I agreed. "Though the privy council believes it's in our best interest to inform Mary of the queen's questionable health. That is why I have been meeting with Lady Katherine. She is malleable and easy to direct. If she inherited the throne, we could carry on as we have been."

"Not to mention that she is Protestant," Drew added.

"It's a mess." I paced to the window. "I have to come to my right mind in 1563, that's all there is to it."

"Perhaps," Drew offered, "if you do not, I can discuss any issues that arise in 1563 with you here and then take your recommendations back to Cecily. Together, she and I will oversee your work."

"You have your own work in 1563."

"Then Cecily can do whatever is necessary."

"I suppose there is no help for it. We will pray that my amnesia clears soon, and we will not have to worry about this."

"We will pray," Drew agreed. "But for now, be ready to leave within the hour. I'll send in a valet to assist you."

After he left my room, I stood at the window and looked down upon Fifth Avenue, trying not to worry about what might happen in 1563. I hoped I would wake up there tomorrow and remember who I was. It was disturbing not to recall half of the day, or to know I didn't even recognize my stepsister.

Surely things would be different tomorrow.

A valet entered the room and began to help me dress for the day.

As he assisted me with my coat, my thoughts turned to Evelyn, as they often did. Why had I asked about her in 1563? Were my feelings for her stronger than I wanted to admit?

An hour later, Drew and I rode in the family carriage on our way to the Whitney Shipping building at 25 Broadway. I tried to forget about 1563, Evelyn, and my time in Newport. Right now, I needed to focus on the farm.

"My father is a reasonable man," Drew said. "I wouldn't be too worried. I inherited my time-crossing mark from him."

I frowned, realizing that I had never wondered before now. "Your father is a time-crosser?"

"*Was* a time-crosser. He chose this path without hesitation. His other path was in the 2030s, and he said it wasn't a hard choice to give that up to be a millionaire here."

"Does your mother know about your time-crossing?"

"Father said he never bothered to tell her. She wouldn't have believed him, and he didn't think it mattered. He only told me as much as was necessary. You've told me more about time-crossing than he has."

"How did Evelyn not know you were a time-crosser? Didn't the three of you discuss it?"

"When I asked Evelyn about it after you told me she was a time-crosser, she said she got her mark from her mother in her other path. I don't even know if Father is aware that Evelyn is a time-crosser. Since she was adopted and we had governesses who saw to all our needs, he and Mother probably never saw the mark on her chest."

"Did she tell you about her other path?" I couldn't help but ask.

Drew shook his head. "She didn't want to talk about it."

I sighed, forcing my thoughts back to today. "Do you think I should tell your father I'm a time-crosser? Might that help my petition?"

"I don't think it's a good idea. He'd want to know about your other path, and that might lead to questions you don't want to answer."

Drew was right. It would be best to keep things as simple as possible.

Broadway was bustling with carriages, omnibuses, carts, pedestrians, and police officers directing traffic. It was only my second time in the city, but I was just as amazed as last time.

When we finally pulled up to the limestone building, I was impressed with its size and architectural style. Large sailboats had been carved into the limestone on either side of the massive windows in the center of the building. It was hard to fathom so much money in one family, and to know that one day, the entire business would rest upon Drew's shoulders.

Drew looked up at the building, and he sighed.

The sun beat down on the asphalt, making me sweat as we walked across the sidewalk into the cool interior of the Whitney Shipping building. Elevators in the lobby took us to the fifth floor, where we got out and walked down a hall to the main offices.

A receptionist greeted us and told us to go right into Mr. Whitney's office. "He's been expecting you," the man said with a nod.

Drew opened the door, and a middle-aged man looked up from the paper he was reading. He resembled Drew, with blond hair and blue eyes. He grinned and rose from the chair, coming around the desk to greet us.

"Hello, Andrew," he said as he shook his son's hand. "I don't think I've seen you since Easter."

"Hello, Father." Drew's shoulders were stiff, though there was affection in his voice. "This is Mr. Charles Hollingsworth."

"Ah." Mr. Whitney shook my hand. His grip was tight and meaningful as he said, "It's a pleasure to meet the man who has convinced my son it's time to step up to his responsibilities."

Mr. Whitney chuckled, but Drew didn't smile. My friend wasn't irresponsible; he just didn't want the obligations his family business would give him.

"I'm eager to hear what has gotten Andrew excited to finally get serious about business, Mr. Hollingsworth. Please, have a seat."

Mr. Whitney sat behind his desk as Drew and I sat across from him. The office was large, with windows offering a brilliant view of Broadway.

After a bit of small talk, Mr. Whitney turned to me, folding his hands on his desk. "So, Mr. Hollingsworth. Tell me all about your business."

It was hard to face the man and know he held the key to my family's possible success—but stranger still was that this man was Evelyn's father. And if he knew I was posing as an earl in his family's home in Newport, he would never allow me to speak to her again, let alone invest in the horse farm.

My nerves wanted to get the better of me, but I wouldn't let them.

Instead, I told him about the horse farm, recounting the success before the war and the difficulty in gaining traction after it. I told him about the various pedigrees we had once bred, and the limited stock we still owned.

"By the time I was old enough to make something of the farm," I continued, "it had gone into such disrepair, it's been impossible for me to make a difference without financial backing. Every little bit we earn from breeding our two broodmares goes into repairs, stud fees, and daily living expenses."

"Before the war," Drew added, "the Hollingsworth horses were in great demand in Europe and all over the US. With the right financial backing, I believe the farm could rise again and be better than ever."

"We have the land, the lineage, and the knowledge," I agreed, "we just need the money."

Mr. Whitney put his finger to his lips as he considered our proposition. "I've heard of the Hollingsworth horses," he said. "My father had a pair, I believe. Good stock."

I sat stiff on my chair, waiting for him to continue.

He tilted his head. "How did you two meet?"

I glanced at Drew, unprepared for this question.

"When I was in Europe," Drew said quickly, "I heard of the Hollingsworth horses. When I returned to the States, I checked into them, and Mr. Hollingsworth and I have been corresponding ever since."

It was completely fabricated, but how could we tell him the truth?

Mr. Whitney took the explanation without pause and then asked me several questions.

Finally, he nodded. "I think this business has good prospects. I never thought I'd get into horse breeding, but it's something that has crossed my mind before." He looked at Drew. "And because it's the first spark of interest I've seen in my son, outside of medicine, I am half tempted to give it a try."

I held my breath. Waiting. Hoping.

Mr. Whitney squinted in thought. "I will do a little investigation of my own, and if everything checks out, I will draw up the necessary paperwork and then we can meet again in a few weeks."

Relief overwhelmed me. Everything I had told him about the horse farm was true, and he would find it to be so.

I stood and shook his hand. "Thank you, Mr. Whitney. You don't know what this means to me and my family."

"My pleasure. Now, how about we have lunch at Delmonico's? We can continue our conversation there."

I grinned at Drew, and he returned my smile, but I could tell that being in his father's office, surrounded by the reminders of his responsibilities, had been hard on him.

Delmonico's was less than a five-minute walk from the Whitney Shipping offices. It was an eight-story building shaped like a triangle and sat on the corner of two converging streets. The structure was impressive, with striped awnings over the lower-level windows and several marble columns near the front entrance. I had never eaten at a restaurant like it, since our family could not afford such luxuries in Virginia, and there was nothing comparable to it in Elizabethan England.

A stiff maître d' led us through one of the public dining rooms. There were several people already seated, enjoying their lunch. Most of them were men, and many of them greeted Mr. Whitney. He stopped to introduce us to some. I recognized names like Rockefeller,

Vanderbilt, Schuyler, Gould, and Webb. Several of them were the husbands of wives who were in Newport, and though I hadn't met any of them before, I suddenly realized how dangerous it was to be dining at Delmonico's. One of the men could have been in Newport for the Wetmores' ball the week before and might recognize me.

Drew must have had the same thought as he put his hand on his father's arm and said, "I'm starving. Perhaps we should get to our table."

"Of course." His father motioned for the maître d' to continue.

Thankfully, we were seated in a relatively private corner of the dining room with potted ferns blocking most of the table. Drew maneuvered so I could be seated near the thickest of the foliage. He gave me a look, and I nodded, understanding his concern.

The luncheon went off without trouble. Mr. Whitney had more questions for me, and I was eager to answer them. Drew was quiet for much of the meal, though Mr. Whitney sent a remark or two toward his son, mostly referring to Drew's eventual takeover of the company. Each time he did, Drew bore the statement with resigned acceptance.

The meal began with cream of artichoke soup and was followed by halibut in hollandaise sauce, watercress salad, sweet potatoes and string beans, beef and noodles, and ice cream meringue with French coffee. It was all delicious, yet I couldn't enjoy it like I wanted, worried that at any minute someone might approach our table and recognize me from Newport. The sooner we left Delmonico's, the better.

"Our compliments to the chef," Mr. Whitney said to the waiter as he cleared some of our dishes.

"Mother misses Delmonico's," Drew said to me as he set his napkin next to his plate. "Her chef has been here, offering to pay top dollar for some of their recipes, but they won't part with them."

"How is your mother?" Mr. Whitney asked, his entire attention devoted to Drew for the first time since we'd sat down.

"She is doing well."

"Is the Earl of Norfolk surpassing all of her hopes and dreams?" His question sounded lighthearted, but I could hear sincere curiosity in it, too.

Drew briefly glanced at me before saying to his father, "I think so. We were just at the Wetmores' party last week, and Mother was formally introduced to Mrs. Astor and Mr. McAllister. Mother is hopeful she will receive a coveted invitation to Mrs. Astor's summer ball very soon."

"I'm glad to hear it." Mr. Whitney leaned back in his chair. "And how is Evelyn? In her last letter, she told me that she and the earl are planning a fundraiser at the Newport Casino. She sounded a bit more hopeful—almost like her old self again."

The mention of Evelyn's name made my pulse pick up speed.

Drew crossed his arms and nodded. "I've noticed a positive change in her, as well."

"Am I to believe it has something to do with the earl?" Mr. Whitney asked. "Will there be an expensive wedding in the near future?"

It took Drew a moment to answer. "I think the earl is responsible for the change in Evelyn." He didn't look at me, but I knew he was tempted. "I hate to admit it, but he's been good for her."

"Hate to admit it?" Mr. Whitney frowned, his shoulders stiffening. "Why? Is he a scoundrel?"

"No—nothing like that. I just don't want to see her get hurt."

"How might he hurt her? Doesn't he want to marry her?"

Drew toyed with his cloth napkin. "I believe he would like to marry her, if he were able."

I longed to speak on my behalf, but it was impossible. I cared for Evelyn—probably too much—but I wasn't a fool. I was nobody here, and her parents would never allow me to marry her, especially after I deceived all of them.

"Why isn't he able?" Mr. Whitney demanded, irritation lacing his words. "Is he not suitable? He's an earl, after all. Is he quite old? I wasn't given that impression. Or is he married already?"

"You know what, Father," Drew said as he lifted his hands.

"These are questions for Evelyn. I know she likes the earl, but I doubt there will be a wedding."

"Doesn't the earl like her?"

"Yes, he does. Very much, I'm afraid." Drew folded his hands on the table. "But I don't think it will work out between them. It's as simple as that. If you want to know more, perhaps you should talk to your daughter."

"I just might," Mr. Whitney said with a decided nod.

Two older men passed our table, deep in conversation. The moment the one nearest our table came into view, my heart thudded to a stop.

Congressman Reinhold.

Drew glanced in the direction I was looking, and then his troubled gaze darted to mine.

I hoped the congressman would not look toward us. I lowered my eyes, as if I was suddenly curious about the tablecloth, hoping that if he glanced our way, he wouldn't recognize me.

"Is something the matter?" Mr. Whitney asked the both of us.

"No." Drew shook his head. "I'm starting to think that perhaps I should head back to Newport on the evening train so I don't miss Evelyn's tournament tomorrow. I should probably leave soon."

"I'll ask for the check." Mr. Whitney lifted his hand to signal to the waiter that we were finished and ready to go.

But the waving of his hand caught Congressman Reinhold's attention, and when his focus landed on me and Drew, his face lit with recognition and pleasure.

He said something to the man he was with and then veered off to come to our table.

My pulse was pounding so hard, I was afraid my heart could not handle the pace. If he greeted me as the earl, then Drew's father would know what we had done—and any hope of him investing in our farm would die. Not to mention that he would insist I not return to Newport, and I would never see Evelyn again.

"Ah," Congressman Reinhold said as he approached with a

grin, "I didn't realize you had come into the city. Imagine running into you here."

"Congressman Reinhold." Drew quickly stood. "It's a pleasure to see you again, sir. May I present my father, Mr. William Whitney."

The congressman continued to smile as Mr. Whitney rose and shook the older man's hand. "It's a pleasure to meet you, Congressman," he said. "How do you know my son?"

"We met in Newport," Drew said before the congressman could answer. Sweat was beaded on his brow. "He and his wife and daughter are summering there."

"Marvelous." Mr. Whitney was about to speak again when Drew interrupted.

"Congressman, may I also present my friend, and hopefully business partner soon." Drew motioned to me.

I was stiff, unsure what Drew was about to do. I had no choice but to go along. I also rose.

"This is Mr. Charles Hollingsworth," Drew said, very slowly and deliberately. "From Virginia. He has a horse farm that I am hoping our family can invest in."

The congressman's smile fell, and he looked from Drew to me, confusion in his face.

I cleared my throat and extended my hand. "It's a pleasure to meet you, Congressman Reinhold." I continued using my southern drawl. "I recognized your name immediately, since we're both from Fredericksburg."

"Hollingsworth," the congressman said as he slowly accepted my handshake, studying me closely. "I knew a Hollingsworth from Fredericksburg once. We were in the war together."

I tried hard to breathe as I nodded. "Was his name Nathanial?"

"It was."

"He was my father."

There was silence between us as the congressman continued to study me, but then he finally said, "How interesting."

He was no longer smiling as he turned to Drew. "When do you plan to return to Newport?"

187

"Today or tomorrow, sir."

"And how is your friend, the *earl*?"

Drew licked his lips and then said, "He is well."

"And will he be in Newport for some time to come?"

"I believe so." Drew nodded. "At least until the tennis tournament, and then he plans to depart and never to return to Newport, I'm afraid."

Mr. Whitney frowned as he listened to their interaction, and I braced myself for the worst.

"How interesting," Congressman Reinhold said again. "I am quite eager to talk to him again. My daughter is fond of the earl, but I have my reservations."

"Oh?" Mr. Whitney joined the conversation. "Should I be concerned? He's a guest in my home with my wife and daughter."

Congressman Reinhold glanced at me again, and then said, "I believe he's harmless, but I don't quite understand what he's trying to accomplish in Newport. I think he means well. However, I think he's going about it in all the wrong ways."

"He's a friend of yours, isn't he, Andrew?" Mr. Whitney asked his son. "Have you invited a rogue into our house?"

"The earl is a good man," Drew said. "Perhaps a little misunderstood, but he isn't a threat to anyone, and he will be gone before we know it. I vouch for him, and I hope that is enough for you to trust him, as well."

"Of course," Mr. Whitney said. "Of course. I know you would not knowingly hurt your mother or sister."

"Never."

Congressman Reinhold continued to look at me with skepticism, but he turned to Mr. Whitney and offered a slight bow. "It was a pleasure to meet you, Mr. Whitney—and you, Mr. Hollingsworth." Then he turned to Drew. "I will see you at the tournament in Newport tomorrow. I look forward to our conversation."

And with that, he left the table.

Mr. Whitney frowned. "What an odd man."

The waiter brought the check, and Mr. Whitney paid the bill, then we left Delmonico's.

When we arrived back at the Whitney Shipping offices, the carriage came for us as we said our good-byes to Mr. Whitney.

"Thank you for lunch," I said to him. "And thank you for taking the time to meet with me."

"My pleasure, young man. I look forward to being in contact with you soon."

After we got into the carriage and it pulled away from 25 Broadway, I leaned my head back and let out a groan. "What am I going to do?"

"Do you think the congressman will reveal your identity?" Drew asked.

"I don't know. He either thinks I'm really the earl and was pretending to be Charles Hollingsworth—or he thinks I'm Charles Hollingsworth, pretending to be the earl. Either way, I think we're safe until he knows exactly who I am."

"He could have asked at Delmonico's. Maybe that means he won't say anything in Newport."

"He didn't have enough time to think." I shook my head. "When he sees us at the tournament tomorrow, he'll have had time."

"Maybe you shouldn't return to Newport."

"I can't leave Evelyn without saying good-bye, especially before the tournament and the fundraiser. She would be heartbroken, and I don't think either of us want to see that happen." I couldn't stop thinking about what he had said to his father earlier. Was I making Evelyn happier? "Besides," I continued, "the worst is done. He already knows I'm a fraud, one way or the other. Even if I'm not there, he could share the truth. I think it would be best to talk to him about why I am pretending to be the earl."

"You'll tell him you're a time-crosser?" Drew frowned.

"No. But I'll try to explain—and hopefully his regard for my father will be worth something."

"Let's hope you're right. If Mrs. Astor or Mr. McAllister find out you've been pretending to be an earl, my mother would become the laughingstock of Newport and New York City. It would devastate her."

I rubbed my forehead as I looked out the window at the passing New York City streets.

In less than twenty-four hours, I would need to face Congressman Reinhold again and come up with a logical reason why I would pose as the Earl of Norfolk.

But I had one day in 1563 before that would happen—and I had a whole different set of problems to worry about there.

15

CECILY

JULY 26, 1563
WINDSOR CASTLE

I both dreaded and anticipated news about Charles as I made my way to his apartment early that morning. My headache was completely gone, but memories of Andrew's gentle care were still with me as I walked along the corridor. His hands had been so tender, and his administration had been exactly what I needed. Just thinking about the massage he'd given me sent a tingling sensation up the back of my neck where his hands had rubbed away the tension.

When I arrived at Charles's apartment, I gently opened the door and found the outer chamber was empty. More than anything, I hoped Charles had woken up and remembered his life here. I was prepared to stay all day and manage my stepbrother's affairs, but I would prefer not to lie to the entire castle. Kat was already making excuses for my absence among the other ladies in waiting today.

Voices from within Charles's bedchamber told me that he was awake. The door was ajar, and I could hear Charles talking. He was just as agitated this morning as he had been yesterday.

"None of this makes sense," he said in his unfamiliar accent. "Why am I here? Why are we not in Newport?"

"I've explained several times," Andrew said patiently. "We occupy both paths, and you had an accident here yesterday, giving you amnesia."

"I know what you've said." Charles was now angry. "But I don't understand any of it."

My heart fell.

He still didn't remember his life in 1563.

I walked to the open door, tentative and hopeful that he might somehow remember me.

"Charles?" I asked.

Andrew sat on a chair, his elbows on his knees and his hands clasped. He looked exhausted and weary.

Charles was in his bed, and though he had hit his head and suffered a concussion, he looked completely normal. No bruises, no wounds, nothing to indicate that he'd been injured.

My stepbrother frowned at me as Andrew rose from his chair.

"Were you here before?" Charles asked.

"Yes. Many times. I'm your stepsister, Cecily."

"I don't have a stepsister." He pulled himself into a sitting position.

"Be careful, Charles," Andrew advised. "I don't want you to hurt yourself further."

Charles closed his eyes, clearly in pain. His face went ashen.

Andrew walked across the room and put his hand on Charles's arm. "If you need to move, I want you to wait for my assistance. Does it hurt?"

"Terribly," Charles moaned.

"It's been less than twenty-four hours since your accident in this path. You must be patient as your body heals."

"I just want to return to Newport and see Evelyn," Charles said.

"She needs to know about Congressman Reinhold. I must speak to her before he does."

"He will not speak to her or anyone else until we have spoken to him," Andrew reassured Charles.

"Why must I wait here until I can see him?" His gaze landed on me again. "Who are you?"

He was behaving like he had yesterday, agitated and angry and impatient. Even after we answered his questions, he repeated them.

"Perhaps you had better leave Charles to rest," Andrew said, an apology in his voice.

I tried not to let Charles's behavior make me upset, but it was impossible. Tears stung my eyes as I thought about all the repercussions of his accident.

But there was no time to feel sorry for myself. I needed to find the letter Charles was writing and intercept anyone who brought work for him.

Andrew motioned for me to leave the bedchamber. He closed the door behind me after we entered the outer chamber and then released a sigh.

"I'm sorry, Cecily. I was hoping there would be an improvement, but it looks like he's in the same state as yesterday."

"How was he in 1883?"

"Completely normal, though he had no memory just before or any time after the jousting injury."

"But he could remember other things about his life in 1563?"

"Yes. 'Tis so strange. I don't know what to make of it all."

I crossed my arms as I paced away from Andrew, trying not to panic.

"There is still time for him to recover," Andrew said, as if he could read my mind. "I will ensure that he stays in bed and bleed him again to see if I can get the swelling to go down inside his head." He approached me. "How does your head feel this morning?"

Warmth flooded my face at the reminder of his touch last night. "Much improved."

"Are your shoulders sore from the cupping?"

"Not at all." The incisions had been so small, there was no sign of injury to my skin, only a bit of faint bruising.

"Do not hesitate to tell me if you experience another headache," he said. "There are things I can do to help."

"Thank you." I hoped I wouldn't need any more assistance because it was too hard to be that near him and not feel the effects. It was time to change the subject. "I will begin to look for the letter."

"I spoke to Charles about it in 1883."

"Did you ask him where it was?"

"He said 'tis tucked inside one of the books on his desk." Andrew walked to the desk in the corner of the room and lifted several books that were stacked there. "He said it was almost finished, but he needed to write a fresh copy. This one has several errors." He pulled it from a copy of *The Prince*, by Machiavelli, and handed it to me without opening it.

"What should I do with it?" I was afraid to read it, too, not wanting to be privy to his and Kat's secret plans. If the queen or the privy council knew they were going against their wishes, it could mean arrest for them both. I didn't want to be implicated with them.

"He asked that you write a fresh copy and have it sent off, as planned, but it needs to look like his handwriting. The privy council believes it will go out this week. Soldiers have been given their orders to take it to Edinburgh as soon as it is ready." He studied me, almost hesitant. "He also gave me a list of other things he'd like for you to do. He said that if we are going to convince the council and the queen that he is capable of writing the letter to Mary, then he needs to perform his other duties."

"Like what?"

"He was also preparing a report for the privy council and the queen on the plague in London. There are several letters from contacts he has in the city, as well as from the Lord Mayor and the aldermen. The situation is dire, and many are asking for assistance. Charles was tasked with being the liaison for the council, and he needs to get the report to them as soon as possible. You will find all the letters in his desk."

"I'm to read them and sort them out to make a report?"

"I believe that's what he wanted. And there are other things—"

"Please." I held up my hand. "I must get a paper and quill and write all of this down."

I went to Charles's desk as a knock sounded on the door.

Andrew walked to the door and opened it.

"Sir Gates," Andrew said, a little surprised. "What can I do for you?"

"I must speak to Lord Norfolk," the Treasurer of the Household said without preamble.

I sat at the desk behind the door, where Sir Gates could not see me. Andrew held the door handle and made no effort to open it farther.

If Charles was not present, it wouldn't be proper for Andrew and me to be alone in my stepbrother's apartment, but if others believed Charles was well and able, there would be no problem. It was yet one more reason to make people believe he was in his right mind.

"I have ordered bedrest for Lord Norfolk," Andrew said. "He is not to be disturbed by visitors, though I am able to bring him your request, and I will see if he is able to address your needs."

There was an impatient sigh, and then Sir Gates said, "We are waiting on a shipment from London with candles, soap, and other sundry items. Our candles are running dangerously low, and I am afraid we will soon be without light. He sent a letter to the Lord Mayor over two weeks ago, and I need to know if he's heard back about the shipment."

"I will inquire and send word to you as soon as possible."

"Fine, but do not tarry. If the shipment is not on the way, I might resort to sending someone after it, and I would hate to compromise one of the queen's servants with the threat of plague."

Andrew bowed and then closed the door.

"I will look through the letters," I said to Andrew before he could turn to me. "And if we do not find what we are looking for, you'll need to ask Charles tomorrow in 1883 if he's had word about the candles."

"Thank you for helping, Cecily," Andrew said.

"I know not what else to do. Charles needs me."

The weight of having others believe Charles was well, while managing all his other duties, and preventing Mary, Queen of Scots, from attacking the castle was suffocating, but I would do it to the best of my ability.

I just hoped I wouldn't fail.

※

My shoulders were stiff from bending over paperwork at Charles's desk all day. I'd found the letter from one of the aldermen regarding the shipment of supplies and penned a missive to Sir Gates, forging Charles's handwriting, letting him know it was scheduled to arrive any day. Andrew had sent the note to the Treasurer of the Household by way of a young page, and then I had turned my attention to the other pressing matters.

Andrew had helped by reading through the various letters sent from London about the plague, and together, we had written the dire report for the privy council. Andrew would deliver it to Lord Burghley the next day with an update on Charles's health. He'd reassure the queen's most trusted adviser that Charles was mending and would soon be recovered.

It was now dark, and my candle was burning low, but I had finished the letter to Mary, Queen of Scots, and was warming the sealing wax. The other courtiers would be playing cards, or chess, or a dice game like Hazard to pass the evening hours. All I wanted was to find my bed after a long, difficult day of work.

The door to Charles's bedchamber creaked open, and Andrew appeared.

"Any change?" I asked, hopeful.

He shook his head, disappointment creasing the edges of his mouth. "I'm afraid not."

I had not been in to see Charles at all that day, but Andrew had sat with him when he was awake, trying to pass the time and make him comfortable. During lunch and supper, Andrew had insisted I join the others so they didn't ask unnecessary questions about my absence. Between meals, Kat had told everyone I was sitting with Charles to keep him company, and they seemed appeased by that excuse.

"He is sleeping now," Andrew said as he closed the door. When he turned to me, there was a smile on his handsome face as he extended his hand.

Frowning, I placed my hand in his and allowed him to help me stand. "What?"

"You'll see." His smile was so infectious that, despite all the heartache I'd recently experienced, I couldn't help smiling and feeling a bit of excitement.

He led me out of the apartment and into the hall, not letting go of my hand. Thankfully the corridors were quiet, though I suspected he would let go if we saw someone.

Lord Wolverton had been at both meals that day, and he had inquired about Charles's health but had not demanded more of my time. Part of me was nervous that he would see Andrew and me stealing through the castle, because his perceptive questions about my feelings for Andrew were still echoing in my heart.

When we came to the door leading onto the North Terrace, Andrew paused. It was dark in the little alcove, with just the two of us standing there.

I stared up at him, my heart thudding against my chest, wondering what he planned to do and knowing I would go along with anything.

Without a word, he opened the door leading outside and drew me along.

The North Terrace was dark without the torches—yet there were dozens, perhaps hundreds, of sparkling lights floating through the air.

"Glow worms," I said as my breath caught.

Andrew's hand tightened around mine as he led me into the heart of the gardens. It was dark, but my eyes had adjusted enough to see the ground, and the moon offered a bit of light for our path.

"I saw them from Charles's window," he said as we stopped in the midst of the light show. "I wanted you to see them."

"I love that you thought to show me."

"I always think of you, Cecily." His words were soft, but they had a powerful impact on my heart.

"I always think of you, too," I whispered after only a moment's thought. It was dangerous to admit the truth to a man who could never be mine—yet he wouldn't be here forever, and what did I have to lose if I reveled in these feelings for the short time we had left? My heart was already breaking at the inevitable parting. Why not enjoy these stolen moments?

He drew me closer to his side, his hand warm against mine as he lifted it to his lips.

I closed my eyes for a moment, drawing in a breath, wishing he had placed his kiss upon my lips.

We walked down the path toward a bench overlooking the hill that led to the Thames River, neither of us speaking.

When we finally took a seat, I pressed close to him, still holding his hand.

"How is your collection of paintings coming along?" he asked, breaking the silence.

"'Tis going well." I enjoyed a safer subject. "Much of what I'm painting is from memory and years of research in 1913, but my memory is not perfect. It could take me years to collect all the specimens I need."

"Can you find them all at Windsor Castle?"

"Not if my book is to be complete. I will need to collect caterpillars from all parts of England. There are some more common here, and others in the northern regions, and some in the southern regions." My mind slipped to Arundel Castle in the south and Lord Wolverton's castle at Alnwick in the north. "But I have enough stored in my memory to keep busy for quite some time."

"You'll need to find a publisher next."

"Aye, but that will have to wait until the plague dies and I can inquire in London."

He was quiet for a moment as he looked down at our entwined fingers and said, "I wish I could help you."

I had to focus on breathing before I could say, "You've done so much already."

"I want to do more. I want to see your dreams fulfilled, probably even more than I want mine fulfilled."

My heart warmed at his sentiments. "To become a doctor?"

"Aye." He lifted his face toward the river. The glow worms were thicker here, away from the terrace. "Charles and I met with my father yesterday in New York City. Father is eager for me to join the family business, but being there—after serving here as a doctor—felt more suffocating than ever before. I don't know how I will survive the next forty or fifty years of my life in that office building. And for what purpose? To gain more money?" He shook his head. "It feels so pointless and hopeless."

I wanted to comfort him as he had comforted me in the corridor the night Lady Agatha had died. I turned my face toward his and squeezed his hand. "I'm sorry, Andrew."

His thumb ran over my forefinger, sending an exquisite feeling up the length of my arm and into my heart.

Comforting Andrew brought me just as much joy as any painting I had ever created or any biology book I'd ever read. Could caring for him be part of my purpose in 1563? My heart longed to soothe him, to give him hope and purpose.

"Are you only choosing 1883 to please your father?" I asked gently.

He took a deep breath. "And to ensure my mother and sister are cared for."

"Do they not have all the money in the world to ensure their happiness?"

He turned to me, his eyes searching mine. "I am the only male heir in my family. I have a duty to perform."

"God made you to be a healer, Andrew. He doesn't make mistakes, as you told me one day in the garden. He is not surprised by anything that happens to us. Could your purpose be better fulfilled in 1563, ministering to the sick?"

Andrew was quiet for a long time, and then he shook his head. "I would be guilt-ridden all the days of my life if I stayed here, Cecily." He let go of my hand and slowly lifted his to the side of my face, his thumb resting on my cheek.

My breath stilled as the glow worms floated on the air all around us.

"And besides," he said as his thumb traced the ridge of my cheekbone, "the only other reason I would stay is an even more impossible dream."

Though I suspected I knew the answer, I still wanted to hear it from his lips. "What dream is that?"

Instead of telling me, Andrew showed me.

His kiss was soft at first, almost tentative—until I pressed into him, my hands against his chest, leaving no room for doubt.

With a groan, he deepened the kiss, his arms encircling me.

Everything else faded as I returned his kiss. All the feelings I'd ever had for Andrew culminated in that one moment, and I did not hold any of them back.

He suddenly pulled away, his chest rising and falling. He stood and paced away from me, his hands on his face. "Cecily—I'm sorry."

"Why?" I asked, standing, one moment anchored to him—and the next adrift.

"I promised Charles—and with him the way he is, I'm even more guilty of dishonoring his wishes."

"Charles cannot control my heart, Andrew."

"What would I have to offer you?" He extended his hands. "You know how I live at Arundel Castle, and even if I became a doctor here, I could never give you the life you deserve."

"I don't want this life. I would be happiest in a little cottage, in the middle of nowhere, painting and being with you."

"I can't even afford a little cottage in the middle of nowhere."

"When you become a doct—"

"And the queen would never approve."

"Then we can be married in secret."

He sighed. "That has never ended well for any of her ladies."

"She eventually comes around," I said pathetically, because it wasn't always true. *Sometimes* she came around, but not always, and only after the couple served time in prison or were separated for years.

We stood several feet apart, staring at one another.

"And I have my other path," he said. "I cannot abandon my family there."

But he would abandon me? It was a selfish thought, and I was ashamed of it immediately. Andrew owed me nothing, and everything he'd said was true.

"I'm sorry, Cecily. I should not have invited you here tonight. It was a mistake, and I am to blame."

I turned toward the Thames, taking several deep breaths. The glow worms were a beautiful sight, one I would have been sad to miss, even if it was a fleeting moment. Just like the one I was having with Andrew.

He'd kissed me, and that was something I could take with me forever.

"Will you allow me to walk you back to the castle?" he asked.

I nodded and took the arm he offered, knowing we could not allow something like this to happen again. No matter how much I wanted it.

16

CHARLES

JULY 26, 1883
NEWPORT, RHODE ISLAND

The train had been delayed leaving New York. I sat on the edge of my seat, my hand on the back of the bench in front of me, willing the train to go faster. I looked at my pocket watch, but less than five minutes had passed since the last time I had checked. It was just after two.

Drew sat next to me, his attention on the passing countryside, his thoughts so far away, it was almost as if I was sitting alone.

The tournament in Newport had already started, but I wasn't supposed to play until three. Even though Evelyn wanted me to compete against the champion in next week's fundraiser event, I had no desire to draw that much attention. As a compromise, I'd agreed to join today's tournament, but she had made me promise to play the winner of the community bracket. If I didn't show up, then the match would be forfeited, and the bracket winner would play Mr. Sears.

We were still several minutes out of Newport and would need to find transportation to the casino from the train station. I hated the thought of disappointing Evelyn.

Yet, the tennis tournament was the least of my concerns.

"What if the congressman has already told everyone about seeing us at Delmonico's?" I asked Drew. "It would be our word against his, but it wouldn't take long for your aunt to learn the truth. All she'd need to do is contact the present Earl of Norfolk to discover that I am not him."

Drew had his elbow resting on the armrest, and his chin was in his hand as he watched outside the train.

I waited, but he didn't acknowledge my comment.

"Drew," I said a little louder.

He finally lifted his chin. "What?"

"You haven't heard a word I've said since we left New York City."

He took a deep breath. "Sorry, mate. I've got a lot on my mind." He turned fully toward me. "What were you saying? Something about the congressman?"

"Aren't you worried that he'll tell everyone the truth before we can get there?"

"Of course I'm worried." His voice was sharper than usual. "But this isn't the only trouble we're facing. There's a lot more going on in 1563 that has me concerned. You still don't remember anything there, the queen hasn't made any progress, and Cecily has shouldered all your responsibilities."

"Did you find the letter to Mary?"

"Yes, and Cecily has rewritten it. It will be sent out tomorrow. I just hope none of the privy council intercepts it or finds out later that you're not well. You and Kat have put Cecily in a dangerous position." His anger began to build. "And what will the council do when Mary doesn't come? Won't they suspect something?"

"I worded the letter in such a way that Mary will respond appropriately but will have no idea the queen is unwell."

"And what if the queen doesn't survive? And someone else sends for Mary? And then they discover what you've done? What Cecily has done?"

His words filled me with apprehension as I sat up straighter. "Is the queen worse?"

"She is stable."

"Then we have nothing to worry—"

"We have everything to worry about, Charles!"

A man and woman sitting nearby looked up at his outburst.

Drew lowered his voice and said, "Don't be so cavalier. A dozen things could go wrong—terribly wrong, and Cecily is at the heart of all of it now. She has enough to worry about. Especially after—" He swallowed, and his gaze darted back to the countryside.

"Especially after what?"

"Nothing." He cleared his throat. "It's my problem, not yours."

I frowned. Drew didn't often avoid hard conversations, and he didn't usually have a difficult time meeting my eyes.

Unless.

Was he feeling guilty about something? I couldn't remember anything that had happened in 1563 yesterday. He had told me that I still didn't know who I was and that I was agitated and angry, especially at Cecily. She hadn't been able to enter my bedchamber but had spent the day in my apartment, alone, with Drew. Had something happened? Or had he only *wanted* it to happen?

I was about to ask when the conductor called out the Newport stop as he walked down the aisle.

Right now, I needed to concentrate on playing in the tournament and deflecting Congressman Reinhold. I could worry about Drew and Cecily and 1563 later.

Within thirty minutes, our hired carriage pulled up to the Newport Casino. I jumped out of the vehicle before it came to a complete stop and ran through the front door.

Dozens of people mingled inside the lobby, and a cheer arose from the lawn behind the casino, telling me there were many more watching the tournament.

But where was Evelyn?

"Lord Norfolk," Isabel called out to me.

My pulse began to thrum until I saw the bright smile on her face and knew that her father hadn't told her about me.

"I've been waiting for you," she said.

I looked past her, trying to locate Evelyn.

"Morgan is playing right now. If he wins this match, he'll be the bracket champion and will play you to see who will go on to compete against the US champion."

"Have you seen Evelyn?"

Isabel lifted a shoulder. "Somewhere. I think she's watching the match."

Congressman Reinhold appeared out of the crowd, his gaze intent on me and his daughter.

He didn't look pleased.

"Isabel," the congressman said as he approached and put his hand on his daughter's shoulder. His tone was serious. "Perhaps you should be on the lawn to congratulate Morgan. His match is almost over, and it looks like he'll be the winner."

"Of course, Papa." She offered me a confused and apologetic smile before she left.

"As for you." The congressman put his hand on my arm and turned me away from the pressing crowd toward the corner of the room. "You and I have some things to discuss."

"I should get ready for my match," I said, attempting to move away from him.

"Now." He motioned to a quiet alcove. "Or I will be obligated to tell Miss Whitney what I learned about you."

"She already knows."

His lips parted. "Miss Whitney knows you're an imposter?"

I hated to admit it, but I nodded.

"What about Mr. and Mrs. Whitney?"

"Mr. and Mrs. Whitney don't know who I really am." I spoke very quietly, hoping no one would overhear us. Thankfully, no one looked like they were paying attention.

Drew entered the casino, and his gaze swept the lobby. He took a deep breath and approached us.

"Who *are* you?" Congressman Reinhold asked. "Did you just make up the Hollingsworth bit because of my connection to Nathanial Hollingsworth?"

"No." I had to come clean—and pray he would let me at least finish the fundraising plans. "My real name is Charles Hollingsworth. I am Nathanial's son from Fredericksburg."

The congressman's frown deepened.

"That's why I brought up his name when we were talking about the war," I continued.

"Why are you pretending to be the earl?"

I glanced out the window toward the lawn, where the match had concluded. Mr. Brent was getting a rousing cheer from the crowd as Isabel approached him.

"I wish I could explain in a way that makes sense," I said. "But the easiest answer is that Drew and I are friends, and he asked me to pose as the earl for the summer to impress his mother's acquaintances. It's as simple as that. I don't plan to hurt anyone, and I will disappear as soon as I help Evelyn with the fundraiser for the orphanage. I won't do anything to make anyone regret my time in Newport. You have my word."

He continued to stare at me. "And Miss Whitney knows you're not really the earl? She hasn't set her cap for you? You don't plan to marry her and abscond with her fortune?"

"No." I said the word with deep conviction. "That was never the plan. Drew can vouch for me."

The congressman noticed Drew standing near us for the first time.

"Charles's visit was only for show," Drew assured him, coming closer and speaking in a low tone. "Nothing more. A bit of innocent fun."

Isabel appeared at the door, her brow crinkled as she watched us from a distance.

"It isn't innocent for some people." The congressman frowned.

"I think my daughter may have fallen in love with you—or, at least, the version of you that you pretended to be." His voice was threatening as he said, "I will not say anything about your real identity, if—" he paused, and there was the promise of murder in his eyes—"*if* you stay away from Isabel and leave the minute the fundraiser is over. Do you understand?"

"Yes." I nodded quickly. "You have my word."

"If I hear that you're causing any sort of trouble, or that you're trying to win the affection of any woman in Newport, I will personally see you on a train and reveal your real identity to everyone. Do I make myself clear?"

"Completely."

"I am only allowing this because I think the fundraiser for the orphanage is a good thing and I would hate to see Mr. and Mrs. Whitney suffer for this reckless practical joke. But if it turns out I'm wrong, I will not be lenient."

"I understand," I said, trying to reassure him that I meant no harm.

Congressman Reinhold narrowed his gaze before he turned and met his daughter to lead her out of the casino.

Isabel looked over her shoulder in confusion several times before they left through the front door.

I let out a breath and would have been relieved—except that we still had a week until the fundraiser, and a lot could happen between now and then.

I had to stay out of trouble at all costs and hope that the congressman was serious about keeping quiet.

Thankfully, Mr. Bennett had a set of tennis clothes he lent to me, and I was able to change quickly into the short-sleeve shirt and linen pants before heading out to the back lawn to play against Morgan Brent.

Hundreds of people stood in the galleries, laughing, drinking, and visiting as I made my way toward the tennis court. Someone noticed me, and a cheer arose as men in white lawn suits and women in light-colored dresses and oversized hats clapped.

"Ah," Mr. Brent said as he sat on a chair under an umbrella, toweling off his face and neck. "You decided to join us after all."

I finally caught sight of Evelyn. She was speaking to a man standing next to a camera, holding a pad of paper and a pencil in hand. Perhaps a reporter? She nodded and smiled, and when she caught my eye, her entire face lit up.

My heart thudded at the sight of her, and when she left the reporter to walk toward me, warmth filled my chest. She made me feel something I'd never felt for anyone before.

Amidst all the turmoil and indecisiveness of both my paths, there was a sudden clarity in my mind and heart. I might be unsure of my plans or how my life would play out, but there was one thing that I knew for certain: I was falling in love with Evelyn Whitney. The realization was both exhilarating and terrifying.

I met her halfway, offering us a little privacy.

"You're here," she said, her beautiful blue eyes shining bright. "I was afraid you wouldn't make it back from New York in time. How did the meeting go?"

It was hard to find my voice as so many thoughts and emotions warred within my heart and mind. The revelation of my growing feelings for her left me speechless, but she needed an answer. And because I had told her the reason for our trip to the city, I was able to say, "I think it went well. Your father was excited about the idea."

Her smile widened. "I'm so happy to hear that, Charles."

"But Congressman Reinhold saw us dining at Delmonico's with your father."

Her smile fell.

"He confronted me in the lobby just now," I continued. "He knows who I am."

She searched my face. "Will he tell anyone?"

I shook my head. "I've promised him that I will leave the minute the fundraiser concludes next week."

Evelyn's smile fell even further. "So you are leaving after the fundraiser?"

"I think it best." I hated the look of disappointment on her face—yet it gave my heart a measure of hope that perhaps Evelyn was starting to have feelings for me, too. But how would we make things work? If her parents knew who I really was, her father would never consider investing in my horse farm, and that would leave Mama and Ada without support. I still hadn't secured a good match for Cecily in 1563, either, and wasn't certain I'd regain my memory in time to help her. If I needed to stay in 1563, I would have to forfeit a life with Evelyn. It was best to forget about my feelings for her and focus on what I needed to do for my family.

A man with a megaphone called for Mr. Brent and me to take our positions on the tennis court to begin the game.

"We can talk later," I told her, lightly brushing her arm. It was all I dared to do in front of the crowd, but I wanted so much more than a simple touch.

The sky was cloudless, and the sun beat down with intensity as I lifted a racket and began to warm up my arms.

Drew joined Evelyn in the gallery, and they started a serious conversation. Neither one smiled as Drew spoke close to her ear, no doubt hoping to avoid being heard. She responded in a like manner, clearly upset with whatever he'd told her as she glanced at me.

I wanted to know what Drew had said, but I had to put thoughts of Evelyn aside as I jogged to the net and shook Mr. Brent's hand.

"You have an advantage," he said to me, his lips smiling though his eyes were filled with annoyance. "I've played two other matches today, and I'm exhausted. You're coming in nice and fresh."

If it wasn't for Evelyn, I wouldn't even compete. But this *was* for Evelyn, and for Laura, and all the friendless children in Newport. So, I simply said, "May the best man win."

"I will."

His arrogance rubbed me the wrong way, but I tried to ignore it.

We parted ways and took our positions on either side of the net. He won the coin toss and chose to serve first. Until now, I had no desire to win, but I couldn't lose on purpose to Morgan Brent. Especially with Evelyn watching.

The ball flew toward me, and I returned it with ease. My muscles were a little stiff at first, and he had the advantage that he was limber and warm. He won the first game, but I easily won the second and third. There were six games to a set and five sets to a match.

The crowd cheered loudly each time one of us scored. I was breathing hard, my attention focused on my opponent and the ball. Even though I had no intention to win, as the game progressed, my competitive nature took over. Each time I lost a point or had a clumsy swing, he gloated. We volleyed back and forth as sweat dripped from my brow, forcing me to wipe it away with the back of my arm.

I won the first set, Mr. Brent won the second, and then I won the third. After the third, we took a break but were quickly back on the court. The fourth set was one of the hardest, and Mr. Brent won it by one point, leaving our sets tied, two to two.

Those who were sitting in the galleries rose to their feet as we began the fifth and final set to determine who would play against the reigning champion the following week at the orphanage fundraiser. The last thing I needed was more attention, and the best thing to do would be to lose. But Evelyn caught my eye and smiled, and I saw how much she wanted me to win. It sent a surge of energy coursing through my body. Not only did I want to prove to Mr. Brent that I could beat him, but I wanted to impress Evelyn.

A movement in the gallery caught my attention as a woman waved a bright yellow scarf. Like a flash of lightning, a memory returned to me from the day of the jousting tournament. The ladies in waiting had waved scarves at us as I had paraded before the joust. I clearly recalled one of them holding a brilliant yellow scarf. At the time, I had felt this same sense of urgency to win.

It was the first memory that had returned to me since the accident. Did it mean I would have my memory when I woke up there tomorrow?

Hope mingled with my desire to please Evelyn, and I faced Mr. Brent with newfound momentum.

The final set was another hard-fought battle, but in the end, I gave it my all and won.

As the crowd cheered, I glanced at Evelyn and found her grinning at me.

It was all the reward I needed.

I hadn't disappointed her, or embarrassed her, or let her down. I had done everything for her, and for her desire to help the orphanage and raise awareness for the friendless children of Newport. And perhaps friendless children everywhere.

"The winner of the community tournament is Charles Pembrooke, the Earl of Norfolk," the announcer said into the megaphone as the crowd erupted into applause and cheers. "He will take on the US tennis champion, Mr. Sears, in next week's fundraiser match. We hope to see all of you back here for that special event."

As I toweled off, Mr. Brent approached and shook my hand, though he wasn't smiling. "I still say I would have beaten you if I hadn't played two other matches today."

"Perhaps you're right." I smiled, not willing to admit that he had made me work harder than I anticipated.

As he walked away, other people approached to congratulate me. When everyone else had moved aside, Evelyn and Drew joined me, and Evelyn's smile was radiant.

Even though I was risking unwanted attention, it was worth it to see her proud of me.

"Congratulations," she said as she put her hands on my arm. "I knew you could do it. I'm confident you'll beat Mr. Sears, as well." She motioned to the reporter she'd been speaking to earlier. He had been standing off to the side with his pad of paper and pencil. "I'd like you to meet Mr. Pendergast," she said. "He's a reporter for Mr. Bennett's *New York Herald*, and he'd like to do a feature story about you."

Alarm reverberated through me as I turned my back to the reporter, hoping he'd take the hint not to approach. "I don't think it's a good idea," I said quietly. "If it gets back to the real Earl of Norfolk that I'm here impersonating him, we could have trouble on our hands. I don't want to be in the newspaper."

Evelyn's lips parted with realization, and she nodded quickly. "You're right. I hadn't thought of that. I'll ask him to leave and find some excuse as to why you don't want to be mentioned in the paper. I'm sorry, Charles. I hadn't even considered what your participation in this tournament could mean."

She slipped away to speak to the reporter as I grabbed my racket and joined Drew.

"I had a memory return from the jousting match," I said to him, searching his face. "What do you think it means?"

"I don't know." He frowned. "But I hope it means the swelling has gone down on your brain in 1563 and you'll regain your memory there."

"I hope so, too. I hate to think that I'm causing Cecily distress."

He lowered his gaze.

"What?" I asked, crossing my arms. "What aren't you telling me about Cecily?"

Drew let out a sigh. "It doesn't matter, Charles. Believe me. I know my place, and I'm staying in it."

I was about to respond when Evelyn rejoined us. Her smile was warm as she said, "The reporter agreed to leave your name out of the article."

I couldn't help but return her smile. "Thank you."

"You're welcome."

Neither of us said anything for a moment, and then Evelyn put her hand on my arm again. "Let's go home. If we only have a week left before you need to leave, I don't want to waste it with a crowd of people."

My heart thudded at the weight of her hand, and the meaning of her words.

But when I looked at Drew, he wasn't smiling.

17

CECILY

JULY 27, 1563
WINDSOR CASTLE

Everything felt different the next morning when I woke up. I hadn't slept well the night before, thinking of the stolen kiss Andrew and I had shared on the terrace. I should have been happy after an experience like that, but knowing it was a mistake, and that it couldn't happen again, made me feel melancholy. My movements were slow, and my mind was distracted as I dressed. Kat had excused me from my chores in the Privy Chamber, but I took my time, uncertain how to face Andrew when I arrived at Charles's apartment.

"There's a page here for you, Lady Cecily," the matron of our dormitory said as she approached with a handful of discarded garments in her arms. She stopped to pick up another, mumbling under her breath about how hard she worked.

It was rare to have a page visit, so I set down the small mirror in my hands and went to the door.

"Doctor Bromley has asked for you, Lady Cecily," the page said.

My heart raced as I thought about seeing Andrew again.

"'Tis about your brother," the page continued.

Excitement and dread mingled as I moved around him and said, "Thank you."

I left the page behind, lifting the hem of my skirts to race toward the stairs that would take me to Charles's apartment. I didn't care if I was breaking the rules of propriety. There were only two reasons Andrew would send for me. Either Charles's condition had improved—or it had worsened.

When I finally arrived at Charles's apartment, I didn't hesitate to enter the outer chamber.

Andrew was pacing, clearly waiting for my arrival. He took a step forward at the sight of me and opened his mouth as if he was about to speak, but then paused.

"What is it?" I asked him. "Is Charles better?"

"Yes. His memory has returned, though—"

I started to move toward Charles's bedchamber door.

Andrew put his hand out to stop me.

Our gazes met, and at the touch of his hand, my world calmed. He slowly removed his hand and straightened. "His memory of this path has returned," he said a little slower, "but he is still in a weakened state of mind and doesn't recall everything. Please be patient and do not distress him."

"Of course not." I began to move toward the door, but Andrew stopped me for the second time by putting his hand on my arm again.

"Cecily, I am sorry about last night. All I could think about yesterday in Newport was what a mistake I had made inviting you outside. I regret what happened, and I hope you'll forgive me."

My body stiffened at his words. A mistake, perhaps—but regret? I did not regret kissing him. I only mourned that it could not happen again.

Did he truly regret the kiss?

"I think Charles suspects that something happened," he continued. "I haven't told him, and I think it best if you don't, either. It would only distress him."

Andrew's touch suddenly felt cool and heavy against my arm. How could he be so detached from what happened between us? My mind filled with a dozen things I wanted to say, but I chose not to speak as I left him in the outer chamber.

The door to Charles's room was slightly ajar, so I pushed it open the rest of the way and found him propped up with several pillows.

He opened his eyes when he heard the door creak, and he offered me a weak smile. "'Tis good to see you, Cec."

"Charles!" I cried out his name and rushed across the room to kneel beside his bed.

He reached out his hand, and I grasped it.

"You remember me," I said, the tears falling down my cheeks.

"I'm sorry for all the uncertainty and work I've caused you these past few days."

The door creaked, and I turned in time to see Andrew close it, offering privacy to Charles and me.

"'Tis not your fault," I said to Charles as I wiped my cheeks. "I'm only happy you are feeling better."

"I wish I *was* feeling better." He grimaced as he tried to reposition himself. "My head is pounding, and my body is stiff and sore. But Drew assures me everything will heal."

"Aye." I smiled and nodded. "You are strong and capable. You'll be back to normal in no time. And I will not have to be responsible for your work."

"Thank you for everything you did yesterday. Drew told me about it all. I'm afraid I might need help for a few more days, but now I can advise you and answer your questions."

"I will happily help for as long as you like."

"Have you sent out the letter to Mary?"

"Nay. I finished it late last night and planned to send it out today."

"Good. I will look over it again before giving it to the guards to have it carried to Scotland. I trust that you did everything correctly, I just need to make sure I said all that needed to be said."

"If you need to rewrite it, I will not take offense."

His smile dimmed as he studied me. "What happened between you and Drew the past couple of days? I know 'tis something, so don't tell me otherwise."

I slowly pulled away from Charles and let go of his hand. "Why would you think something—?"

"'Tis written all over his face—and yours."

Andrew's comments returned to me, and all I could focus on was the word *regret*. I didn't want to tell Charles about something that had no consequence. I would not allow myself to be with Andrew alone ever again, because I could not bear for him to regret his time with me.

"Nothing of consequence happened between us," I told him, trying to convince myself it was true.

Charles was quiet for a moment, but then he said, "I will not press you, if neither one of you want to talk about it, but I know something happened." He was quiet for a moment before saying, "There is no hope for a future with him, Cec."

"What about you?" I asked, trying to make my voice sound light and unaffected. "You spoke of Evelyn quite often while you had amnesia."

"Did I?" He leaned his head back on his pillows and closed his eyes, taking several deep breaths.

"Tell me about her, Charles." I watched him closely for his response. "Are you in love with her?"

His lips pressed together in a subtle, fleeting tell. When he finally opened his blue eyes, I saw the truth in their depths.

"You do love her," I whispered in surprise.

"It matters not." He looked toward the window, where the sun was shining brightly. "Just as you and Drew cannot follow your hearts, Evelyn and I cannot, either."

"Does she return your affection?"

He continued to look out the window as he said, "If she does, she has not told me."

"But you suspect she cares for you."

When Charles met my gaze, I saw the pain. "'Tis foolish to want something that I cannot have."

I knew his pain better than anyone. It was hard enough to bear it on my own, but to know my stepbrother suffered the same heartache, after everything he'd sacrificed for me, was too much. Why must we both suffer?

"What if you stayed in 1883?" I asked quietly.

"What do you mean?"

"Could you find a way to marry her if you stayed there?"

He shook his head. "Her mother thinks I am the Earl of Norfolk. If she knew my real identity, she would never approve of the match—not only because I have deceived her, but because I am nothing more than a horse farmer from Virginia. Worse, her father would withdraw his financial help for the farm, and if others learned about my deception, it would be hard to convince them to invest. I would have no means to support her, or Mama and Ada."

I took his hand in mine. "You are so much more than a horse farmer from Virginia, and you know it. And one day, when you have the means, you will return your farm to something magnificent, and you will not only gain riches, but also status. Her family could not deny you then."

"'Tis a hopeless idea."

"Nothing is hopeless," I told him, wanting to believe it for myself as much as I did for him.

"Worry not, Cecily," he said with a tired smile. "You, Mama, and Ada are my only concerns right now. God has given me a responsibility to my family, and I will not abandon my duties to chase after a fantasy."

"But if you had no duty toward me," I said, holding his hand tighter, "and you only had 1883 to worry about—do you think it would be utterly impossible to win her heart?"

He was fatigued from our conversation, and I did not want to burden Charles, though I did want to know the truth. I couldn't perform a miracle, but if I got out of his way, became one less duty, then perhaps he would not have to sacrifice his love for Evelyn.

Charles was quiet for a moment, but then he said, "The Bible tells us that nothing is impossible for God. It might be impossible for me—but I don't have all the answers."

I sat up a little straighter. "Then 'tis possible to win her heart?"

He sighed and closed his eyes, clearly finished with our conversation. "I am tired, Cec."

There was nothing left to say as I slowly rose to my feet.

But there was something I could do, even if it broke my heart. Charles had sacrificed so much for me and Ada and his mama.

It was time to sacrifice for him.

※

Queen Elizabeth loved to dance, and she required that her courtiers were adept at the skill. So, despite her illness, she insisted that the court continue as usual, which meant that there was a feast that evening, with dancing afterward.

I sat with the other maids of honour, half hoping and half dreading that Andrew would attend the meal. He had been scarce most of the day as I had stayed with Charles. Between my stepbrother's naps, we worked on his council responsibilities. I had completed the report about the plague and had it delivered to the privy council for their consideration. I had also handed the letter off to the queen's guards, who would ensure it was brought to Mary, Queen of Scots.

When Andrew had come to check on Charles, I hadn't spoken to him about anything other than Charles's health and well-being. What was there to say? He had made it clear that he regretted our time together, and even if he hadn't, I knew what I must do. There was little other choice for me, and the sooner I accepted my fate, the sooner I could come to terms with it.

Lord Wolverton sat at one of the long tables in St. George's Hall, across from Aveline. She had told me that he had approached her on two occasions to ask questions about my character and to encourage her to speak to me about his proposal. She had relayed the message but given no indication as to whether she thought it was a good idea or not.

That was for me to decide.

"'Tis time to clear the hall for dancing," Lord Burghley said as he stood from the head of the table, close to where the queen usually sat.

Tonight, there would be no performance for the queen, so we would dance together.

As the musicians began to warm up, Lord Wolverton made his way to my side.

"You look well tonight, Lady Cecily," he said as he bowed over my hand. "I have heard that your brother is doing much better today. I am very happy for both of you."

"Thank you," I said. "'Tis a burden relieved."

A group began to form for the first dance, a simple branle.

"Will you dance, my lord?" I asked him.

He wrinkled his nose and looked at the others, and then he turned back to me and earnestly studied my face. "Will it please you if I do, Lady Cecily?"

His question caught me off guard, yet I could see he was sincere.

"It would."

Lord Wolverton offered me a bow. "Then I will endeavor to do my best."

He took my hand, and we joined the circle of dancers. The tempo was slow, and the footwork was easy, but Lord Wolverton still struggled as he watched the other dancers closely.

Despite the pit in my stomach, I couldn't help but smile at his efforts.

When the dance came to an end, I curtsied, and he bowed.

"Thank you," I said and began to walk away.

He put his hand on my arm to stop me.

We were standing close, and he said, for my ears only, "If you marry me, I cannot promise that your life will be everything you hope or desire, but I will do my best to make you comfortable and happy."

For the first time, I realized his eyes were hazel, and when he looked at me with such honesty, I could almost believe that things might not be so bad at Alnwick Castle.

I dipped my head in deference to him and then left his side to find Kat.

She was not in the hall, and one of the maids said that she had been called back to the Privy Chamber at the queen's behest.

It was probably better this way. It was the queen I needed to speak to, and Kat was the person who might give me access.

I tried to hold my head high as I walked along the darkened corridors of Windsor Castle, away from the light and the lively music in St. George's Hall. But tears began to prick the backs of my eyes as I faced the reality of what I was about to do. Whether I agreed to marry Lord Wolverton or some other aristocrat, it mattered not to me. If I could not have the man I wanted, then all I needed was a good man who would treat me well and ensure my protection.

It was as simple as that.

Dim wall sconces offered just enough light for me to see my way to the queen's apartment. There was no one in the halls, and I preferred it that way.

When I arrived at the Presence Chamber, the ushers let me pass without comment, and I entered the Privy Chamber.

It was rare to find the room empty, though I could hear voices in the queen's bedchamber, so I knew there were people attending Her Majesty. She was never alone, not only for safety's sake, but to protect her reputation and because she didn't like to be by herself.

The door opened, and Andrew appeared, wiping his hands on a clean cloth.

He paused and then slowly closed the bedchamber door.

"I did not expect to see you here," he said.

My chest rose and fell on deep breaths. It was hard enough to know what I was about to do, but then to face Andrew, unexpectedly, made it even harder. "I came to speak to Her Majesty."

A frown marred his forehead. "She has not allowed an audience in weeks. What makes you think she'll see you now?"

"I have an important question for her that cannot wait." I tried to stay calm as my emotions tore at my heart. "And all I need is a simple yes or no."

He stared at me, and I could see the uncertainty in his eyes. "What do you need to ask her?"

I pressed my trembling lips together, knowing that I did not owe him an answer but wanting desperately for him to stop me. "I must ask for her permission to marry Lord Wolverton."

Silence filled the Privy Chamber as we stood facing one another, and though we were only a few feet apart, obligations, expectations, and centuries divided us.

"If I marry him, Charles will be free to stay in 1883 to rebuild his farm and care for his mama and sister—and, perhaps—" I paused to swallow—"marry the woman he loves."

"Has he demanded this of you?" Andrew clenched the rag in his hands.

"No. I am approaching the queen of my own free will."

A war waged within Andrew, playing out on his face, and for a heartbeat, I thought he would deny my request to speak to the queen. Hope budded to life in my heart.

But then something flickered in his gaze. Acceptance? Resignation? Surrender?

He slowly lowered his eyes and took a sidestep away from the queen's bedchamber door.

"I will not stand in your way," he said just above a whisper, and then he strode out of the Privy Chamber without a backward glance, leaving me alone and bereft.

I closed my eyes as my heart broke into a million little pieces, and the weight of the grief I'd been carrying for months flooded my soul again.

Yet, I refused to cry, knowing that if I started, I might not stop, and that was the worst feeling in the world.

Instead, I took a deep breath and opened my eyes to face the reality set before me.

If I had learned anything, it was that I was strong and capable, and even if it felt like God had abandoned me, Mama and Papa had taught me that He never left my side. My life wasn't a surprise to Him, and the obstacles He'd placed in my path were there for a reason. I didn't know why God would allow me to love Andrew, but I also didn't know why He chose for me to lose 1913, or why Aveline had lost her parents, or why the queen was so ill. Trusting God didn't mean I wouldn't have heartache, but it did mean that I needed to lean on Him and follow the path He had laid before me.

With a heavy heart, I knocked on the bedchamber door.

Kat answered it a moment later, concern on her face. "What is it, Lady Cecily?"

"May I have an audience with Her Majesty? I have one simple question and only require a yes-or-no response."

She was not blind, and she had a finger on the castle's pulse like no other, so I knew that Kat wouldn't need me to explain.

With a sigh, she stepped aside and said, "Her Majesty is feeling a little better today. But please be brief and do not debate with her if she refuses to speak to you."

I nodded as I stepped into the dark interior.

Queen Elizabeth was on her bed, propped up with several pillows all around her and a blanket over her body. Her red hair was in a simple braid, and her pockmarked face was devoid of makeup. It was swollen, as were her hands, which held an embroidery hoop. When I entered, she looked up in surprise.

"Lady Cecily," she said. "I hope you do not bring bad news. Doctor Bromley has assured me that your brother is doing well."

"He is, Your Majesty." My voice quivered with emotion, despite my earlier resolve, as I gave a low curtsy. "It does my heart good to see you again."

She lowered the embroidery hoop to her lap. "Why have you come?"

I slowly rose to face her, knowing that once my request was made and her response was given, there was no going back. Yet, what choice did I have?

"I have come to ask your permission—" I swallowed the nerves racing up my throat.

"My permission for what?" she asked impatiently.

"To marry Lord Wolverton, Your Majesty," I said quickly before I changed my mind.

"Ah." She was quiet for a moment, and then said gently, "Is this what you want, Cecily?"

I pressed my lips together and clasped my hands. "'Tis what I need that matters more."

"Aye." She let out a weary sigh. "We rarely get what we want."

I didn't answer, since there was no point.

"You could do little better," she continued. "He is wealthy and loyal to the throne. I think your stepbrother has done well in choosing Lord Wolverton for your match."

It wasn't quite permission, but almost, so I looked up at her. "Are you granting permission, Your Majesty?"

"Come here." She motioned for me to join her and patted the bed.

I glanced at Kat, who raised her eyebrows. Neither of us often saw the queen's tender, motherly side.

"Leave us, Kat," the queen said.

Kat did as she was told, and I approached the queen's bed, tentatively lowering onto the mattress to face her.

Her brown eyes searched mine. "You're in love with Doctor Bromley, are you not?"

My lips parted in surprise.

"Because he is in love with you," she said matter-of-factly.

I briefly closed my eyes as tears stung them once again.

"Listen closely," she said as she put her hand over mine and made me look at her. "Love is fickle and untrustworthy. It does not last, and it offers no protection or guarantee. My mother loved my father, and he beheaded her." Her voice was fierce as she spoke. "If Doctor Bromley was a nobleman and he had a home to offer to you, I would tell you to marry him—for those reasons alone. I would not take into consideration that he loved you. That would be a secondary bonus. But he has none of those things, so he is not an option. Love is not enough for a woman of your position."

I nodded, unable to use my voice.

"Marry Lord Wolverton and move as far away from Doctor Bromley as possible," she continued. "Then, and only then, will you find peace."

Queen Elizabeth was speaking from experience, as I knew she loved Lord Robert and kept him close at hand. His presence rarely brought her peace and often resulted in difficulties I couldn't begin to understand.

"You have my permission," she said. "Now, go and start to make plans. I'm certain Lord Wolverton is eager to leave Windsor. I will pray that I am well enough to attend your wedding."

My legs felt weak and heavy as I stood and curtsied before leaving her bedchamber.

Kat looked up from her needlework as soon as I entered the Privy Chamber, a question in her eyes.

"She has granted permission." I choked on the words.

Setting aside her embroidery, Kat joined me in the middle of the room. "He is a good man. He will do right by you."

I nodded, unable to speak past the emotions in my throat.

"How is your brother?" she asked quietly. "Doctor Bromley tells me he has regained his memory. Are all his correspondences in order?"

Again, I could do nothing but nod.

"You may leave." Kat returned to her needlework, dismissing me.

I was tired of feeling used and discarded, of being a second thought to everyone.

God included.

18

CHARLES

JULY 27, 1883
NEWPORT, RHODE ISLAND

I didn't have an appetite that morning, so I skipped breakfast and found myself in the dim library instead. Gray clouds hovered low over the ocean, and a misting rain made rivulets of water run down the windowpanes at Midcliff. I stood at the window, watching the Atlantic roll toward the cliffs in massive waves, my mind filled with all the problems I faced in both paths.

My time in Newport was quickly coming to an end, making me both relieved and anxious. Thankfully, my memory had come back in 1563, and Cecily had been available to help me continue my work. I should have concentrated on the plague that devastated London or the succession issue and who would sit on the throne. But no matter how hard I tried, I could think of little else but Evelyn.

Cecily had been quiet and withdrawn all day. Her melancholy, and the way she had treated Drew when he came to my apartment, confirmed that something had happened between them. Drew had stayed with me after Cecily had gone to supper, but then he'd left to check on the queen and not returned to my bedchamber before I had fallen asleep. I was eager to find out how the queen's health was faring and to ask him about Cecily. While I had resolved to let it go, I wanted to know if I needed to be concerned.

At least, more concerned than I already was.

"I was wondering where I might find you." Evelyn appeared at the library door.

My heart skipped a beat at the sight of her. I would never tire of the way she looked at me. All I wanted was to be near her, to ease the longing within me. To see her face and hear her voice. The desire thrilled me and scared me at the same time.

She was wearing a simple gray gown, but it was fashionable and fit her perfectly. She stood out amongst the dark wood paneling and shelves of books.

"I kept waiting for you at breakfast." She entered the room and joined me by the window. "Drew didn't come down, either, so I ate alone."

"I'm sorry," I said, pleased that she had wanted to see me, too. "I didn't have an appetite."

Concern slanted her brow. "Is something bothering you?"

I smiled at the question as I considered all the things that were bothering me in both paths—yet they somehow slipped from my mind when I was with her.

"Congressman Reinhold?" she asked.

"Among other things."

"You can tell me, Charles. I might not know how to ease your burdens, but I would love to try. You've done so much to help me."

I had told her little about my other path out of habit. It was best not to share, to risk changing history—yet I wanted to tell Evelyn. She was the first person I longed to trust with both my lives.

She took my hand and gently led me to a set of chairs in the corner of the room. She was about to sit down, but I didn't let go of her hand, and she was forced to stop and turn to me. "What?" she asked.

"I want to tell you," I said. "For the first time in my life, I want to tell someone—you—everything. But it scares me, Evelyn."

She still held my hand as she moved closer. "Why?"

Her eyes were so wide and beautiful as she stood close to me. My heart pounded with certainty that I loved her, but that also terrified me. I had never loved someone the way I loved her, and I wasn't sure what I would do without her.

"It scares me, because I'm afraid that I will bare my heart and soul to you, but you won't feel safe to tell me about your past."

Her eyes clouded over, and she began to pull away, but I held her hand and grasped the other one. "I know it frightens you, too, Evelyn. Sharing our pain requires us to be vulnerable, because we don't want to be hurt anymore."

"It's not that." She shook her head. "I know the past can't hurt me, but if you knew what I've done . . ." She swallowed and gently removed her hands from mine. "I don't think you'd look at me the same way again, Charles, and that's something I couldn't bear. Right now, you see me as innocent and loving—but if you knew—"

"I do know."

Her lips parted as she frowned. "How could you possibly know?"

"I know Laura is your baby."

Her frown disappeared as an incredulous look came over her face. "What?"

"I put all the pieces together. Drew said that you changed drastically about a year and a half ago, and with the way you despised me when you met me, I realized that someone had broken your heart. And when I saw you with Laura—not only does she look like you, but you care so much for her, and you're doing so much for the orphanage. It all makes sense."

She took a step back, the incredulity gone, replaced with pain. "Laura is not my baby."

It was my turn to frown.

"The reason I help at the orphanage is not because I got into trouble in this path." Tears gathered in her eyes. "It has nothing to do with this path. Everything I do in 1883 is driven out of my pain and guilt from my other life. And no matter how much penance I serve, I can never undo what I did there."

I took a step closer to her. "I want to understand, Evelyn. I want you to trust me enough to share that part of your past with me. I understand—"

"You can't possibly understand. Each time-crosser's experiences are unique and complex, and even though you have two lives, you can't begin to know what it was like for me."

"I want to know."

She shook her head. "I don't think you do."

I took another step, drawing close, and put my hands around her waist. "Let me decide that for myself."

Evelyn studied my face for a moment, her emotions raw and, for a fleeting second, hopeful. But then sadness filled it again. "And what if you decide you don't like what you learn about me?" She swallowed. "What if you realize what I've always known?"

"What have you always known?" I whispered.

"That I am unlovable."

I lifted a hand to her cheek, every inch of my body aware of her nearness, of the scent of her perfume and the softness of her skin. "What if you realize what I know?"

She looked up at me, questions in her tender blue eyes.

"That you *are* lovable—because I'm falling in love with you."

A tear slipped down her cheek. "How could you be in love with me? You don't know who I truly am."

I wiped away her tear with my thumb. "I know you are kind and thoughtful and good. You love the children at the orphanage, and you would do anything for them. You have a gentle and pure heart, Evelyn."

She started to protest, but I continued. "The reason I know your heart is pure is because of the remorse you feel for your past. An evil, hateful, vindictive person doesn't regret their transgressions. You are lovable, despite everything you've done in your past. And that's not just my opinion, it's God's truth. You are not the sum of your mistakes."

Evelyn closed her eyes and pressed against me in a hug that took my breath away. Not because of her strength, but because of her weakness.

She rested her cheek against my chest, and I wondered if she could feel my heart beating.

I laid my lips against the top of her head and wrapped my arms around her, loving how she fit perfectly in my embrace. I wanted to know all of Evelyn Whitney, because even the dark moments had shaped her and created the woman I was falling in love with.

"I want to tell you," she whispered, "but I need more time, Charles."

I inhaled the scent of her soap and nodded, though she wasn't looking at me. "I will wait as long as it takes."

Yet, even as the words slipped out, I knew I didn't have much time left.

In a week, I would leave Midcliff and Evelyn, and the chances of us ever seeing each other again were impossibly small.

She finally pulled back, wiping the tears off her cheeks. I reached into my pocket and removed a clean handkerchief and gently placed it in her hand.

"Thank you," she whispered. When she was done, she looked up at me. Her blue eyes were brighter than usual, swimming in tears. "Are you really falling in love with me, Charles?"

My heart felt like it was going to tear in two, divided by all the things that could keep us apart. Yet, I couldn't deny the truth. "I am."

Her gaze filled with wonder as she reached up and placed her hands on either side of my face.

"I don't deserve your love," she whispered, her breath warm upon my mouth. "But I want it, with all of my heart."

I couldn't wait another moment as I drew her close, capturing her mouth in a kiss.

She wrapped her arms around my neck, pulling me closer, increasing the desire building inside of me. I'd kissed other women before, but none of them had been anything more than flirtation. This was different—in every way possible.

Despite all the obstacles in my way, the impossible choices I had to make, and the mess I'd gotten into pretending to be the Earl of Norfolk in 1883, there was one thing I knew for certain. I loved Evelyn Whitney.

But as we separated from our kiss and sat in the corner of the intimate library for most of the afternoon with the rain falling, as I told her about Cecily and Queen Elizabeth and Mama and Ada, I realized something I didn't want to acknowledge.

Evelyn hadn't said that she was falling in love with me. And until she trusted me with her other path, I didn't think she could.

That evening, Evelyn and Mrs. Whitney attended a house concert for the American Red Cross, leaving Drew and me on our own for supper. I hadn't seen him all day, but I wasn't sure if it was because I was avoiding him, or he was avoiding me.

A footman told me that Drew was in the billiards room, so I made my way there as darkness started to descend over Newport. It was still raining, and ominous clouds hung over the ocean, portending an oncoming storm that might be more powerful than we expected.

I heard the billiard balls before I entered the room and found Drew bent over the table, a cue in hand, as he prepared to strike again.

He glanced up at my arrival but did not greet me as he usually did. Instead, anger radiated off him, and he scowled.

"What do you want?" he asked as he struck the cue ball.

I paused, frowning. Had he seen Evelyn and me in the library? Was that why he'd been avoiding me all day? Was he angry that I kissed her?

"Your mother and sister just left," I said cautiously as I entered the room. It was a large space with green- and cream-colored tiles on the walls, ceiling, and floor. Curved arches around the doors and windows gave it an Italian flair.

Drew was playing English billiards, and he didn't respond as he positioned himself to hit the next cue ball, turning his back to me.

In all the years I'd known Drew, he'd never been this angry at me, and I couldn't blame him. He didn't want me to pursue Evelyn, just as I didn't want him to pursue Cecily.

"I'm sorry," I said, though I didn't regret kissing Evelyn or telling her I was falling in love with her. She hadn't told me she was in love with me, but her kiss had confirmed that she cared for me.

When it was all said and done, however, it wouldn't matter if she loved me or not. I needed to take care of Mama and Ada, and I couldn't do that without Mr. Whitney's investment. It was one of the reasons I'd come to Newport in the first place. He could never learn the truth about me. And even if I was willing to sacrifice his investment and tell the world I wasn't Lord Norfolk, the scandal would ruin Mrs. Whitney, which would irreparably hurt Evelyn and Drew. I couldn't do that to two people I cared so much about. It would be selfish, and I wouldn't get what I wanted in the end anyway.

For the first time in a long time, I realized I couldn't rely on my own strength in this situation. It was something I'd done since my fathers had died, trying, in vain, to manipulate things to work in my favor. Even going against the privy council by not telling Mary, Queen of Scots, the truth about Queen Elizabeth was me trying to control the situation, as if I knew what was best.

Perhaps I had never known what was best. I was at the end of my own abilities. All I could do was trust that God had a better plan than me, because I'd messed everything up.

"Did you come to tell me you are sorry, Charles?" Drew finally asked, standing straight to face me.

"I'm sorry that I've upset you," I said, unwilling to apologize for kissing Evelyn. Perhaps it had been a mistake, but I wasn't sorry for it.

Drew shook his head and scoffed as he positioned himself to hit the ball—but he stood suddenly and glared at me. "Why don't you let her decide what she wants? Why force her?"

I crossed my arms, feeling defensive. "I would never force her to do something she doesn't want. She was the one who initiated it."

"Because she feels guilty."

"Guilty?" I lowered my arms. "She didn't do it because she felt guilty. What kind of a man do you think I am if I would allow that? I hope she did it because she loves me—or, at the very least, regards me with affection."

"Of course she loves you," he said. "But she's confused and hurting, and she thinks she's doing what's best for you."

"Do you really think she loves me?" I asked. I couldn't help it.

He frowned as he stared at me. "Of course she loves you. Cecily adores you."

"Cecily?" It was my turn to frown.

"Yes, Cecily." He set the end of his cue stick on the ground and gripped it. "Who did you think I was talking about?" Realization dawned on his face. "Did you think I was talking about Evelyn? What did Evelyn initiate?"

I didn't respond as Drew came closer.

"Did something happen, Charles?"

It was my turn to get angry. "I can ask the same about you and Cecily. What happened when I was suffering from amnesia?"

Drew pulled back—just enough for me to know that my suspicions were correct. Something *had* happened between him and my stepsister.

"You're being a hypocrite," I said. "It doesn't excuse my behavior, but it doesn't justify yours, either. Both of us want someone we can't have, and we feel powerless because of it. That doesn't mean we have to turn on one another."

"I'm not turning on you because of Evelyn." He leaned against the billiards table and set the cue stick beside him. He looked as if he carried the weight of the world on his shoulders as he said, "Cecily sought the queen's permission to marry Lord Wolverton—and the queen granted it."

"What? When?"

"Last night after I left your apartment, I went to check on

the queen. Cecily arrived as I was getting ready to leave, and she told me she was there to ask permission to marry that boring—tedious—northerner!" He stumbled over the last words as his anger mounted. "Kat told me that the queen has granted Cecily permission and instructed Cecily to start planning the wedding." He rubbed his face as he growled and then looked at me. "She's going to be miserable—and she's doing it for you."

"Me?"

"She wants you to have a chance with Evelyn." He motioned toward the mansion with an irritated wave of his hand. "Even though it's impossible, she doesn't want to be the reason you're forced to stay in 1563."

With a heavy sigh, I joined him at the billiards table and leaned against it, shaking my head. "I don't have a chance with Evelyn."

"You do. But there are so many obstacles, Charles, ones of our own making."

I ignored the hope that tried to spark inside my heart at his words. Even if I had a chance to win Evelyn's heart, I was foolish to think we could overcome all the other things standing in our way. "I don't want Cecily to marry a man who would make her life miserable. Lord Wolverton *is* a bore."

Drew crossed his arms but didn't speak.

"But she needs to marry someone." I looked up at him. "And while you're at Windsor Castle, she won't give her heart to anyone else."

He slowly lowered his arms. "What are you saying?"

I turned to him, knowing what needed to happen. "You're not able to help the queen, so there's really no point in you staying at Windsor any longer. It would be best for everyone if you went back to Arundel Castle. Hopefully, Cecily can meet someone else and fall in love before March, and then she and I can both have what we need. She'll be in an advantageous marriage with someone who can provide properly for her, and I can stay here and take care of Mama and Ada."

Drew ran his hand over the back of his neck and moved away

from the billiards table to pace. "I can't leave the queen—not yet."

"Drew—"

"She needs me. I can't tell you why, but she does. After that, I will leave Windsor Castle. I promise."

"How long will it be?"

"Not much longer. The minute the queen is out of danger, I will leave Windsor Castle and never look back. You have my word."

"And until then?" I asked as I pushed away from the table. "What will you do about Cecily?"

"I'll keep my distance. I already told her I regretted what happened." He paused and then shook his head. "I kissed her—the other night—but I knew it was wrong, and it won't happen again."

"You told her you regretted it?" I grimaced.

"I realized my choice of words wasn't smart the minute they were out of my mouth. That was yesterday, before she asked permission to marry Wolverton, and I suspect it's part of the reason she went to the queen."

"*Do* you regret it?" I asked him.

He shook his head. "I will never regret kissing Cecily. Or falling in love with her."

"You love her?"

Drew slowly nodded as he took a deep breath. "I do love her, but just like you, I know it's impossible and I need to keep my distance. I wish you'd do the same with Evelyn. We can do nothing but hurt them if we continue to be selfish and ask them for things they cannot give us—and that we cannot give them."

I rolled the cue ball across the billiards table, not wanting to admit he was right. But I had no other choice. The last thing I wanted to do was hurt Evelyn.

"I'll keep my distance," I said to him.

"And so will I."

I nodded as I turned and left the billiards room, needing some time alone.

19

CECILY

AUGUST 2, 1563
WINDSOR CASTLE

The small dormitory where I slept with the other maids of honour was as black as ink on that hot, humid night. Our elderly chaperone lay snoring in her narrow cot in the corner, only adding to my insomnia and discomfort.

It had been almost a week since I'd visited Queen Elizabeth and received her permission to marry Lord Wolverton, but I had not yet told him of her decision. The following day, the queen had taken a turn for the worse, and I did not feel it was prudent to share news of our impending nuptials—not even with him—until she was better.

If she got better.

At least, that's what I kept telling myself.

There was a part of me that wanted to put off the announcement indefinitely, especially after Charles had told me the next day that I need not marry the Earl of Wolverton, unless I wanted the match.

Since no one else knew about my visit to the queen except Kat and Andrew, I suspected that one of them had told him, and my bet was on Andrew.

I turned to my side, wishing I could sleep, though the blessed relief would not visit me. I'd spent most of my week with Charles, helping him with his work, but he was doing so much better, I would no longer need to assist him. Kat would expect me back in the Privy Chamber to serve the queen, but with her worsening condition, there was little for any of the maids to do. The entire castle held its breath. There had been no feasts, no games, no tournaments, no dancing—nothing to offer entertainment or joy. Aveline and I had stopped planning her masque because we didn't even know if the queen would survive to see it.

The only thing that helped me pass the time was my painting. I spent hours and hours in the tower, lost in my world of butterflies.

I turned on my cot again, wishing for a bit of fresh air. The stuffy dormitory made it hard to breathe. The weight of the queen's illness, and my distress over marrying Lord Wolverton, started to make me feel panicked. I needed to move, to pace, to set my mind on something good and hopeful.

Mama's voice from 1913 whispered into my heart, as if she were there with me, reminding me I needed to pray.

As quietly as I could, I slipped out of my bed and tiptoed through the room. Thankfully the other maids were asleep, and no one stirred as I made my way into the dressing room that adjoined the dormitory.

I had to feel my way around to find my kirtle and gown. I would not bother to put on my farthingale, but I needed to be dressed properly in case a servant came upon me in the corridors.

It took some maneuvering, but I was able to dress and leave the dormitory without our chaperone realizing what I was doing. Most maids who snuck out at night left to have a tryst, and some of them were able to return in the morning without our chaperone any wiser. Others who were caught faced harsh punishment, including house arrest and banishment from the court. There were still several hours before sunrise, and I would return long before then, so I wasn't worried. It wasn't the first time I'd gone for a late-night walk to clear my head.

Our dormitory wasn't far from the queen's apartment. I walked down the long corridor as beams of moonlight poured through the high windows and made squares on the opposite stone wall. It was still hot, but the air was fresher out of the dormitory, and I could take a deep breath.

I wasn't even sure where to begin with God as I thought through everything that had happened in the past year. My grief was still with me, and I was certain it would always be there, but it wasn't as piercing or as raw as it had been. Painting had helped to heal my pain, and finding joy in creating a book had given me purpose again. Working with Charles had been good for me, not only to keep my mind occupied, but also to spend time with my brother.

Perhaps I didn't need to worry about what I wanted from God tonight. He already knew. He understood the desires of my heart, even better than I did. Maybe I needed to use my late-night walk to simply thank Him for all the ways He'd already cared for me.

So I did just that.

As I moved down the corridor, the only sound I heard was the quiet rustle of my skirts, but then a faint whisper caught my attention as I came to a turn in the hall.

I paused, afraid I might interrupt a midnight tryst—or worse, someone who had gotten into the castle to cause trouble. More than once, people had broken into the castle to do harm to the queen. Her ushers were always on guard and could call for help at a moment's notice, but there were no guards near me now.

"There is a family in Hedgerly, in Buckinghamshire," a female voice whispered just around the corner from where I stood. "The man is named Robert Southern. He was summoned to the castle a month ago and told to be ready at a moment's notice. He won't ask any questions."

I slowly pressed myself against the wall, trying to steady my breathing. The woman speaking was Kat.

"His home is on the main road?" a male voice asked, and I immediately recognized it as Andrew's.

My heart started to beat harder. Why were Andrew and Kat meeting in the middle of the night? Discussing a man from another village?

"Aye, 'tis a simple cottage, unremarkable," Kat said. "The second one you'll come to on the south side of the road once you pass over the bridge. He was instructed to keep a candle burning in the window by night and to hang a wreath on his door."

"We cannot awaken anyone in the castle," Andrew whispered, "or draw any unwanted attention by calling for a horse. 'Tis only seven miles. I will go on foot."

"If you go quickly, I think you can get there before daybreak."

"I must act fast. There is no time to lose."

"The guards on duty have been told to let you pass. They know not to question me."

Before I could move, Andrew and Kat stepped out of the adjacent hall and came face-to-face with me.

My lips parted as I stared at them.

"Lady Cecily!" Kat said, her hand going to her heart in surprise. "What are you doing up this late?"

Andrew tenderly held a blanketed bundle in his arms, and my focus went from the bundle to his face, a dozen questions demanding answers.

"Cecily," Kat said as she put her hand on my arm to gain my attention. "What are you doing here?"

"I—I couldn't sleep. I—" I didn't know what else to say.

The bundle in Andrew's arms began to move and there was a quiet sound, almost as if—

"Is that a baby?" I asked.

Andrew and Kat glanced at one another, and then Andrew nodded.

"Aye," Kat said with a sigh.

The baby's whimper started to grow louder.

"We must get him out of the castle," Kat said as she turned me around and nudged me to move. "Now that you are here, Lady Cecily, you will be of great help."

I didn't ask any questions as we quickly walked down the corridor and Kat pushed open a secret side door onto the North Terrace.

"Lady Cecily will accompany you, Doctor Bromley," she said as she walked us outside into the humid night. "If anyone stops you, tell them 'tis her baby. They will be less likely to ask questions if there is a woman present with a newborn."

"My baby?" I asked, still stunned.

Kat reached into her skirt pocket, pulled out a pouch of coins, and handed it to me, her voice low and serious. "In case you need anything. I will make excuses for you while you are gone, but the longer it takes you to return, the more likely this will cause a scandal, and we cannot afford for anyone to ask questions. Do you understand? Do not come back during the daylight. Wait until tomorrow night to make your way to the castle. I do not want anyone to associate your errand with the queen. Do not share your real names and do not, under any circumstances, tell them where this baby came from."

"Where *did* it come from?" I asked.

"We need to leave." Andrew put his free hand on my lower back. "It will take a couple of hours to walk to Hedgerly, and the baby will be hungry and making its presence known to the world if we wait too long."

"We cannot allow that." Kat started to retreat into the castle, but right before she closed the door she said, "Godspeed."

I stared at the closed door as Andrew took my hand in his.

"We cannot tarry," he said, his voice low. "We must be away."

"What's happening, Andrew?"

"There is no time to explain now, but I will tell you as soon as we are away from the castle." The moon was so bright, it offered me a clear view of his dark brown eyes. "Please trust me."

I nodded, knowing Andrew would not do anything to harm me or anyone else.

Through Each Tomorrow

We began our trek away from Windsor Castle as quickly as we could. The baby quieted in Andrew's arms, allowing us to pass through without awakening anyone or causing alarm.

When we arrived at the Thames, the bridge was guarded since the queen was in residence at the castle. My heart beat wildly as we approached, but the guard on duty simply nodded once as we passed by and then turned to look in the opposite direction.

What was happening?

We walked down High Street, past homes and businesses, which were closed for the night. Neither of us spoke, but the longer we stayed silent, the more questions I had.

I was thankful I had chosen a simple dress, one that would not raise too much suspicion if we were seen. I wasn't wearing my farthingale, which also helped, since commoners rarely wore wide skirts.

When we finally passed Eton College and were on the outskirts of Windsor Village, I turned to Andrew, perplexed and uncertain.

"Will you tell me now?" I whispered.

We continued to walk, though Andrew slowed the pace as he looked down at the sleeping babe in his arms.

"'Tis the queen's."

I stopped in my tracks. "The queen's?"

He took my hand, tugging me to continue. "We cannot waste a moment, Cecily."

I started to walk again and stared down at the baby. "The queen's?" I asked again.

"Aye. He was born just a few hours ago, so we must hurry. He'll be wanting his first meal before too long, and it will be hard to go unnoticed when he begins to cry."

"How long can a baby wait to eat after he's born?"

"They should eat as soon as possible, but he can wait for six hours or so. The family we are taking him to has an infant in the home, and the mother has agreed to take on another child."

"As a wet nurse?"

"No." Andrew's voice was serious. "As the baby's new mother."

"Does the family know who the real mother is?"

"No. And they must never know. They are distantly related to Kat and think the baby was born to an unmarried servant in the castle."

"Who else knows the queen had a baby?" I tried to keep up with him.

"Shh." He put his finger to his lips. "You cannot say that again, Cecily. If anyone hears, there could be disastrous repercussions."

"Who else knows?" I asked quieter.

"Just Kat, you, and me."

My mouth parted as a new question formed. "Who is the father? Does he know about the child's existence?"

Andrew was quiet for a moment and then shook his head. "He does not know a child exists."

"But you know the father's identity?"

"Aye. The queen told me, but it matters not."

"Is it Lord Robert?"

Andrew didn't answer, but he didn't need to. I saw the truth on his face.

The moon paved our path as we continued down the road and it turned into a country lane. Very little stirred this late at night, and even the crickets and frogs were silent. It was so hot, I longed for some wind or a breath of fresh air, but everything was still and quiet.

"Why was the queen so ill?" I asked.

"I believe she suffered from a sickness called toxemia. There is little known about it here, and not much more known about it in 1883, but it causes toxins to build up in the system during pregnancy. Sometimes, it can be deadly, and the baby is often born early and small." He looked down at the child. "This one is no more than four and a half pounds. 'Tis a miracle he's alive."

My heart warmed at seeing Andrew with the baby in his arms, cradling him protectively, risking everything to get him to a safe home.

"Will the queen recover?"

"Aye." He nodded. "She will soon return to normal, and if we are fortunate, no one will learn about the baby or the pregnancy. The scandal would give her enemies justification to hate her and overthrow her power. And if anyone knew the queen had an heir—even an illegitimate heir—the queen's life would be in danger. A male on the throne is more desirable than a female, and one so young can be manipulated and used by people in authority. There are those who would kill the queen to see this boy become king." He looked up at me. "You must never breathe a word to anyone, Cecily. The queen and Kat have worked hard to keep her pregnancy a secret."

"I would never betray my queen." I thought about all the times I'd seen the queen, noticing that she'd put on weight, but she'd always had a tray of sweets with her, and I'd just assumed that she had been eating too many. Even when I saw her in her bed the other day, there had been so many pillows and blankets around her, I hadn't noticed an enlarged stomach.

"Thank you," Andrew said. "I wish you weren't put in this position, but I know we can trust you."

I suddenly realized that if he and I were caught, and someone learned our real identities, my reputation would be ruined. My chances of marrying a Lord of the Realm would disappear, and then Charles would not be free to leave 1563.

We could not be caught.

It took over three hours to reach the outskirts of Hedgerly, north of Windsor Castle. We had passed no one on the road, for which I was thankful, and the sky was still dark, though daybreak was not far off.

Andrew and I had spent much of the walk in silence. We had not been together for this much time since the night we'd kissed, and I wasn't sure what was left to say between us.

The baby started to fuss, and Andrew bounced him gently as he spoke soft words of comfort, but the baby didn't settle.

"He's getting hungry," Andrew said.

"May I try? My sister had a baby in 1913, and I spent a lot of time with her before—" I couldn't finish the sentence. I didn't like to talk about my death.

Andrew slowly transferred the baby into my arms.

The little bundle was warm and lighter than I'd imagined. He wore a soft nightgown, and he smelled of fresh soap. My heart ached for the baby, knowing what he would face if anyone ever learned the truth about his identity—and mourning for both him and the queen. It must have been torture for her to give up her child. I prayed the family in Hedgerly was kind and good to him.

The baby continued to cry, so I gently placed my little finger on his bottom lip. He latched on without effort and began to suck, quieting his fussing for a little while, perhaps.

Andrew watched me, his face filled with tenderness. "You look natural with a baby."

I couldn't meet his gaze, my longing for him—for this—so fierce it took my breath away. "I miss my niece." It was all I said, though I wanted to say so much more.

A candle came into sight as we walked over a little bridge.

"There," Andrew said.

The baby started to lose interest in my finger and began to cry again as we hurried our footsteps to the cottage.

Neither of us spoke as we walked up the path to the front door, where a wreath hung.

I glanced around to see if anyone was awake in the village—but I saw no movement.

Andrew knocked on the door, and it sounded louder than normal as the rest of the village slept. He waited a moment and then knocked again.

Finally, there was a sound in the cottage, and the door slowly opened.

A bleary-eyed man appeared. He was clean-shaven and had a pleasant face.

"May I help you?" he asked—but as soon as he saw the baby in my arms, his eyes opened wide.

"We've come to bring the baby," Andrew said.

"Aye." The man didn't hesitate, didn't even blink as he reached for the bundle in my arms.

I was both relieved and sad to let the baby go, but I handed him over, thankful that he would get something to eat.

"Thank you," Andrew said.

The man simply nodded and then closed the door without another word.

Andrew and I stared at the closed door for a second—and then the candle in the window was snuffed, and our job was done.

I felt Andrew's hand on my elbow as he said, "We need to find an inn. We'll wait until tomorrow night to make our way back."

The weight of the coins in my pocket reminded me that our job wasn't quite done, after all. We needed to get back without being detected.

How would Kat explain my absence from court? I had a feeling she would go to the chaperone in my dormitory and ask for her complete silence, and then they would fabricate a story for the other maids and ladies in waiting—perhaps that I was ill and sequestered in another part of the castle, or with Charles again. Whatever story they told, I would be apprised when I returned so I could play along with the ruse.

"Is there an inn in Hedgerly?" I asked Andrew.

"'Tis best we move on to a different village. This one is too small, and if anyone realizes the Southern family has a new baby and saw two strangers come through, they might start asking unwanted questions."

"Where will we go?"

"Let's return the way we've come. Farnham Heath is a larger village, and I saw an inn there."

We turned and headed back. Farnham Heath was about thirty

minutes behind us. My feet ached, and I was exhausted, but I wouldn't complain.

The darkness started to soften as we came into the village. The path curved, and several buildings came within sight. There was one that looked like an inn or a pub, with candles in the windows, though there was no movement outside.

As we drew closer, I saw *The Olde Bell Inn* sign above the door.

Andrew paused before entering the building. "Mayhap we should say we're married. It would raise fewer questions."

I had not anticipated any of this, but I nodded, knowing we had little choice.

He opened the door, and we passed inside. The ceiling was low, and the room was dark. There were two men at a corner table, cups of ale in front of them. Both were clearly drunk, and one was in a stupor.

"Frank," the other one called in a slurred voice, "you got some fancy customers."

There was a shuffling noise, and an older man appeared through a short doorway next to the bar. He wore a dirty apron, and his face needed a shave. "What can I do for you?"

"My wife and I need a room," Andrew said without hesitating or stumbling over his words.

I stepped closer to him as the men inspected me. My dress was simple, but it was still made of the finest material and craftsmanship. It would draw attention in a place like this.

"I have one room available," the man said as he reached under the counter and pulled out a key. "Do you and the missus need something to eat?"

Andrew looked at me, and I shook my head.

The less I talked, the better. I didn't want any more attention than we were already getting.

The innkeeper handed over the key and told us which room we could use on the second floor. Andrew paid for the room as the innkeeper brought us a candle.

When we were ready, Andrew led me toward our room.

"I'm sorry, Cecily," he whispered as we climbed the narrow stairwell, concern in his voice. "'Tis not an ideal situation—none of it."

"I will be fine." I admired the way the candlelight flickered on his handsome features. "We are doing this for our qu—" I paused, not wanting to say more than I should, in case someone was listening.

Andrew unlocked the narrow door, and we passed inside.

The candle sent shadows to the corners of the small room, and what I saw caused me to shrink back, pressing into Andrew. It was dirty, run-down, and, if the disheveled, soiled bedding was any indication, probably infested with vermin.

Andrew's free hand slipped around my waist. "I'm sorry," he said again. "I know this isn't what you're used to."

"I cannot sleep in that bed." I didn't want to sound like a spoiled or sniveling child, but I was certain I would regret laying my head on the pillow.

"Aye." He slowly closed the door. "We'll sit on the floor, against the wall. You can lean on me and try to get a bit of sleep. 'Tis not ideal, but we have little choice."

He walked to the far wall, which was less than ten feet away, and set the candle on the floor. Then he slowly lowered to the ground and reached out his hand toward me.

His eyes were so calm, so reassuring, despite our circumstances. I couldn't help but feel safe.

I joined him, sitting on the ground beside him.

Neither of us spoke for a moment as my shoulder pressed into his arm. I watched the candlelight, trying not to look at the room.

"Thank you for coming with me tonight," he finally said. "I know things have been a bit . . . awkward between us."

A scampering noise in the opposite corner made me press closer to him, and he put his arm around me.

I wasn't usually skittish, but I didn't want to know what else was occupying this room.

"Charles has asked me—" He paused. "Now that the queen is on the mend."

I looked up at him. "Charles has asked you what?"

He turned his face toward me, and we were so close, my heart began to beat a wild rhythm.

"He thinks 'tis best if I return to Arundel Castle," Andrew said softly.

"Leave?"

"Aye."

I didn't respond. What could I say?

Instead, I laid my head against his shoulder, and his arm tightened around me.

"I will miss you, Andrew," I whispered, tears gathering in my eyes.

"I want you to be happy." He took my hand in his and ran his thumb over my fingers. "I wish I could be your knight in shining armor and rescue you from the choice you have to make, but I will trust and pray that whatever plans God has in store for you, you will find happiness."

"I cannot imagine it to be possible." I wiped my tears with the back of my free hand. "But I'm learning that I can survive hard things."

He laced his fingers through mine and gave them a gentle squeeze. "He never leaves us, nor forsakes us, though sometimes, 'tis hard to understand His ways."

God had been with me through each hardship and difficulty, and He would be my strength through this one.

We were quiet again as the sky lightened beyond the one, small window in the room. I was tired in body and soul, but I could not sleep.

"Thank you," I finally whispered.

"For what?" he asked as he rubbed my hand again.

"For helping me find joy and purpose again."

He slowly lifted my hand to his lips and placed a kiss there.

"I don't know how I'm going to explain all of this to your stepbrother," Andrew said with a sigh. "We have a busy day in Newport tomorrow. Evelyn and Charles have planned a fundraiser.

He won't know, yet, that we've spent the night at an inn together until he and I come back here. But it's going to be hard not to say anything to him tomorrow in 1883."

"Why would you need to explain? Surely Kat will make some excuse for us. And if the worst happens, you can just tell him the truth, that we came here to take care of the baby."

"Charles can never know about the baby, Cecily." He pulled away slightly, so I would look up at him. "You must never tell him or anyone else—no matter how inconsequential you think it might be."

I nodded and quickly said, "I promise I won't."

He relaxed again, and I laid my head on his shoulder.

"It just feels dishonest not to tell him that we're at this inn together," Andrew said. "If anyone knew . . ." He didn't finish the sentence, because I knew what would happen.

"No one will find out," I assured him. "We'll wait to return until night, and Kat will do everything to protect our reputations."

His hand tightened around mine, but he didn't speak.

Ever so slowly, I drifted off to sleep. And, despite the unpleasant room around us and the threat of being discovered, I'd never felt more comfortable or peaceful in my life.

Andrew had been a godsend. A gift amidst the heartache and loss.

20

CHARLES

AUGUST 3, 1883
NEWPORT, RHODE ISLAND

The day was overcast, but there was no rain as I stood on the tennis court, warming up for my match against the US Tennis Champion. Evelyn and I had come to the Newport Casino right after lunch to oversee the plans for the match, as well as the dinner and dance that would follow. Tickets were sold out, and the event had become the talk of the town. Even now, the galleries were full, and more people were coming onto the grassy lawn to watch the match.

I was happy for Evelyn and the Newport Home for Friendless Children. We'd exceeded our fundraising goals, and the orphanage would benefit beyond what Evelyn had hoped.

But, despite the success, there were so many things weighing on my mind, and my mood was as gray as the clouds.

Queen Elizabeth's worsening condition had created near panic among the privy council. I had finally been well enough to join their meeting, but the division among the council had been exhausting. The letter that I'd sent to Mary, Queen of Scots, would not have arrived yet, and even if it had, the others believed it would encourage the Scottish queen to make haste to Windsor. I knew differently. There had been talk of sending a special messenger on horseback to get to Mary faster than the armed guards who carried the letter. But I worked hard to convince the council to wait another day, hoping Queen Elizabeth would recover. I'd spent much of my time trying to convince the council that Lady Katherine was a better choice to replace the queen, should it come to that. But several were hard to sway.

Drew had been with the queen all day and had shared no word about her status. When I had woken up in 1883, I wanted to talk to him to see if the queen had made any improvement the day before, but I could not find him. If I didn't know better, I would think he was avoiding me. He hadn't joined us for breakfast or lunch, and I hadn't seen him since Evelyn and I had arrived at the casino.

A cheer arose from the crowd as Mr. Sears appeared, wearing a white shirt and a pair of white trousers. The third annual US Tennis Championship would begin tomorrow, and many people had come early to get one more opportunity to watch Mr. Sears play. I wasn't under any delusion that I would beat him, but I would give it my best shot—especially because Evelyn had come out onto the lawn with her mother and a few other friends to watch.

As the audience cheered for Mr. Sears, Evelyn's attention was on me. She smiled, and I smiled back, but something had changed between us that day in the library. Her old reserve had been put back in place. It wasn't as intense, but it was there to protect her. Would she never trust me with her past?

Today was the last day I would be in Newport. That had to be heavy on her mind, as well. Would we ever see each other again? I tried to be stoic about the whole thing, but I'd told her I loved her in the library, and she had not returned my feelings. I didn't expect her to, though I longed for her to say she loved me. Yet—what could come of such a declaration? Perhaps she was wiser than me and would not allow herself to say something she might regret as the years came between us.

I forced myself to put thoughts of Evelyn and 1563 aside as I jogged to the net and shook hands with Mr. Sears. I'd met him earlier, but it was still proper etiquette to greet one another before the match began.

A newspaper reporter snapped a picture of us, but I tried to turn my face so he would not get a good image of me. Mr. Sears was a congenial man with a wide mustache. He was athletic and lean and would be a fierce competitor.

"Thank you for agreeing to participate in this match," I told him. "The orphans will benefit greatly from today's events."

"I'm happy to help," he said with a nod. "May the best man win."

We left the net and took our places. I would serve first, which I did as soon as the head referee gave me the signal.

Mr. Sears was a tough competitor, as I knew he would be, though I held my own against him and ended up winning two of the five sets. In the end, he took the fifth and final set and the crowd cheered.

When it was time to shake hands again, I was sweating and tired, but proud of playing my best. "I wish you success in the tournament tomorrow," I told him. "I have no doubt you'll be the champion again."

"Thanks." He glanced at Evelyn, who was approaching. "But I'm looking forward to attending the dinner and dance tonight." He nodded in her direction. "Is she spoken for?"

My hand tightened around Mr. Sears's, but I had to be honest. "I don't believe so."

He let go of my hand and gave his full attention to Evelyn.

She smiled at Mr. Sears, offering her hand to congratulate him, but her gaze kept trailing to me as he spoke to her.

I toweled the sweat off my brow as others came up to congratulate me for a job well done.

When everyone else had moved away, Helen Whitney approached. "And to think," she said, "if you hadn't come to Newport at Drew's invitation, none of this would have happened, *Lord Norfolk*."

The way she drew out *Lord* was concerning, though I might have imagined it.

"You are correct," Evelyn said as she left Mr. Sears and joined me to face her aunt. "We are so fortunate he came when he did, or the orphanage would not be the recipient of the largest donation in their history. The money will allow them to have better care, more nutrition, and updated clothing. Not to mention more awareness in the community."

"That's what I was just thinking," Evelyn's aunt said with a tight smile as she lifted her eyebrow at me. "Awareness is so important, is it not, *Lord* Norfolk? But the most important thing is what we do with the information we've been given. Sometimes, we should act immediately—and other times, we should keep the information close and put it to use when it is most beneficial."

My pulse ticked high as Helen kept her cool eyes on me. Thankfully, there was no one close enough to hear our conversation.

Evelyn lifted her chin, steel in her eyes as she said, "Only when the information is used for good, and not to hurt innocent people." Her gaze traveled to her mother, who was congratulating Mr. Sears. She lowered her voice. "Not everyone is privy to the information."

Helen's lips pursed as her eyes narrowed. "I can't believe that some people who should know are unaware."

"Unfortunately, it's true." Evelyn's voice didn't waver. "And I would hate for someone innocent to suffer for something they didn't do—no matter how much it might benefit someone else. Some things are not worth the damage that could happen."

The two women stared at each other for a heartbeat, and then Helen turned and walked away.

"I wonder how long she's known," I said quietly.

Evelyn's jaw was tight as she watched her aunt blend into the crowd. "Long enough."

"Will she try to cause a scandal—or blackmail us?" I ran the towel over the back of my neck to look nonchalant, but every one of my muscles was tight with concern.

"I don't know, but she is biding her time. She could have made it known right now but chose not to."

"Perhaps it's best that I'm leaving tonight."

Evelyn looked at me, and for the first time all week, I saw vulnerability in her eyes. She had been pretending that my departure wasn't affecting her, but I could see it was.

"You cannot leave before Mother's ball."

I frowned. "Ball? What ball?"

"It was meant to be a surprise for both of us. I think she was hoping she might convince you to propose to me if she could impress you with all the important people she knows. I only found out about it this afternoon when one of her friends accidentally told me."

"A surprise ball? To draw out a proposal from me?" I couldn't help but smile.

If only it was that easy.

"She has it planned for two days from now."

"But I promised Congressman Reinhold that I would leave after the match today. If I stay, he will tell everyone what he's learned."

"I've spoken to Congressman Reinhold," she said, "and explained the situation. Mother invited Mr. McAllister and Mrs. Astor, and they've both accepted. She's elated, because they've never accepted one of Aunt Helen's invitations. Once the newspapers hear that Mrs. Astor was at Mother's ball, it will solidify her success and triumph over Aunt Helen once and for all. Congressman Reinhold was not happy, but he understands and does not want to force my mother to answer uncomfortable questions if you should happen to leave before her ball."

I studied Evelyn as she spoke, trying to understand what *she* wanted. "Do you want me to stay, Evelyn?"

She was quiet for a moment as her blue eyes sought mine. "I wouldn't have begged the congressman to give you two more days if I didn't want you here."

My heart warmed at her words. "And what about your aunt?"

"I have a feeling she's known about your identity for a while and hasn't chosen to reveal it, yet."

"Perhaps she's waiting for your mother's ball, to cause a scandal in front of everyone."

Evelyn put her hands on my arm. "I will speak to her, Charles, explain that Mother doesn't know who you truly are and that she welcomed you into our home in good faith."

I was very aware of the weight of her hands on my arm, and I had to stop myself from putting my hand over hers. "I don't think it'll stop her."

"Whether you leave or stay," she said, her voice still quiet so that no one around us might hear, "she knows the truth. Stay—for a little while longer. For me."

I would probably regret my decision, but I couldn't say no to her. If we only had two more days, it would have to be enough.

"I'll stay," I said. "For you—and for your mother's ball."

Evelyn's smile was warm as she nodded and removed her hands from my arm. "Thank you."

"Have you seen Drew?" I asked.

Evelyn shook her head as she scanned the galleries. "No. I spoke to him briefly before we came to the casino, and he said he was going to be here, but I saved him a seat and he never came to sit with Mother and me."

I also scanned the galleries, but I couldn't see him, either.

"Should we be concerned?" she asked me.

I let out a heavy sigh as I set my towel over the back of a lawn chair. "I think he's avoiding me because something happened in 1563, but I don't know what it could be. The queen has been very ill. I hope something didn't happen to her and he has been waiting for me to learn about it tomorrow so it wouldn't affect my day here."

"We'll both hope for that," she said. "But for now, we need to prepare for the dinner. Hopefully Drew will come soon. He has a ticket for the meal and the dance tonight."

I hoped so, too, but I wasn't sure he'd make it.

Something was wrong, and Drew didn't want me to know.

The dinner went off without trouble, and then the ballroom was cleared for dancing. The orphanage directors, Mr. and Mrs. Flanders, were invited to attend as guests of honor, and they seemed to have the most fun of all. Evelyn had arranged childcare, and the older couple were taking advantage of the night off, smiling and visiting and answering questions about the Newport Home for Friendless Children. Attendees had been making donations above and beyond their ticket prices, and Evelyn's eyes shined bright with the success.

I had not had a moment alone with Evelyn since the match ended, and I searched the room for her now. We'd been seated at different tables for dinner. Congressman Reinhold had one eye on me from where he sat, and Helen Whitney had another eye on me from her side of the room.

Neither one made a move to reveal my identity, but it was only a matter of when and not if they would. Congressman Reinhold had no reason to share the truth unless I threatened his daughter in some way or didn't leave after Mrs. Whitney's ball. But Helen was a different matter. Could Evelyn convince her aunt not to say something, especially now that Mrs. Astor had accepted Minnie's invitation? Did Helen know Mrs. Astor would be at Mrs. Whitney's ball? Would Helen use the information to finally win the war with her sister-in-law?

I caught a glimpse of Drew as he stood with his mother near the ballroom doors. He'd arrived in time for the dinner but had been seated at a different table. Though he'd acknowledged me, he hadn't sought me out, and, if I wasn't mistaken, he was about to leave now as his mother pleaded with him to stay.

As I approached, he spoke quickly to Mrs. Whitney and then started to walk toward the door.

I jogged to catch up to him as he entered the dim lobby. It was empty, except for a young clerk who manned the front desk on the opposite side of the room.

"Drew."

He paused, his shoulders stiff as he turned to me.

"What's going on?" I asked him. "Why have you avoided me today?" I took a step closer to him and lowered my voice, though the clerk was so far away, he wouldn't be able to hear us. "Is it the queen?"

"No." He glanced toward the door leading out of the casino, clearly eager to get away, but said, "She is doing much better. I think you'll be pleased with her improvement over the coming week."

Relief washed over me. "That's great news! Why have you avoided telling me?"

"I haven't avoided telling you." His tone was short. "You've been busy. I thought the news could wait for tomorrow."

Drew was easy to read—at least, he had been before he came to Windsor Castle. Something else was bothering him. "What's wrong?"

"Nothing." He lifted his chin. "I'll prepare to return to Arundel tomorrow. You won't need to worry about me anymore."

So that was what was bothering him. He was no longer needed and would have to say good-bye to Cecily.

I put my hand on his shoulder, knowing exactly how he felt. "I think it's best."

He didn't meet my gaze but nodded and then said, "I'm heading home. I don't feel like dancing tonight."

"I don't blame you."

Drew left the casino without another word.

"Is something wrong?" Evelyn asked as she walked up behind me, surprising me with her arrival.

I turned toward her, taken again by the lovely gown she wore. It was dark blue, pulled up to a bustle in the back with a slight train. The color made her eyes sparkle, even in the dim lobby. She was stunning, and my longing for her only increased.

"I think Drew is having a hard time saying good-bye to Cecily."

"Your stepsister?"

I nodded. "He's in love with her."

"But he's a commoner there?"

"Yes. And he has responsibilities here."

She glanced toward the door where he'd just left, and there was complete understanding in her face. When she looked back to me, she asked, "Is there any way for them to be together?"

I had to shake my head.

Her shoulders fell, and anger mixed with her sadness as she went to a sofa in the corner. There were ferns to offer privacy, so I followed her there and took a seat next to her.

"I hate this burden we carry," she said.

"Even if he didn't have his responsibilities to his family here, he still couldn't marry her in 1563. The queen would never approve—and to be honest, I wouldn't, either."

"Why not?"

"It's not because I don't think he would make her happy," I added quickly. "But she needs financial security and a titled husband, two things he couldn't provide for her."

"Ever since I was young," she said as she studied my face, "it has amazed me that the same time-crosser could occupy two paths and possess all of the same character qualities, personality traits, and morals—and yet, the only thing that determined their perceived worth to the world was where they were born."

"I think you've landed on one of the biggest problems with humanity." I gently took her gloved hand into mine. "I am the same man both here and in 1563, yet it is my birth that dictates my value and how I might live my life . . . and who I might love."

She looked down at our hands and slowly turned hers over, so our palms touched, and laced our fingers together. "No one can tell you who you might love," she said in a whisper. "Your birth cannot determine that for you."

I inhaled at the feeling of her fingers wrapping around mine.

Her lips parted as if she was going to say more, but then she hesitated.

"What is it?"

Her face looked so much younger—so fragile and uncertain. "I want to tell you about my other path, Charles. I want you to know, so that after you have all the facts, you can decide if your love for me is strong enough to overcome the truth."

"There is nothing you could say that would change how I feel about you."

"I wish it was true, but I cannot let you leave without telling you about my past." She let out a sigh and shook her head. "I know it doesn't matter—that we cannot change the outcome of our lives. You need the investment from my father, and if he learned that you pretended to be the earl, he would not only withdraw his support, but he'd forbid me from seeing you again. If I disobeyed his wishes and people learned the truth, the scandal would ruin my mother, and I couldn't live with myself if I hurt her. But there is a part of me that knows I must be honest with you. You deserve nothing less."

"I deserve nothing," I said, longing to know all of Evelyn, though she didn't owe me an explanation.

"You do, and that's why—"

"There you are!" Mrs. Whitney appeared beside the fern but paused as she saw us holding hands. Her surprise turned to delight and then sheer triumph. "Well, look at this."

I stood and helped Evelyn to her feet and then let go of her hand.

"It's not what it looks like, Mother," Evelyn said, her cheeks turning pink. "I mean—it is—but—"

"Say no more." Mrs. Whitney ran her gloved fingers over her lips as if she was buttoning them. "We will not make an announcement until the ball in two days."

"Mrs. Whitney." I stepped forward. "There will be no announcement."

"Of course there will." Her amenable voice turned rigid for a moment, revealing a new side of her I hadn't seen until now. But she quickly covered it with a smile. "I've suspected for several weeks that you two had fallen in love. It's written all over your faces." She stepped into the little alcove created by the ferns and took Evelyn's hand. "Now, I will not let you out of my sight until after the announcement, Evelyn. If someone else had come across the two of you, what would they think? It would start rumors before we're ready to share the good news." Her face became serious again as she said, "I eagerly wait for you to become my son-in-law, Lord Norfolk. This match will be good for all of us. I will become the mother of a countess! Can you imagine how many doors that will open for our family? And you, Lord Norfolk, will have a beautiful heiress—with a tidy dowry, I must add—to help with your castle."

I opened my mouth to protest again, but Mrs. Whitney whisked Evelyn away before I could speak.

Evelyn glanced at me over her shoulder as they disappeared. She hadn't told me about her other path, so I followed her and Mrs. Whitney into the ballroom, hoping to get another chance to speak to her.

But Mrs. Whitney was true to her word. She didn't let Evelyn out of her sight again.

21

CECILY

AUGUST 4, 1563
FARNHAM HEATH, ENGLAND

I slowly opened my eyes and winced as I lifted my cheek off Andrew's shoulder. My neck was stiff, and my bottom was numb.

"Good morrow, Lady Cecily," Andrew said gently, his voice clear, telling me he'd been awake for some time but had let me sleep.

"Good morrow," I said, feeling self-conscious as the early morning daylight brightened the room, making me aware of my appearance. I hadn't taken the time to style my hair the night before, and the hem of my gown was soiled from the long walk from the castle.

The room didn't look as bad in the light of day as I had imagined the night before, though the bedding needed some attention. There were no cobwebs in the corner or dust on the simple furniture.

"What time is it?" I asked with a yawn.

"I'm not sure, but it can't be past seven."

"Seven?" I looked toward the window. "Then we haven't slept long."

"You can sleep longer, if you'd like."

I slowly shook my head. "I need to use the necessary. And I'm hungry."

He stood and offered me his hand, helping me off the ground.

When I was on my feet, I touched my hair, smoothing back the loose strands.

Andrew smiled. "You look beautiful."

I slowly lowered my hand and returned his smile. "Thank you."

He went to the door and placed his hand on the knob but paused. "'Tis a risk to be seen in the tavern together. 'Tis still early enough, though, so hopefully there won't be many people here. We'll sit in a quiet corner and hope we're not noticed."

Andrew opened the door, and we both stepped into the narrow hallway.

Everything looked different in the daylight as we walked down the hall to the stairway. It was enclosed and just as narrow as everything else in the inn. Andrew allowed me to walk ahead of him, but he reached out and grasped my waist when I stumbled over a broken floorboard.

I briefly closed my eyes, loving the protective feel of his hands on me. I wasn't sure if he was aware of what his touch did to me, but I never wanted him to stop.

When we entered the tavern, I was relieved to see that there were few people inside. The innkeeper was behind the bar, and there were two tables with patrons, all men, who were eating breakfast. Everyone looked up at our arrival, but I kept my face lowered, while Andrew kept his hand on me.

The innkeeper told me where to find the necessary, so I slipped out the side door as Andrew ordered our meal.

The humidity was still thick, and the heat was oppressive as I quickly took care of my needs and then left the necessary and entered the yard. Farnham Heath was a significant village, and people were busy on the street.

As I walked toward the inn, a man caught my attention. He stood out among the commoners, dressed like a nobleman with his richly colored clothing and feathered hat. He was limping as he walked toward the inn, scanning the street—until he saw me and paused.

My heart thudded to a stop as I recognized him.

Lord Wolverton.

I quickly stepped into the inn as dread filled my heart.

Andrew sat at a table in the corner. He smiled at my arrival, but his smile quickly fell. "What's wrong?"

"Lord Wolverton," I said as I bumped into a chair, trying to get to Andrew. "He's here—outside."

The door to the inn opened and Lord Wolverton's gaze swept the room, falling on me and then on Andrew.

Andrew rose from his chair and put his arm out, as if to protect me.

Lord Wolverton stood at the open door, allowing light to filter into the dim tavern.

The innkeeper and the other patrons stared at him, and then looked at Andrew and me.

No one said a word.

Finally, Andrew stepped away from the table. "Perhaps we should take this conversation outside."

The innkeeper looked disappointed.

Andrew turned and offered me his hand. I took it, tentatively, a question in my eyes.

We walked out of the tavern and met Lord Wolverton on the road, but Andrew didn't stop there. He led me around the side of the tavern to the backyard, where the necessary was located.

"What is the meaning of this?" Lord Wolverton asked, his face red from anger. He was limping hard as he followed us. "Lady Cecily, I knew you loved him, but I didn't think you would be foolish enough to anger the queen and throw your life away for him."

Despite the threat of being discovered, something softened in Andrew's eyes. Didn't he know I loved him?

"Well?" Lord Wolverton asked.

Andrew turned back to him. "How did you find us?"

"I followed you," he said, as if it was obvious. "I couldn't sleep last night and was on the terrace to try to get some relief from the heat. I saw you leave with a bag and suspected that you were running off together to elope."

A bag? He hadn't known it was a baby? No matter what happened, Lord Wolverton could not find out about the queen's child.

"But I didn't get far before I twisted my ankle," he said with a growl as he motioned to his leg. "I was too far away from Windsor Castle to turn back, so I asked for the nearest village to find a horse and was told to come here." He glared at Andrew. "Imagine my surprise to see Lady Cecily in this repulsive place. If you are going to marry her in secret, the least you could do is treat her like the lady she is and bring her to decent lodgings."

"Marry?" Andrew asked.

I squeezed his hand to quiet him.

Lord Wolverton's eyes opened wide. "Surely you are married!" He took a menacing step forward and then winced. "If you have taken her virtue and not married her—"

"He would never take my virtue." My heart pounded so hard, I was afraid I might faint. If the news returned to the castle that Andrew and I were married—and then people found out it wasn't true—we'd be in more trouble than we already were. But I didn't know what else to say. "Of course we're married."

Andrew studied me, a thousand questions in his eyes. Finally, he turned to Lord Wolverton. "This was the closest location we could get to before daylight. My wife needed to rest."

It was one thing to lie to the innkeeper, but another entirely to lie to Lord Wolverton. The innkeeper would have no way of knowing if it was true. Lord Wolverton, on the other hand, could easily demand proof.

"I have never been more appalled or disappointed in my life," Lord Wolverton said to me. "To think I've wasted all this time. Why didn't you just tell me that my suit would be rejected?"

I pressed my lips together, realizing how close I'd come to promising to marry him. If I had, and then I'd ended up here with Andrew, Lord Wolverton could have demanded Andrew's arrest. An engagement was almost as binding as a marriage, and a commoner running off with a nobleman's wife was unimaginable.

"I'm sorry, my lord," I told him, truly contrite. "I did not mean to hurt you."

"I'm not hurt," he spat. "Just angry and disappointed." His jaw muscles twitched. "And in need of a horse so I can go back to Windsor and gather my things to return to Alnwick." His lips turned down in a scowl as he said, "The queen will be made aware of this union as soon as I reach the castle."

And with those portending words, he limped away from the inn.

I still held Andrew's hand as I turned to him. "I'm sorry I had to tell him we were married," I whispered. "I didn't know what else to say. He couldn't know about the baby."

"What will Charles think when he hears? It was bad enough that I kept you overnight in an inn."

"There was no other excuse for us leaving in the middle of the night," I continued, realizing the ramifications of my reckless statement could haunt me forever. I let go of Andrew's hand, panic tightening my throat. "There's nothing else to be done, Andrew. We'll need to be married before we return to the castle. If we don't have proof, things will be far worse for both of us."

"I could not do that to you. You are a noblewoman, Cecily. The queen would never approve, and I could not be the cause of your ruin."

"We are doing this for the queen. Surely she'll understand when we explain what happened. She knows why we left the castle, and Kat will vouch for us."

He lifted his troubled gaze to me. "I hope you're right, but she will still be forced to punish us. What would people think if she simply allowed a secret marriage between her maid of honour and a lowly doctor? It would draw unwanted questions."

I nibbled my bottom lip as I realized he spoke the truth. The queen could not let this go unpunished if she didn't want to raise suspicions. Would marrying Andrew make things better or worse?

"But if Lord Wolverton tells the castle he saw us together," Andrew added, "and we do not have a marriage certificate, it would be detrimental to your reputation. The marriage would need to be in name only, and once I leave 1563 and you become a widow, at least you can still marry a nobleman. But if we do not have a marriage certificate, you will be ostracized, and no one would marry you then."

My breath caught as his words pierced my heart.

As soon as he left.

Even if Andrew married me, he would still choose 1883. Nothing had changed.

But he was right. It would be better to be a widow of a commoner than a fallen woman.

"I think we must marry, Andrew. We have few other options."

We looked at each other for several seconds before Andrew said, "Only if you're certain."

I nodded, though my heart was breaking. This was not how I had imagined this moment.

It took us all day to find a vicar who was willing to perform a wedding ceremony without the reading of the banns, or a special license from the bishop of the diocese. In the end, we were able to persuade a vicar in Wexham, about three miles away from Farnham Heath, with the bag of coins Kat had given me the night before.

He told us to return around dusk so we drew less attention.

As the sun set, Andrew and I stood in a little stone chapel in Wexham, with the vicar's sweet wife acting as witness.

I had tried to freshen up, but my gown was a mess, and I was exhausted from the lack of sleep. It was not the wedding of my dreams—yet, when I stood facing Andrew, none of it mattered. I was marrying the boy I had loved as a child and the man I had fallen in love with again as a young woman. My heart wanted to burst with joy, yet my mind tempered those feelings by reminding me that this wasn't going to be a real marriage. It would be in name only. A way to protect me once he was gone.

His brown eyes were warm and gentle as he took my hands in his. "I, Andrew Patrick Bromley, will have and hold you from this day forward." His voice was so serious, full of such conviction, my heart wanted desperately to believe this was real. "For better, for worse, for richer, for poorer, in sickness and in health." He paused again as his hands tightened around mine. "To love and to cherish you, Lady Cecily," he said tenderly, "till death us do part."

Tears stung my eyes, wishing that he was not marrying me out of obligation, but because he wanted to spend his life with me, all of it.

"'Tis your turn, Lady Cecily," the vicar said to me.

I repeated after him as I looked deeply into Andrew's eyes. Perhaps he couldn't promise me forever, but I could promise it to him. My vows could be real. "I, Cecily Abigail Pembrooke, take thee, Andrew Bromley, to be my wedded husband." I inhaled. "To have and to hold from this day forward, for better, for worse, for richer, for poorer, in sickness and in health, to love, cherish, and to obey, till death us do part."

"Forasmuch as Andrew and Cecily have consented together in holy wedlock," the vicar said, "and have witnessed the same before God and this company, and thereto have given and pledged their troth, each to the other, and have declared the same by joining of hands; I pronounce that they be man and wife together, in the name of the Father, and of the Son, and of the Holy Ghost." He made a cross with his hands. "Amen."

"Amen," I whispered.

"Amen," Andrew echoed.

The vicar said a final prayer, and then he nodded and smiled as his wife joined us to give her best wishes.

"You're a lovely couple," she said with a knowing smile. "If this one isn't a happy union, Thomas is in the wrong business."

"My dear," the vicar said with a laugh, "of course it will be a happy union. Just look at them."

They turned their approving smiles on us, and I felt like an imposter as Andrew entwined our fingers and stepped closer to me.

"Thank you," he said to the vicar, handing him the bag of coins. "We appreciate your willingness to marry us so quickly."

"Of course." He handed Andrew the marriage certificate. "Go in peace."

We left the little chapel and stepped into the hot August evening. The sun had set, but there was a bit of light in the western sky, turning the world a soft shade of pink.

In less than twenty-four hours, my world had shifted. I had the very thing my heart desired, yet it was just a mirage. Something that would disappear as if it had never been.

"Do you want to go back to Windsor this evening?" he asked quietly.

I shook my head. "The damage has already been done. The sooner we return, the sooner we will face punishment."

I felt a yawn come over me, but I tried to hide it from him.

"You haven't slept," he said. "You need some rest."

"You need rest, too."

"Truth be told, I'm uneasy about going to bed. No doubt word has gotten back to Windsor Castle and Charles knows what we've done. I'll have to face him in 1883 tomorrow, and he will be very angry."

"Angry is an understatement." I would have to face him, too, but he would not be as kind or understanding with Andrew.

"Let's find an inn for a proper meal and some rest," he said. "Our fate will await us later."

He offered his arm, and I accepted it. We walked down the lane to the village center with the soft glow of sunset all around us. And though our wedding wasn't planned or desired—at least by Andrew—everything felt different. For better or worse, I had a husband, the man I loved. Even if he wasn't planning to stay in 1563, I had him until his birthday in December. Four months.

It wasn't long, but I wouldn't be the first or last bride to lose a husband so quickly. Might I persuade him to love me, for the short time we had left?

I had taken my marriage vows seriously. I would love him and honor him until death parted us. Despite my earlier intentions, I wanted a real marriage, no matter what that meant.

But how did I convey that to Andrew? And what if he didn't want what I wanted?

We found a quaint inn and ordered a warm meal. This time, I didn't feel a twinge of guilt when Andrew called me his wife or asked for a single room to share. We were married in the eyes of God and man, a reality that sent a bittersweet thrill up my spine.

When our meal was done, we walked up the steps to the second floor and Andrew unlocked our room.

Though it was small, this room was clean and well kept.

I stepped inside, a candle in my hand, as Andrew followed me and closed the door.

My pulse was thrumming as I tried to even out my breathing.

"I'll sleep on the floor again," he said. "You should have the bed."

I slowly turned to him, a new thought on my mind.

Was he betrothed or married to someone else in 1883? Was that why he didn't want to make our marriage real?

"Andrew," I said tentatively, not sure how to approach the topic as I set the candle on a nearby table.

"Aye?"

"Are you—do you—"

He lowered himself to the ground and settled against the wall. "What are you trying to ask me, Cecily?"

It didn't pay to circle the issue. We were married now. I would need to be open and honest with him, no matter how uncomfortable it might be. "Do you love someone else? Someone in 1883? Are you married or betrothed there?"

His face was serious as he said, "No."

I walked across the small room and slowly lowered myself to the ground, facing him.

He watched me, his thoughts unreadable.

I was being bold, but I didn't care. I'd already lost 1913 and was facing the loss of the man I loved in December. I was tired of playing coy and unaffected. I was ready to make my life what I desired. We would face consequences for our marriage, so why not enjoy the benefits from it?

Gently, I reached for his hand and whispered, "I want to have a real marriage, Andrew."

Several emotions warred within his eyes as he laced his fingers through mine. Desire, regret, joy, sadness. "You know I can't stay, Cecily."

"I don't care." I moved a little closer to him. "I want you, for as long as I can have you. I love you."

He groaned quietly as he placed his hand on my face and leaned his forehead against mine. "I love you, too," he said softly. "And as much as I want to be selfish and have you for myself, I know I can't promise you forever."

"No one can promise forever," I whispered, tears in my eyes. "We don't know what the future holds."

"I know it doesn't hold a place for me here." His voice was strained as he lifted his forehead off mine. "If I could choose you and 1563, I would do it in a heartbeat, without a second thought. But I've always known I have a responsibility to my family in 1883, Cecily. I can't be selfish there, either."

I placed my hand over his and closed my eyes, knowing he was right. *I* was being selfish, asking him for something he couldn't give me. Even if we lived as man and wife for the next four months, there was the chance of a child, and it would be even harder for him to leave me and an unborn baby behind.

"Cecily." He put his other hand on my cheek and lifted my face toward his. "Your title was stripped from you today. You are no longer a lady, and as soon as the queen learns about your marriage to a commoner, you will no longer have a place in her court. We will be required to return to Arundel Castle, and you will be a commoner in a place where you were once the daughter of an earl. I've already taken so much from you."

"You've taken nothing that I haven't freely given. If you recall, it was I who told Lord Wolverton we were married. I was the one who got us into this mess."

He caressed my cheeks with his thumbs. "If you recall," he said, "I didn't put up much of a fight." With a sigh, he added, "But I cannot risk leaving you with a child and no way to support it. I love you too much to give you that life."

I took a deep breath and nodded as I lowered my gaze, embarrassed that I'd even asked for more.

He put his finger under my chin and lifted it until I looked at him.

"But I took my vows seriously when I said them today." He spoke softly. "I will have and hold you from this day forward. For better or worse, for richer or poorer, in sickness and in health." He moved his thumb from my cheek to my lips and brushed them, sending a shiver down my spine. "I will love you and cherish you, until my last breath—here and in 1883."

My tears fell as he captured my lips with his. His kiss was tender and gentle, but it deepened as I moved closer to him.

I felt restraint in his affection—but it was a restraint born of love and sacrifice, not disinterest.

And when I laid my cheek on his chest and felt his arms wrap around me, I slowly drifted off to sleep.

22

CHARLES

AUGUST 4, 1883
NEWPORT, RHODE ISLAND

The moment my eyes opened in 1883, I tore off my covers and leapt from the bed. I didn't wait for the valet to assist me and instead dressed as quickly as I could, anger radiating off my body in waves.

A storm was raging outside Midcliff, and the Atlantic Ocean was in turmoil. It matched my mood as I pulled on my pants and buttoned up my shirt.

How could Drew have run off with Cecily in the middle of the night? Lord Wolverton's arrival back at Windsor late the night before, claiming that he'd found Andrew and Cecily at a run-down inn in Farnham Heath, seemed preposterous. My level-headed stepsister would never do something like that, and Drew wouldn't dare. But when I went looking for them, and no one knew where they had gone, my anger knew no bounds. It was after midnight, so I went to sleep knowing I could confront Drew a lot faster crossing time than if I got on a horse and rode to the inn.

As soon as I was dressed, I rushed out of my room and went down the hall to Drew's bedroom but found it empty.

If he had run off here, too, to avoid speaking to me, I would move heaven and earth to find him. Was that why he had avoided me yesterday? Because he and Cecily had already left Windsor Castle?

Drew was a cad of the worst sort, and I would hold him accountable.

I could hardly see straight as I rushed down the steps and crossed the entrance hall to the breakfast room.

I'd been looking forward to today so I could finally speak to Evelyn about her past. She'd almost opened up the night before at the dance, but Mrs. Whitney had kept her daughter close to her side the rest of the evening.

Now, all I could think about was Drew and Cecily and the repercussions of them running off together.

I still couldn't believe they'd be so foolish.

I entered the breakfast room and found Evelyn and Drew both at the table. Evelyn looked up with a smile, but Drew looked ill.

"I can explain, Charles," he said as he stood.

"How could you?" I asked as I circled the table, never so angry in my life. "You've taken everything from her, and what do you have to offer in exchange?"

Drew went the other way, keeping the table between us. "It's not what you think. I married her—"

"That's *exactly* what I was thinking!" I growled.

Prescott entered the room, but then turned and exited as Evelyn looked between us, truly perplexed.

"You *married* someone?" Evelyn asked Drew.

"Keep your voice down," Drew said to me as we continued to circle the table. "What will the servants think?"

"I don't care," I said. "How could you have taken her away from a future of certainty to one of—of—"

"I promise you"—Drew put up his hands—"it's not what you think. If you'll calm down, I'll try to explain."

"How can you expect me to calm down?" I asked, breathing heavily. "She was going to marry Lord Wolverton, and you took that future from her. Now she will suffer the consequences of the queen's ire, and you've ruined her for future prospects."

"She didn't want to marry Wolverton, and you know it. You told her yourself that she didn't have to. Was that just a ploy to get her to comply?"

That was the wrong thing to say. I raced around the table, but Evelyn stood up and blocked me, putting her hands on my chest.

"We will not get to the bottom of this unless you calm down, Charles." She motioned to the door with her head. "Let's go somewhere private, since the whole household will quickly know something is wrong if we continue to shout in here." She looked at her brother. "And based on the little information I've gleaned, they will never understand what you're talking about. Do you want all of Newport to think you've run off and married someone, Drew?"

I was breathing hard, but the pressure of Evelyn's hands on my chest started to calm me, if only slightly.

"Go to the veranda," Evelyn told her brother. "Charles and I will join you shortly."

Drew kept a cautious eye on me as he left the breakfast room.

After he was gone, Evelyn slowly lowered her hands. "I know you're angry," she said, "but you need to let him explain. Think about Drew. He wouldn't hurt you or Cecily for anything in the world. If he says things aren't as they seem, then let him tell you why. You will only cause more trouble jumping to conclusions."

"You don't understand." I tried to refocus my thoughts. "Her life there is ruined, and if Drew is still planning to leave 1563 on his birthday, then she will be a destitute widow. And if there is a baby . . ." All I could think about was how miserable Ada was after her husband's death. She was a pregnant widow, and all she had was me for support. Who would Cecily have if both Drew and I had to leave her? "I'm not only upset for her—but for me." The truth felt selfish, but it was there, nonetheless. "I can't possibly leave Cecily in a situation like that. I will have to forfeit this path, and my ability to help Mama and Ada, to stay in 1563 and take care of Cecily. Drew's actions don't just affect him and Cecily, they affect me and my family here."

"I realize that," she said. "But please, let him tell you what happened. There must be a reasonable explanation."

I took a deep breath. "I doubt it, but I'll listen."

"Good." She nodded, her face serious. "And when you two are done, I'd like to talk to you, too."

It took me a moment to calm my breathing enough to say, "So would I."

We left the breakfast room and found Drew pacing on the veranda. The storm raged outside, pushing against the canvas covers that had been secured to keep the veranda dry. It was cooler than usual, and rain slipped past the canvas.

Evelyn closed the door behind us.

I crossed my arms as I faced Drew. "Tell me why you did it."

Drew ran his hand over the back of his neck as he glanced at me. "I can't tell you why—"

"Drew." I took a step forward, but Evelyn put her hand on my arm to stop me.

"What I can tell you is that we didn't have a choice," Drew said. "I needed to leave the castle at a moment's notice, per the queen's request, and I ran into Cecily as I was leaving. I am not at liberty to tell you why, but it was important that she went with me. We planned to sneak back into the castle last night, no one the wiser, but Lord Wolverton came upon us at the inn. Cecily told him that we had left to get married."

"You didn't get married?" That thought made me angrier still. If he'd been caught with her and refused to marry her, Cecily's life would be ruined beyond repair.

"We *did* get married," he said as he continued to pace. "After we saw Lord Wolverton. I took her to a village chapel in Wexham, and the vicar agreed to marry us. I have the certificate—" He took a deep breath and faced me. "And I mean to honor my vows, Charles. I will be a faithful husband to her."

I took another step forward, my chest rising and falling. "What does that mean?"

Drew put up his hands. "Not what you think. Cecily wanted—" He paused, and I was thankful he did, because I was about to lose my temper again. "What I mean," he continued, "is that I will stand by Cecily's side until my last day in 1563. I will do everything—"

"You don't mean to stay there?"

"You know I can't."

Evelyn stepped forward. "If you love her, stay."

Drew's sad gaze shifted to his sister, but he shook his head as his shoulders lowered. "You know as well as I do that the entire Whitney empire rests on my shoulders."

"What I know is that there is nothing as painful as losing the person you love."

I turned to her, but she didn't look at me.

"I lost someone I love in my other path," she continued as she let out a breath and the weight of it all seemed to wash over her. "Nothing is worth giving up a person you love. The grief will eat you alive, especially when you could have made a different choice. My other path was stolen from me, but you can choose. The Whitneys will figure out how to go on without you. Father has years left to find a replacement and the rest of us have enough money to survive, even if the shipping business closed tomorrow." She walked across the veranda to her brother and put her hands on his forearm. She was so small and delicate next to him and looked as if she carried a lifetime of burdens. "Don't give up on love, Drew. Cecily is worth everything you might lose here. Trust me."

"You forget," I said, hating to be the one with common sense, especially given Evelyn's vulnerability. "I didn't give my blessing. What kind of life could you provide for her, Drew? Yes, she might think she can give everything up for you and you for her, but she's never known want or poverty. What happens if you die there and she has several children to feed? Do you know how difficult life is for a poor widow in 1563? Even in 1883, life is hard for widows. I should know. Both my mother and sister have suffered at the hands of poverty. Is that the life you want for Cecily?"

They turned to me, and I could see the hurt in Evelyn's eyes.

"I know what's best for my sister," I said. "And what I want for her. She's my responsibility, not yours, Drew. I will go to Wexham in the morning and demand an annulment from the vicar. If he refuses, I will take the matter to the bishop in Winchester and tell him what has happened."

"What about Cecily?" Drew asked, upset. "Won't that be worse for her? To return to the castle with a marriage annulment? People will spread the rumor that she was never married and that you found her with me and brought her home, a fallen woman."

"Do you see the mess you've put her in?" Anger burned anew in my chest. "No matter what happens, Cecily suffers." I tightened my jaw. "But I will demand an annulment nonetheless and defy anyone at court who spreads false rumors. I will take the matter to the queen, and, if what you claim is true, she will acknowledge that Cecily had to leave at her request, and she will help quell the rumors."

"The queen doesn't know Cecily was with me."

"You just said—"

"I said that I had to leave at the queen's request, but Cecily just happened to be at the wrong place at the wrong time."

I stared at him for several heartbeats as I tried to control my fury. "Regardless, I will tell the queen that Cecily was forced to go."

"The queen cannot know that you are aware of her request, either." Drew turned to me and gave me his full attention. "No one must know anything about that night."

A frown creased my brow. "What are you hiding?"

He stared back at me. "I am not at liberty—"

"I am a member of the queen's privy council. If there is something, I should know."

"Charles." Drew's voice filled with a warning, "I cannot and will not tell you why I left the castle. You need to trust me, especially with years of friendship between us."

The seriousness of the situation intensified as I realized this wasn't just about Cecily, but about the queen and something she wouldn't tell her most trusted advisors.

"You cannot tell anyone that I left the castle for the queen's sake," Drew said. "The ramifications could be catastrophic."

"Why can you know and I cannot?"

"I am her physician—a role that you invited me to take. You need to trust me, Charles."

What could the queen have possibly asked Drew to do in the middle of the night? And was it the first midnight rendezvous he'd taken for the queen? Would it be the last?

"If the queen asked you to leave," I said, "then she knows that you left the other night for her sake and Cecily was an innocent bystander. Hopefully, she is feeling benevolent and will allow Cecily to remain part of her ladies in waiting if I can arrange an annulment."

Drew shook his head in frustration and turned away from me.

I had the right to protect my stepsister, and I would do whatever was necessary to make sure she was unscathed.

"If it wasn't for your mother's ball," I said to Drew, "I would leave Midcliff today. But I have promised I will stay, and I want to keep my word. I think it best if we avoid each other until then."

Without another word, I left the veranda and returned to my bedroom. It would be a long day before I could get back to 1563 to rescue Cecily, and with the storm raging outside, I would have little to keep me occupied.

※

The storm gained strength throughout the day. At times, it blew so hard, the house shook and the windows rattled. Trees on the Whitney property bent at impossible angles, and some snapped in half. The rain came down in sheets and prevented me from seeing anything beyond Midcliff's back lawn.

I spent most of the day pacing, thinking through the options I had concerning Cecily. Drew was right. An annulment might look worse than if they returned to the castle as a married couple, but it was still something I would consider. An annulment would allow Cecily to remain a lady in waiting, *if* the queen was benevolent to my stepsister.

I didn't join the Whitney family for lunch, but by suppertime I was starving, and I couldn't avoid them all day. Mrs. Whitney would be concerned, and I didn't need to trouble her. More importantly, I had promised Evelyn that we would talk, and she didn't deserve my silence.

My valet helped me dress for supper, and then I left my room, tugging at the sleeves of my evening suit. Everything felt off and uncomfortable today.

It was too early to go into the dining room, and I didn't want to join the family in the parlor. Instead, I went to the library, which was one of my favorite rooms of the house. Not only because it was there that I told Evelyn I loved her, but also because it was private and quiet.

The cool day had turned into a cooler evening as the storm continued. A fire had been laid in the hearth to banish the chill. It crackled softly as I entered the room.

Evelyn sat on one of the chairs in the corner, wearing her evening dress, with a book in hand.

Her blue eyes were gentle as she regarded me.

"I was wondering when I might see you again." She closed her book and set it on the table beside her as she rose. "I didn't want to disturb you today until you were ready to talk."

My temper had settled, but I was still upset and knew that seeing Drew would be hard. But none of it was Evelyn's fault, and I didn't want her to be at the mercy of my bad mood.

"I'm sorry."

She walked across the room and stood in front of me near the fireplace. "I'm sorry, too. I know how much Cecily means to you, and I also know that it's not simply a matter of what is best in 1563. There is a lot to think about."

Her skin looked so soft tonight, and her sapphire earrings glimmered in the dancing firelight. They made her eyes look bluer than usual.

"I'm the sorriest that we didn't get a chance to talk today," I said. "I needed to calm down before I could give you the time and attention you deserve."

She nodded as her focus dipped to my cravat, and she took a deep breath. "There is a lot I want to tell you, but perhaps it isn't a good time with everything—"

"I want to know, Evelyn." I put my hands on her upper arms, drawing her gaze back to my face. "I want to know more than you can imagine."

Her past was the only thing between us, holding both of us back from truly knowing each other, and I didn't want to wait another moment.

I took her hand and led her to a window seat. It was still raining hard, but the wind had settled, and darkness had started to descend. Here, in the intimate alcove, we could have more privacy.

We sat together, slightly turned so we could face one another. I didn't let go of her hand and loved the feel of her skin against mine.

"Tell me whatever you want to say," I said. "I promise it will not change my opinion of you."

"Perhaps you'd better wait to make that promise until after you learn about my other path."

I didn't respond but waited patiently for her to begin.

She took a deep breath. "I was born in Sandwich, Massachusetts, in 1672. I had a very large family there. Many of them were time-crossers. My father, John, was a time-crosser, and my mother, Patience, was the personification of her name. We were Quakers, and my life revolved around my large family and my church." She let out her breath as she shook her head. "I was loved, deeply, but it was such an oppressive, difficult life. Quakers were hated in the Massachusetts Bay Colony, and we suffered all kinds of persecution. It was especially difficult because I had this life to compare it to." She waved her hand toward the elegant library. "I wanted freedom in my other path. I didn't want to be associated with the Quakers. I struggled in my relationship with God, trying to understand my time-crossing gift. I decided it was easier to cast Him aside and go my own way." She lifted her shoulder. "Much like the prodigal son, I left my loving family and went to Boston to become a servant in the home of—" She paused and removed her hand from mine as she looked down at her lap. "His name was Josias Reed."

I listened intently as she spoke, wanting her to trust me more than I'd ever wanted anything in my life.

She finally lifted her face to look at me. "Josias was a very wealthy merchant who left England and moved to Boston several years before I arrived at his home. He was married and had one son, but he'd left them in England, and his wife had no plans to come to America." She stood and paced away from me before turning around to say, "I never intended to fall in love with Josias, but he was so charming and handsome, and he told me everything I'd ever wanted to hear."

I sat up a little straighter. She'd fallen in love with a married man?

"Looking back"—she clasped her hands together and lifted her face to the ceiling, as if she was trying to control her emotions—"I can see that he was seducing me, that he only intended to use me, but I fell in love with him and thought he loved me. When he said he was moving to Salem and asked me to go, I knew he was asking me to be his mistress." She said the word so quietly, I almost missed it.

It was hard to hear her talking about her other path, about a man she loved but who had misused her. Everything she'd assumed about me when we first met was starting to make sense. Josias Reed had told her all the things she wanted to hear and convinced her he was in love with her.

But how did it end?

"Did you go with him?" I asked, making sure my voice and tone were neutral.

"I did." She crossed her arms. "I rejected my Quaker family and everything I knew and loved, and went to Salem to be his mistress, but really, I was still his servant." She shook her head. "There, I was a servant, here I had servants."

"What was your name in Salem?"

Evelyn uncrossed her arms and returned to the seat, where she faced me. "My name was Rachel Howlett."

I frowned. "It wasn't Evelyn?"

She shook her head. "My full name in this path is Rachel Evelyn Whitney, but I don't use my first name here. It never felt right to have the same name in two different lives when I felt like two very different people. So here, I'm Evelyn Whitney, and there, I was Rachel Howlett. But Rachel died in 1692 and no longer exists."

"She does exist," I said. "She will always be a part of you, Evelyn. We can't separate our two lives, no matter how hard we try."

With another sigh, she said, "I haven't finished my story." She played with the lace of her dress, not looking at me again. "It wasn't too long after we arrived in Salem that I realized I was pregnant, and I had to go into hiding. The punishment for adultery was severe in Puritan Massachusetts. Thankfully, no one outside of Josias's house even knew I was there, but it became a very lonely existence. The one bright spot was that I believe Josias came to love me toward the end, though it was of little consequence. He soon learned that his wife had changed her mind and was on her way to America with their son. I couldn't stay at his home, and I couldn't return to my parents, so I walked to Salem Village, where my cousins Hope and Grace lived. But it was at the height of the witch hysteria, and when their stepmother learned of my identity, she had a fit and accused me of being a witch. I was cast into the gaol, eight months pregnant."

Tears slipped down her cheeks, but she wiped them away.

I didn't move as I listened, unsure what to say as the horrors of her story tightened inside my chest. I couldn't imagine what she had gone through, especially during the witch hysteria.

"I was tried and convicted of witchcraft," she said simply,

though her tone was dry and unemotional. "It was a farce, the whole thing. But because I was pregnant, I was not hanged with the others. Instead, I was sent back to the gaol in Salem. I was so despondent, especially because Josias never came for me. He didn't fight for me or stand up for me at any time." She lifted her gaze to mine, so many questions in the depths of her eyes. "Why wouldn't he fight for me, Charles? Am I not worth fighting for?"

My heart broke as I took Evelyn into my arms, holding her close, wishing I could take away all her pain.

"I had the baby in the gaol," she whispered. "A little girl with a time-crossing mark on her chest. I never held her. My cousin Hope was there with me, and I made her promise to take the baby to my family in Sandwich. And that's all I remember. I woke up here the next morning, and I never went back to 1692. My only explanation is that I died in that gaol, abandoning my daughter."

I continued to hold her as the weight of her pain pressed against my heart. "I'm so sorry, Evelyn. I'm sure Hope was able to get the baby to your family."

She pulled away and shook her head. "She didn't. I did a little research soon after I realized I had died there, and I learned that Josias's wife and son had died on the passage to America and Josias took our daughter, who he named Anne, to South Carolina."

"What happened after that?"

"I don't know. I couldn't bear to do more research. It hurt too much. I can't imagine what Anne did without a time-crossing guide. Josias had no idea I was a time-crosser. That's why I wanted Anne to be with my family, so she would understand the gift." Her breathing became shallow, and she pulled away to stand up. "This is why I don't talk about it," she said as she struggled to catch a breath. "I feel so panicky. The thought of my daughter not knowing why she is a time-crosser—I can't." She looked up at me, her eyes frantic.

I stood and placed my hands on her upper arms. "Take a deep breath in through your nose, and let it out slowly." I had her do it several more times until she began to calm down.

"I'm sorry," she said. "I know this isn't your problem."

"Evelyn." I had her look at me. "What happened was out of your control—perhaps not your relationship with Josias, but he was just as much to blame, if not more so, since he was in a position of authority over you. But losing your life in Salem, and Anne not having a guide, is not your fault. God allowed that to happen for a reason. I won't begin to pretend that I know what that reason might be, but we can trust Him, that I know for certain." I'd learned it in my own life. Though I wasn't sure how God would fix all the brokenness in my paths, I had to believe He had allowed all of it for His purpose.

She nodded, though I wasn't sure if she believed it.

I slowly guided her back to the bench as the storm continued to blow and the fireplace crackled with heat.

"That was the day I saw the orphanage in New York City," she said after a moment. "And my heart bled for them in a different way. I had been an orphan once, in this path, and had tried to ignore that fact as I grew up in this opulent lifestyle. I used to turn my back on orphans, pretending I had nothing to do with them. But after I lost Anne, I started to see motherless children in a different light. I began volunteering in New York, and when we arrived in Newport, I inquired about an orphanage here. When I saw little Laura and realized she was about the same age my Anne would have been, I felt a deep bond with her. She had blond hair and blue eyes, just as I imagined Anne might have." She let out another breath and shook her head. "I knew it would be a miracle, but I asked Mrs. Flanders if Laura had a birthmark like mine."

"Does she?"

Evelyn shook her head. "But a part of me heals every time I'm with Laura and can make her life a little easier."

"Sometimes the best way to heal is to help others."

Evelyn rubbed her hands together and took a tentative look at me. "Do you think less of me, Charles, knowing the truth about my past?"

My heart beat hard as I placed my hands on either side of her beautiful face. "I think more of you, Rachel Evelyn Whitney. For all that you've endured and sacrificed."

Tears glistened in her eyes again, and she entered my arms.

I held her tight, wanting to convince her that my love was unconditional.

"You are the woman I love because of everything in your past," I said. "It has made you the person you are today, and though I wish I could take all your pain away, it shaped you into this version of you—the version I've fallen in love with."

"Charles," she said as she pulled back. "I love you, too," she whispered. "Thank you for seeing *who* I am and not *what* I am."

She kissed me, melting into my arms without effort as her beautiful words warmed my heart and soul.

Evelyn loved me.

23

CECILY

AUGUST 5, 1563
WEXHAM, ENGLAND

For the second day in a row, I woke up at an inn as morning sunshine streamed through the window. This time, however, I was lying in the bed.

Frowning, I turned to look at the wall where I'd fallen asleep in Andrew's arms. He was sleeping on the hard wooden floor, having rolled up his doublet to use for a pillow.

I couldn't remember walking to the bed. Had he carried me in the middle of the night?

Warmth filled my chest at his thoughtfulness, and I lay for several moments just watching him sleep. Even if our marriage was in name only, I was proud to be Andrew Bromley's wife. I vowed I would not make him regret marrying me, even if the wedding had been forced upon us.

Especially because it had been forced upon us.

A noise in the hall made me sit up.

Andrew stirred on the floor, and he blinked awake a moment before someone pounded on the door.

"Cecily!" Charles said from the hallway. "Open this door immediately."

I was fully clothed, but I still felt exposed and vulnerable as Andrew hurried to stand and pull his doublet on over his linen shirt.

"Charles was understandably angry yesterday in Newport," Andrew whispered as he buttoned his doublet. "I had hoped he'd be calmer by now."

"Cecily!" Charles called again. "Don't make me break this door down."

"Clearly, he is not." I got off the bed and smoothed down my hair before I unlocked the door and opened it.

Charles stood on the other side, breathing heavily, fire in his eyes. He glanced over my shoulder at Andrew and then back at me. "Get your things. We're going to the vicar."

"The vicar?" I frowned. "Why the vicar?"

"I'm demanding an annulment." He strode into our small room and came face-to-face with Andrew.

Neither one spoke, and I had a feeling that they'd already said all there was to say in Newport.

"Are you ready?" Charles asked me, turning away from Andrew.

I shook my head, still rattled by his unexpected arrival. "I'm not asking for an annulment, Charles."

"I'm not giving you a choice, Cecily. The queen will not allow you back into her household if you're married to a commoner. We cannot return there until we have your marriage certificate and annulment in hand, and even then, she might not allow you back."

"I don't care if I can't go back. All I've ever wanted is to return to Arundel Castle, anyway. I'll travel there with Andre—"

"'Tis not that easy." He studied me, disappointment and frustration in his eyes. "There will be consequences for your actions. You cannot marry without the queen's consent, and you cannot leave court without her consent, either. She would have you brought to the Tower if you tried to go to Arundel Castle now. You're not thinking clearly."

I pushed past Charles to stand next to my husband. "I've never been more clearheaded in my life. I left Windsor Castle of my own free will, and I married Andrew of my own free will. I refuse to go to the vicar, and because I vowed to love, honor, and obey Andrew, you can no longer order me to do anything."

Andrew stood stiff beside me as we looked at Charles.

"Then I will appeal to your *husband*," Charles said, "and demand that he asks for an annulment."

Andrew's hand found mine in the folds of my dress.

"I also took vows," he said, "and I will not break them by giving in to your demands."

Charles stared at Andrew, so many emotions playing over his face. "You will break them the moment you choose 1883."

Andrew didn't flinch or waver as he stared back. "I spent all day yesterday thinking about Evelyn's words on the veranda. She's right. I do not want to give up the woman I love." His fingers entwined with mine. "My father has time to find a different heir, someone who will do the company proud." He turned to me, searching my face. "I cannot offer much, but I will apprentice with a doctor and pursue medicine here. It will not be the life you've always known, but I will do my best to give you the life you deserve."

My heart fluttered with joy as I realized what he was saying. He was choosing me, and I would choose him, a thousand times over. "I will go anywhere and do anything with you, Andrew."

"You've given me no other choice." Charles's voice sounded tired and defeated. "I must challenge you to a duel for Cecily's honor."

"Charles! You cannot be serious." I stepped forward. "Dueling is illegal, and even if it wasn't, it's foolish and barbaric. The queen would never approve."

"Name your weapon," Andrew said from beside me, his voice level.

"No." I turned to face Andrew. "You're both being absurd."

"The rapier," Charles said.

"You cannot do this," I protested, "either of you. How will this solve anything? I might lose one or both of you. Will you challenge each other to a duel in 1883, as well? Will you not be happy until one of you is dead in both paths?"

"I cannot allow your honor to go unchallenged," Charles said without looking at me.

"You're talking about hurting Andrew," I told him—and then looked at my husband, "and hurting Charles. You two are not only best friends, but you share a time-crossing bond. Neither of you need to defend my honor. I can defend my own honor. I am responsible for my choices. I do not need a knight in shining armor to save me."

"I will go to the livery and rent two horses to take us back to Windsor," Andrew said to me. He let go of my hand and walked past Charles. "And when we return to the castle, I will honor your challenge, Lord Norfolk."

"Andrew." I took a step toward him, but he left the room before I could stop him.

Charles ran his hand through his hair and took a seat on the bed, dropping his arms to his knees.

"How could you?" I asked.

He shook his head. "Don't even start, Cecily."

"I love him."

Taking a deep breath, he straightened, and I saw anguish in his blue eyes. "If that was all you needed, I would throw you the biggest celebration in the kingdom. But 'tis not enough. I, of all people, know it to be true."

Despite my anger and frustration, I saw something deeper in Charles's gaze. It wasn't just his fury at me and Andrew—he was mad at the world. Perhaps at God.

I slowly walked to the bed and took a seat next to him. I wanted to appeal to his tender side to convince him to give up the duel. Charles was chivalrous, but he wasn't a fool.

"Tell me what's really bothering you."

"Where would I even begin?"

"Perhaps with Evelyn."

Charles leaned on his forearms again and looked down at the wooden floor. "She finally told me about her other path."

"You didn't know about it?"

"Nay. She was afraid to tell me because she thought I would think less of her."

I frowned. "Surely it wasn't that bad."

He finally looked at me. "It was bad, but nothing she said made me think less of her. It only made me more compassionate. She made some poor choices, but then other things were out of her control." He sighed. "I don't know how to help her."

"Being a time-crosser is difficult, but being a female time-crosser might be a little more challenging, especially if she was born into a path that was harder for women."

"She lived through the Salem Witch Trials," he said in a grave voice. "Or rather, she died at the hands of it."

My breath stilled as my pulse escalated. Charles rarely spoke about his other path for fear that he might tell me something that would jeopardize his choices there. And for the first time, I wondered if I should question him further, because my time-crossing grandmother, Grace, had also lived through the Salem Witch Trials. Did she know Evelyn? I'd never told Charles about anyone in my other family besides my parents and siblings. He didn't know that my grandmother had lived at that time.

"How did she die?" I asked quietly.

"I don't want you to think less of her, either, Cecily."

"I won't. I understand how complicated time-crossing is. I don't blame her for anything she might have done in a different time and place."

He ran his hands over his face before saying, "She was accused of witchcraft and died giving birth to a child in the gaol—a child sired by a married man."

I sat a little straighter, recalling a story my mother had told me about Grandmother Grace's cousin, in gaol during the witch hysteria. "What was her name?"

"Rachel Howlett."

My lips parted as I stood in surprise. Rachel Howlett was the name of my grandmother's cousin.

"Rachel Howlett?" I whispered.

He turned to me, his eyebrows wedged into a frown. "Do you know her?"

I slowly shook my head, not wanting to alarm him. I didn't *know* Rachel. I knew of her, but I wasn't sure how much I should tell him.

He studied me for a moment. "You're hiding something from me, Cecily. What is it?"

I paced away from him. "I—I'm just surprised, that's all."

He also stood. "About what?"

"I've heard her name before."

"How?"

I wasn't sure it was wise to tell him, but I couldn't think of a reason it would cause problems. "Rachel Howlett was my Grandmother Grace's cousin in Salem in 1692. My grandmother's twin sister, Hope, was in the gaol with Rachel when she died."

It was Charles's turn to look shocked—and then he looked a little sick. "Does that mean that Evelyn and I are related?"

"No," I said quickly, wanting to put his mind at ease. "I'm related to Rachel through my time-crossing family in 1913." I laid my hand on his arm to reassure him. "And even if I was related to her in this path, you and I are not blood relatives, Charles."

Relief eased his features as he took a deep breath. "It doesn't really matter. There is no future for her and me either way." He paced away from me and then turned. "Do you know what became of her child?"

"Anne?" I nodded. I'd heard the story from my mother, but it was heartbreaking. "'Tis a sad tale, though Anne's daughter, Caroline, had a happier ending."

"Tell me."

"Do you think 'tis wise?"

"I don't care anymore. I'm so tired of trying to make all the right decisions when everything seems out of my control anyway."

I knew how he felt and took a seat on the bed again to tell him the story.

"Anne's father, Josias Reed, took Anne to South Carolina and raised her on a tobacco plantation, but she ran away with a man at the age of thirteen."

Charles's eyebrows rose in surprise.

"A year later, Anne brought her daughter, Caroline, back to South Carolina and left her in Josias's care. Then she returned to the Caribbean, where she lived as a pirate and died on her twenty-first birthday."

"Evelyn would be heartbroken to hear it."

"The tale doesn't end there. Caroline found Hope in Salem in 1727 and told her the rest of it. Caroline had no guide, so she had gone on a quest to find Anne. She eventually located Anne in her other path in 1927 and learned that Anne was a notorious criminal there."

Charles frowned. "That's horrible."

"It is," I agreed, "but Caroline reconciled with her mother Anne in 1927 before Caroline chose to stay in 1727 with her husband. According to Hope, Caroline and her husband lived a happy and prosperous life together in Boston. But I do not know what became of Anne in 1927."

"There is some redemption in the story, at least," Charles said.

"I don't know if Evelyn would think so."

"Why does she go by Evelyn in 1883?"

"Her real name there is Rachel Evelyn Whitney, but she never felt right having the same name in both paths."

I nodded, understanding her feelings. "What will you do with the information?"

"I know not. Mayhap nothing."

Neither of us said anything for several moments, and then I rose from the bed and met Charles in the middle of the room.

"Please withdraw your challenge from Andrew," I begged. "No matter what you think, I do love him, and I am willing to make sacrifices to be with him. I'd much prefer to live a simple life as his wife than a grand life as Lord Wolverton's wife. Surely you can see that."

He shook his head and sighed. "I will not pretend to be happy about the situation, Cec. But if he is willing to stay with you in 1563, and he has vowed to protect you, then I will withdraw my challenge and leave your fate in the hands of the queen."

With a cry of happiness, I threw myself into Charles's arms. "Thank you."

He hugged me back, but when he withdrew, he said, "Do not underestimate the queen, Cecily Bromley. She will not accept your marriage without severe punishment. It could be years before you and Andrew are released to live as husband and wife, and that is only if it benefits the queen. There are some still living in exile from the court, on house arrest, for lesser offenses."

I worried my bottom lip, knowing that he spoke the truth.

In my excitement to learn that Andrew would stay in 1563 and Charles would not challenge him to a duel, I'd forgotten that we still had to face Queen Elizabeth and the rest of court.

That fate could be worse than all the others.

24

CHARLES

AUGUST 5TH, 1883
NEWPORT, RHODE ISLAND

Drew and I were quiet during breakfast the next morning at Midcliff. Yesterday when we arrived at Windsor Castle, I had gone to my apartment without another word to him and Cecily. I didn't know what had become of them. Whether Cecily had gone to Andrew's apartment or back to the maids' dormitory, I hadn't bothered to ask Drew. Their fate was now in the hands of the queen, and there was nothing I could do for either of them.

Evelyn looked between us with concern, though she didn't broach any subject that would cause division.

As we ate in silence, I thought about Cecily and what she had told me about Evelyn's daughter's tragic life. Would Evelyn want to know? I wasn't sure I would ever tell her. Her guilt about leaving Anne was already so profound.

Mrs. Whitney entered the breakfast room like a burst of wind, and all three of us looked up in surprise. She never ate breakfast with us.

"Good." She put her hands on the back of a chair and faced us. "I have some exciting news."

The three of us waited as she took a dramatic pause. In all the chaos of the past two days, I'd almost forgotten about her upcoming ball and the knowledge that Helen knew about my real identity.

"In light of the announcement that will be shared at my ball tomorrow," she said, giving Evelyn and me a pointed look, "we will have a special guest in attendance."

"What announcement?" Drew asked.

Mrs. Whitney clasped her hands in excitement. "Lord Norfolk and Evelyn are engaged to be married."

Drew stood so quickly his chair fell to the ground behind him. Mrs. Whitney's eyes opened wide, and she took a step back.

I, too, rose as Evelyn's face went ashen.

"You hypocrite!" Drew turned to me. "You proposed to Evelyn?"

I held my hands up. "There's been a misunderstanding."

"Oh, really?" Drew's jaw tightened as he crossed his arms.

"A misunderstanding?" Mrs. Whitney asked, the spark of obduracy I'd seen at the casino the other night revealing itself again. "That can't be. I saw you and Evelyn in the secluded sitting room in the lobby at the casino. A man doesn't get that close to a proper young lady unless he's proposed to her."

"Mother." Evelyn finally rose to her feet. "Lord Norfolk has not prop—"

"Not yet," Mrs. Whitney said, "but I will expect a proposal before the day is done, or your father will demand he is held accountable for taking liberties with you."

"He did not take liberties at the casino." Evelyn's voice lowered as her cheeks turned pink.

"Perhaps not at the casino, but a maid saw the two of you in the library, *kissing*," she stressed. "If that doesn't warrant a proposal, I don't know what does."

Evelyn looked to me with helplessness.

"I've already hinted to our guests that this ball will also be an engagement party," Mrs. Whitney continued, clasping her hands together again, not welcoming debate. "Mrs. Astor included. I'll be the laughingstock of Newport if there isn't a proposal. And your father will be angry that he's making the trip from New York."

"What?" Drew asked. "Father is coming here?"

"He is coming by yacht and should be here any minute." Mrs. Whitney's piercing gaze speared me in place, and I realized that the sweet and gentle exterior she'd exhibited during my earlier visit was an act. "What will become of me when everyone finds out there is no engagement, Lord Norfolk? Helen will gloat like never before, and the papers will be full of scandal. I'm certain Mrs. Astor only accepted my invitations because I am the future mother-in-law to an earl."

"How can there be a scandal when there was no proposal?" Evelyn asked.

"Why would you invite Father?" Drew demanded.

My heart rate intensified as sweat broke out on my brow. I couldn't face Mr. Whitney—not as Lord Norfolk—and I couldn't hide the fact that I had lied about my identity all summer. He would know moments after his arrival that I had misled everyone.

"There's nothing left to do but to propose to Evelyn," Mrs. Whitney said to me. "It simply must be done."

All I could think about was escaping Midcliff.

Prescott entered the breakfast room, his face serious. "Mrs. Whitney, the police superintendent, Officer Francis, is here to see you. I've brought him to the drawing room."

"The police superintendent?" She frowned. "Whatever for?"

"I couldn't say, ma'am, but he asked to speak to you and said perhaps your children should be there, as well."

Mrs. Whitney's eyes grew wide as she looked to Drew and then Evelyn. "What could he want?"

Drew moved around the table and offered his arm to his mother. "Let's not keep him waiting."

She nodded and then said to me, "Lord Norfolk, escort Evelyn to the drawing room and join us."

I quickly offered Evelyn my arm, and we followed them out of the breakfast room.

Evelyn's eyes filled with unease as she looked up at me.

I gently squeezed her arm and tried to give her a reassuring smile, though my mind was reeling with everything Mrs. Whitney had just told us.

"Officer Francis," Mrs. Whitney said as we entered the drawing room. It was decorated in shades of white like the rest of the rooms in the public part of the house. "How can we help you?"

"Good day, ma'am." The police superintendent held his blue hat in his hands, clearly uncomfortable. "Perhaps you'd like to have a seat."

Mrs. Whitney didn't speak for a moment as her face went from uncertainty to resolve. "I'm certain that what you have to say is unpleasant, so please just say it."

He nodded. "I hate to be the bearer of this news, but there was a maritime accident yesterday afternoon off the coast of Southampton, during the storm." He paused. "Unfortunately, there were no survivors."

Mrs. Whitney placed her free hand on Drew's arm as if to steady herself. "And who was in the accident?"

"Besides the staff of five, your husband, Mr. William Whitney, was one of the casualties, ma'am. I'm very sorry."

Evelyn cried out in shock as Drew caught Mrs. Whitney from collapsing. He led his mother to a chair as she shook her head and said over and over, "It cannot be true. William wouldn't make me a widow."

Drew's face lost all its color as Evelyn began to weep silently beside me.

"I'm so sorry," I said to her, putting my arm around her.

It took several minutes for the shock of the announcement to pass. Mrs. Whitney held a handkerchief to her mouth, but she did not cry. Finally, she looked at Officer Francis. "Who else was on the yacht?"

He glanced at Drew, Evelyn, and me as he tightened his grip on his hat.

"Well?" Mrs. Whitney demanded. "I'm certain there was someone else."

"Besides the staff? A Miss Molly O'Leary, ma'am."

Mrs. Whitney took several breaths before asking, "And *who* was Miss Molly O'Leary?"

"From what we can tell," Officer Francis said, "she was a showgirl at Harry Hill's Variety Theatre in New York City."

Evelyn slowly lowered into a chair as Drew paced to a window and looked outside.

"And what kind of a *theatre* is Harry Hill's?" Mrs. Whitney asked.

"I-I hate to say," the police officer stammered.

"Tell me."

"It was a burlesque theatre, ma'am."

Mrs. Whitney pressed her handkerchief to her lips again as she turned away from Officer Francis, and for the first time since receiving the news, tears gathered in her eyes.

"The yacht was unsalvageable, as you can imagine," Officer Francis said to me, since I was the only one looking at him.

"That's the least of our concerns right now," Drew said from the window.

"Of course." Officer Francis fidgeted. "I'll send a mortician to see you tomorrow, to make plans for the funeral."

Mrs. Whitney wiped her nose and then stood. "We'll plan the funeral in New York. We'll return there directly. Thank you for coming, Officer Francis."

"Of course." He nodded and then started to move to the door where Prescott materialized, no doubt waiting just outside in the hall. "If there's anything else I can do for you, please don't hesitate to call on me."

"Thank you," I said, since the other three didn't seem to hear him.

After Officer Francis had left the room, Mrs. Whitney didn't waste a moment. "We'll need to cancel the ball and return to the city tonight. I'm certain there will be legal things you need to deal with, Drew. We don't want Clarence and Helen to get their hands on—"

"Father died." Drew turned away from the window. "Can't you take a moment to mourn?"

"We don't have a moment." She clasped her hands. "I will mourn in private, but in public I will always remain stoical. There is no other choice. We must look strong to stay strong, and no doubt Clarence will try to take whatever he can from the family business. This is your time to shine, son. The moment you were born for."

A look of dread overcame Drew as he turned back to the window.

"What's wrong with you?" Mrs. Whitney asked. "Whitney Shipping is your legacy. I'd think you'd want to honor your father's memory by keeping it strong. It's time to step up and be a man, Drew. Take the company to new heights."

"Is that all life is to you?" Drew asked, facing her again. "Just money and power? I lost a father, and now I'm being asked to give up a life with—" He choked on his words, and I knew what he had wanted to say.

He was being asked to give up his life with Cecily.

"I'm being asked to live a life I don't want," he corrected himself. "I might need a few minutes to process everything that's just happened."

"We don't have a few minutes," she said. "Clarence and Helen are vultures. We must read your father's will as soon as possible and see how he's left the company. He was the majority stockholder, but I don't know what his father's will said, should William die before Clarence. We need to get our hands on that will as soon—"

"Enough!" Drew roared.

Evelyn and Mrs. Whitney jumped.

"I need space to think." Drew ran his hand over the back of his neck. "Give me a minute," he said, a little calmer.

She pursed her lips. "I will instruct the staff to pack our things and purchase train fare back to New York for this evening. You have until then to enjoy your *space*, and then I need you to take your rightful place at the helm of Whitney Shipping."

And with those final words, Mrs. Whitney swept out of the drawing room.

Drew looked at me and slowly shook his head. "My entire world just crumbled around me. What am I going to do?"

Evelyn rose from the chair and rushed across the room to enter Drew's embrace.

I quietly slipped out of the room, my heart breaking for Evelyn and Drew—and for Cecily, who would soon learn that Drew no longer had the liberty to stay in 1563.

The house was solemn that morning, though the staff was busy preparing to move the family back to New York. I wasn't sure how much space to give Drew and Evelyn, or if Drew would even want to speak to me. The shock he'd endured pierced my heart because I knew what it felt like to lose a father tragically. It was a unique kind of grief, the loss of a parent.

I waited for a couple of hours and then inquired with the staff where I might find Drew. He was in his father's study.

With a heavy heart, I knocked on the study door and waited for him to answer.

"Come in," he said.

Slowly, I opened the door and found Drew standing near the window, looking out at the Atlantic Ocean. He had his hands in his pockets and glanced briefly in my direction.

"My father loved his yacht," he said in a monotone voice. "Mother hated it, for many reasons, but especially because he often brought showgirls with him when he used it."

"I'm sorry for your loss."

"I can't believe he was bringing one here," Drew continued, as if I hadn't spoken. "I'm sure he intended to keep *Miss O'Leary* on the yacht while he made an appearance at the ball and then return to her after his obligations were done."

I stood just inside the study, realizing that Drew didn't need me to talk.

"I wonder if she was a new acquaintance, or if she was a steady mistress," he mused, though I knew he wasn't looking for my opinion. "What I'd like to know is why." He finally turned to me. "Why would he not take his vows to my mother seriously?" He swallowed his emotions and shook his head. "I know I might be naïve, but the vows I made to Cecily a couple of days ago are seared into my heart and soul for eternity. I would rather die than break them. How could my father justify his immoral choices?" He put his hands to his face and took a few deep breaths, then lowered them and said, "I don't want to become my father, Charles. I don't want the life he had—not a single part of it. I don't want the money or the homes or the yacht or the company. The only thing I want is Cecily. And now?" He turned back to the window and wiped his eyes. "Why would God allow this to happen? I'll be eaten by guilt if I leave Mother and Evelyn at the mercy of my uncle Clarence, and I'll be plagued if I break Cecily's heart. I am a prisoner of time, and no choice I make will be good enough for the people I love."

"What will be good enough for you?" I finally asked.

He scoffed. "It doesn't seem like God wants my opinion on the matter."

"Do you want my opinion?" I left the door and walked to the window to join him.

Drew used his shoulders to wipe his eyes and shook his head. "I can about imagine your opinion."

"What do you think I'll say?"

"You'll tell me that I should give Cecily an annulment and then stay in 1883 to take care of Evelyn and Mother."

I shook my head. "You should do what *you* want to do, Drew. It shouldn't matter what I want, or what your mother wants. You should take some time to pray about it and then make the choice that you feel convicted to make—not guilted to make."

For years I had operated out of guilt and obligation, and it had brought nothing but strife and resentment. I had tried to play the part of God, and He had showed me that no amount of striving, manipulation, or cajoling could alter His plans.

"I've learned the hard way that God doesn't work through guilt," I continued. "Conviction, yes, but not guilt. If you're feeling guilted to stay in 1883, and you're convicted to stay in 1563 and honor your vows to Cecily, come what may, you should do that. But, if you feel guilty staying in 1563 because of your vows, but convicted to stay in 1883 because you're the heir to the Whitney legacy and are now required to take care of your mother and sister, then do that. I can't make that choice for you, nor will I presume to try."

Drew sat on the window seat and put his forearms on his knees while clasping his hands. "I'm so raw with grief right now, I couldn't tell you if I'm coming or going. I have no idea what to do."

"You don't need to choose right now. But—" my voice became stern—"if you don't know whether you'll choose Cecily, I'm asking you not to consummate your marr—"

Drew looked at me sharply.

"I know," I said, holding up my hands, "but it's not fair to her if you don't plan to honor your marriage vows."

"You don't have anything to worry about. I'm not a blackguard."

Neither of us spoke for a minute, and then Drew finally stood and sighed. "I can't make my final choice for several months, so I might as well get busy doing what I can here." He studied me for a moment. "Will you return to Virginia or come with us to New York?"

"As Lord Norfolk?" I shook my head. "I should return to Virginia." I paused. "I don't want to add more to your plate, Drew, but one of the reasons I agreed to do this was to get financial investment for my farm."

"I am not sure what my father's will entails," Drew said, "but I'd be shocked if I didn't inherit all his shares in the company, making me the majority stockholder. No matter what, I will ensure that the Whitney company invests in your farm. It could take some time for all the legal work to be done, but you don't need to worry about your mother and sister anymore."

Relief and gratitude overwhelmed me, and I reached out to shake Drew's hand, gripping it hard. "Thank you, Drew. I know that things have been awkward between us lately—"

"Say no more, Charles. You came here to do me a favor, and now I will do one for you."

"Thank you," I said again.

"I want you to talk to Evelyn. The last thing she needs right now is more grief. If she wants you to come to New York with us, as our guest, please consider her request. If she'd rather you go back to Virginia, I'd like for you to honor that, as well."

"Of course."

I left the study, thankful that Mama and Ada would be taken care of. That meant that I could stay in 1563 with Cecily.

And if Drew ended up staying in 1883, I might have no other choice.

I should have felt relieved that everyone would be taken care of, but I wasn't.

Evelyn was in the garden at the back of Midcliff, facing the ocean. The sun shone bright, such a stark contrast to the storm that ravaged the Atlantic the day before and took the lives of those on Mr. Whitney's yacht.

"My father created this garden for my mother when they had the cottage built ten years ago," she said without taking her eyes off the ocean. "He knew how much she loved flowers and wanted her to have this space to read or host lawn parties. They were so happy then—at least, they appeared to be."

"I'm sorry for your loss, Evelyn. Is there anything I can do to help?"

"Sit with me." She finally turned to me and placed her hand on the stone bench next to her.

I walked through the dahlias, black-eyed Susans, and zinnias. I knew the names of the flowers because Cecily loved them and had spent hours in the garden growing up. She and Evelyn would be good friends, I was certain, though they would never get to meet.

I took a seat next to Evelyn, and she reached for my hand.

"Thank you for being there for me when Officer Francis gave us the news."

"I wouldn't want to be anywhere else."

She looked at the ocean again, and I saw the remnants of tears in her eyes. "Nothing will ever be the same. You would think I was used to change and loss, but I hate it more than ever."

I lifted her hand to my lips. "I wish I could take your pain, Evelyn."

"I know." She leaned her head on my shoulder. "Charles, I can't even think about you leaving right now. Will you return to New York with us?"

I sighed. "I would like nothing more, but our separation is inevitable. If Congressman Reinhold learns that I've traveled with your family to New York, I'm certain he'll tell your mother the truth about me. And we have your aunt to think about. She's been waiting for the perfect opportunity to hurt your mother, and what time would be better than now?"

Evelyn lifted her head off my shoulder. "Aunt Helen wouldn't dream of hurting Mother at a time like this."

"Do you really believe that? If their rivalry is as ruthless as I've heard, I wouldn't doubt she'd try."

"Not now," Evelyn said with certainty. She gently squeezed my hand. "Will you stay, at least through the funeral? Everyone would think it odd if you didn't."

I wasn't sure that it was wise, but I couldn't say no to Evelyn, especially at a time like this. "Of course," I said, lifting her hand to my lips again. "I would stay forever, if I could."

Tears gathered in her eyes again, and she leaned into me for a hug.

I wrapped my arms around her, willing to hold her for as long as God would allow.

But I was done trying to manipulate Him and His plans. It was time to surrender my own will and start to trust His.

Come what may.

25

CECILY

AUGUST 6, 1563
WINDSOR CASTLE

Despite Andrew's declaration that he was going to stay in 1563 and honor his vows to me, dread overwhelmed me as I sat at the window seat in his apartment the next day. I wrapped my arms around my bent knees and placed my cheek on them. At any moment, the queen might summon us, and we would face our punishment.

Below me, the North Terrace was bright with the colors of late summer as the early morning sun shined upon the castle grounds. A gardener was busy trimming shrubs, peacefully going about his work.

How I longed to be in the garden to look for caterpillars and take them to my tower to paint.

There was a light knock on the bedchamber door, causing my heart to pound.

"Cecily?"

Relief overwhelmed me as I realized it was Andrew and not the queen's guards.

"Come in." I slipped my feet off the window seat and turned to face him.

The door opened, and Andrew entered. His face was still lined with sleep, and he was only wearing his linen shirt and hose. His feet were bare, and his hair was still tousled from being abed.

He'd never looked so handsome or inviting. I ached to be in his arms.

With each passing day, my love and desire for my husband grew. Seeing him in such intimate surroundings, wearing only a shirt and pants, made my pulse escalate.

"Good morrow," I said, allowing the joy of seeing him to banish the melancholy I'd been feeling all morning. When he didn't return my smile, I knew something was terribly wrong. "What is it?" I rose to my feet. "Is it the queen? Have we been summoned?"

Ever since we'd arrived at the castle the afternoon before, we'd been anticipating a page or guards to be sent to Andrew's apartment. We'd spent the previous day dreading the summons, yet no one had come. As night had fallen, Andrew had insisted I sleep in his bedchamber while he took the couch in the outer room. Neither of us wanted our marriage as husband and wife to start under the strain of uncertainty.

"Nay," he said as he joined me, taking one of my hands to lead me back to the window seat. "'Tis not the queen."

There was so much sadness in his voice and movements. I stopped him. "What's wrong, Andrew?"

When our gazes met, his face crumpled and he drew me into his arms.

My lips parted as I clung to him, starting to fear the worst. "What's happened? Is it Charles? Did you two duel after all?"

"Nay." He shook his head. "'Tis my other path."

"Tell me, Andrew," I begged. "Did something happen to Charles there?"

He finally pulled away but didn't let go of me. "My father was killed in a yachting accident on his way to Newport. There was a terrible storm, and no one survived on the boat."

I stared in shock. "I'm so sorry, Andrew. How terrible."

"We traveled to New York City yesterday," he continued. "When I wake up there tomorrow, I will have to deal with all the business details while Mother and Evelyn plan the funeral." He studied me as he spoke. "This isn't how I imagined everything would go. Father was supposed to have years left to find a replacement for me."

I shook my head in denial. I'd just started to hope that we could have a life together. He said he was going to choose me. "What do you mean?"

"I don't know what I'm going to do. I can't live my father's life. It would destroy me. But I can't abandon my mother and Evelyn right now, either. There is no one else to fill my father's shoes except my uncle Clarence, and he will run the company into the ground. Hundreds of employees depend on Whitney Shipping for their livelihoods, not to mention my relatives. It's not just Mother and Evelyn, but my aunt and cousin, as well." He shook his head. "I'm sorry, Cecily."

My heart was breaking, but Andrew was in pain, and he needed me to be strong. "You have nothing to be sorry about, my love," I said, slipping my hand up to his face. "'Tis not your fault."

He hugged me again, and I clung to him.

"Is there time enough to find a replacement for you?" I asked, hopeful.

"There are so many unknowns. Once my father's will is read, I will know more, but I can't think of anyone my uncle Clarence would approve if I tried to find someone else." He placed his hand on my cheek, and I placed mine over his. "I love you," he whispered. "The only thing that got me through the horrors of yesterday was knowing that I would come here today and see you. Hold you." He kissed me then, and I wrapped my arms around him, wishing I could hold him forever. When he pulled back, he said, "I don't know how I would survive a life in 1883 without you. Running the family company is not my dream, but to do it while grieving the love of my life seems a penalty too great to bear."

"We will find a way," I promised, though I'd already suffered so much loss and disappointment, and a small voice in the back of my head told me to prepare for the worst. Very few things had gone as I had hoped or planned in my life, so why did I think this would work in my favor? Bitterness wanted to take root in my heart as the tears began to fall.

Yet, I could almost hear my mama's voice, whispering in my mind and heart not to let anger win. She'd been a time-crosser and understood the difficulties. As I had been sick in 1913, and we were certain I would not live, she had made me promise not to let bitterness win. To remember all the things she and Papa had taught me, to love God and trust Him and pray. Always pray.

He leaned his forehead against mine. "I'm sorry," he whispered.

"'Tis not your fault."

A loud knock echoed throughout the chamber, causing both of us to stiffen.

"Doctor Bromley!" a man yelled. "The queen has summoned you and your wife to her Privy Chamber at once!"

I clung to Andrew as panic raced up my throat.

"Fear not," he whispered to me as he kissed me again. "God has gone before us in this and all things. We must trust Him, Cecily."

I briefly closed my eyes, trying, with all my heart, to believe him. Would God listen to my prayer if I asked Him to protect us? He hadn't answered mine or my parents' prayers in 1913 when I became sick. Was it because He had a better plan? *This* plan?

As the door to the bedchamber opened, Andrew laced his fingers through mine, and we faced the queen's guards together.

"Pray, my love," he whispered.

So I did.

We followed the guards through the halls of Windsor Castle at a fast pace. I imagined many who had gone before us, summoned to the English monarch, some with more tragic fates than others. Yet, I knew their dread. The queen was at liberty to exact any punishment she saw fit for the unapproved marriage of one of her maids. My only hope was that she would be lenient with us, knowing why we had left the castle.

We walked through the Queen's Ballroom, past dozens of courtiers apparently waiting there to see us. People stood in small groups, whispering with disapproving glares.

Would all this attention cause people to question Andrew's past? What if someone discovered that he hadn't apprenticed with a doctor? Would he be at risk for further punishment?

I didn't want to even contemplate such a thing.

Aveline was among those who stood in the Queen's Ballroom. The moment our eyes met she stepped forward, but there was nothing she could do. The guards walked so quickly I wouldn't be allowed to speak to anyone.

Her eyes were filled with worry as we passed her, and I wondered what would become of her if the queen banished me from the castle. Aveline's hope of becoming a maid of honour was now ruined, and she would be forced into a convent.

"Where is my brother?" I asked Andrew as I searched the faces of those present.

Andrew inhaled as we continued toward the Presence Chamber. "I know not."

"Are things any better between you?"

"I'm thankful he was there for us yesterday." It was all Andrew would say.

As we entered the Presence Chamber, the familiar room looked menacing. I tried not to panic. Just beyond the door at the other end was the queen—and our fate.

Andrew's fingers tightened around mine as one of the ushers opened the door to the Privy Chamber.

We walked through the door and found the queen sitting on her couch. She wore her makeup, but I could tell she was still weak and exhausted from giving birth to her son. Her swelling had gone down considerably since the last time I'd seen her, and her eyes were creased with the depth of her loss.

Kat stood behind the couch on one side, and Charles stood on the other.

I met my stepbrother's cool gaze briefly as I let go of Andrew's hand and curtsied to the queen while Andrew bowed.

"Rise," the queen said in a hard voice.

Panic wrapped around my heart as I stood straight.

"Step forward, Cecily."

It did not escape my attention that the queen had failed to call me Lady Cecily.

I stepped forward and dipped my chin.

"Is it true that you left the castle in the dead of night with Doctor Bromley?"

"Aye. 'Tis true, Your Majesty."

"And that you married Doctor Bromley, without my consent, at a chapel in Wexham?"

"Aye."

"Do you deny this charge, Doctor Bromley?" the queen asked him.

"I do not, Your Majesty."

"Why did you do this thing without asking me?"

"Because—" He paused, and I saw the war waging within him. He had done it to protect the queen and her son, but he could never admit that to anyone, the queen included. "Because I love Cecily."

There was a pause, and I glanced up to find the queen looking at him. Her emotions were masked and hard to read. Was she testing his loyalty to see if he would reveal the truth about the baby? The only person in the room who didn't know was Charles, and he would be trustworthy with the news. She had to know that. She could have chosen anyone else to be present.

"I have asked Lord Norfolk and Kat to be my witnesses," the queen said, still sitting on her couch. "So I ask them now, do either of you have anything to say on behalf of Doctor Bromley and his wife?"

Hope filled my chest as I looked at my brother and then at Kat. Charles could petition the queen to grant us leniency because he was one of her favorites, and because he knew that the only reason we'd married without her consent was because Lord Wolverton had seen us. And Kat could appeal to Her Majesty because she knew why Andrew and I had left the castle in the middle of the night. She had all but forced me.

Yet neither of them spoke as an awkward silence filled the Privy Chamber.

Was the queen testing their loyalty, as well?

"Your Majesty," I finally said, "may I—?"

"There is nothing you can say that would convince me of your innocence," the queen said in a sharp voice. "You have blatantly disobeyed my orders by marrying without my consent, and for that reason, I am banishing you from court and putting you on house arrest until further notice."

"My queen," I said as I bowed my head, "I beg you—"

"You are fortunate the plague is ravaging London," she barked. "Or you would find yourself in the Tower! Charles, call in the guards and have them remove Doctor Bromley and Cecily to their rooms."

Andrew stepped forward. "Your Majesty—"

"I do not want to hear your pathetic excuses," the queen said as she slowly rose to her feet. "You have betrayed me and my confidence in you." She turned to me. "Not only have you married without my consent, but you married beneath you, Cecily. I cannot tolerate a member of my household, or a member of nobility, marrying a commoner. Anyone with access to my person must be of the highest character, trustworthy, and willing to do whatever is necessary for the safety of the crown. You have done none of those things."

Charles moved past us and opened the door to summon the guards.

"Charles," Andrew said as he turned back to the room. "You know—"

"Silence!" the queen said. "If you utter one more word in my presence, I will send you to the dungeon."

Andrew pressed his lips together as his gaze met mine.

I shook my head as tears filled my eyes.

Why didn't the queen pardon us? She had to know why we left.

And why didn't Charles come to our defense? Or Kat? There were things they could say without betraying the queen.

Two guards took hold of Andrew, and the other two took hold of me. Mine walked me out of the Privy Chamber just ahead of Andrew.

When Andrew came out, his face was filled with both fury and grief.

"I love you," he said to me.

"I love you," I replied as tears fell down my cheeks. "I will not stop praying."

We were pulled in two separate directions, but I did not take my eyes off my husband until he was out of sight.

26

CHARLES

AUGUST 10, 1883
NEW YORK CITY

I should have left after the funeral the day before, but I couldn't return to Virginia when Evelyn was still grieving. She'd relied heavily on me to get through the day, and she'd asked me to stay until after the solicitor read her father's will. There were still so many unknowns, and she wanted me there if things didn't go as they hoped.

Yet, what could I do?

We were avoiding the inevitable.

I paced outside Mr. Whitney's office in the Whitneys' brownstone mansion on Fifth Avenue as the family met with the solicitor. Clarence and Helen had come to listen to the will, and the biggest question was whether Clarence would inherit the majority of the company or if it would go to Drew.

Helen's glare had been cool as she'd passed me in the hall on her way into the office. She had been biding her time, as I knew she would, and hadn't said a word about my identity yet. Was she waiting to see if I would try to marry Evelyn? Or had she decided not to say anything because of Mr. Whitney's death?

After today, none of it would matter. I would have no reason to stay in New York. Despite what was happening at Windsor Castle, and my inability to defend him and Cecily, Drew had reassured me that if he retained a majority in the company, I would still receive the promised investment. He knew as well as I did that there was nothing I could have said to stop the queen from exacting punishment. My defense might even have made things worse.

At the moment, Drew's investment in my farm was the least of my concerns.

Grief tore at my heart as I briefly closed my eyes. How was I going to say good-bye to Evelyn?

Shouting erupted inside the office, muffled by the closed door, but it brought my head up. I wasn't sure who was yelling, though I had a suspicion.

A moment later, the door opened, and the solicitor quickly appeared with his briefcase in hand. He was an older gentleman with a mustache and a balding head, and when he saw me, he gave me a look that suggested he was eager to leave the mansion.

The office door was left open, and I had the opportunity to hear the conversation seeping into the hallway. I also had a good view of the room.

Drew, Evelyn, and their mother sat on one side of a table while Clarence and Helen sat on the other.

Clarence stood and slammed his hand on the table. "This is ludicrous. Who ever heard of giving their *daughter* a share of the company? I would never dream of expecting Marianna to run Whitney Shipping or make important decisions regarding the company. She's a—a *woman*."

"Why would William do such a thing?" Helen asked, her face filled with disgust. "Did he want our family to lose everything?"

Drew slowly rose and looked at Evelyn.

She had her hands clasped as she stared at the table, clearly shocked at the turn of events.

"I believe my father saw what I have known for years," Drew said. "Evelyn is intelligent, capable, and hardworking. She will be an asset to Whitney Shipping, in whatever capacity she chooses to participate."

"I can't understand why William would do this to me," Clarence said as he paced away from the table. "To give Drew fifty-one percent of the company and Evelyn nine percent while I maintain forty percent is ludicrous and a slap in the face for all the years of hard work I dedicated to our family and this company."

"Most of those years," Mrs. Whitney said, "you spent more time wasting money than making it, Clarence."

He turned and glared at her. "How dare you?"

"How dare I what? You know it's true. Perhaps William wanted to ensure that Evelyn was self-sufficient, and that even if you fritter away forty percent of the company on your extravagant lifestyle, there will still be sixty percent left over for everyone else."

"Or maybe," Helen said as she stood and joined her husband, "William thought Evelyn needed all the help she could get to attract a husband—preferably an aristocrat. Heavens knows she can't do it by her own charms."

I took a step forward, but Mrs. Whitney started to round the table toward Helen.

"There is no need for Evelyn to use her money to attract an aristocrat," she said, lifting her chin. "I have it on good authority that she will be announcing an engagement to Lord Norfolk as soon as our period of mourning ends. And that was agreed upon *before* she owned nine percent of the company."

Helen laughed. The sound was loud and obnoxious, making the hairs on the back of my neck rise.

Heat gathered beneath my collar as the conversation shifted in my direction.

Evelyn noticed me outside the door and stood.

"Look," Helen said as she stopped laughing abruptly and a scowl filled her face. "The *earl* in question is eavesdropping at the door as we speak."

Mrs. Whitney's pleading gaze met mine. "Tell her, Lord Norfolk. Tell her how you plan to marry Evelyn."

Drew and Clarence turned to look at me, and suddenly, I was at a loss for words. More than anything, I wanted to declare my love for Evelyn and whisk her away, but this grieving family had more important things to worry about than whether I would marry Evelyn or not.

There was nothing left for me to say or do. The ruse was up, and if I didn't confess to Mrs. Whitney, Helen would do it for me.

I couldn't live with myself if I wasn't the one to tell her. She deserved better.

Drew grasped the back of a chair and lowered his gaze. He was just as guilty as me, but I wouldn't lay fault on his shoulders. I wanted him to remain blameless in his family's eyes. He was already suffering enough here and in 1563—and I'd done little to help him in his other path.

With a fleeting glance at Evelyn, I put all my focus on Mrs. Whitney.

"The last thing I want to do is hurt you or your family," I said to her, "especially at this difficult time. But it would be impossible for me to marry Evelyn, no matter how much I might love her."

Evelyn bit her lower lip and looked away from me.

Pain sliced through me, knowing it wasn't just Mrs. Whitney who would suffer because of my choices.

"Whyever not?" Mrs. Whitney asked, her voice desperate. "You're not already married, are you?"

"No." I swallowed and decided to forge ahead. "I can't marry Evelyn because I'm not who you think I am."

Helen's feline smile was hard to miss as she watched Mrs. Whitney's reaction.

"Who are you?" Mrs. Whitney asked, frowning.

"Perhaps," Helen said, "the better question to ask is who he *isn't*."

"Who aren't you?" Mrs. Whitney demanded.

Drew turned toward the window as Evelyn continued to look at her hands.

"I am not Charles Pembrooke, the Earl of Norfolk," I said, my voice steadier than I expected.

Shock stole over Mrs. Whitney as she stared at me. The color drained from her face, and she slowly lowered herself into a chair.

"So, you see," Helen said to Mrs. Whitney, crossing her arms and gloating, "your son and daughter have been fooling you all summer, Minnie. They knew that this—man—was not a real earl. I don't know who they invited to your home, but he is no aristocrat, and I intend to tell the world that you knowingly tried to pass him off as one. Can you imagine what Mrs. Astor will think of you then? You'll never be allowed in polite society again."

"Who are you?" Mrs. Whitney asked me in a choked whisper, ignoring her sister-in-law.

I owed her the truth, though I felt as small as an ant. "I am Charles Hollingsworth of Virginia, ma'am." I let my British accent slip and returned to the cadence of my Virginia roots. "I am a farmer."

"Good heavens." Mrs. Whitney looked like she would be ill. "I've been entertaining a *farmer* all summer?" She put her fist to her mouth. "I'll be ruined when word of this gets out."

"There's no need to ruin anything." Clarence lifted his hands to calm the ladies. "We can come to an agreement, I'm sure."

"What kind of agreement?" Drew asked, frowning at his uncle.

"I want fifty-one percent of Whitney Shipping for our silence," Clarence said, crossing his arms. "And I want Evelyn removed from the company entirely. Drew, you can retain forty-nine percent of the company, but you will also take over your father's position in the office so I can maintain the lifestyle Helen and I have become accustomed to."

"But—" Helen's mouth parted. "You're not going to let me tell the world about this, Clarence?"

"Not if it benefits us to remain silent." He turned toward Drew. "What will it be?"

"You want the majority of the company," Drew said, the muscles in his cheek jumping, "but you don't want to do any of the work?"

Clarence nodded. "I've put all the time and effort into the business that I'm comfortable sacrificing. It's time for you to step up and take over."

The dread Drew had been living under was written all over his face. This was not the life he wanted, and it was only getting worse as he faced running a company that he wouldn't have a majority ownership or say in.

He looked at his mother, but she was staring at her hands, so he then turned to Evelyn.

Instead of looking at her brother, she lifted her eyes to me. I couldn't read her thoughts as she stared at me.

"We will need some time," Drew finally said to Clarence. "I want you to promise that you won't utter a word about this until we give you a decision."

Helen's mouth slipped open in utter astonishment as she waited for her husband to respond.

"You have twenty-four hours," Clarence said as he gathered a few pieces of paper on the table. "If you don't give us a satisfactory answer by this time tomorrow, I will allow Helen to contact *The New York Times*."

Drew nodded. "But not a word can be leaked. If anyone hears about this, the deal will be off."

"Agreed," Clarence said.

"Clarence." Helen tripped after her husband as he walked out of the room. "You won't let me tell anyone? Not even my closest friends?"

"No one." Clarence walked toward the doorway.

I stepped aside to let him and his wife pass.

Helen continued to beg as Clarence strode down the hall and the two disappeared.

I stepped into the office, wanting to fix this situation. To assure Mrs. Whitney that I wasn't a monster.

She slowly lifted her cold eyes and pinned her glare on me. I paused.

"Do not take one more step into this room," she said as she stood.

"Mother." Drew put his hand on her arm.

"Don't touch me," she hissed at him, pulling her arm away as anger and resentment seethed from her lips. "How could you, Drew?" She turned to Evelyn. "And you. My own children. You've betrayed me beyond words. And worse, my greatest enemy gloats over me. How long has she known?" She closed her eyes briefly and then turned to me again. "You—you—evil man. How could you deceive me this way? Was it your idea to manipulate my children into this? And what did you hope to gain? Wealth? Fame?"

"Mother," Drew tried again. "I asked Ch—"

"It was my idea," I said, taking the blame from Drew. "I had hoped to gain an investment in my family's horse farm. Nothing more."

"You will never get it." Mrs. Whitney's voice was half crazed. "As long as I draw breath, you will eat the dust of your labor. I never want to see you again. Leave my house immediately."

"Mother," Evelyn said as she, too, tried to reach for her. "Charles is not the only one to blame."

"Please," I said to Evelyn. "Don't try to take responsibility. I'm the one who chose to deceive all of you." I took a deep breath, trying to maintain my dignity, though there was little left. "I'll pack my bags and leave as soon as possible."

I didn't wait for anyone to respond but turned and strode down the hallway toward the stairs.

The time had come to face reality.

I could no longer pretend to be the earl, I wasn't getting the investment for the farm, and once Drew left Cecily in 1563, there was little hope that I could find a good husband for Cecily before my next birthday.

Nothing had changed, despite my best efforts.

Instead, everything was worse—and I had no one to blame but myself.

※

It didn't feel right to take any of the clothes that Drew had purchased for me, so I changed into the suit I'd worn to New York from Virginia and took a moment to stare at my reflection in the mirror.

How had I found myself in this position? The plan had been simple. Impress a few people and then leave.

But it had turned out to be anything but simple.

And the worst was that I had fallen in love for the first time, and I was now in possession of a new sort of heartbreak I'd never known before.

"Charles," Drew said as he knocked on my door, "may I come in?"

I opened the door and stepped aside, allowing him to enter.

"I'm sorry." Drew shook his head. "Nothing was supposed to go this way."

"It's not entirely your fault. It was foolish of me to come here. I should have known better."

Drew ran his hand across the back of his neck. "Why is nothing going as planned? It seems that everything I put my hand to fails."

I knew he was talking about him and Cecily. I hadn't spoken to either of them in 1563 since the queen had put them on house arrest. They'd been taken to different parts of the castle, and I didn't even know where to look for them.

"How is Cecily?" he asked, waiting intently for my answer. "They won't tell me where they've taken her."

"I haven't spoken to her. They won't tell me, either."

He lowered himself into a chair, looking forlorn and melancholy. "I can't stop thinking about her. She fills my every waking moment, both here and in 1563. Even at my father's funeral, when I should have been focused on him, all I could think about was how much easier this would all be if Cecily was at my side." He put his face in his hands and shook his head. "I've never known such misery in my life, Charles. And to know that I'll wake up tomorrow and not be able to see her there, either—it's unbearable."

The ache in my chest was so deep and painful, I knew the misery he spoke of. "I wish I could say I didn't understand."

He shook his head. "I keep forgetting that you know exactly how I feel." He stood and paced to the window. "Why is God allowing this misery?"

"We were wrong to deceive everyone." I lifted my hat off the bureau and held it in my hand. "I don't think God is allowing us to succeed because we tried to manipulate people to get what we both wanted. He obviously has a different plan than us. It's taken a lot of heartache to realize I can't manipulate or cajole Him to do my bidding."

"My uncle's plan is nothing more than manipulation and blackmail. Why would God let Clarence get away with it and not us? We didn't do what we did for our own selfish gains. We were trying to take care of our families."

"In his own way, so is Clarence."

Drew stared at me, his countenance heavy. "If I give in to him, he'll own the majority of the company and you won't get your investment, Charles."

The truth felt like a knife in my gut. "I never had it to begin with." I put my hat on. "It was a wild gamble, and we lost. Nothing more. Nothing less."

"If I don't give in to him," he continued, "and they tell the newspapers, the scandal will follow you to Virginia. And no matter how much money I pour into your horse farm, your reputation will be tarnished, and the very people you hope to sell your horses to will turn their backs on you. Not to mention how the scandal will impact Mother and Evelyn."

"If you don't give in, at least Evelyn will have nine percent of the company, and she can be independent. You could also retain your majority vote and have control over the company to do with it what you will. I would rather my reputation be tarnished than take that away from you and Evelyn. Actually, I insist."

Drew frowned. "What will you do about your mother and Ada?"

"I'll do what I've always done. I'll take care of them and pray for a miracle."

"What about Cecily? Who will take care of her?"

Frustration and fear stole over me. "She wants you."

He paced away from me. "How can I leave now when I'm most needed?"

I slowly shook my head. "I can't answer that question for you. What I do know is that you're going to end up hurting someone. You need to ask yourself which broken heart can you live with."

Without another word, I left my room, closing the door behind me.

My heart pounded as I walked down the hallway, needing to say good-bye to Evelyn. I wasn't sure where I might find her or if she'd want to see me, but I couldn't live with myself if I didn't try.

I descended the stairs and headed to the library. It wasn't as cozy as the one at Midcliff, with views of the Atlantic Ocean, but it was just as impressive. And if Evelyn waited for me anywhere, it would be in the library.

If she wasn't there, then she didn't want to see me.

Taking a deep breath, I opened the door to the library and allowed my eyes to scan the room.

Two of the walls were covered with bookshelves, while a third had a massive fireplace. Windows on the fourth wall were flanked by wingback chairs.

Evelyn sat in one of the chairs, looking out at the courtyard behind the mansion, her chin in her hand. The sky was cloudless, and sunshine brightened the room.

When I entered, she turned, and in one fluid motion, she was out of her chair and walking across the room to enter my embrace.

I held her tight, my heart pounding as relief overwhelmed me.

She wasn't angry at me.

"Charles," she said through her tears, "I don't want you to leave."

"I'm sorry," I whispered.

"I can convince Mother to change her mind."

I couldn't get enough of her as she pressed against me, her arms around my back as her face lay against my chest.

"She would never let me stay, and even if she did, I have nothing to offer you, Evelyn."

She pulled away. "I will have nine percent of Whitney Shipping. What more could we need?"

I placed my hands on her cheeks, my heart breaking as she grasped for hope. "Only if your family chooses to reveal the truth about me, and knowing Helen, she will do her best to ruin all of you in the process. Your mother would never approve, and neither would society. I couldn't do that to you."

"Then we'll go to Europe," she said. "The scandal will eventually die down."

"I love you," I whispered as I placed a kiss on her lips, "but I wouldn't be any sort of man if I allowed you to provide for me at the expense of your family's social ruin. It would be one thing to accept an investment in my farm, which I could run and manage, but another entirely to live off your income without contributing. And I couldn't leave Mama and Ada alone on a failing farm to gallivant around Europe. I have responsibilities. Plus there is Cecily to consider. If Andrew stays here, I need to find a way to care for her, and that might mean staying in 1563."

She closed her eyes as a tear slipped past her eyelid. "I'm sorry." She lowered her face. "I'm being selfish. I know—" She paused and took a breath. "I can't ask you to leave any of them. Please forgive me."

I kissed her again, allowing my lips to linger on hers, savoring the sweet pleasure it gave me, hoping it gave her the same feeling. I wanted to capture this moment forever, to impress the memory on my heart.

Because it couldn't last. Evelyn and her family had a lot of things to work through, and I would only be in their way.

Finally, I pulled back, placing a kiss on her forehead. "I love you, Rachel Evelyn Howlett Whitney."

Tears fell down her cheeks and dripped off her chin as she swallowed. "I love you, too."

"I'll pray for you every day," I promised as I took a step back from her.

She nodded. "I'll pray for you, too."

We stared at each other for a heartbeat. "Good-bye, Evelyn."

"Good-bye, Charles."

And with those final words echoing in my heart, I left the Whitney mansion.

Walking away from Evelyn was the hardest thing I'd ever done. And as much as I wanted to stay and forsake all the other people in our lives, it would only cause more heartache.

I wasn't sure what the future would hold, but it wouldn't be in New York City.

27

CECILY

AUGUST 11, 1563
WINDSOR CASTLE

I stared at the farmland outside the window of my apartment, longing for the view of the North Terrace. It had been raining for two days, and everything was gray—the sky, the land, the castle walls, and my mood. The sun was setting behind the western horizon, and soon it would be dark once again. I shivered, longing for Andrew's arms around me, because I knew that his presence would banish the melancholy I felt.

It had been five days since I'd been sentenced to this room somewhere in the southern wing of the castle and as far removed from the queen's apartments as I could get in the Upper Ward. The apartment was comfortable, but lonely. There were no books or painting supplies. Nothing to fill the long hours. The only person allowed into my chamber was a servant who brought my meals three times a day, and she didn't speak to me.

I wiped a tear as it slid down my cheek, wondering where Andrew was being kept and if his punishment was worse than mine.

I was afforded a nice apartment because I was the daughter of an earl. Andrew was a commoner who had disobeyed the queen's commands and married a noblewoman.

There was an ache in my chest that was growing stronger with each passing hour, and a yearning that pierced my soul. What if I had to live like this until Andrew's birthday in December? Might I never see him again? Would the queen demand I remain on house arrest even after he died here?

I hugged myself as I continued to stare at the bleak land, knowing no worse fate than being kept from Andrew.

A knock at the door signaled the arrival of the servant—except that I'd already eaten my evening meal. Why had she come back? Unless it was someone else.

Soon, a key rattled in the lock, and the door opened.

I wiped the tears from my cheeks and turned to see who would enter.

It was Kat.

Anger and resentment wound around my heart, squeezing tight. I wanted to yell and scream and demand answers, but all I could do was give her a cold stare. She knew what she had done to Andrew and me. Yet she displayed no remorse. I had helped her and Charles with the letter to Mary, Queen of Scots, putting myself at risk, and I was shown no mercy or benevolence. Did she have no heart? Had my sacrifices meant nothing?

"Good evening, Cecily," she said as she slowly closed the door behind her.

"Why are you here? To delight in my misery?"

Kat frowned. "Of course not." She clasped her hands in front of her gown. "I've come to move you to a different part of the castle. Her Majesty would like you closer to her apartments."

"Why?" I crossed my arms.

Kat let out a sigh. "Why must you ask, Cecily? Why can't you simply accept a small gesture from the queen?"

"A small gesture?" I motioned to the apartment. "I'm on house arrest because I was forced to leave the castle for—"

"Stop." Kat stepped forward, a dire warning in her voice and face. "Not one word about that night," she whispered. "Or you will be silenced. For good."

My heart pounded hard, and I swallowed the panic that ran up my throat.

"Now listen closely." Kat moved closer to me. "This arrest has far more to do with what you know than with what you did. This is just a taste of what might happen if you utter one misplaced word, do you understand? You're fortunate that you're not in the Tower of London right now."

"But it's not my fault that I know."

"It doesn't matter." Kat put her hands on my upper arms and looked directly into my eyes. "What matters is that you do know, and you and Doctor Bromley are now the greatest threat to the monarchy. It is not a power you should take lightly, nor is it something that the queen will ever allow to be used against her." She lowered her hands. "But, if you comply and follow the queen's commands, you will be treated fairly. Do I make myself clear?"

I nodded, but then asked, "This arrest has nothing to do with my marriage to Andrew?"

"To everyone else, it has everything to do with your marriage. But to the queen, it is more about the knowledge you possess. And that is the greater fault you carry at the moment."

"Why does the queen want me closer to her apartments?"

"'Tis not a matter of wanting you closer," Kat said, "but offering you leniency to see if you will comply. If not, you will be sent to the Curfew Tower until we return to London."

The Curfew Tower was in the Lower Ward, near the military portion of Windsor Castle. It contained the dungeon and several prison cells and was the very opposite of the comfortable apartment I'd been in.

"Gather your things," Kat said.

"I have nothing."

She looked around the chamber and nodded. "Then come with me."

I left the apartment and followed Kat through the maze of the castle toward the state apartments on the north side. Would I have a view of the North Terrace again?

We passed people in the corridors and rooms, and many of them stared at me as if I was a criminal. I held my head high, not wanting anyone to know how I truly felt.

When we were alone in a passage, I finally asked, "Where is Andrew?"

"That is none of your concern," she said without missing a step.

"He is my husband."

"Not unless the queen allows it."

"But he is my husband," I said again.

She finally stopped and stressed the words, "*Not unless the queen allows it.*"

We were now in a familiar part of the castle, not far from the tower where I painted.

My heart began to pound hard as Kat stopped outside an apartment connected to the tower. She opened the door and allowed me to enter.

The outer chamber was a little more comfortable than the one I'd occupied in the southern part of the castle. Here, there were books on a shelf and a crackling fire lit in the hearth. Though it was now dark outside, I knew I'd have a view of the North Terrace in the morning.

My heart leapt at the thought for just a moment.

"There are two doors that lead up to the tower where your paints are still waiting," Kat said to me. "One is in the hall and is now locked from the outside. The other is in this room, and you will have unlimited access to the tower." She clasped her hands, looking neither happy nor upset. "It was Doctor Bromley who made this request for you, Cecily. He knows how much you love to paint and asked that the queen give you this one gift for his service to her."

Tears sprang to my eyes as a sob caught in my throat.

Kat put her hand on my arm. "The queen knows you were placed in a difficult position, Cecily. She is not heartless. You will enjoy the comforts of a lady, though you gave up that title of your own free will. But you will still be on house arrest until further notice as the queen decides your fate. You must prove trustworthy, or you might remain this way indefinitely."

My tears fell as I embraced Kat. "Thank you," I whispered. "Please tell the queen how grateful I am. I will take her secret to my grave."

Kat returned my hug and then nodded. "I will tell her."

Without another word, she left the apartment, locking the door behind her.

As the tears continued to trail down my cheeks, I lit a candle and found the door to the tower stairwell, eager to return to my paintings and caterpillars.

Candlelight flickered off the familiar stone walls of the tower as I climbed the stairs. It would be too dark to paint tonight, but it had been almost a week since I'd been in the tower, and I simply wanted to savor the moment. Several of my caterpillars had cocooned and turned into butterflies, and I'd let them go. But there were others that I hadn't had the opportunity to check on, and I was eager to see their progress.

The sound of the rain tapped against the windows as I made my way up. It was cold, but I didn't care. My pulse thrummed with the knowledge that my days could be filled with painting again.

Light bounced off the wall up ahead near the top of the stairs, making me pause.

Had Kat already brought a candle to my tower room?

I slowly climbed the rest of the way, and when I came to a stop in my room, my heart nearly burst out of my chest.

"Andrew!" I cried as I set down my candle and raced across the room.

Andrew turned at the sound of my voice and opened his arms to embrace me, showering my face and neck with his kisses.

"Cecily." He exhaled my name as he kissed me over and over.

I captured his mouth as it touched mine and slipped my hands to the back of his head, sliding my fingers into his hair, deepening the kiss. The yearning within me was so keen, it took my breath away.

His hands went around my waist as he drew me closer, pressing the lengths of our bodies to one another.

I could not get close enough.

Tears continued to fall down my cheeks, but they were now tears of joy.

"Cecily." He pulled back, just enough to speak. "It feels as if I've been parted from you for a lifetime."

I kissed him again and then slowly released my hold, looking into his dear eyes. "How did you get here?"

He smiled, and it was the most glorious thing I'd ever seen. "Kat brought me here earlier today and said that she was going to return with a surprise. A gift from the queen."

My own smile could not be dimmed as I fell into his arms again. "Do you think this means she'll let us stay together?"

"For now," he said, kissing the top of my head. "And I will savor every moment, Cecily."

I pressed my cheek against his chest, loving the sound of his pounding heart against my ear. My own heart was galloping so fast, I was certain it was racing with his.

"I've missed you so much," I said as my tears changed once again. Pain filled my voice as I pulled back to look at his handsome face. "Kat said that you requested this room for me. Is that true?"

He lifted his hand and moved aside a tendril of hair that was lying on my wet cheek and tucked it behind my ear. "Aye. I knew you could bear almost any punishment, but you couldn't live without your paints."

"Or you."

His thumb traced my cheek as his eyes caressed my face. "I love you, Cecily."

"I love you, too."

"The last five days—ten, for me—have been the worst of my life." He kissed me again, as if he couldn't get enough, and I allowed him, because I couldn't either. When he finished, he told me about his father's funeral and his uncle's blackmail, threatening to reveal Charles's identity. "My father's will was read yesterday in 1883," he continued, "and he is granting me fifty-one percent of Whitney Shipping, while nine percent will go to Evelyn. That is, if we decide not to give in to my uncle's demands."

I had to ask the question that had been plaguing me for days. "Will you leave me here alone in December?"

He placed his hand on my cheek and shook his head. "I made up my mind in my other path, and it's solidified now. I've been so miserable for the past ten days. I couldn't go a lifetime without you. I've decided to make a will that will give Evelyn fifty-one percent of Whitney Shipping, and my mother will get nine percent. Uncle Clarence will retain forty percent, which makes Evelyn the majority stockholder when I forfeit 1883 on my birthday. 'Tis not ideal for them, but they will be protected and taken care of, and I can leave there knowing I've done the best I can for them."

"But what of your uncle's blackmail? Won't he tell the world that Charles was a fraud?"

"Perhaps he will, but Charles insisted that I do. And even if it hurts, our family will survive. Mother can go to Europe and have a fresh start there if she wants. And Evelyn—"

"Evelyn can do whatever she wants, as well." I smiled at him. "Perhaps marry whomever she wants? But won't the scandal hurt Charles's business?"

"That is my greatest concern, but I will pray that the scandal will die quickly, and he can focus on building his life. I think this is the only way." He kissed me again. "But now it is time for me to talk about what I want."

I smiled, feeling my cheeks grow warm at the way he was looking at me.

"I love you," he whispered, "for better, for worse, for richer, for poorer, in sickness and in health, to love and to cherish, till death us do part."

He kissed me then, and this time, he did not stop.

28

CHARLES

SEPTEMBER 17, 1883
FREDERICKSBURG, VIRGINIA

Caroline Street was bustling that September morning as I maneuvered the family wagon toward the post office, my hands on the reins and my thoughts three hundred miles away.

It had been almost a month since I'd left Evelyn in New York City, and not a day—not an hour—went by that she wasn't on my mind. I'd had no communication from her or Drew or Whitney Shipping, and I wasn't sure if I'd ever hear from them again. If they had given fifty-one percent of the company to Clarence for his silence, there would be no investment for the Hollingsworth Horse Farm.

"I just need to make one more stop," I told Ada as she held her sleeping infant next to me on the wagon seat. "Will the little guy be content to wait?"

Ada grinned as she cuddled her son a little closer. "He'll be just fine."

"And Mama is doing well at home, you think?"

She placed her free hand on my arm. "You should stop worrying, Charles. We're all doing fine. Mama is feeling much better since the baby was born, and we're getting by. Take care of whatever business you have."

I returned her smile, though there'd been little to smile about besides the new baby. Mama had been feeling better, but without the financial investment from Whitney Shipping, our farm was in the same predicament it had been in before I turned my life upside down in Newport.

I pulled the wagon over to the side of the road and set the brake before securing the reins. I hadn't spoken to Drew or Cecily since the day the queen had placed them on house arrest. No one even knew where they were being sequestered, and when I asked Kat for information, she refused to answer me. I'd even petitioned the queen on Drew and Cecily's behalf, but she silenced me when I brought up their names. There was no telling if or when I'd see them again, or if Drew would stay with Cecily on his birthday. And until I knew, I wasn't sure if I was staying in 1883 or in 1563.

I hated feeling unsettled and dissatisfied. But I was done trying to manipulate God's plans for my life. I had found a sense of peace in the not knowing, in trusting that whatever plans He had for me, I could and would walk confidently forward.

At least the queen was feeling like her old self again and the immediate threat to the throne had abated. There had been no word from Mary, Queen of Scots, and the privy council had assumed that she heard Queen Elizabeth was on the mend and that's why she hadn't come after receiving my letter. I was thankful a war had been avoided, but the privy council was more adamant than ever that Queen Elizabeth marry and produce an heir. Over the past month, I had searched high and low for another possible suitor, but to no avail. With the plague still raging in London, we had to focus our resources on dealing with the catastrophic loss of life. A suitor would have to come later. Perhaps the archduke of Austria would prove a suitable match when he visited in the spring.

I entered the post office—and stopped short.

"Congressman Reinhold." I took my hat off as my pulse picked up speed.

The congressman turned from the counter, a congenial smile on his face until he recognized me. "Mr. Hollingsworth."

"How are you, sir?"

He walked away from the counter and met me near the door. His face slowly shifted from disdain to curiosity. "I'm doing fine. How are you, young man?"

I didn't want to admit that I was struggling, but his look was so earnest, I conceded. "I've been better."

"I imagine you were relieved when the story broke in New York."

Frowning, I crossed my arms and shook my head. "What story?"

"About Vicomte Deville," he said. "It was all the newspapers were talking about for the past several weeks."

"I haven't seen any newspapers from New York." The truth was, I had avoided anything to do with New York.

Congressman Reinhold lifted his eyebrows. "Apparently, Miss Marianna Whitney, Clarence and Helen's only child, ran off to Europe with the Vicomte Deville the day after William Whitney's funeral and married the vicomte before they could stop her. The real scandal is that it turns out he wasn't a vicomte after all, but a destitute schoolmaster from Luxembourg."

I stared at him, dumbfounded.

"Helen tried to curtail the scandal by claiming that her sister-in-law had entertained a counterfeit earl for the summer, but nothing could quell the rumors and gossip about Marianna. Clarence and Helen whisked themselves off to Luxembourg to talk some sense into their only daughter, but she's apparently smitten and refuses to leave her husband."

"I had no idea." I couldn't quite wrap my mind around it.

"So," he said, his face growing serious, "it appears that Drew and his family avoided a scandal where you're concerned."

"I'm sorry for Helen and Clarence," I said, "but I'm happy for Mrs. Whitney and Evelyn. They didn't deserve to put up with a scandal of my making."

"I couldn't agree more." He studied me. "I've been doing some research since coming home from Newport. It turns out that you've been a very diligent steward of your father's farm. And, other than your little foray into Newport, you're an upstanding, hardworking young man with a good reputation. You remind me of your father."

I pressed my mouth together, accepting his compliments and wondering why he'd bothered to investigate me.

"I like you, Mr. Hollingsworth," he continued. "I can't pretend to know why you posed as an earl, but I think your intentions were honorable and you've learned your lesson."

"I have."

"Good. I won't cast a stone, since I have a few choices in my past that I would rather forget." He smiled. "I think most of us would."

I glanced at the counter, wanting to grab my mail and then be on my way. As much as I enjoyed seeing the congressman, his presence was a harsh reminder of all I'd lost in Newport.

"I hope to serve as a congressman for a few more years," he continued, drawing my attention back. "But I'd like you to consider running for my seat one day. I think you'd be a good politician and diplomat. There's something about you—something I can't quite put my finger on—but I have a feeling you'd be a natural."

I couldn't help smiling. In 1563, I was the youngest member of the queen's privy council, the highest governmental position in England. I wasn't sure if I was a natural politician, but I enjoyed the challenges of the queen's court and would consider his suggestion—if I stayed in 1883.

"What do you think?" he asked. "I'd love to mentor you and get you ready for the job. Perhaps start with some local political seats maybe a county clerk or school board member. One day, if I think you're ready for the job, I'll personally endorse you for office."

I slowly nodded. "I'd like that. Thank you for thinking of me."

He clapped my shoulder. "Good." He paused and then said, "Isabel refused Mr. Brent's marriage proposal. I imagine she would be pleased to see you again."

I wasn't ready to rekindle a friendship with Isabel, but I smiled at Congressman Reinhold and nodded. "Perhaps one day our paths will cross."

"Perhaps." He smiled. "I'll be in touch, young man. And I have a lot of good stories to tell you about your father." He chuckled to himself as he left the post office. "A lot of good stories, indeed."

I stood there for a moment, trying to imagine what it would look like to be a congressman one day. It wasn't something I'd considered in the past, but the more I thought about it, the more it appealed to me. I could run the Hollingsworth Horse Farm and provide for Mama and Ada while fulfilling the part of me that loved diplomacy.

And there was also the promise of learning more about my father.

I just needed to make sure Cecily was cared for.

"There's a letter for you, Mr. Hollingsworth," the postmaster said, holding up an envelope. "Just came in today from New York City."

Anticipation filled my chest as I stepped forward and took the envelope, nodding my thanks. Had Drew finally reached out to let me know about the investment?

My heart ached for a letter from Evelyn, but I knew better than to play with fire. If we couldn't have a life together, there was no point in drawing out our pain.

I didn't even look at the return address but put the letter in my pocket and left the post office, eager to get back to Ada and the baby and read the letter in private.

Ada was singing to her son as I approached the wagon. When I stepped up, she turned and smiled at me. "Any letters?"

"One. From New York."

She put her hand on my arm as soon as I settled. I'd told her all about my time in Newport, so I knew she was eager to learn about the contents of the letter. "Who is it from? The Whitneys?"

"I don't know."

"You didn't look?"

"Not yet."

"Charles! How could you wait?"

I unlocked the brake and tapped the reins against the backs of the horses, and the wagon went into motion. "I want to wait until we get home."

"Why?"

"For some privacy."

Ada shook her head and sighed. "You've been waiting a whole month."

"I can wait a little longer."

"I can't."

I turned to her and saw the expression on her face. She was not interested in being patient.

"Fine." I pulled the letter from my pocket as I maneuvered the wagon down Caroline Street, toward home.

She took the letter from me—but she hesitated.

"What?" I asked.

"It's not from Whitney Shipping." Disappointment filled her voice.

"Who is it from?" I glanced at the envelope.

"It's a bill for Mama's subscription to *Leslie's Weekly* magazine." Her voice was heavy as she lowered the envelope. "I'm sorry, Charles."

I turned my face away from her so she couldn't see my pain.

Neither of us spoke on the way to the farm. I wanted to consider Congressman Reinhold's suggestion and share it with Ada, but all I could think about was Evelyn. Memories of our time together played continually in my mind. I tried to push them away, wanting to forget about my feelings and try to move on, but they refused to obey. For whatever reason, God wasn't letting me forget.

I prayed someday He would, because this was torture.

That evening, as the sun was setting, I closed the barn door and stopped at the yard pump to wash up before supper. Both Stella and Faye were in foal and doing well. The farmhand I had hired for the summer had done a good job with them—and, if I wasn't wrong, had taken a liking to Ada. I'd already sent him ahead of me into the house for supper as I closed everything up for the night.

The sky was a brilliant shade of pink, coloring the whole world. I glanced at the farm, seeing it as it should be and not as it was. I'd dreamed of a new horse shed and expanding the corral. The house needed paint and a new front porch. The current one was starting to rot and would soon be unsafe.

The barn could use a new roof, and the fence could be strengthened. There were so many things that needed attention, it was hard to prioritize which project should happen first. And harder still, wondering where the money would come from. The foals would help, when it was time to sell them, but that would be many months from now and would have to go toward our debt. It was a vicious cycle.

Dust on the road tore my gaze off the farm. It wasn't often that people passed by at this time of day. Most neighbors were home, eating their evening meals.

I finished washing my hands and let them air-dry as I walked toward the house.

But the buggy started to slow by our drive.

With a frown, I paused to see who had come, since it was rare to get visitors.

The buggy pulled into our drive and followed the lane up to the house.

Before the driver came to a stop, I caught a glimpse of her, and my heart leapt in my chest.

"Evelyn." I said her name like the answer to a prayer as I began to jog toward the buggy. Excitement filled my chest, and I felt like whooping for joy. She'd come.

Evelyn had come.

Yet—why had she come? Was this good news or bad?

The moment I saw her smile, I knew the news was good. Her face was as bright as the morning sun and just as promising. She was wearing a beautiful blue traveling suit with her blond hair twisted up under a jaunty hat with a short mesh veil. It stopped at her chin, accentuating her slender neck.

She brought the buggy to a stop, securing the reins as she looked at me, drinking in my appearance like I was drinking in hers.

It had been a month since I'd seen her in 1883, but it had felt like two months to me. I hadn't forgotten what she looked like, but she was prettier than my memory recalled. Her eyes looked bluer, and her smile was dearer than before.

"Charles," she said as she started to leave the buggy.

I stepped up, offering her my hand, but before her feet hit the ground, I wrapped my arms around her and held her close.

Tears stung my eyes as she returned my embrace, burying her face into my neck.

"Charles," she said again, tears in her voice. "I can't believe I'm finally here."

I never wanted to let her go, but I slowly lowered her to her feet so I could look at her beautiful face. I'd missed it so much.

She smiled up at me and said, "Hello."

I returned the smile, my heart beating so hard, I was afraid she could hear it. "Hello."

We looked at each other for so long, she finally giggled. "Aren't you going to ask me why I'm here?"

I put my hand on her cheek, running my thumb over the soft skin. "It doesn't matter to me why you've come," I said, "just that you're here."

She put her hand up to my wrist and gently encircled it, her eyes filled with so much joy.

As a time-crosser, I didn't dream, but I was certain this was what it felt like.

"Charles," she said, slowly lowering my hand, laughter in her voice. "I have official business to conduct."

I finally took a step back and gave her my full—if distracted—attention. "Why have you come, Evelyn?"

She held up her finger for me to pause and went to the buggy, where she took out a satchel and removed an envelope. "I have something here that I think you'll want to see."

I took the envelope and found the Whitney Shipping return address on the corner, smiling to myself at God's sense of humor.

I pulled several papers out of the envelope as her eyes glowed. "What is this?" I asked her.

"It's the legal documents that Drew had drawn up for Whitney Shipping to finance the Hollingsworth Horse Farm." She clasped her hands again. "I know you haven't spoken to Drew in over a month, but there's something you need to know. He plans to stay in 1563 with Cecily."

I stared at her, unsure how to process the information.

"That means," she said with a tender smile, "if you want to stay here and take care of your mother and sister, there is nothing keeping you in 1563."

For almost a year, I'd been uncertain about my future. To know I finally had a choice again was the most liberating feeling in the world.

"I'm sorry it took so long for me to come," she said. "Father had begun the legal work for the investment, but with his death and all the other things that needed attention, it took more time than I anticipated. So much happened this past month, and I wanted to hand-deliver this news to you myself."

Even though I'd heard the rumors, I still asked, "What happened after I left New York? Your aunt and uncle had threatened to tell the newspapers about me if Clarence wasn't given the majority of the company."

"The day Uncle Clarence and Aunt Helen left our home, they

were told that Marianna had run off with Vicomte Deville—or whatever his name is. They were so scandalized, they left for Europe immediately. Of course, once news broke about Marianna's marriage, Aunt Helen tried to tell *The New York Times* about you, but the editor thought it was a feeble attempt to distract people from the real story. You'd already left our home quietly and the *Times* had no interest in investigating Aunt Helen's claims. We don't expect Uncle Clarence or Aunt Helen to return home any time soon, and when they do, any danger of a scandal about the Earl of Norfolk will be so old, no one would care."

"I just heard about Marianna today. I'm sorry."

"I'm not." She grinned. "Marianna wrote and told me she's sublimely happy. I think she's just glad to be away from her parents. She seems to genuinely love her new husband, and that's all that matters to me."

"Then I'm happy to hear it."

She slowly took the papers out of my hand and returned them to the satchel. When she faced me again, there was a new look in her eyes. A tenderness and vulnerability I'd never seen before.

"There's another reason I've come, Charles," she said as she took my hands in hers.

I moved closer to her, every nerve in my body on fire.

"I once told you that the greatest tragedy of my life was that the man I thought I loved didn't fight for me."

I nodded, hating to think about Josias Reed and how he'd misused and hurt her.

"So, I decided to fight for myself." She laced her fingers through mine. "And I'm here to fight for you, too."

"What about your mother? Won't the scandal ruin her social ambition?"

"She won the rivalry with Aunt Helen as soon as news broke about Marianna. And even though only a month has passed, Mother's being courted by Anthony Belmont, one of the old-money bachelors. He's quite smitten with her, and I believe they will marry once her mourning period is over. There are few scandals that could ruin her social standing now." She studied my face. "Is it too late for us, Charles?"

"Too late?" I took her into my arms, relieved that Cecily would have Drew and that Mrs. Whitney would survive the scandal. "You're right on time, my love."

"Will you have me, Charles? Even with all the brokenness in my past?"

"I will, Evelyn, if you're willing to accept all my brokenness." I kissed her with all the longing I'd felt for the past month. I kissed her thoroughly and deeply, leaving no question in her mind as to how I felt about her.

When I finally pulled back, her eyes were a little dazed but filled with joy.

"I know you claim the scandal cannot hurt your mother," I said, "but what about you?"

"I won't need to worry about society because I don't want to live in New York."

"Where do you want to live?"

"Here, of course." She motioned to the house. "I grew up on a farm in Massachusetts in my other path, and I miss it more than I realized I would."

"Will you be happy here, Evelyn?"

"Exquisitely."

I grinned. I couldn't help it.

"We have a lot of obstacles to overcome," she said to me, "but I promise to never stop fighting for us."

I lifted her hand to my lips and kissed it. "And I promise to never stop fighting for us, either. Or trusting that God is fighting on our behalf."

Her smile was so beautiful, it made the longing in my chest tighten.

"Will you marry me, Evelyn?" I asked, not wanting to wait another moment.

She threw her head back and laughed. "I thought you'd never ask, Charles Hollingsworth!" But then she sobered. "I hope you don't mind, but Drew has made a will, and when he leaves here in December, I will become the majority shareholder in Whitney Shipping."

"Mind?" I laughed. "I will support you in whatever you do, Evelyn. I hope you don't mind that I plan to operate this farm and, one day, possibly run for Congress."

"It sounds like we will be very busy, Mr. Hollingsworth."

"Not too busy to do this," I said as I kissed her soundly.

29

CECILY

SEPTEMBER 18, 1563
WINDSOR CASTLE

Sunshine poured in through the tower window as I sat in front of my easel, studying the picture I was painting. It was a chrysalis in intricate detail. I'd been working on it for days and was about to add it to the growing pile of paintings I'd created since the queen had allowed me back into my tower.

"Lunch was brought," Andrew said as he entered the room with a tray and set it on a nearby table.

I wrinkled my nose. "What is that smell?"

"Cabbage and bacon soup." He stood behind me, his hands on my shoulders, and studied the painting with me. "'Tis remarkable, Cecily. It doesn't even look like a painting, but more like a colored photograph."

It would be many centuries before photographs were invented, long after I was gone.

The smell of the soup hit me again, and I had to turn away from it, afraid I might gag. "Could you please take that downstairs?" I asked, grimacing. "'Tis a wretched smell."

Andrew frowned as he lifted the tray and brought the soup up to his nose to sniff. "It doesn't smell spoiled."

"I don't think 'tis spoiled," I said, "but the smell does not agree with my stomach."

He placed a kiss on my temple before leaving the tower room to return the tray to the apartment.

Our lives had slipped into a familiar and comfortable pattern. During the day, as I painted, Andrew spent his time studying the medical textbooks he'd found in the castle library. He was anxious to leave house arrest and find a doctor to apprentice with so he could begin his work in earnest. In the evenings, we would sit by the fireplace and talk for hours. There was so much I didn't know about his other path, and so much he didn't know about mine. And, at night, we would lie in each other's arms, dreaming about an unknown future.

Though it was just the two of us, I loved married life, and I woke up excited to spend another day with him. Somehow, each day was better than the last.

The smell of the soup still lingered in the air when Andrew returned, this time with a serious look on his face. "Kat is here."

I turned from my painting and slowly stood. We hadn't seen Kat since the day she'd brought us together. "Why?"

"The queen is summoning us to her Privy Chamber."

A cold sweat broke out on my brow as my stomach turned again.

Andrew stepped forward and placed his hand under my elbow. "What ails you, Cecily?"

I put my hand to my forehead. "I know not."

He studied me with a critical eye, but we didn't have time for him to do a medical assessment.

"The queen will be waiting," I said.

We walked down the stone steps and found Kat in the outer chamber.

She looked me over and nodded once. "Marriage becomes you, Cecily Bromley."

My cheeks grew warm as I glanced at Andrew. He smiled at me and placed his hand on my waist.

"We should hurry," Kat said as she motioned to the open door. "The queen is waiting."

It had been strange to live in the castle and watch the activity on the North Terrace but not know what was happening within the castle walls. We hadn't spoken to anyone and didn't know any of the news that had transpired. We'd been sheltered away in our own little world for the past five weeks, and I didn't mind in the least.

Although I couldn't escape, Andrew still spent a day in 1883 while I slept. He told me about his time there and all the things he was doing to prepare for his departure. Evelyn had embraced her role in the family company, and his mother was thriving as a widow, though she was being persuaded to consider marriage again.

We left our apartment and entered the hall, following Kat down two flights of stairs to the main level of the castle. Though I hadn't disliked our seclusion, it felt good to be free of the same four walls.

Andrew slipped his hand into mine as we walked, and I glanced up at him. His brown eyes were so gentle as he regarded me. And though he had proven his love to me, every day, the way he looked at me left no doubt or hesitation in my heart.

We entered the Queen's Ballroom, and it was bustling with activity as tables were being set up and decorations were being hung.

"Is there a celebration happening?" I asked Kat, eager for a little news.

"Aye."

I waited for her to say more, but she didn't.

Aveline was among those decorating the ballroom, and when she saw me, she hastened to my side, giving me a hug as we moved through the room.

"Cecily!" she said. "I have wanted you to know but had no way of telling you."

"What?" I asked.

"The queen has made me a maid of honour, to take your place."

I smiled—a wide, heartfelt smile. "I'm happy for you."

"Thank you," she said as Kat gave us a look that suggested we needed to move on.

"I'll talk to you later and fill you in on all the news," Aveline said as she waved and was off.

"Come," Kat said. "We don't want to upset Her Majesty."

Andrew and I followed her into the Presence Chamber and past the ushers.

Kat opened the door, and I took a deep breath, nerves twisting my stomach.

Andrew's hold on my hand tightened as Kat crossed the threshold into the Privy Chamber and we followed her.

Queen Elizabeth sat at a table with a quill in hand. She looked healthier than ever and was dressed in a stunning gown, with her red hair twisted at the back. Her painted face was white, and her lips were red. When her gaze swept over me, I lowered my eyes and offered a deep curtsy while Andrew bowed next to me.

"Rise," she said as she left her chair and walked closer to us.

Kat stepped into the corner, but there was no one else in the room.

I'd missed Charles and hoped he would be there, but he was nowhere in sight.

The queen inspected us, looking at us up and down, though I wasn't sure what she was trying to find.

"How have you enjoyed your honeymoon?" she asked.

I glanced at Andrew and felt my cheeks growing warm again.

"'Tis been the happiest month of my life," Andrew said.

"And you, Cecily?" the queen asked. "Have you been happy with Muscles?"

Hearing her use Andrew's pet name again was a good sign that she was in a favorable mood and that she was no longer angry at him.

"Excessively, Your Majesty." I smiled. "Thank you for allowing us to share an apartment."

"That must be our little secret—one of several, I fear."

"Secret?" Andrew asked.

"We must let the others believe you've been in separate apartments, in isolation," she said. "Because you married without my consent, it would only be natural that I punish you, which was exactly what I did." She smiled. "In a way."

Andrew took my hand in his and said, "It was far from punishment."

"As I suspected."

The queen's spirits were high, and my heart raced with hope.

"I believe Kat explained the other reason for your house arrest," the queen continued. "It was a warning to both of you. Especially you, Cecily."

I nodded. "I understand."

"Doctor Bromley was under oath to me the whole time and never once broke his vow of silence on the matter." She crossed her arms, and I saw a hint of regret in the depths of her eyes. "He knew immediately the condition I suffered and was loyal to the end."

Andrew dipped his head in deference to her.

"But I needed to be certain of you," she said to me. "And I still do. Though I believe five weeks is long enough to keep up pretenses. My favor has been returned to you, and I am hosting a wedding celebration tonight to honor your union. However, before we can proceed with the festivities, there are a few things I need to do first." She motioned to the paper on the table where she'd just been sitting. "As a gift to Doctor Bromley for saving my life, I am bestowing upon him a barony and the gift of land near Guildford in Surrey."

My lips parted at the news. A barony was a noble rank—one of the lowest, but nobility nonetheless.

Andrew's face lifted as he stared at the queen.

"There is an old castle in Guildford," she continued, "used until the fourteenth century by the King of England, and more recently as a hunting lodge. I have no use for it, and it is falling into disrepair. I will gift it to you and your heirs, along with a thousand acres of land to do with as you will."

I was speechless as I grappled with the news.

"Thank you, Your Majesty," Andrew managed to say. "I am not worthy of your gift."

"Perhaps you aren't," she agreed, "but I want to keep you close at hand to serve as a royal physician, and I cannot have your wife serve as a lady in waiting if you are not nobility. You've given me no other choice."

"You want us to remain at court?" I asked, stunned. "And you want me to be a lady in waiting?"

"You are a favorite, after all."

I had never been called one of her favorites, and it brought more joy to my heart than I realized it would.

She went back to the table and picked up the quill again. "Guildford is close enough to London that you will be allowed to return home whenever needed, though I must insist that you and your husband stay close. You are both indispensable to me."

She scratched out a signature on the paper. "I am finishing this letters patent, and with my signature, it is binding." She looked up at us. "You are now nobility, Lord and Lady Wharton."

Kat smiled in the corner of the room.

"Thank you, Your Majesty," I said as I curtsied again. "I cannot begin to—".

"Then don't try." She rose again, and her face became serious. "All I ask in return is that you swear fealty to me." She approached and laid one hand on Andrew's shoulder and one hand on mine. "To the world, this gift is given because Andrew saved my life. But to me, personally, it is because of the kindness you both showed to me on the worst night of my life." She lowered her hands and pressed her lips together as tears filled her eyes. She blinked quickly and took a deep breath, lifting her chin again. "Now, let us speak no more about it. We have a wedding to celebrate, and I intend to enjoy myself." She motioned to Kat. "Let us remove to the bedchamber to give Lord and Lady Wharton a moment of privacy."

As the door closed behind them, I turned to Andrew, shaking my head.

He grinned as he lifted me in a hug that brought my feet off the ground.

"Did you hear that?" he asked.

I laughed. "Yes."

He hugged me close before setting me down. "God has answered our prayers, Cecily. He's made a way where there seemed to be no way. And though we suffered, He was faithful."

Tears gathered in my eyes as I nodded. Just when I thought all was lost, God had brought Andrew back into my life. And when I thought I'd lost Andrew again, God had shown me that He had other plans. The trusting and waiting had been almost unbearable, but the reward was priceless.

The queen did not spare any expense or extravagance for our wedding celebration that evening. The ballroom was filled with food, dancing, music, and laughter. Andrew and I sat at the head of the table, on either side of the queen, and enjoyed the entertainment.

My stomach was still unsettled, though it felt better than it had earlier in the day, and I started to suspect that I might be pregnant. When I glanced at Andrew on the other side of the queen, his smile was so warm and full of promise that I knew he'd be as thrilled as I was.

Having the barony, with lands and a home, made all the difference. We would still be required to live at court with the queen, but many of the queen's ladies in waiting had large families, and it did not deter them from serving faithfully.

As long as Andrew and I could be together, I didn't care where we lived.

Yet, how would we convince the castle that we had been separated for the past month when a baby would appear in only eight?

I smiled to myself, not worried in the least.

"Ah," the queen said as the maids of honour finished their

dance and the musicians played a song to fill the space. "There is my Eyes."

I glanced in the direction that she was looking and found Charles entering the ballroom.

My heart leapt with joy at seeing my stepbrother. "May I be excused, Your Majesty?" I asked. "I'd like to speak to him."

"Of course." She waved us away. "You both must go."

Andrew rose and helped me from my chair. He offered me his arm as we rounded the large table and approached Charles.

He stood near the door, waiting for us, his expression difficult to read.

My heart started to beat hard, wondering what he might tell us. "Have you spoken to him in 1883?" I asked Andrew.

"Not since he left New York last month."

"Charles," I said, wanting to run to his embrace but uncertain of my welcome.

He opened his arms and smiled—banishing all my fears.

I went into his arms and gave him a tight hug before letting go. "'Tis been too long."

Andrew and Charles shook hands, and though they'd been friends for a long time, I knew the trouble between them had changed things.

"Can we go somewhere to talk?" Charles asked us.

I nodded and then took Andrew's hand as we followed Charles out of the ballroom and into an alcove in one of the corridors.

There were wall sconces, but it was still dim. I stood close to Andrew as we faced Charles.

"Congratulations, Lord Wharton," he said. "I've heard the queen has given you a noble title."

"Aye." Andrew nodded. "I don't deserve it, but I will do my best to please the queen. She has requested that I remain on as a royal physician."

"Does she know that you did not apprentice?" Charles asked.

It was my own fear, but Andrew put that to rest.

"She knows that I did not acquire my knowledge in the typical fashion, but she does not care. She trusts me, and that is all that matters. I will do my best to continue my studies."

"Evelyn told me that you are planning to stay in 1563." Charles smiled. "I could not be happier to hear it."

Andrew put his arm around me and nodded. "Then you've spoken to her."

"Aye."

My heart filled with warmth as I watched Charles's expression transform to pure joy.

"Did she show you the papers?" Andrew asked.

I turned to my husband. "What papers?"

"Whitney Shipping is investing in Charles's family farm," Andrew told me. "And, if my suspicions are correct, Evelyn will be living on the farm sooner than later."

Charles's smile turned into a grin. I'd never seen him look so happy or carefree. But it slowly faded as he said, "Evelyn no longer has a father, so I am asking for your blessing to marry her, Andrew."

Andrew let go of me and clasped hands with Charles as he put his other hand on Charles's shoulder. "I give it without hesitation."

"Thank you." Charles nodded and then looked at me. "Will you be fine without me?"

I smiled as I went into his embrace once again, thinking of the possibility of a baby, and a castle in Guildford, and a lifetime with Andrew. "I will be better than fine. And I wish you and Evelyn all the happiness in the world."

Yet, sadness started to weigh upon me as I thought about never seeing Charles again.

He must have known what I was thinking because he said, "There's no reason to be sad. I have several months before my birthday, and I'm not going away any time soon."

I smiled, blinking back my tears.

"Let's return to the celebration," Charles said as he touched my shoulder. "We have much to be thankful for."

"You go ahead," Andrew said. "I need a little privacy with my wife."

Charles winked at us and then disappeared into the ballroom.

Andrew turned to me and took my hands into his, bringing them up to his lips. "Are you happy, Lady Wharton?"

"Exceedingly." I echoed what he had told the queen earlier. "Are you happy, Lord Wharton?"

"My heart could not be fuller."

I lowered his hands and placed one on my stomach. "Is there enough space in your heart for a child?"

A grin lit up his face, and he gathered me into his arms. "That's the beauty of a heart, my love," he whispered. "It never runs out of room."

I wrapped my arms around him and reveled in the gift of our family.

A few months ago, I thought I had no room in my heart for anything other than grief, yet God had brought Andrew back into my life to prove me wrong.

Epilogue

CHARLES

JUNE 10, 1914
NEW YORK CITY

The RMS *Olympic* was docked in the New York harbor as I stood near the gangplank. Sunshine glistened off the gently lapping waves of the East River below us as the stretcher was moved through the passengers who were waiting to disembark.

"Please make way for the stretcher," I asked a woman in a fur coat who gawked at the patient. "We must get Mrs. Wells to the ambulance."

The patient's daughter, Libby, stood nearby, clasping her hands as she watched her mother being removed from the ship. She was a beautiful young woman I'd met on the voyage home from England. We'd spent hours conversing at the captain's table over meals, and earlier that day, before she'd learned her mother needed an ambulance, I'd discovered that she was a time-crosser.

A time-crosser who went between 1914 and 1774—the same years as my son, Henry.

"Thank you, Congressman Hollingsworth," Libby said as she

approached me. "I don't know what I would have done without your help."

"Let me escort you to the ambulance," I said, offering her my arm.

Her green eyes were filled with concern as she nodded and took my assistance. Her maid followed behind us as we trailed after the stretcher, down the long gangplank to the waiting ambulance.

"Do you need assistance at home?" I asked. "My wife and son are coming to the harbor to fetch me, but we are at your disposal."

She shook her head. "Thank you for the offer, but I believe our family doctor is meeting us at the ambulance, and my father was notified of our impending arrival. He should be waiting for us at home."

"If there is anything I can do for you," I said, "please don't hesitate to call on me. I live in Virginia, but we are in the city often for business." I didn't bother to tell her that the RMS *Olympic* was owned by Whitney Shipping, right here in New York. Evelyn still held stock in the company and was on the board of directors, which brought us to the city several times a year.

Libby smiled at me, but I could tell her thoughts and concerns were with her mother.

The boxy ambulance was waiting at the base of the gangplank, and a man in a suit approached Libby as soon as we stepped onto shore.

"Hello, Dr. Payne," she said. "Thank you for coming."

"My pleasure," he told her, tipping his hat. "We'll get your mother home as soon as possible and see what we can do to help her."

"Thank you." Libby let go of my arm and turned to me. "Again, your assistance has been invaluable. I won't forget you, Congressman Hollingsworth." She smiled and touched my arm. "Or our timeless connection."

I put my hand over hers and nodded. "It was a pleasure, Miss Wells. I hope our paths cross again one day."

Libby's mother was placed in the ambulance, and Dr. Payne waited to help Libby get in with them.

"Good day, my dear," I said, patting her hand. "God be with you."

She gave me one final smile and then slipped into the ambulance.

The doors were closed, and the vehicle drove away.

A crowd had gathered to welcome home the ship, and they were forced to move apart to make way for the ambulance.

I stood there, watching to make sure they made it through.

"Father!"

I turned to the sound of my son's voice as he pushed through the crowd on the opposite side of the dock as the back of the ambulance disappeared.

Henry was tall and handsome, with brilliant blue eyes and a passion for American history that he'd come by honestly from his path in 1774.

I smiled to myself, suspecting that I knew who Libby might be. From the moment I'd learned she was a time-crosser, I had to smile at God's gracious love. Henry had spoken of Libby many times from 1774, but he knew from his studies at The College of William and Mary in this path that he was going to become the first spy hanged in the American Revolution in 1775. Because of it, he wasn't at liberty to give his heart to her.

Little did he know that Libby also occupied this path. It wasn't something I could tell him, not only because it wasn't my place to interfere with God's plans, but also because God's timing was perfect. I knew that without a doubt. And if he intended to bring Henry and Libby together in this path, nothing could stop Him.

Because Libby was so surprised to meet another time-crosser, I assumed that she didn't realize there were so many of them. I had chosen to keep a lot of information to myself. She'd asked if I knew of any other time-crossers, and I had told her I didn't. She would learn the truth at the right time, I was certain.

But, for now, I would wait to see what God had planned.

"Charles!" Evelyn said as she moved through the crowd beside Henry.

I met her midway and embraced her. "Hello, darling," I said as I kissed her. "Did you miss me?"

She laughed, her blue eyes sparkling. "More than you'll ever know. Thankfully, I've been busy with meetings and spending time with Laura's family."

I smiled at the mention of our daughter, Laura. Soon after we'd married, we returned to Newport and adopted her from the Home for Friendless Children. She had filled our lives with joy and was now married with children of her own and living in New York.

"How are the grandchildren?" I asked.

Evelyn glowed with happiness. "Wonderful. They're expecting us for supper tonight. I hope you didn't forget to bring them presents."

"How could I? Little Whitney wrote to me twice to remind me to bring her something special."

The laughter in Evelyn's voice warmed my heart.

"What about the summit?" Henry asked me. "Was your trip to Europe successful?"

I'd been meeting with European powers in England as a senior United States Representative from Virginia, trying to convince them to reduce armies and navies. Another war was looming, and we were doing everything to stop it from happening.

"It was . . . disheartening," I said to Henry. "I'd rather hear about your meetings."

His face lit up with excitement. "I introduced Dr. Goodwin to John D. Rockefeller. I think we're close to convincing Mr. Rockefeller to take a look at Williamsburg. He's interested in our vision to restore the town as a museum and is considering how he might invest in the venture."

"I'm happy to hear it."

"I know it'll take some time," Henry said, a shadow falling across his face, "but once I leave my other path, I'll have nothing but time."

My gaze wandered in the direction of the ambulance, and I couldn't help but wonder when or if Libby and Henry's paths would ever cross again. I hoped they would.

"Let's get your things," Evelyn said as she slipped her arm through mine. "And we can keep talking on the way home. Henry, I want to hear all about your ideas for Williamsburg. Your father and I would also like to be considered as investors."

"And as a congressman," I added, "I can help you get other funding."

"I appreciate the offer," he said. "We have a lot of work ahead of us, but I'm happy that we're moving in the right direction." Henry grinned as he put his hand on my back. "I'll go speak to the porter about your luggage."

I watched Henry walk away, his hands in his pockets and focus on the horizon. I prayed for his endurance to face the coming years.

"What's on your mind, Charles?" Evelyn asked as she wrapped her arms around me and watched our son.

"I just met Libby on the ship."

She pulled back. "*The* Libby?"

"I believe so."

"Interesting." She returned to my embrace. "I both envy and dread what Henry will go through over the next few years, but if I know anything, it's that God is faithful, and He will not leave Henry's side."

"I don't know what will happen," I agreed, "but I have a feeling it will be beautiful."

She smiled at me. "If it's anything like our story, it will be."

"I don't think it will be anything like our story," I said as we started to follow Henry. "But if it ends as well as ours, then it will be amazing and worth all the trouble to get there."

Evelyn chuckled and took my hand. "Come. It's getting late, and I'm eager to get you home."

I glanced toward the gangplank where I'd said good-bye to Libby, but something told me it wasn't good-bye forever.

Only time would tell.

Historical Note

Once upon a time, I created a character named Congressman Hollingsworth. He appeared briefly in *When the Day Comes*, the first book in my TIMELESS series. At the time, I never imagined that he would become the hero in book six, so I had him make a random comment about his other path starting in 1541. Six books later, I realized that he not only needed a story, but also a first name. Until now, I've chosen to set each book in a period that was familiar to me. But if Congressman Hollingsworth—now known as Charles—was born in 1541, his story would take place approximately twenty-five years later, and I had very little knowledge of the 1560s. I quickly learned that the most interesting events happening at that time were the intrigue in Queen Elizabeth I's court and the plague ravaging London. I decided to have Charles live at court with his stepsister, Cecily, and thus began my quest to learn all I could about Queen Elizabeth and her courtiers. I read several books and articles for research, but the most helpful book by far was *Elizabeth I and Her Circle*, by Susan Doran.

Since I wanted to set the story during the plague, I needed Charles to be twenty-four in 1563. Unfortunately, I had already given him a birthdate of 1541, so I had to fudge the years a little. If I could time-cross back to *When the Day Comes*, I would have had Congressman Hollingsworth's other path begin in 1539. I hope you can forgive this little change.

I only knew the basics about Queen Elizabeth when I began my research. I didn't know anything about her courtiers or life in the palace in the sixteenth century. But everything I learned was so fascinating, I couldn't wait to include it in *Through Each Tomorrow*. One of the things I learned was that Elizabeth played favorites with the men in her life, and she was drawn to handsome, confident, intelligent men, especially those who were good dancers (who isn't?). Her closest male companion was Lord Robert Dudley, a friend from childhood. It was well known that they were in love, and he wanted to marry her, but Lord Robert was already married to someone else. When Lord Robert's wife mysteriously died falling down a flight of stairs less than two years after Elizabeth became queen, the scandal was so intense, Elizabeth knew that they could never marry. But that didn't stop them from being close or from living in adjoining apartments.

It's no wonder, then, that there were rumors that Elizabeth and Lord Robert had a child. In 1561 (not 1563, when my story is set), the queen was bedridden with an illness that made her body swell, and she was kept from the eyes of the court. Twenty-six years later in 1587, a man named Arthur Dudley was detained by the Spanish after a shipwreck on the Biscay Coast, under suspicion of spying. When questioned, Arthur claimed to have been born in 1561 and that he was the child of Queen Elizabeth and Lord Robert Dudley. There are three letters that still exist from his interviews. He claimed that Elizabeth's lady in waiting, Kat Astley, summoned a man named Robert Southern to the castle to take a newborn baby. The child would be raised as a gentleman in London, taught how to dance, and speak several languages. Upon Southern's deathbed, he confessed to Arthur about his royal origins, fearing for both his and Arthur's lives. Soon after Arthur recounted his story, he disappeared from history and was never heard from again.

Scholars refute the claim that Arthur made, but I thought the story was too good to pass up! It was purported that Queen Elizabeth was a virgin throughout her life and took pride in that title. She never married, despite the advice of her privy council, and eventually the crown was passed to her distant cousin, James VI, the son of Mary, Queen of Scots (who had been beheaded for conspiring against Queen Elizabeth).

By 1578, Lord Robert had proposed to Elizabeth several times and was tired of being rejected. He married Elizabeth's widowed cousin, Lettice Knollys, in a secret ceremony, without the queen's knowledge or consent. The queen was so enraged, she banished Lettice from court and never allowed her to return, and she did not speak to Robert for several years. Lettice was one of the queen's maids of honour and someone who played a part in my story. By 1563, when my story is set, Lettice had been a maid of honour for four years. She was considered one of the most beautiful women in the court and was often paraded in front of visitors and dignitaries as the standard of English beauty. Elizabeth felt betrayed by her cousin and her favorite when Lettice and Lord Robert married, and she never fully recovered.

As for nicknames, the queen offered them to her favorites, and it was Lord Robert that she called Eyes. I chose for her to call Charles Eyes in my story because in previous books, Charles's blue eyes were commented on as being brilliant and unique.

The queen loved competitions and entertainments and was fond of royal tennis and jousting, to name a few activities. When I learned that there was a royal tennis court at Windsor Castle (also known as real tennis), built in the fifteenth century, I was so excited! I had already planned a tennis fundraiser in 1883 and loved this time-crossing connection.

As for jousting, I learned that King Henry VIII, Elizabeth's father, sustained a brain injury in a jousting match in 1536. He was unconscious for two hours, and it's believed he suffered lifelong complications, some affecting his personality. It wasn't long after his accident that he had his second wife, Anne Boleyn, beheaded. Elizabeth was only two when her mother died. It was this accident that gave me the idea for Charles's amnesia. I had often wondered what would happen to a time-crosser if they suffered amnesia in one path, and this was an opportunity to find out.

Cecily was introduced in *Every Hour Until Then*, book five in my TIMELESS series. She is Kathryn and Austen's daughter and inspired by several of the maids of honour in Queen Elizabeth's court. There is little known about these women, but they were noblewomen who served the queen with devotion and dedication. They weren't allowed to get involved in political matters but were relied upon to keep their eyes and ears open, and report back to the queen. The maids of honour slept in a cramped dormitory with a chaperone, and even after they were married, they continued in the service of the queen, some through multiple pregnancies. It was rare to have a position open up in the queen's household, but when one did, the competition was fierce for those coveted spots.

When I began to brainstorm *Through Each Tomorrow*, I was sitting with my daughter Ellis. I knew that one path would have to be in the 1560s and the other would have to be in the 1880s, since Charles appears in *When the Day Comes* as an older gentleman in 1912. As I thought through the cast of characters who had already been introduced, and who might be living in the 1880s, I remembered Hope and Grace's cousin, Rachel Howlett, who had died giving birth to a child in the Salem gaol in 1692. She had made a comment to Hope when they met, saying, "My other path is 1882. 'Tis a grand life there. Nothing like this one. There, I have servants. Here, I am one." The moment I remembered that comment, I sat up and looked at Ellis and said, "I know who the heroine of this story will be!" I had to do a little maneuvering to make sure no one was related to each other, and then I began to put the pieces of the puzzle together. I quickly realized that this was the perfect opportunity for Rachel/Evelyn to heal, and I love a good redemption story.

As for the Whitney family, I fashioned them after the Vanderbilts, who were a fascinating group of people. The feud between sisters-in-law, the way the Whitney family made their fortune, and their rise in social status in New York and Newport all come from the Vanderbilts.

Alva and Alice Vanderbilt's rivalry was world famous and often reported about in the newspapers. Among other things, Alva Vanderbilt built a ginormous summer cottage in Newport called Marble House between 1888–1892. Not to be outdone, one year later Alice Vanderbilt began to build The Breakers, easily the largest and grandest home in Newport (I could fit four of my houses in her great room alone, since it measures 250 feet by 150 feet, and is 50 feet tall). Sadly, Alva's marriage to William Vanderbilt ended in 1895. It was well known that William entertained showgirls and domestic servants on his yacht and did not hide it from his wife. He had a mistress in Europe and flaunted her in front of Alva, which caused the final rupture in their marriage. Their divorce was scandalous, especially since the elite rarely divorced, but Alva was granted full custody of their children, the right to remarry, and Marble House in Newport. To learn more about the Vanderbilts and the other wealthy Gilded Age families, I highly recommend a book called *The Husband Hunters: American Heiresses Who Married into the British Aristocracy* by Anne de Courcy.

In 1883, the grandest of the mansions had not yet been built, but the social elite had already descended upon the town for their summer holidays. It was a very common pastime to attend fundraisers in Newport and to go to the Newport Casino for tennis, lawn bowling, billiards, dancing, etc. I loved discovering that the International Tennis Hall of Fame is currently at the Newport Casino in Newport, Rhode Island. It was there, in 1881, that the first US Lawn Tennis Championship was held. The winner was Richard Sears, who won the title for seven years in a row. This championship eventually became known as the US Open.

During the Gilded Age, young people would picnic, swim in the ocean, or, a bit later, have bicycling parties. Afternoon teas were popular, as were evening dinner parties and balls. And every afternoon there was a grand promenade on Bellevue Avenue as people went calling on each other. Newport society was run by the wives and daughters of the wealthiest families, and the husbands and adult sons often stayed in New York City, only coming to Newport for weekend trips or special occasions. They were known to come by yacht or private train cars. For this reason, there was a shortage of young men for dances and parties. It wasn't uncommon for a hostess to inquire from a commanding officer at Fort Adams to send over officers, from good families, to play bridge or to dance. These men were required to wear their uniforms so none of the young heiresses would waste their time on them.

Since I knew that orphans would play a part in my story, I was happy to discover that there was an orphanage in Newport. The Newport Home for Friendless Children was created in 1866, right after the Civil War, at 24 School Street. The organization has undergone many transformations over the years, and it eventually became a charity organization that helped thousands of families during the Great Depression and offered a daycare for working mothers. When orphanages became obsolete in the 1960s, they transformed into an emergency short-term care center. In the 1990s, they opened a homeless shelter for women and children and expanded to other locations. In 2009, after 145 years at School Street, they built a new multi-service community center in Middletown, Rhode Island, and now run as a state agency called Child & Family. You can learn more about their history by visiting their website www.childandfamilyri.org/our-history.

There are so many other little details, real people, and events that I tucked into these pages. I hope this story, and the others in my TIMELESS series, inspire you to dig deeper. As always, it is a pleasure to bring real history to life. Thank you for allowing me space to share my passion.

—Gabrielle

Discussion Questions

1. This story is set in two very different centuries, 1563 and 1883. If you had to pick one of these two eras to live in, which one would you choose and why?
2. In 1563, this story explores the intrigues of Queen Elizabeth I's court. What do you think was the most interesting aspect of this lifestyle?
3. Would you have wanted to live at court with the queen?
4. In the sixteenth century, there was very little known about the origin of insects, allowing Cecily to be the first to "discover" it. If you went back in time, what is one thing you'd like to discover? (It can be scientific, an invention, new land, etc.)
5. In 1883, we get a peek at the opulence in Newport, Rhode Island. Have you ever visited there? What is one aspect of the lifestyle you'd love? What is one you would dislike?
6. This story explores the idea of family obligations. Can you relate? What are some things you've sacrificed for family or loved ones?
7. An overarching theme in the TIMELESS series is dealing with disappointment when life doesn't go the way we hope

or plan, and God's faithfulness to meet us amid those disappointments. How has this played out in your life?
8. Ultimately, Andrew chooses to remain in 1563 with Cecily, and Charles stays in 1883 with Evelyn. Were you happy with their choices? Would you have chosen differently?

Acknowledgments

I am blown away that this is my sixth novel in the TIMELESS series! What began as a seed of an idea for books one through three has grown into a complex world of time-crossers, with more on the way. I'm thankful for my acquisitions editor, Jessica Sharpe, who has been one of the biggest fans of this series. Every time I throw a wild idea at her, she's quick to encourage me and see where it goes. A special thanks goes out to my editors, Jessica Sharpe and Bethany Lenderink, as well as my amazing marketing team of Rachael Betz, Raela Schoenherr, Joyce Perez, Emily Vest, and Lindsay Schubert. Thank you for partnering with me to share my books with the world. I also want to give a special thank you to my cover designer, Jennifer Parker, who outdoes herself with each new cover. Wow. The entire team at Bethany House inspires me to dig deeper and dream bigger.

Thank you also goes out to my agent, Wendy Lawton, and the whole team at Books & Such Literary Agency. I also want to thank my mastermind group, Fellowship of the Pen, and my writing friends, both near and far, who encourage me, equip me, and cheer me on with each new book.

And finally, I want to thank my family. I couldn't write without their love and support. The very first time I spoke to my husband on the phone when we were sixteen, I told him I was going to be an author. From that day until now, he has believed in my dream without wavering. Every hero I create has a piece of Dave's heart, character, or personality. When I started to write for publication, my children were 7, 5, 2, and 2. Now, they are 21, 19, 15, and 15. It has been difficult to balance being a full-time mom and author, but my children are my biggest cheerleaders and love the adventures my books take us on around the world. My daughters, Ellis and Maryn, are now adults and are often my brainstorming partners, first readers, and founts of inspiration. My twin boys, Judah and Asher, can't remember a time when I wasn't writing books, but with each new release, they are just as proud as if it was my first. Thank you, Meyer clan, for being the most incredible humans on this planet. I love you to the moon and back.

I always reserve my final thank you for my Heavenly Father, the Author and Perfecter of my faith. Before one word of the TIMELESS series was written, God was preparing my heart for the stories I would tell. I'm honored, humbled, and blessed to write for His glory.

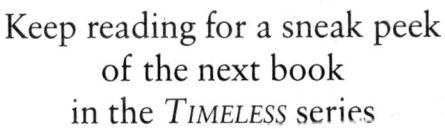

Keep reading for a sneak peek
of the next book
in the TIMELESS series

Available summer 2026

1

SAN FRANCISCO
AUGUST 29, 1849

If I didn't get help soon, my father would die.

"Can someone help me?" I held him upright in the small rowboat that had taken us from the *Eugenia* to shore. "My father is not well."

Hundreds of men moved along the shores of San Francisco. Every conceivable race of humanity pushed and shoved as cargo was unloaded from the incoming ships and dozens of men scrambled from the boats to descend upon the city. Countless vessels sat in the harbor, abandoned and forgotten as their crews made their way to the goldfields in the Sierra Nevada foothills, a hundred or more miles to the east. Their masts reached toward the cloudless sky as their anchors dug into the muddy bottom of San Francisco Bay.

"Please," I said as my father's limp body weighed heavy against me. "Anyone."

"Our daddy is sick." Hazel's small voice was lost in the din of confusion.

"Looksee here," a man in a blue flannel shirt said as he stopped on the dock nearest our boat. "It's a sunbonnet and a child!"

All the other men who had come with us from the Isthmus of Panama on the *Eugenia* had been so excited to get to California, they hadn't stopped to ask if we needed help. They'd recently been in the East with their wives and children. But these men on the dock, clearly starved for the sight of a woman and child, were suddenly eager to assist.

"Do you need a hand up?" the first man asked me.

"Yes, please. Our father took ill with malaria in Panama City," I explained. "He hasn't been well since."

It was an understatement. Father had been near death for six weeks. His illness had prevented us from taking the first ship that had come to Panama City after our arrival, and it had been another four weeks before the next one was available. Thousands of people had been waiting in Panama City because so many of the ships that sailed into San Francisco were abandoned by their crew and only a few made the return trip. The space was so limited, the ship had three times the number of passengers it should have carried, and we had spent ten times the reasonable amount for passage.

Which meant we were late to California and had no money left.

Several men stepped into the rowboat and lifted Father out as Hazel moved close to me. At the age of six, my half sister was far braver than I felt. She'd weathered the voyage from Boston to Colon, the city on the northern shores of the Isthmus, and then laughed and sang her way through the eighteen-day trek by boat and pack mules to Panama City. Not once had she complained or whined.

Even now, she stared at the teeming mass of men with a look of awe but not concern. I hoped it was because she believed I would take care of her, but I was having my own doubts.

Thankfully, she was too young and naïve to understand our dire circumstances.

Another miner in a red flannel shirt offered his hand to me, and I stepped out of the rowboat with Hazel not far behind.

The sun scorched my neck as the brim of my bonnet shaded my eyes. From the dock, I had a better vantage point of San Francisco.

It looked nothing like the city I knew in 1929.

"This old man can't be your husband," one of the miners said to me as he motioned to my unconscious father.

"He's our father."

"You'll be looking for a man, then." He took off his stained bowler hat, revealing a tan line on his forehead and greasy, thin hair. "I'd have need of you, miss. We can go to the parson right now."

I stared at him as my father was manhandled onto the dock. Not knowing what to say, I simply stepped around him and went to Father's side. Though he was unconscious, sweat beaded on his ashen brow.

"Can someone tell me where I might find a room to rent?" I asked the men who were congregating around us. "Preferably close, since my father is unable to walk. And I'll need a doctor."

Even as I said the words, I had no idea how I would pay for anything. We didn't have a single penny to our name.

Hazel slipped her hand into mine as the men crowded closer. Some touched her golden braids or patted her head.

"Please," I said as I moved her away from one man who was far too familiar. "We need a place to stay. Preferably fifty cents a night. Could someone point us in the right direction?"

"You won't find anything for less than ten dollars a night," a rough-looking man with a British accent said as he stepped forward. He had a strange gait, and ragged scars wrapped around his neck and into his jaw.

The other men parted, either in respect, awe, or fear of the menacing man.

"Bess will put you up." He nodded to the men who were holding my father by the arms and legs. "Take the old man to Bess's Place."

Unease slithered up my spine as the men began to haul Father away without waiting for my response. No one seemed to question the newcomer.

"Wait." I took a step forward and called out to the others to stop. "Is Bess's Place respectable?"

A chorus of laughter erupted as Hazel pressed closer to me. I knew what I was getting into when I talked Father into leaving Massachusetts, but I hadn't realized it would take us this long or that we'd lose all our money getting here. We needed to travel to the Yuba River by the end of September to be primed for the next big gold strike. It was the only chance Father had to restore his finances, though he had adamantly refused to look for gold. He thought we were coming to start a school.

I had other plans.

But the end of September was only a month away. If he didn't get better soon, or I didn't find a job in San Francisco to pay for the hundred-and-forty-mile trip by ferry and then pack mules, I would have put Father and Hazel at risk for nothing.

"It's as respectable as they come in this city," the British man said. "Tell Bess that English Jim sent you. She'll treat you right."

"Or else," another man said under his breath.

English Jim either didn't hear or ignored the man as he nodded for the others to continue carrying Father.

"Do you have luggage, miss?" an older miner asked. "I'd be happy to carry it for you."

I pointed to the trunks and bags we'd brought with us, trying to keep one eye on Father as I held Hazel's small hand.

"Go on," the man said in a kind voice. "We know where Bess's Place is. We'll be right behind you. I'll make sure your things get to you without being mussed."

I had little choice but to trust him.

The sound of hammers, saws, and shouts echoed across the dock as Hazel and I followed the men carrying Father. Hundreds of canvas buildings climbed the hills of the city, with several in the middle of construction. There were a few brick and adobe buildings sprinkled throughout, but the majority were hastily built of boards and canvas. Shelters made of sticks and clothing dotted the landscape, but very few trees softened the scene. To the right was a tall, rugged hill, different than the others.

"That's Telegraph Hill," said a man near my elbow. His stench suggested he hadn't bathed in months. "You'll find Bess's Place at the base of it."

Thankfully we didn't have far to go.

Father's head lolled back, and I prayed that the movement wouldn't be the end of him. He had started to recover from the malaria when we boarded the ship in Panama City, but the close, dank quarters of the *Eugenia* had brought on another bout of sickness. He'd been feverish and delirious for the past two weeks and had passed out when they lowered him into the rowboat earlier.

If he died, I wasn't sure what I would do. I didn't plan to stay in 1849 on my twenty-fifth birthday on November 3rd. That's why I needed Father to get well and get him to the gold strike near Nevada City. I knew about the gold discovery from my life in 1929, and though I couldn't change history and have Father be the first to find the gold, I could have him there, before thousands of other miners descended on the Yuba River.

If Father died or was penniless, who would look after my little sister? I couldn't leave her to fend for herself as an orphan—but I didn't want to forfeit my life in 1929, either. As a time-crosser, I would have to give up one life on my birthday. I had no other choice.

The closer we came to the start of the dock, the more crowded it became with men of every shape, size, and color. Foreign languages mingled with unfamiliar English accents, and no matter how hard I tried, I couldn't see a woman among them.

Hazel and I followed the men along a level, dusty street that ran parallel to the shoreline. Signs on canvas buildings promoted everything from gambling halls and saloons to restaurants, banks, laundry services, real estate brokers, and general stores. We passed several hotels and boarding houses, but *No Vacancy* signs hung on the doors.

The closer we came to Telegraph Hill, the rowdier and louder the crowd became. Here, there wasn't as much diversity in appearances. Most of the men looked like they were of Western European descent. Their accents were English or Scottish or Irish.

And there were women, standing on porches, lounging at the end of alleys, and sitting in upper-floor windows—all of them scantily dressed.

"Welcome to Sydney Town," a man said as he followed us and spit into the dusty street. "Best watch your back, miss. This is the meanest piece of God's green earth."

Sydney Town?

My pulse began to race as I realized where they'd taken us.

The most notorious and dangerous place in the burgeoning city. Perhaps in the world.

The men pushed open the door into Bess's Place before I could stop them. A hand-painted sign at the front of the building said *Hotel and Restaurant*, but I wasn't convinced that was all I would find.

"Please," I said as I pushed my way through the group to get to the front, my hand clasping Hazel's in a death grip. "Is there nowhere else we can—?"

"What's going on?" A young woman entered the front room of the building, wiping her hands on an apron. Her British accent was just as strong as the others.

The room was full of a dozen roughhewn tables, surrounded by three-legged stools.

"We got us some newcomers, Bess," a man said. "English Jim sent them your way."

I scanned the wood floor of the flimsy canvas building, looking for a trapdoor. A movie I'd seen in 1928 had been about Sydney Town and the gang known as the Sydney Ducks. They were hardened criminals who had escaped from the British penal colonies of Australia. The story was about one of the more infamous gang leaders among them, Sam Kendal. It was rumored that the Ducks had trapdoors in the floors of their buildings to capture unsuspecting customers. The men would be sold to the ship captains to be pressed into service, and the women—I didn't even want to think about what they did with the women they took captive. The movie had been violent and garish, highlighting the atrocities of the vicious gang that had wreaked havoc on San Francisco until a vigilante committee broke them up in 1851.

That was two years from now.

I lifted Hazel into my arms, holding her tight. I couldn't remember the last time I'd held her on my hip, but I did now. Had they brought us here to abduct us?

Bess looked me over without emotion. I wore a simple cream-and-brown-checkered cotton dress with a brown bonnet. It wasn't fancy or expensive, but serviceable and proper. She was young—perhaps in her early to mid-twenties—but she looked hardened by life, and her clothes were worn and simple. She was still pretty, but her eyes lacked sparkle, and her skin lacked luster.

"The lady and her father need a place to stay," one of the men said to Bess, a bit of awe in his face. "And the little one. English Jim thought you could put them up."

Bess sighed. "Of course he did." She lifted her chin at me. "You have money to pay?"

My mouth slipped open to say no, but I couldn't bring myself to speak, so I shook my head.

She pressed her lips together in disapproval. "What about your father? What ails him?"

"Malaria," I finally said, choking on my voice, anxious to get out of there. "We can go someplace else. Just point us in the right direc—"

"There's nowhere else that will take you without money." Bess nodded at the men who held Father. "I don't have any empty beds. You'll have to put him on the floor upstairs."

"We can't stay—" I stepped forward.

"You don't have much choice." Bess looked me up and down as the door to the back room opened and a little boy walked in. He stepped next to Bess, and she put her hand on his shoulder without taking her eyes off me. "What's your name?"

I swallowed as dozens of eyes stared at me. All the men who came from the dock had filed into the room, and there were many others who had been sitting at the tables when we walked in.

"Ally Adams," I said, trying not to sound panicked as some of the men disappeared up the stairs with Father.

"And where are you from, Miss Adams?"

"Concord, Massachusetts." I stepped closer to her. "Please. We can leave. I don't want to be an imposition."

"It's too late for that. You and the girl look like you're about ready to collapse. I can feed you and give you space for the night, but you'll need to work it off."

My throat tightened as I stared at her. What kind of work did she have in mind?

"I could use some help in the kitchen," she said, lifting an eyebrow, as if she had read my thoughts.

I had been a teacher in Massachusetts in Father's school. My stepmother, Hazel's mother, had seen to all the domestic work before she passed away. In 1929, my family owned a movie studio, and I had been acting since I was a child. I didn't have any experience in a kitchen and wouldn't even know how to help. But I couldn't tell Bess, because I had no other choice.

"The rest of you can get out," Bess said to the men, "unless you're here to eat."

"Come on, Bess," said a man at the back of the group. "Miss Adams is the prettiest thing I've laid my eyes on in months. I'll pay you just to look at her."

"I don't run that kind of business," Bess said. "If you're looking for that, go on down to the Boar's Head or the Jolly Waterman."

There was a chorus of protests until a large man stepped out of the corner of the room and they quieted. He was broad and bulky, and the scars on his hands and face suggested that he had seen his fair share of brawls, though his eyes lacked a depth of understanding or recognition.

"Paddy will see that you men stay in line," Bess said to the crowd, and then she motioned to me. "Come into the kitchen."

I followed her and the little boy into a back room, still holding Hazel. The kitchen was small and warm, with a cookstove, a work table, and various kitchen utensils. A cupboard sat against one wall, and hooks hung from the ceiling with pots and pans dangling overhead. Barrels of salt pork, flour, and sugar sat alongside bags of beans, coffee, and oats. Jars of pickled cucumbers and honey sat on a shelf with various spices. There were no windows in the room, but the thin canvas walls offered enough light.

"You and the child will sleep in here," she said to me. "It won't be safe, but it'll be safer than sleeping upstairs with the men or out on the street. I'll have Paddy guard the room at night."

My eyes opened wide. I couldn't help it. "Surely there would be a better place for my father and sister."

"Perhaps," she said as she put a few sticks of wood into the cookstove and pulled a coffee pot over the front burner. "But your father doesn't look like he'd make it up the hill to Portsmouth Square, where the more respectable people find lodging, and no one would take you without money." She turned from the stove, and her gaze landed on the boy.

He looked like he was six or seven, and he was strangely quiet as he watched her with large brown eyes. "Besides," she said as she drew him to her, "Johnnie could use the companionship of another child. He hasn't seen one in months."

Hazel was growing heavy in my arms, and when she wiggled to get down, I set her on her feet. She looked at the little boy with open curiosity, and he stared back at her.

The back door opened, causing me to jump.

A man stopped in his tracks as his gaze met mine. He was tall, but it was the breadth of his shoulders and the size of his arms that made me draw in a breath. A scar drew up his left eyebrow, almost giving him a sinister look, but he was still dangerously handsome. He was bronzed with the sun, and though he couldn't have been more than twenty-five, the wrinkles at the corners of his eyes suggested he'd spent a great deal of time outdoors.

His brown eyes were hooded as he took in the full length of me.

"Sam," Bess said. "We have a few new guests."

Slowly, Sam entered the kitchen, and the size of him made the space feel much smaller and warmer. He wore a simple button-up shirt of gray flannel and a pair of canvas pants, held up by black suspenders. His shirtsleeves were rolled at his muscular forearms, and his top button was undone, revealing a white shirt underneath. His dark brown hair was worn a little long, and his brown beard was trimmed short and suited his handsome face.

I backed up, putting my hand on Hazel's shoulder to take her with me.

His expression didn't change as he said, "Why would you come here?"

I swallowed the apprehension climbing my throat and was about to speak when Bess said, "Her father is upstairs on his deathbed. No doubt he was the fool who thought he could make it rich like all the others."

"It wasn't Father's idea," I finally said, finding my voice and courage. "I convinced him to come."

"Then you're the fool," Sam said, his British accent matching Bess's. "Only fools and convicts come to San Francisco."

I shuddered to think what he must be.

"The girl your daughter?" he asked, nodding at Hazel.

"My sister."

"Keep a close eye on her. Never let her out of your sight, especially here in Sydney Town. There's no telling what would happen to her."

I pressed my hand against Hazel's shoulder.

"I'm Sam Kendal," he said. "You're welcome to stay as long as you don't cause trouble, but the sooner you leave, the better."

My heart fell as his name sounded an alarm inside my troubled mind.

Sam Kendal. The most notorious Sydney Duck in San Francisco.

Which meant the woman was his wife, Bess Kendal, the person who would betray him and cause his downfall.

And soon, if I wasn't mistaken.

Gabrielle Meyer is a Christy Award–winner and ECPA bestselling author. She has worked for state and local historical societies and loves writing fiction inspired by real people, places, and events. She currently resides along the banks of the Mississippi River in central Minnesota with her husband and four children. By day, she's a busy homeschool mom, and by night she pens fiction and nonfiction filled with hope. Find her online at GabrielleMeyer.com.

Sign Up for Gabrielle's Newsletter

Keep up to date with Gabrielle's latest news on book releases and events by signing up for her email list at the link below.

GabrielleMeyer.com

FOLLOW GABRIELLE ON SOCIAL MEDIA

Gabrielle Meyer, Author   @Gabrielle_Meyer   @MeyerGabrielle

Be the first to hear about new books from Bethany House!

Stay up to date with our authors and books by signing up for our newsletters at

BethanyHouse.com/SignUp

FOLLOW US ON SOCIAL MEDIA

@BethanyHouseFiction